DAGGER
IN THE
SEA

CAT PORTER

WILDFLOWER INK, LLC

Dagger in the Sea
Cat Porter ©2018
Wildflower Ink, LLC

Editor
Jennifer Roberts-Hall

Content Editor
Christina Trevaskis
www.bookmatchmaker.com

Proofreader
Penelope Croci

Cover Design
Lori Jackson, Lori Jackson Designs
& Cat Porter

CONTENTS

for my father

PROLOGUE
TURO

I'VE ALWAYS HATED HAMLET.

Hamlet never got the job done. Entire play goes by, and the Prince of Denmark does nothing. Bottom line, he couldn't deal with the truth, nor could he handle what that truth required of him.

Masking the truth is easy for some of us. You become an artist, painting pictures for yourself with your lies. A dash of richer color here, a broader stroke there.

The lies you paint for yourself are the most brutal though, because you need to believe them, wrap yourself up in them. We fight to make them defy logic, remain digestible, real, three dimensional, and oh so pretty as we insist they pirouette on our stage again and again and again.

But when they're ripped away, because eventually they will be, they hurt the most and leave the deepest wounds, the ugliest scars. They're the ones that reveal the vileness that we've been working so damn hard to disguise. That rawness can never truly be obscured, no matter how hard we try.

I know because I've been trying. For years.

Unlike Hamlet, I've been brave enough to hunt, maim, kill

when needed. And tonight I needed to. I had to for reasons that seem so fucking inconsequential all of a sudden, and only one that seemed real. Her. I needed to do it for her.

There is one spark of hope in the whole damn play for me. Just one—that forced journey of Hamlet's across the sea. That journey to England had allegedly renewed his determination, and he returns home to Denmark full of grim purpose and ire. Finally. This was going to be good.

Wrong.

Still, the ass is incapable of getting the job done. Still he philosophizes and watches from a distance, still he admires the boldness of his peer, the warrior prince Fortinbras and envies him, still he puts on a show. And at that show, that sword fight, he hasn't prepared for every outcome and ends up getting himself and his mother poisoned, leaving others to speak for him, others to rule.

Fuck no.

I'd always been filled with purpose and ire, but I was bound by thorns that my ambitions kept sharp. My own journey across the sea, however, has loosened those bonds, stripped me bit by bit.

Tonight, I took up the gauntlet that fate offered, and I rose to the challenge. Now I was the pawn, again. The means to someone else's end. Inconsequential.

And in that flickering, loud darkness, in that surreal stillness, the cold, hard metal of that gun slick in my sweaty hand, expectations like flames licking at me, the jagged music of that violin ripping through me, the power of that bullet waiting to be unleashed under my touch, I'd seen my lies and the emptiness that lay beneath. Everything I thought I knew, everything I'd been clinging to for so long slipped from my hold as my fingers moved around that trigger.

Only the heavy click, that horrible gasp between my roar and the foul silence.

To be or not to be?

Oh, I am, fuckers. I am.

My heart thrashed in my chest once more, and there, in every hard pound, in the rush of blood, through the smoke, her eyes held mine. *She* remained. She knew.

That was the victory. That was the only triumph. She was the only truth.

And that scared me more than all the lies.

CHICAGO

1

TURO

1993 - Ten years prior

I'D NEVER MET my father before that moment.

"*Arturo.*"

That unusual, rich baritone voice saying my name in Italian made my heart leap in my chest. I was being summoned by an unknown force of nature right there on the sidewalk.

He cut a cool figure from my very own imagination—dark hair, dark eyes, dark suit, sly aura. I was speechless. The tone in his voice expressed he knew things, understood secret shadowy things about life. *About me.* Things that I had no concept of, but that a small, burning piece of me had always been intrigued by.

"Arturo, I'm your father," he said.

He'd been a capo on the rise when he'd hooked up with a University of Chicago freshman, Erin Cavanaugh, and then left her lovelorn and pregnant. He couldn't marry her, he'd explained, she wasn't Italian, but he'd make sure his kid was taken care of. My mother was furious at herself for her lack of self control and lack of birth control, and for not being aware that he was so deeply connected to a crime family. She'd been duped, swept away by his dark allure and her own deep feelings.

"First love is blinding—" she'd told me on several occasions over the years, *"—it grips you viciously, fiercely, and refuses to let go no matter how you chop away at it. Beware."*

She'd refused any more contact with him. Erin came from a wealthy, old Chicago, Irish American family and she didn't need his pathetic attempts at child support—once, twice, then nothing. She made it clear that he wasn't allowed to see me or come near me. She'd given me her grandfather's name, Arthur, and her own surname.

He'd walked away, hands in the air.

In 1993, the year after I'd gotten out of grad school and was working with my mom at her company, I went outside on a break to grab a coffee from the new gourmet coffee shop down the street, when a man approached me. When I heard the voice.

"Arturo," he repeated, his dark eyes glimmering.

This is my dad, this is my dad, raced through me right there on the sidewalk, numbing me and setting me on fire on a freezing, windy autumn day in Chicago. I had a father who was completely unlike any man I'd ever known. Utterly unlike my mother's husband, who was a clean cut old moneyed WASP from Michigan, kind yet devoid of any sort of complexity. No, no. Here *he* was, and he'd found me.

Mauro Guardino and I began meeting regularly. For pizza, for panna cotta and espressos. For focaccia sandwiches with incredible homemade mozzarella and sweet tomatoes. We bonded over veal parm, and messy, luscious piles of sausage and onions. He called me "Turo" short for Arturo, and I liked it. Suddenly my world was richer, more colorful.

Then he asked me to do him a favor.

"I'm in a jam, Turo, and I really need your help."

He needed money laundered.

I knew it was wrong, of course, but he was in a tough spot. My mother ran several companies under many corporate identities. I had access to a lot of arteries within those holdings. He obviously didn't have the advantages I grew up with. He was in a bind, and I could help. Just this once.

I did it.

My father was grateful, impressed. I thought it was a one time deal, but he kept feeding me cash, kept saying, *"Just this once more. Come on, buddy. You're really doing me a huge one here."*

And again.

And again.

That last time, when I'd sworn to myself that I'd tell him this was it—when I'd started to get uncomfortable about it, because frankly, how long can any good yet underhanded thing really last?—My mother found out. Of course she'd found out. She'd stormed into my office one evening, face red, eyes hard and sharp, drilling holes into mine.

"How could you steal from us? And for him? Expose us this way? Why? Do you hate me that much?"

"I don't hate you, Mom."

But she'd been right. A piece of me hated her all these years for keeping my father from me. No phone calls, no birthday cards even. What the hell would have been wrong with that?

"Then why?" she'd yelled uncharacteristically, tears filling her eyes. Tears that never spilled down her cheeks.

"He's my father. He asked me to help him. That's all. I wanted to do one thing for him. Something."

"You're not this naive!"

No, I wasn't. "Why can't you understand that I want some sort of contact with my own father? There's nothing wrong with that."

"He contacted you and immediately immersed you in illegal activity."

"Immersed? How dramatic."

"I told you from the very beginning that he was trouble. He's evil," she said.

"Evil? What does that make me then?" My voice shook.

She shut her eyes, a quake shuddering through her body, but she controlled it. She was that disgusted, that horrified?

All my life my mother had insisted that I remain spotless, above reproach, and I'd made it my mission to excel at that. To impress her, make her notice, gain her glorious approval. Top of my class, captain of the hockey team, captain of the lacrosse team, an excellent tennis player to partner with her and play at her charity events, to accompany her to dinners and openings and converse politely and appropriately. Always well-dressed and well-groomed. I'd done it, enjoyed it even. I followed her into the business she'd created.

But a part of me had been so curious about the other side of the life I knew. That other side was exemplified by my father.

Her eyes narrowed. "I won't tolerate this behavior." Her voice had lowered, her words pointed. "You have a choice to make."

"A choice?"

"Yes."

She was asking me to choose between them? Always keeping me and him at a distance. This was the first time she'd actually articulated such an absolute ultimatum.

"I won't do that."

"You need to."

We stared at each other for a hard moment, her body clenched, my heart pounding. Neither of us willing to show our cards. True to form, Mom made the first move. Explicit and emphatic.

"Get out."

My ears stung, my skin flared with heat. "Out?"

"Out."

"Mom?"

"I cannot have anything about that man touching us. Not one thing. It's an absolute for me. I've been perfectly clear on this subject from the very beginning."

My father was a *subject*, not a person. I did understand intellectually, but I wanted to get to know him. I deserved it. It was basic. Fundamental. How dare she—

"The apartment, the trust fund are yours. But don't ever come back here." She turned on her heels and strode off.

A roar raged out of my throat, and I lunged at my desk shoving at everything. Computer, paperweight, folders, documents, coffee cup, pens, all flying, smashing, crashing.

I left the company.

For two days I sat in my apartment in silence and stared at the city through my grand windows that my housekeeper always kept spotless. I'd have to get rid of her now. Time to budget.

I had the urge to work at a simple job, not think, not analyze, only do. To sweat with the common man for a change. I got a job as a waiter at an Italian restaurant my mother didn't own. It was startling to function in the business I knew from the very inside, from kitchen to table, from chef to customer. Now, I was on the front lines, I was the foot soldier, and I liked it. And then one day, my father walked in with another guy and three very young women, and the hostess seated them in my section. My father stared at me without saying a word as I passed out the menus.

"Would you like to hear the chef's specials for tonight?" I said, forcing my plastic hospitality smile to transform my facial muscles against my will.

"Is there veal Marsala? I love veal Marsala," said one of the women.

"It's a house special, I highly recommend it. One veal Marsala." I jotted down on my pad. "What would you like, ma'am?" I asked the next blonde and she told me her choice.

"Sir? What would you like?" I finally turned to my father.

"What are you doing here?" he muttered under his breath.

"I'm sorry, what was that?"

A charged pause. "Linguine alla Vongole," he said tersely, hitting those ugly consonants with relish.

"Very good, sir."

I'd served them their cocktails, their antipasti, their dinners, a second bottle of wine and then a third, their cheesecakes which the women fed each other while my father and his buddy laughed, egging them on. After I brought over the Anisette liqueurs, the espressos, the cappuccinos, my father cornered me in the hallway leading to the kitchen.

"What are you doing here?" he asked me.

"What does it look like?" I flung back at him.

"What? You quit your job?"

"Seriously? My mother found out what I did for you, and she fired me."

He knocked his head back and laughed. A laugh that sheared through me. My pulse jammed in my neck. Was he laughing *at* me? I'd told him my greatest tragedy and for him it was the greatest joke ever?

My jaw stiffened. "That's funny? She kicked me out on my ass for helping you."

"So fucking easy," he spit out. "Just like I thought she would."

"What? What are you talking about?" I breathed, my chest suddenly numb.

"You think I needed you?" he said. "All that was for her benefit. All these years that bitch kept you away from me. You're my son, too, so I hit her where it hurts. She got the message this time." His lips smacked together, a smirk streaking his face.

My own father had used me as a pawn to make a statement to my mother. Couldn't help himself, had to express his vengeance upon her somehow even all these years later. A vendetta.

I froze, my heart slowing to a thud in my chest. "You used me to get back at her?"

"Yeah."

"I thought you—"

His eyes gleamed. The enthusiasm for his plan was still stamped on his face. "What?"

I'd thought he needed me. I'd thought he'd wanted a relationship with me, with his son. He didn't give a rat's ass about me. This was about sticking it to my mother with a sharp blade.

No enemy should ever go unpunished, he would later tell me after I'd completed my first assassination for him.

"Look, kid, it had to be done. End of story."

"How nice for you, but it's not the end of the story for me. I lost my job, I betrayed my mother out of some sense of loyalty to a father I don't even know, out of—fuck knows!"

"Calm down, dammit. I get it, I do." He clapped a heavy hand around my bicep.

"No, no, you don't." I pulled myself out of his grip, but he dragged me back in, his face suddenly stern. He was annoyed with me. I was being disobedient, childish.

That word *father* had lost its luster for me right then and there. *Father* had been a cherished desire, now *father* was shattered into shards of broken glass I'd slid into, scraped and cut myself, made myself bleed.

And I wasn't quite sure how to clean up the mess.

"You think she didn't use you all these years to show off to me that you're not like me?" he said on a growl. "That you never would be? Every little academic achievement, every athletic championship. Every educational and professional score." His voice was laced with the acid of mockery. "Yeah, guess the bitch got that wrong, huh? I hope she's loving this feeling right now. I got her. I finally got that Irish cunt good."

He shoved me back, and I stumbled. My stomach lurched, sour bile shot up my throat. I'd played right into his hands. He'd used me. I'd been duped by him, just like my mother.

My father had been her shameless dirty adventure on the wild side, and although she'd deeply regretted her stupidity and carelessness, as had her parents, she didn't get rid of me or give me away for adoption. She stashed me at her parents' country house in Saugatuck, Michigan with a nanny while she finished college and then sent me to the finest boarding schools out East. Three, actually. I got kicked out of one for my anger issues, and another for instigating a fight which sent a kid to the hospital. Through the years, through my mother's marriage, I remained, I grew up. I was the reminder of her feverish mistake of stepping out of the family coach and into a dirty puddle on the sidewalk in the big, bad, dark world. And Mauro Guardino knew it and enjoyed taunting her for it.

"Come on—" Mauro held a hand out to me, and I blinked. "You shouldn't be working like this. Let me do something for you." His voice returned to that thick, velvety tone. I took his hand and got up from the floor. "She tossed her own son out to the wolves. Look at you now." His hands gestured with that flair of Italian despair at my jeans and white shirt, the red waiter's smock I wore. A wink. Mollification. "You call me tomorrow and come in, and I'll have something for you. Least I can do."

The least. Yeah, the least.

"I'll do right by you," he said.

I snickered. "Yeah, okay."

He slapped a heavy hand around my neck yanking me close to him once more, I flinched. The cigar smoke, the women's perfume mixed with his too spicy aftershave filled my nostrils. "Tomorrow at noon. You come over, you little shit."

"Okay."

At twelve noon the next day I went over. What the hell. I was curious. And he owed me. What was he going to offer me? He'd told me he was in construction, real estate, looking into some new business venture online.

I met him at an Italian deli that had tables and chairs in West Loop. Muscled men hovered, elderly people slunk around him, glancing this way and that.

"Boss, he's here," said a huge, bull-faced goon who showed me to his table and stood behind him.

I held his gaze, my heart pounding. My father was the fucking boss of the Guardino crime family.

He'd really lied to me. It had all been a performance to ensnare me, to humiliate my mother. He'd played himself out to be a lowlife thug always behind the eight ball—*Cut me a break, son. I wish someone would, I really regret not being able to be there for you when you were growing up, believe me.*—when, in fact, since my birth he had risen the ranks to king.

I had been royally played. Duped. Fucked with.

"You don't talk to no one here about us, you got that? They'll know I hired you myself, so there won't be any questions asked. But no one can know you're my kid. No one. You understand? I have a wife, a daughter, a son. They're my family. Don't expect no special favors out of me either. I'm giving you an opportunity here, you got that? You got to prove yourself like everybody else. We'll see how you work out then I'll give you special assignments." That wink again. "First, you prove to me you can take it, that you're a man."

Yeah, because, at the end of the day, he wanted to know that my balls were as tough and as big as his. He wanted them to be. I was his son. My balls were as tough and as big as his, and I could prove it. To him, to my mother, to the whole fucking world.

I'd done everything my mother had asked of me and I'd fit into her world spectacularly. Honor student, championship athlete, well read, articulate, masters degree. I'd pranced on her stage brilliantly and earned the applause and the passport into her business. I'd brought everything she'd cultivated in me into her company and had been an asset for her.

Then she dumped me.

I could achieve in Mauro's world, be his asset. I'd make him respect my balls and regret he'd ever turned his back on me. I'd make my mother shudder and regret that she'd turned her back on me.

I took the challenge and took his job. He introduced me

around using that nickname he called me, 'Turo.' With his help, I changed my last name to something Italian so I'd fit in, but there would be no hiding the fact that I was half-Irish.

No resumes necessary, no interviews to pass. No scrutiny by middle of the road minions. Just me. Me in action.

On call all hours of the night and day, I collected money on the street, transported packages, picked up packages, delivered all sorts of "messages" on the Boss's behalf. Got paid sporadically at best, had to pick up the tab countless times for my overseers. Dirty work, crazy, and the craziest part?

I liked it.

I could feel the fear in a room when I approached. My temper was now a useful commodity, not a shameful thing to be punished for. The harder I was, the thicker the fear I invoked. That gleam in people's eyes? Panic. Dread. Respect.

Three years went by, and then I finally got a regular gig in one of his many businesses. "I guarantee it's better than waiting on tables." He winked at me, a lift to his chin that said this conversation was over.

I had to pick up money. Nothing new there. Seedy, run down large apartment, flowery sweet scent spritzed all over, thick dark curtains on all the windows, votive candles trying hard to lend some sort of atmosphere. Women were seated on a grouping of worn out sofas in various stages of undress, looking bored on the edges and looking like they were capable of blowing my cock to the next galaxy the minute they caught my stare. Disney SexWorld for a horny twenty-something like me.

"Turo, you gotta wait a bit, all right? Sorry about that. Ms. Morantz ain't ready yet," said Eddie, the madame's bodyguard, at the entrance where I waited.

"No problem. I'll go grab some coffee and come back." I turned to leave, but my eye had snagged on a curvy redhead in the corner.

Eddie nudged my shoulder. "Go ahead, man. Go for it. It's on the house. Mr. G said anything you wanted anytime."

"Oh yeah? He said that?"

"Yeah. You like Suzy over there, huh? It's been a slow morning. Warm her up for her work day. You'd be doing us a favor." He let out a laugh. "G'ahead. Get to know the product. Hey, Suzy!" Eddie slanted his head in my direction. Suzy uncrossed her legs and smiled big as she rose from the sofa, her short purple negligee falling open revealing huge, bare tits and a tiny thong. She prowled toward me, my pulse throbbing louder and louder with every *click clack* of her very high, very garish heels on the scuffed wood flooring.

Click clack. Click clack.

Her dark eyes focused on me like sonic lasers burning into my flesh. "Hey, baby," her voice soft and inviting.

Eddie brushed her chin with his fingers. "Be good to Turo. He's working with us for Mr. G now. We'll be seeing a lot of him from here on in."

"Oh, nice," Suzy's voice cooed as she put my hand on her formidable ass, leading me to a tiny bedroom in the back. Something told me this would be very different experience from the college girls and office and bar hook ups of my past. Once in the room, Suzy got on her knees and went down on me. She slid off at the perfect time and we fucked, her coaxing me to go harder, faster, moaning wildly like I was the best she'd ever had.

Something *click-clacked*, all right, as I pumped inside her furiously, coming like I'd never come before. This was a game, a game I liked. A game I was always guaranteed to win. A game played by whatever rules I wanted and I didn't have to convince the girl under me to like it, and I sure as hell didn't have to pull myself back from being as rough as I wanted. We fucked non-stop until Eddie knocked on the door telling me the money was ready.

Optimum job satisfaction reached that day. In the weeks and months that followed, I got to know all the girls.

Mauro Guardino was a very smart man. He kept my dick entertained, kept me hitched to his wagon and his businesses always with the hinted, unspoken promises of more, more, more. And as the years went on I'd taken on more and more to get that more, more, more. Assassinations, clean ups, heists, threats, clever accounting. He appreciated my Ivy League white collar background and used it with certain clients, and I proved my worth over and over again. When the time was right, I told him I wanted to run his whore business.

He gave it to me to manage.

I was a success.

But I hadn't forgotten my mother. So I devised a stinging, crude plan. I seduced her friends one by one, her close circle of three—one was divorced, the other married, the other newly separated.

They were flattered by my attention, obviously attracted to me, my manners, my repartee, my sexual suggestiveness. I already knew each one's interests and did further homework. I planned each one carefully, and one by one down they fell.

Boom. Boom. Boom.

The first was a one night stand at her apartment where I'd fucked her against the wall in her foyer the moment she'd led me through her front door. The other gave me head in her chauffeured limo after the ballet. The third dragged it out into a two week sex fest, meeting me at hotel rooms on her lunch breaks. Yes, everyone gave in to their dark little desires eventually. And I was happy to satisfy them.

I made sure Erin noticed. Once at a gallery opening, another at a ballet premiere, a fundraiser at one of her restaurants. I wanted to provoke her. To show her I was indeed the blight on her great moral compass. I wanted her anger and indignation. I wanted her to be offended and horrified. A duel. But each time Erin Cavanaugh Bradley would ignore her friend, glare at me for one long moment, her cold eyes spearing mine, then look away and glide on. Not quite the explosive response I'd hoped for. Fuck it.

Mauro was married and had a son and a daughter a few years younger than me. Sometimes, he'd invite me to have a drink at his favorite bar, just the two of us. He would tell me that one day, when his two kids got a little older and settled, he might share with them that I was their brother. "Sure," I'd say. "Sure. Whatever you think, it's up to you." He'd raise his glass at me, his eyes suddenly glassy and wink, saying a soft, *"Salut."*

He appreciated my understanding. I liked that, that was good. I felt liberated from any constraints. I was the master of my own life now.

Or so I thought.

2

TURO

"I NEED TO SEE YOU."

Simple words. A simple request from a mother to her son. If we were an ordinary mother and son.

Erin Cavanaugh Bradley and I hadn't spoken in the ten years since she'd fired me. We'd seen each other around town on occasion, but had only exchanged heavy looks. She remained unapologetic, and I bitter. Yet my pulse had raced the second I heard her clear firm voice on my cell phone. The blare of horns and sirens on Michigan Ave fell away as she invited me to her office.

Eyes followed me as I moved through my mother's spectacular new corporate offices in River North, a loft in a converted factory on the Chicago River. I recognized a few faces from when I'd worked at the company years ago. The sleek, minimalistic space was impressive. I'd read the article about her moving the company here in *Chicago Magazine,* seen the photographs.

"Hello, Marjorie."

Erin's personal assistant stared at me, eyes wide behind her glasses. She stood, her posture erect, stiff. "Let me take your coat."

I handed her my Burberry trench and her thin lips pressed into a barely recognizable smile, like being polite to me was bitter medicine she had to swallow. So loyal.

Marjorie asked, "Would you like coffee or—"

"Nothing, thank you." I smoothed a hand down my suit jacket.

"She's waiting for you." She opened Erin's office door.

I strode in, and my mother stood and came around her massive desk. Her eyes—my eyes, we shared the same amber hazel color, she and I—held mine.

As beautiful and well maintained as ever. Not a lock of that professionally blown out honey golden hair, which fell to her shoulders, was out of place. We both stopped moving and took each other in. To be in her presence again, after having worked side by side, learning from her, making decisions, brainstorming, getting excited, complaining together, arguing, laughing.

"Turo."

She used my nickname. She knew all about me, it seemed. Accepted my new life.

"Mother."

Her chin lifted a degree at the sound of that familiar yet now somewhat foreign word. "Thank you for coming. Please, sit." She gestured at the sofa beyond her desk in front of the huge swathe of windows revealing a cloudy, rainy Chicago.

"Would you like coffee or—"

"No, thank you." I sat down on the sofa, my fingers smoothing down my trousers along my thigh. "I just came from a breakfast meeting." A business meeting where my cock ended up being breakfast for two prostitutes. They *were* my employees after all.

One well-groomed eyebrow arched ever so slightly as she sat and crossed her slim legs, her posture as straight as a ballerina's. I pressed my back against the stiff red leather sofa. I couldn't wait to hear what she needed from me.

"I'm about to open a new restaurant in a month's time," she said. "Everything's on schedule, except for a few minor things, and one major thing: the liquor license."

I suppressed the smirk that began its creep along my lips. Ah, now she needed my help. My under the table magic. I'd been waiting for this moment for years. That one day she'd call on me and be desperate for the help only I could provide in this town.

"I've tried every avenue possible," she continued. "Everything and everyone I know."

"You need me to grease the right wheels for you?"

"No, this isn't about that. I've been cockblocked."

"Cockblocked?" I let out a dry laugh.

"Yes." Her gaze leveled with mine. "And it's not the first time."

She crossed her legs in the other direction. Graceful and elegant as all hell even when she was laying down the law, going for the jugular, giving no quarter. I'd seen many a man taken aback by her in this mode, and it had always made me proud. I took in a breath.

"I need you to get your boss to let it go," she said.

My boss. "You think it's Mauro?"

"I know it's him." She never said his name. She detested him that much.

"How do you know that?"

"He told me so himself."

My pulse twanged. "You spoke with him?"

"He misses no opportunity to speak with me. We've been playing a chess game for years. His pocketed politicians and city planners against my political friends and city planners."

I shifted on the sofa, leaning forward, my jaw set. I had no idea.

Her lips pursed, her face remaining cool. "You didn't know?"

"No. I've never been party to any discussion about your business."

"Well, he spends a great deal of time and energy on my business. The Cuban restaurant we opened last year?"

"Aja de Bolero?"

"Yes." Her brow furrowed and relaxed. Was she surprised I knew? I kept track. I went to all her restaurants.

She cleared her throat. "He held up construction for months. The renovation on The Chophouse the year before? One inspector after the other had issues. I could go on."

My back went rigid. "I had no idea."

"This opening is very important to me, Turo."

"Every opening is important to you, Mother."

"Yes, it is," her voice dipped. "It takes an extraordinary amount of time and energy and focus for me to deal with these issues. With him. This time, I'm asking you for your assistance."

"Why?"

"Why?" Her eyes narrowed at me.

"Why this time?"

She took in a deep breath. "This time he threatened me."

A chill razored up my spine. "What do you mean he threatened you?"

"He said he'd stop me. He's annoyed that I'm a member of the Mayor's task force on cleaning up West Loop. I suppose it's one of his...commercial centers? His territory?" Her eyebrows peaked.

I gave her my best blank face chiseled in titanium. The one I'd learned from her. She lobbed hers back at me.

"That's where this restaurant is located," she continued. "A lot of arrests have been made lately, buildings condemned. He called me and let me know that I'd better stop, pull out, or else he was going to show me how unhappy he was with me. He's never spoken to me like that before. Not in those terms at least. The point is, I'm truly concerned. His past actions were him pissing on fire hydrants, making messes I had to clean up, him needing to have the last word. As always. But this is different. I know it is."

Wasn't all that acrimony between them done with? I was over it. He'd won. He got me on his side of the tracks.

"I'm asking you to see if you can get him to pull back, to see reason," she said. "That neighborhood renovation is inevitable, and it's happening. He can't stop gentrification. The city has invested big money in making that happen, people are excited. He can't stop it. He's worried, frustrated, and picking on me and my business is obviously his way of lashing out, but he's always had it in for me."

Mauro frustrated was never good. Mauro vengeful, even worse. He never forgave, this she and I both knew. Once an enemy, always an enemy.

"I'll talk to him."

"Thank you."

I slanted my head. "It might make it worse."

"No worse than it already is," she replied, rising from the sofa, a hand quickly skimming down her perfect fitting pencil skirt. "I have a conference call in ten minutes," she said, plucking her tortoise shell eyeglasses from her desk.

We were done.

"Of course." I rose from the sofa.

She took in a breath and exhaled slowly, the edges of her lips curving up ever so slightly. That almost smile that expressed satisfaction, yet also served to tamp down and press emotions into a vacuum sealed bag, leaving me still, after all these years, with that raw urge to rip it open and look inside.

Her penetrating gaze roved over me. "You look good, Turo. You seem well."

My throat thickened, my lips parted to speak, but nothing came out. I could see us having a genuine, frank conversation. I could see us putting the last ten years aside and picking up where we'd left off. Clean slate. Mutual respect.

My chest tightened. Fuck, I'd missed her.

I lifted my chin. "I am. Very well."

"Hmm." Her eyes searched mine. "Are you happy?"

"I'm good, Erin." I shut down her attempt at an inquiry.

She lifted that eyebrow again, her gaze traveling over me once more. "Thank you for coming."

"I'll be in touch."

"I appreciate it."

We stood there motionless, once mother, once son. Two business professionals exchanging pleasantries, a promise to cooperate, forging an agreement. How civilized of us.

Her smile faded, and something nipped at my insides. I strode from her office and, shutting the massive door behind me with a heavy *click*, separated us once more.

As I took my coat from Marjorie, I let out a heavy breath, but it didn't bring any relief. The burn of Erin's fierce gaze still radiated through me along with the buzz from having seen her again. The elevator doors closed, and in the ride down the burn faded, but that buzz of excitement at seeing my mother remained. The same buzz of excitement I'd once felt as a child when she'd invite me out with her.

When I was in elementary school and would be home on school breaks, my mother would pick a day and take me out for a museum exhibition, and lunch at our favorite French restaurant, and shopping. She was very busy at graduate school and working at Grandfather's office. This was our special time, just the two of us, and I loved it. We both did.

On one of these occasions, after seeing a Picasso exhibit at the Chicago Art Institute, we had an incredible meal at Ambria where we had our favorite appetizer, *escargots* in a garlic butter sauce with pignoli nuts. Afterward, we headed up Michigan Avenue to Nordstrom.

. . .

IN THE FITTING room in the boys' department, she pulled up the collar on the stiff white Polo dress shirt she'd chosen for me and ran a hand through my new haircut. "Very sharp. So handsome." Her hands rested on my shoulders, our gazes locked, and that warmth raced through me. We were a perfect pair in style and look; same color and shape eyes, same color hair, too, although mine had gotten darker the past year, and I wasn't sure I liked it.

Mom's blonde hair was swept up today and she wore her favorite wrap dress along with perfect makeup and those big, sparkly diamond earrings Grandmother had given her last Christmas. We could be in a magazine spread together, that *Town & Country Magazine* that Grandmother subscribed to and they enjoyed pouring over together.

We got to the cashier, whose face reddened as she announced the total, over one thousand dollars. My mother took out one of her many credit cards from her Louis Vuitton wallet and paid the bill. Two other salesladies folded my new clothes, making neat piles and packing them carefully into great big shopping bags. I took two of the Nordstrom bags and she the other two.

My mom grinned at me. "Let's go."

"Let's go!" I repeated.

"Erin! How are you?"

Mother stopped in her tracks, her face locking into a tight smile. "Paige, hello."

"You didn't come to the last Foundation tea and I've been meaning to call you to tell you the news."

"News?"

"Oh yes, there's this big controversy going on about — Oh." The lady's blue eyes blinked and honed right in on me. "And who's this?"

"This is my godson. Arthur," my mother replied smoothly.

I froze. My heart thudded dully in my chest. My skin suddenly heated.

Godson.

Godson.

"Such a handsome young man. Hello there, Arthur."

"Hello," I mumbled, my mouth suddenly very dry.

I'd never heard her say it before. "Godson." I stole a glance up at her. Her skin was paler than usual. She listened to Paige's flow of words about the meeting of the organizers of the Garden Show, the latest hot chef and could my mother introduce her, the fashion show she'd gone to in New York. My mother smiled, but I noticed the fine press of her lips. She wanted to escape and quickly.

"We really have to go, we have dinner reservations," my mother finally interrupted her friend.

"Of course. Call me, won't you?"

"Will do."

"Goodbye, Arthur."

"Goodbye, ma'am."

I stumbled to keep up with my mother's long stride, her quick pace. The big shopping bags I held kept bonking into my legs, slowing me down. "Mom, wait—"

She pivoted on her heels and leaned down into me, her blue eyes flaring. "Don't call me that. Not here. Not now. Jesus."

A painful rip tore through my insides. My breath caught in my chest and choked there. The full shopping bags grew as heavy as fifty pound weights strapped to my arms.

She spun once more and kept walking, charging out of the store until we got to the curb. Our driver pulled up within moments. We climbed into the Town Car quickly.

"Take us home, please," she said.

"Very good." The driver's gaze flicked to mine, and I sank deeper in the leather seat and examined the throbbing red marks the shopping bag handles had left behind.

There was no excited chatter, there was no trip to Unabridged Books to explore new books—cooking, art and design for her and science fiction, fantasy, and historical adventure for me—and bring home shopping bags loaded with our treasure. There was only a young woman across the backseat from me with her hands folded rigidly in her lap as she stared out the window for the entire ride. My mom who wasn't supposed to be my mom. Or something.

Once through the front door of the apartment, she handed off her shopping bags to the housekeeper.

"Go on." My mother's fingers ruffled quickly through my hair, but she didn't meet my gaze. She disappeared down the long hallway that led to her bedroom.

I lumbered up to my room upstairs and fell back onto my perfectly made bed and stared at the ceiling, willing the sickening churn of my stomach to cease, for my thoughts to numb. I was good at that. Very good.

When I was in high school my mother and her new husband were featured in the pages of *Town & Country Magazine* sitting in their newly purchased penthouse apartment remodeled by a top architect and interior decorator. I read the article. Even though she'd recently gotten married, the new Mrs. Cavanaugh Bradley managed to transform her father's company and lead it to the top of the heap in Chicago. She was a businesswoman to admire, a role model for all young women, a new generation of entrepreneur. Erin Cavanaugh Bradley knew how to balance her career and personal life.

She sure did.

I wasn't included in the photos in the magazine, nor was I mentioned in the article. Eventually my mother's uptightness about having an illegitimate child eased, and once I got to college, she'd begun to introduce me as her son without explanation. But that day at school, I'd thrown the magazine into a trash can and lit it on fire on my way to Lacrosse practice.

That day the coach ousted me from the field for excessive aggression, and I was barred from playing in the next match. They should have ousted me for the rest of the season, but the fuckers couldn't do that. Not only was my grandfather a star alumnus, I was the Captain of the team and we were in the play-offs for the cup; they needed me. My mother was informed, and she expressed her deep disappointment in my behavior. But it was my grandfather who flew out to see me. He always made time for me, but I knew for him to fly all the way out to Massachusetts for the day from his golf vacation in Florida was a huge deal.

"You have to learn the art of self control, Arthur," he said. "Take this time and use it wisely. Regroup and prepare yourself, and when you have the privilege to be back out on that field, you do what needs to get done. I have every confidence that you know what that is and that you will accomplish what you set out to do. Remember, actions always speak louder than words, that's what remains in people's minds—what you do, how you react, the choices you make. The rest is hot air. You show them all what you're made of. You show them who you are."

My pulse raced at his words. "Yes sir, I will."

"Good." He hugged me. "Your grandmother and I will be coming to see you play in the finals."

"You are?"

"Yes, we are. And we're bringing your mother too. See you then."

"See you then, Grandpa."

In the weeks that followed, I released my steam on the track, in the swimming pool, and in the weight room every day until I was allowed to play again.

We got to the Final and we won that goddamn title.

3

TURO

I DROVE over to the Boss's house in Oak Brook. I'd called ahead, of course, and he said to stop by. I wanted to discuss my mother with him right away. Alone. This could get messy very fast. It already had gotten messy, and I was the one playing fucking catch up.

The timing sucked. I had good news to share with him. News I'd been sitting on for a while now, waiting for the right time to impress the fuck out of him.

The housekeeper opened the door, and told me to go on to his office, but unfortunately, I encountered his son in the hallway.

Valerio glared at me, scaling me like a fish with a sharp scrape of his eyes. "Look who it is. I have a question for you, Turo."

"Call me. Make an appointment."

"Did you kill that biker?" he asked.

"What are you talking about?" Of course I knew what he was talking about, because, a week ago I'd killed Med McGuire, a meth-making bike club president from Kansas. His was the type of outlaw bike club you didn't fuck with. The Smoking Guns were a huge criminal organization that worked for the Tantucci family, our historical enemies on the landscape of Chicago and the Midwest.

I'd killed Med because he was a vital resource for the Tantuccis drug trade. But I enjoyed killing him because he deserved it for what he'd done, for his brutality. Me, the avenging angel.

Valerio leaned into me. "I'm going to feed you to the Tantuccis for this."

"Excuse me?"

A slight smile flickered on his lips. "You used to be a useful tool, DeMarco."

A tool. That summed it up in the Outfit, didn't it? A network of useful tools. Actually, my parents had taught me that first. In their own ways both of them had gotten me to do their bidding, yet always kept me at arm's length, dangling their carrots in my face to keep me at it. The rewards had once seemed so damned promising. Glittering.

Artificial starlight.

I was thirty-three, yet that lesson from some ten years back still stung fresh in my veins. Working for Mauro had given me the agency to break out of Erin's treasured mold. But Mauro wasn't simply the "other side" of the life that I'd been raised in. He was the underside.

Both worlds were similar. Both bet and parleyed for the same things. Both needed each other. And I found I enjoyed playing in that long, wide field between the two teams. In fact, the Boss had come to rely on my opinion on a great many things, much to Val's consternation. I'd found myself savoring that. But after ten years of working for Mauro, making his bordellos major moneymakers and an established system that generated important contacts, I was still not a "made man." Everyone knew I was only half Italian and half the dreaded Irish. I may have had the sheen of Mauro's favor and, therefore, accepted, but up to a point. My blood was sullied. Not to be completely trusted.

Over the years I thought things would improve for me on that score by way of the results I consistently brought in. That wasn't the case, however. Tradition was tradition. A fact Val enjoyed.

"You killed him, Turo. Didn't you?" That smile stretched across his pretty boy face. Was he waiting for a reaction? He wasn't going to get one. "Such an arrogant son of a bitch."

I let out a deep sigh. "Valerio."

"I'd love to see Mr. Tantucci blow his stack when he finds out that you're the one responsible for killing his precious meth maker. They've been losing big bucks across several states ever since."

"You have proof?"

He let out a dry laugh. "Your new boy, Little Anthony, is mine, fuckhead."

Little Anthony was a newbie soldier who'd just joined my crew on the Boss's insistence. I'd had him checked out. I'd been thorough. *How the hell—*

Val slid a five by seven photo from his suit jacket and held it up for me to see. Med's bloodied body strewn on that burnt orange motel bedspread flashed before me. The musty smell of that trashy motel room in southern Indiana on that hot and muggy afternoon came rushing back to me.

I'd snuck into Med's room as he'd been taking a hit from a pipe, utterly mesmerized as he watched a bikini clad girl, one of my most trusted prostitutes who I'd planted in his path, crush a piece of cake with her ass on the dresser (people's addictions to fetishes never ceased to intrigue me). While he got busy desperately trying to get himself off, I slid my blade into his neck, pushing him back onto the bed, the smell of him foul. He'd actually smiled, laughed, the high bastard. Then he got pissed, his eyes narrowing, a low growl escaping his lips as his body bucked once, twice. Sweet, sweet panic, that struggle for one more breath, the frantic then slow thump of his heart as I held him down, blood oozing. He gave in to me, and he was finally gone.

"I helped Little Anthony with his mamma's medical bills recently," Val said. "He owes me big time. No health insurance is a good thing for some of us."

What a fucking moron. A moron who had me by the balls at the moment. I shifted my weight. "You think doing this would be good for the family?"

"Don't talk to me about family, you fuck. I know my father didn't order this hit, I asked him about it. He didn't like it much." He jabbed a finger in the air at me. "You did this. Your head's too big for your own good, and the sooner my dad sees that the better."

"Entitled punk," I shot back.

Val's chin jutted out and he lunged at me, grabbing at my collar. I shoved him off. "Don't you fucking touch me," I said on a hiss.

The boss entered the hallway, and Val moved away from me, his fingers rubbing over his creased forehead, nostrils flaring. I smoothed down my collar, my tie.

"Good, you're here." Mauro Guardino's eyes went from me to his son and back again, his lips set in a firm line.

"Yes, I'm here." I ground my jaw, adjusting my suit jacket. I was the one who was always here.

Val was a few years younger than me, and was comfortable sitting on the arm of the throne in a well-made suit and his gold chains and diamond Rolex, the family initial on a gold pinky ring, nodding his head and making faces, while his dad made all the tough decisions. Perched there until the moment came when his father would be gone and he would just slide into the seat.

Or so he assumed.

That's not what it was about. It was about hard work, hours pounding the streets, getting dirty, real dirty, stealing, haggling, beating, making contacts, giving shitheads the time of day, being respected, feared. That's how you got what you wanted.

Mauro threw a newspaper on his desk. "Look at this shit."

A column's headline blared about Med's "biker assassination" and how the Smoking Guns Motorcycle Club was up in arms as were their enemies. How the Feds were bracing for a war between bike clubs and would be investigating Med's chapter, and his ties to a host of criminal organizations in the region.

"Not good." Mauro shoved the newspaper across his desk and it flew onto the floor.

"Why not, Dad?" asked Valerio, his eyes sliding to mine. "If the Tantuccis catch some heat this way, isn't it good?"

"Not necessarily. These bikers are idiots. What if one of them starts talking to point the finger at the other?"

"Yeah, this gang versus that gang, all hell could break loose," said Val.

"They're clubs, not gangs," I said.

Valerio rolled his eyes. "Who gives a shit?"

"We've worked with a few off and on, but never long term," said Mauro. "What if they all start pointing fingers to make deals to stay alive? This sucks dick. And why leave the body out like that? Why not get rid of it? Was this some sort of vendetta? Jesus, I don't like it at all."

"Fascinating, huh, Turo?" Val asked me, a cold smile brightening his sour but handsome face.

Mauro's hard gaze shot to me and back to Val. "What's going on?"

I'd been looking forward to finally telling him about my crippling a vital artery of the Tantucci drug apparatus and now finally cutting it off at the head by killing Med. But instead, I had Val threatening me and the Boss in a snit over Med's death.

And I needed to discuss what the hell he was doing to my mother.

I'd been lucky. Through my girlfriend I'd met Serena, a new friend of hers who came to me for a favor one day. I did a little more digging than I had to into this girl because she intrigued me, and I discovered that Serena was Med's ex "old lady" whom he'd kidnapped as a teenager and held prisoner until she'd escaped. She owed me and we struck a bargain. Information on Med as payment for her debt to me. She agreed.

Med and his crew were vagabonds, and Serena fed me information about his hiding places, his manic thought process, his maneuvers. His insanity. I hit him over and over again as no one else ever had. One by one I'd set off explosions in Med's path. I was Lawrence of Arabia watching and waiting for my carefully laid dynamite to ignite along the Tantucci-Smoking Gun train tracks, then I'd charged into the sand dunes on a triumphant roar, looting the spoils, humiliating them, defeating them.

Med was a drug-addicted sick fuck. Under my constant attacks, paranoia reigned supreme in his camp, affecting his trade and rattling the Tantuccis. Their dependable routines had been broken, business was down, reputations suffered, finger pointing abounded. Killings. I'd jammed their symphony with a sudden, long, driving violin solo. I was the masked conductor of this brutal orchestra.

Je ne regrette rien. Fucking truth, Edith Piaf.

My stomach hardened under Val's gaze. A wolf waiting for a sign of his prey's weakness. *Motherfucker.* I'd planned on this getting me more in to the Guardino Outfit than ever before. It was a smart plan. But I hadn't planned on Val stalking me.

Val slid the photo on his father's desk. "You need to see this, Pop."

Mauro stared at it. "What the hell is this?" He lifted his fierce gaze to mine. "Did you do this?"

"Holy shit, you didn't know?" said Val. "I thought you'd ordered the hit yourself."

"What have you done?" Mauro bellowed at me.

"I ruined this biker's business and his life, and made the Tantuccis miserable, and then I took him out," I replied.

The Boss's eyes flickered, his one cheek twitched. "You took him out?"

"Yes."

"Without my permission? Without consulting me?"

Val crossed his arms over his chest his eyes darting between us.

I said, "I had an opportunity, and I—"

"And you took it."

"I took it."

Mauro chewed on his thin lips. His glare heavy.

"I told him, Dad." Val couldn't help but jump in and splash in our muddied waters. "I told him it was wrong. I figured it out. I had him watched. I knew it'd come to this. He just does whatever the hell he wants. It's gotta stop, right? I mean, there's no telling what else he'll get up to if you give him the legroom."

Mauro's hand shot out and clasped the edge of the desk. "There's something to be said for initiative and enterprise, but I'm the fucking boss, here."

"Do something about him already!" Val raised his voice in the eerie silence, his face streaked with red. "He goes overboard. He needs to be punished."

"Don't you ever question me!" Mauro thundered. "At the end of the day, Turo delivers."

And Val didn't deliver. That I knew, we all knew. But Val was the crown prince. That I also knew.

"He delivers?" Val's face dropped along with his tone.

"Yes, he delivers. And you're whining, I'm sick of it!" Mauro turned to me. "You—if I had known you were taking out Med, that you had an opportunity, I would've told you not to. The FBI had a lead on him recently, a huge sting operation in the works. They were getting ready to arrest him and his band of nut jobs. And I was gonna sit back and watch the circus. But no, you had to go in and be the goddamn dragon slayer. What the fuck! What the fuck, Turo?"

I ground my jaw.

He sucked in a breath. "Who knows, they probably saw you

take him out. Maybe they have you on video, and now they're gonna turn this into some kind of all out war. They're gonna sniff out every connection to these freaks. I do not need this shit right now!"

My insides twined like a tight rubber ball. The blood rushed to my head.

The Boss's hand slammed on his desk. "Judge Connelly won't be able to do a damn thing for me if they got one of my men on fucking video."

"I—"

"Shut up!" The veins in Mauro's thick neck bulged.

My feet cemented to the floor, but I didn't avert my gaze. His fierce glare held mine.

"Jesus, dad, why don't you just cut him off already?" Val's voice seethed from behind his father. "Because I swear I will!"

"No, you won't!" Mauro snapped.

Val stiffened, saying nothing, his eyes bursting from their sockets.

"Arturo."

An icy jag razored through me at the hiss in his voice.

"Get out."

4

TURO

"Turo, are you okay?"

I blinked. Francesca, Val's sister, stood in the foyer of the house. Val's luscious little sister who had a crush on me. The boss's daughter.

My half sister.

"Hey," I said.

Her lips parted and she blushed. A blush that extended from her cheeks over her chest and down beneath her bikini top. A pair of small, too small, triangles of a fine burgundy colored crochet material.

Francesca's crush on me had been cute once upon a time. Now it was a burden. A grave burden. We'd seen each other at a dinner party at a supper club a few weeks ago. She was with a cousin, looking bored two tables over. I was with my girlfriend, Ciara, fingering her under our table as Francesca stared at me thinking the look on my face was about her. Then she blushed violently and looked away when she realized the truth.

"I'm just heading off to the pool," she said, voice breathy.

"Enjoy. It's unusually hot for May."

"Very hot." Her glance shifted to my mouth.

Voices rose from down the hall, behind the closed door of Mauro's office. "Daddy not happy with Val again?" she asked.

"You could say that."

She rolled her eyes. "I wish he and Stella would move into their new house already. It was supposed to be finished last month, but Stella keeps changing her mind about the counter-tops and the bathroom tile and the carpeting." A soft giggle escaped her lips. "God help us all when she gears up to do the baby's room."

"She's pregnant?"

"Hmm."

"That's nice. I didn't know."

Stella. *That bitch.* I'd thought she was so into me, into us, but it had all been a sham.

My first summer working for Mauro, Stella and I would meet secretly in cars, in hotels, in clubs, to consummate and be consumed by our roaring lust. She certainly had an appetite for me which, along the way, I'd stupidly mistaken for real feeling. All my little heated declarations to her were always met with an equally heated series of *"yes, yes, yes!"*

When I told her I was falling in love with her, her response had been, *"What are you talking about? We're just having fun. Geez, that's all this is, I thought you understood that?"* An amused look was on her face like she was genuinely stunned and rather mortified. She never again answered my calls.

Shock seized me at my failure of judgement. Anger at my pathetic desperation to believe what wasn't actually there. At being stomped on and ridiculed. Again.

Never again.

Stella had been Val's girlfriend, but I hadn't known that. I'd only been her play toy that summer while Val was on a post college graduation trip through Europe with his buddies, prob-ably fucking his way from Amsterdam to Paris to Rome. The night he'd returned home, she was on his arm, eyes sparkling. He eventually put a ring on her finger and they'd gotten married five years ago.

"Only family knows she's pregnant," said Francesca bringing me back to the here and now. "But soon my mother will be having a party to celebrate. She loves to throw a party."

"Yes, yes, she does."

"I hope you'll be there," said Francesca, inching closer to me, her shoulder leaning against the wall, her throat at an angle.

I moved back from her. "If I'm invited, I'll be there."

"Of course you'll be invited."

She inched closer toward me again. I could smell her light perfume, flowers, honey. Oh, she was honey all right. "Don't you dare bring a plus one, though," she whispered.

"Francesca..."

"I like your tie." She pressed her fingers down my navy Armani tie. All the way down my chest, my abs. "You're always dressed so nicely." Her hand slid down over my belt buckle, and I cuffed her wrist, stopping it from going any farther south. She smiled up at me, a lazy smile, a smile sodden with lustful promise and capitulation.

Jesus.

"Francesca?" Val's voice sliced between me and his sister.

Francesca's body stiffened, and she immediately stood at attention, tugging at her cover-up. "Turo and I were just talking."

Val glared at me then his sister, at me again. "I thought you'd left, DeMarco."

"Francesca and I were...catching up." I wiped a thumb down the corner of my mouth. Sometimes you had to make your point viciously clear, damn the cost.

Mauro came up behind his son, his dark eyes glimmering at all three of us. His children. He said nothing but the roar screaming in his mind was obvious.

"Get lost, Fran," Val said to his sister.

She rolled her eyes, planting a hand at her waist and

remained put. She was a sweet kid, but not a kid anymore, that was for sure. Francesca was twenty now. A woman.

I shot her a final grin. "Enjoy your swim."

She grinned back, her face rosy. "See you." She bit her lip and turned down the hallway, opening the French doors to the back-yard and sashaying outside on her wedge heeled sandals, the robe flaring around her bare legs. An exit worthy of a music video diva.

"What the fuck do you think you're doing?" Val bit out.

I let him think the worst. That was how these things worked. By indirection. Underhanded, slithering indirection. Letting his imagination do all my work for me.

"Saying hello," I replied.

"You leave my sister alone, motherfucker!" Val seethed. "I don't want you anywhere near her."

"Get out of my way. I'm leaving."

"Leave and don't come back, you prick."

We're all bastards of some kind, me more than others. Val was certainly in a class all by himself though.

Oh, wait, "bastard"—that's me.

Mauro stood motionless in the distance, a stone mountain in the hallway, his eyes burning into mine. Shit, I still had to talk to him about my mother.

"Leave," Mauro's voice seethed.

And now was not the time. Fuck.

I got out of their house, their pompous fucking six bedroom house with the gaudy Italian lacquer furniture Mauro's wife loved, my stride long and quick. Getting in my car, I gripped the thick leather steering wheel as I got the hell of out their neigh-borhood.

5

TURO

I LET OUT A HEAVY BREATH, my head knocking back against the headrest as I got on the expressway and headed back into the city. I brushed a hand down my face.

This started with a girl.

I'd cheated on Ciara with her friend Serena, the former biker girl. Serena was beautiful in an odd way. She was funky vintage clothes, too much crazy colored hair, too many tattoos, and for all that exhibitionism, she was anything but an exhibitionist. Introverted, not very smiley, body language tight and in control. She was a woman of few words, yet the ones she used were careful and straight to the point like a sleek blade. But those clear blue-green eyes...oh, those gorgeous orbs told a thousand tales. I wanted to be fucked by those eyes alone.

An unusual desire for her had taken hold of me over the time that she'd been feeding me information about Med. I'd initially chalked it up to lust, but no, it had been more. Her last night in Chicago before she'd taken off for parts unknown with a new name and identity which I'd provided, I seized what I wanted—sex. She'd given into me, but she hadn't surrendered. I tried to fuck her into submission, or at least earn some sign of appreciation, but nothing worked. Not the orgasms, not the intensity, not the pushing of every boundary. She remained remote, detached. Later, I realized that by screwing me she was setting fire to herself and her life up until that moment. A phoenix.

Thoughts of her had stayed with me long after that night, which was unusual for me. It was more than just a satisfying fuck with a sexy woman or the appeal of her imperiousness. I wasn't sure, but it lingered for a long while like an exotic fragrance I couldn't place and couldn't forget. That fragrance festered inside me, but I ignored it.

A few months ago, three years after I last saw Serena, I met Finger, the man who had helped her escape from Med's madhouse, and it all came together. Finger was a biker from another club, a club just as outlaw as Med's—his rivals, in fact. Med had taken him prisoner and tortured him years ago like he had Serena, leaving him scarred and maimed.

Nonetheless, Finger had gone back in to Med's lair and freed Serena and then brought her to Chicago where she lived in hiding. They kept their relationship secret. Unfortunately, Finger had gotten arrested and sent to jail for a few years, and Serena got spooked and took off having changed her identity again thanks to my help. After he got released, Finger came to me looking for her.

I'd listened to his deep, husky voice demanding answers from me about her, and that's when I knew—it was his blood that pumped though her heart, his soul wrapped in hers if such a thing were possible. The fierceness in his eyes that night as he'd questioned me about where she'd gone, what her new name was —burning ashes. Full of torment and yearning just like her eyes had been, only she had learned to mask her pain with opaque ice.

He had a will of iron that had been forged in his raw passion for her, and it raged from him. It was palpable and pushed at me, like a wave in the ocean. This was being in love? This burning incineration?

I braked in the traffic on the exit ramp. Had he ever found her? Were they together now? Oh, for fuck's sake, why the hell did I care?

Finger was a fearless, intelligent man, and I ended up hiring him for a job that Val had fucked up. Finger delivered, and the payoff for both of us had been undeniably huge. Boss was impressed, capos silenced, Val livid. So good.

Then and there I decided to keep my connection to Finger to myself. I had ruined Med's stellar reputation in a matter of months thanks to Serena. I'd scored big on the Outfit's resourcefulness scale with my Finger connection. But would any of those successes trump the blood issue? Would anything, ever?

No.

I knew that, so did Val, so did the Boss.

The Boss knew he could rely on me, though, and I'd worked hard to prove that to him over and over again. I provided steady income, no excuses, no complaining. But no matter how much I accomplished to lift myself up, I was dragged underfoot. Being a "consultant" as the Boss had named me was fine, running his prostitutes was fine, but it had gotten to the point I wanted more —my own territory, my own business within the business.

Rules were rules. Tradition was essential. My blood would always be an issue. I was the Tom Hagen of the Guardino crime family, for fuck's sake. But this wasn't a Hollywood film.

I was *in*, but at the end of the day, on the periphery, out.

———

I MANEUVERED through the usual traffic in Lincoln Park and guided my black Range Rover into its parking spot in the garage under my building. José, the uniformed doorman, greeted me in the lobby and hit the button in the elevator that led to my apartment.

Once inside, I threw my trench coat on the vintage leather

Barcelona chair my mother had given me as a housewarming gift when I'd bought the apartment. An ache raced over my skull. I needed a drink.

At my bar, I poured myself a Laphroig in my favorite glass and drained it in one swallow, my throat burning. I poured another.

Swirling the bracing liquor in my mouth, I took in the Chicago skyline. Earlier, when I'd gotten dressed and taken in this very same view, I'd felt more sure of myself, of my place, my future. Over the years I'd become good at kicking any self doubts to the curb before they flowered like a deadly plant releasing noxious fumes, rendering me immobile. I relished problems, finding a way out of their maze, breaking their code, solving, squashing.

Today, though. Fuck, today there had been no resolving.

I put down my empty glass. I knew what I wanted, needed. I dialed my soldier, Paul.

"Did you find Salazar?" I asked.

"Perfect timing. Just tying him up."

My pulse ticked in my neck. "I'll be right there."

I took a cab to Bridgeport and walked up and over the three blocks to our basement holding cell in a pawn shop owned by Paul's cousin. The tension in my muscles pounding, I charged down the winding metal steps and pushed through the door.

Paul's eyes widened at the sight of me and he quickly stepped aside. He knew.

"Well, hello, Mr. Salazar," my voice filled the dank, dark space.

Salazar strained against the chair he'd been tied to. He groaned, his body pushing against the chains around his chest and legs.

"He ain't talking," Paul said.

I sniffed in air. "You'll talk to me though. Won't you?" My fingers flexed and Salazar's bloodied eyes darted to the movement. I took off my jacket and handed it to Ricky, Paul's boy. "Be careful with that."

"Yeah, 'course."

I reached for the tire iron, and a low moan heaved from Salazar. Paul cleared his throat, shifting his weight. "You don't have to talk yet." I stroked Salazar's face with the heavy metal bar. "It's my turn now."

Thwack.

Bone cracked, and he screamed. I hit his leg again at the knee.

"Aaaah!" Salazar's body jerked, he shuddered violently. His head slumped forward, hanging on his chest.

I lifted his swollen face with the tire iron. "*Now* it's your turn," my voice hissed. A cockroach crawled to my left and I squashed it with my shoe. "For fuck's sake, Paul, you have to get an exterminator in here." I threw down the tire iron and grabbed the hammer.

Paul jumped over and untied Salazar's one hand, tying it to the small table to the right. I slanted my head at Paul and he held Salazar's head, making him focus on his hand on the wood table that was scratched and dinged with knife marks and poundings.

"No! No! Please!" Salazar squawked.

"I need the address of that Tantucci drop off location. And I need it now."

Salazar's face froze. I'd caught him double dealing with a Tantucci soldier. He was a low worker bee in our Outfit, but at this level was where you found the buried riches, where the trail began, at the lowest denominator.

My fingers squeezed around the taped handle, and my hammer flew. With every scream of his agony my heart jolted in my chest, adrenaline coursing through my veins.

Valerio's scowl, Francesca's inviting smile, Mauro's controlled rage, my mother's politeness, Serena's body yielding to mine as she turned her face away. I stood back from Salazar and waited. He muttered through his groans and cries. Next to me, Paul's face glistened with sweat, pale in the one fluorescent light bar buzzing over us as he asked him detailed questions and received replies. Ricky chewed on his lower lip behind him.

"That's better," I said.

Paul handed me a paper towel and I wiped off the blood and muck. Ricky held out my jacket. I slid it back on and left. Outside in the fresh air I took in a deep breath, but the high I'd felt two moments ago had already faded. My nerves twitched. I'd hyped myself up instead of calming myself down in that basement. I needed something else. Something to take the edge off my edge.

Something more.

6

TURO

I WENT BACK HOME and drained another whisky. I had to talk to Mauro about my mother, and I needed to do it fast. His threatening her was a hazardous chemical seeping into my nicely dammed reservoir. Poisonous. The buzz of the concierge phone in the foyer of my apartment clipped the rush of my thoughts.

"Mr. DeMarco? Ms. Ciara is here to see you, sir."

Dammit. I'd missed her performance tonight.

"Send her up, José, thank you."

I returned the phone back to its cradle by the front door, unlatched the lock, and went back to my bar. I was going to need liquid fortitude for this.

Ciara waltzed into the apartment like a Valkyrie, her long blonde hair floating over her shoulders, the door slamming behind her in a *boom*. She knew I hated that. Detested that. She strode toward me in a long, body hugging, coral dress and strappy, high-heeled sandals that I'd bought her just last week. Fifteen hundred dollars worth of thin leather straps and stiletto.

"I didn't forget," I said. Own up up front was my motto.

"That's all you have to say to me? Really?"

"No. How about—"

"You never used to forget anything. Always prompt, always reminding me of my little shortcomings, my tardiness. But this takes the goddamn cake."

"Ciara—"

"Tonight was my debut, Turo! My premier at the Fuego Club. You knew how important this was to me. I've been talking about this for weeks, months ago when I got this gig! Where the fuck were you?"

"I had a meeting I couldn't get out of."

She let out a heavy breath. "Yes, this meeting, that meeting. Always a meeting."

"What the hell do you want from me, Ciara?"

Her eyes flashed at me. "Wow. That says it all. You're just not willing, are you? I used to be willing to put up with all this. You know, I always thought you were a lot of fun—different but fun. You always kept me at a distance, but I didn't mind. There were rules I had to follow in order to be with you, and I wanted you badly enough that I followed them. I didn't care. But those rules were quite convenient for you. I've come to realize you're not just distant, you're totally empty inside. No better than a well-dressed robot. You feel fucking nothing, no matter how hard I try."

"I am a robot, Ciara. You're absolutely right. You want more and I—"

"I don't want more, you idiot! That's not what this is about! I never expected a ring from you, but I did expect quality, because I'm worth it, goddammit!" Tears filled her eyes, and something in my chest pinched.

I didn't like seeing her upset. I didn't like being the cause of it. Ciara had been good to me, and I'd figured being generous with her in bed and with gifts, a well-planned dinner date here and there, would be enough. It had been enough for a long time. A couple of years, in fact.

Years? Jesus.

She had a point. Obviously, I hadn't been paying too much

attention. She had filled a role in my life very nicely and I'd just rolled along with it.

"Not even a fucking apology? An attempt to be sorry, to show you give some kind of a shit?" she said. "This past year you've been a real asshole, you know that? I've put up with a lot from you. A whole hell of a lot. But this, tonight? No."

She posed on those heels, a lean leg posturing out of the high slit in her dress. Was she waiting for me to protest? Ciara was a beautiful woman, but her beauty didn't hold me in its grip. Neither did she.

She was right. I really didn't care. And I'd had enough of people glaring and bitching at me today. Expecting whatever they expected. For me to pay, for me to be there to do and to be what they needed. Ciara had agreed to my terms when we'd first started this, and she'd certainly enjoyed all the many treats and trinkets that I'd provided her. She should cut and run like a good girl.

I filled my glass again and, holding her gaze, I drank. Her heavily made up eyes flared as she grabbed the vase filled with peonies on the mahogany console table to her left and hurled it at the antique Venetian mirror. *Crash. Crack.*

I raised my glass at her. "Well done."

Venom snaked in the curve of her lips. We'd been content for a while. At least, I'd been. What a bloodless, lukewarm word that was. *Content.* I certainly wasn't a lukewarm person, and neither was she. I liked Ciara, but was I devoted? Eh. Burning? No. Obsessed? God no.

I raised my glass. "Is the romance drama over now? I've got a hell of a lot going on tonight."

"I hope you die alone, you bastard, because that's what you deserve."

"Get out of my apartment. Now."

"Fuck you, Turo! Fuck. You." Spinning on her heels, she

charged out of my apartment. I grit my teeth at the chop of her shoes over the marble flooring.

Good for her.

And thank fuck that was over.

I picked up the concierge phone. "José, Ms. Ciara is no longer welcome at my home. Do not let her into the building ever again. Is that clear?"

"Yes, sir, Mr. DeMarco."

I hung up the phone and drained my glass, tearing off my tie and tossing it on the bar. So what if I was thirty-three and had never been in a long, successful love relationship? So what if I'd never been engaged or married? I'd saved myself the thousand irritations and petty annoyances that came with it. A few of my college buddies who'd been married for about five to seven years now were already bitching and complaining and looking war weary. The tedium was real. I certainly wasn't going through that crap.

My mommy and daddy had been just a flash of lust in the dark for a handful of weeks, and then it was done, nothing more than an opportunity for a con and a smack on the face for her. Even I'd felt the sting of that crack. Me? I distilled my needs and wants perfectly with women.

I caught my splintered reflection in the broken mirror. My face was drawn, dark circles under my eyes. My hand rubbed against the edge of my jaw. I was the fine, upstanding, not so young anymore, citizen of my community from a well-respected family. But I was also an underground killer and a fixer and a pimp for hire.

"But a shadow in both worlds," a voice whispered in my ear.

A chill raced over my flesh, and I let out a tight breath shaking those words away, yet a hit of tension knifed my gut. Fuck that. I dialed Tricia's number on my cell. My madame.

A classmate and study partner in business school, Tricia had a hard time paying her undergrad and graduate student loans once we got out into the real world. I offered her a managerial position which needed her looks, poise, and merciless organizational skills. She hadn't been offended. Like me, she appreciated cash and had no moral qualms about sex. Business was business. We made a good team.

"Hello there," her singsong voice magnified the swirl of my anticipation.

"Tricia, send me someone."

Her voice perked up even more. "Any preferences this evening?"

"Short to medium height, pale skin, blue eyes. And tattoos."

"I have just the girl. But she's a newbie, still in training, and I don't want you to be disappointed."

My dick hardened in my trousers. "Sounds perfect. In fact, I'll make sure she's ready for you. It's been a long time since I've done any training."

"It certainly has. Um, are you okay? You sound—"

"Send her over now. With a goody bag."

"You've got it."

When my father had given me his small brothel business to run, I first focused on cleaning up the accounting, then the seedy locations that were used. Then I got down to the product, the centerpieces, the stars of the spectacle. I showed the women not just sexual moves hungry men would go for, but the way to talk to a client, how to change up their demeanor according to tastes and preferences in order to make the fuck all the more satisfying and tailor made. How to *engage*. You wanted that john to remember the experience, to leave him desperate for more, to be convinced he needed more. Return, steady clients were top priority. I even had a couple of top executive gay women who were steady clients.

Tricia and I chose our stable carefully, kept our girls clean, healthy, and happy with good pay, clothing allowances, regular doctor visits, and client screening. Unlike in my father's day, when all he gave a shit about was getting the most bang out of his buck—literally—and not giving a shit about anything else. Completely wrong. Yes, online porn was the rage now and a great moneymaker for the Outfit, but prostitution was the greatest theater of them all, and it was sorely taken for granted.

"Turo, before you go, I have some news for you," Tricia brought me back to the present.

"What is it?"

"I just got another call from Mr. James Bradley," she said, her voice liquid honey over the phone. She knew I'd be pleased. "He requested Nari again."

"Did he now?"

"He did. Third time in two weeks."

My stepfather had an obsession with Korean pussy.

About a month ago, I had sent a girl his way one afternoon when I knew he'd taken off work to go sailing, his favorite hobby. I'd sent Julia, our WASP princess who knew how to sail, had just graduated Northwestern, having majored in chemistry and wanted the job as she was heading for an expensive med school in the fall. They'd flirted, he'd propositioned her, and she'd let him know she was on the clock. He'd been surprised at first, she'd said, his manly ego taken aback that for her this was about business and not desire.

We men can be such idiots.

But then the power of his smug self-indulgence had taken over, as I'd hoped it would.

Three hundred dollars later, fuck him she did. Over a catered lunch on the boat the next week, he asked her about her "friends," and expressed a particular desire for an Asian girl. Enter Nari, our new Korean American asset. James blew through a five hundred dollar session with Nari. Of course I'd asked my ladies how James was in the sack, and they'd both reported that he was adventurous, but not very attentive. Poor girls had to do all the work.

James came from money, but he hadn't managed it well over the years. My mother had taken over whatever brokerage accounts and trusts he had in his name and put him on a salary as a senior VP of her company which seemed to work out well. I thought of it as an allowance really, because he never did much of anything at the office. He would show up, always very well-dressed, look official, make a few calls, sign a few documents, and leave.

James shined on my mother's arm at the restaurant openings, the dinner parties, the foundation fundraisers. An excellent conversationalist, an avid theater-goer, book reader, and symphony subscriber, he was top notch on Chicago's socialite list of invitees. He was handsome and that handsome had aged extremely well. He and my mother made a very attractive couple and they were popular. They'd always been affectionate with each other, but now, knowing what kind of man he really was, it only made me sneer when I thought of him holding her hand, kissing her on the cheek, helping her with her coat.

I'd wanted her to sting, but now I wanted to punish the idiot who paraded at her side and slept in her bed at night.

He'd been a kind stepfather to me over the years, but a disinterested sort. They'd been married since I was fifteen, yet his presence still felt like nothing more than a temporary guest's whenever I'd been home. Frankly, I'd been the guest. Boarding schools from the time I was in first grade then onto college. Then my own place. Home for holidays, the meal mostly, and joining them for the grand vacations once a year. But not really home ever.

James was nothing better than a paid consort, wasn't he? But maybe that's the way Erin wanted it. A partner who didn't bother her, didn't demand. Did my mother know about his extracurricular activities? I doubted it, why would she stand for it? Erin didn't suffer fools.

Me being a prime example.

So I fucked with him because I could. I did this because I couldn't *not* do it. I tested him, and he scored brilliantly. I'd wanted to know if James Bradley would bend and dip. And he certainly did. One day soon I'd share the information with her, the proof. One day.

Years ago when my mother got tangled with my father, she had bent, been bitten, and gotten stung. And it had shocked her into a rigid autonomous independence. After I'd misbehaved, she'd drawn her battle lines with me. Now, I could show her where her squeaky clean intentions had gotten her.

I would bring a new art project home from school.

Look, Mommy. Look!

———

WITHIN THE TIME it took me to clean up the mess Ciara had left behind, a short, blue-eyed girl with long black hair entered my apartment. The hair was not what I'd hoped for, but otherwise, she was perfect. I sat back on my leather sofa and motioned for her to approach.

"Strip to your panties and let me see your body."

She followed instructions, turning around. A long tattoo of musical notes twisted over her round ass and up her back. Cliché, unfortunately.

"Face me and come closer." She did as I said, and I kneaded her full, stiff plastic tits. Her face reddened, and she let out a gasp, glancing up at me. "Don't move and don't look at me," my voice commanded. "But lick your lips. You want whatever I'm giving."

She averted her gaze downward, her tongue wetting her bottom lip, and my cock got impatient at the sight.

"Good girl. Get on the floor on your knees and lean your head back against the sofa." It had been a long, long day, and I needed immediate attention where it mattered the most.

She got on the floor, and I slid off my shirt, belt, trousers, boxer briefs. Her eyes widened at the sight of my demanding erection as I angled her head back onto the edge of the sofa, cuffing her neck with my hand.

"Show me you want this cock."

Her tongue darted out and her lips glistened, a moan escaping her throat. Taking my cock in hand, I slid it past her wet lips and thrust in deep. She let out a cry, but she didn't gag.

"Good," I said, my voice low. "Work my balls, and show me you love this, you want more."

She moaned, her body bouncing back against the sofa with my every sharp thrust, saliva dripping down her chin. Her one hand rubbed my balls and the base of my cock perfectly, the suction of her lips just right. I fucked her mouth and pulled out of her. She blinked as I sprayed her face and chest with my cum. She opened her mouth, her tongue curling, lapping.

"Ahh. A plus plus for you, honey."

She rubbed my cum all over her tits, a hand sliding down to her pussy where she stroked herself, her legs spreading wider for my perusal.

"That's it." I got down on the floor and slid two fingers up inside her slick pussy, her hips jerking to my fast pace. "Always consider how the customer can get the best view," I said.

Her chest arched back, tits bouncing. She came, her head lolling back on the sofa cushion. I dug my fingertips roughly into a breast. "Now get on your hands and knees. I want that ass in the air." I twisted a nipple and she shrieked.

I fisted her hair and pulled. "No, no, no. You don't have to like it, but I do. You moan when I do that. Again." I twisted her nipple harder, pinching it, and this time she moaned loudly.

"Better."

"Sorry, I'm just real sensitive there."

I twisted her other nipple and she pressed her lips shut against another gasp. "You say, 'Oh yeah.'"

She smiled softly. "Oh yeah."

"Hmm. Ass."

She flipped over onto her knees, and I spread her ass cheeks and spit, carefully fingering her tight hole. "Have you done this before?"

"Yes." She rocked her ass back and forth.

"My fucking lucky night then." I had lube ready and squished a dollop into her. I slid my dick in between her ass cheeks, and stroked. She moaned, rocking against me, and I got hard again. Condom on, I nudged my cock past her tight ring, inch by slow inch.

"Play with your clit," I gritted out.

Pleasure pulsated through me as she began to push back, her grip strangling my hard length, her hand working fast between her legs.

Robot.

Robot.

Hollow robot.

Fuck you, Ciara, for your tears.

Fuck you, Serena, for making me want to want more.

Gripping her hips tightly, I pulled out slowly. "With every pound of my cock, you fucking moan."

She moaned.

I controlled my orgasm. I wanted this one long, long, long, and hard won.

She pressed her head against the sofa for stability, her hand steadily working between her legs, as I burrowed deep into her perfect tightness, finally allowing myself to blow.

I released her. "Bedroom. This way." I pointed toward my guest bedroom.

She tottered in there on her heels, her ripped panty hanging on an ankle, a damp sheen in between her legs. My artwork in the making. I followed her into the room, pushing her back on the bed, and she lay there, hips twisting, tattoos fluttering on her flesh.

Reminding me of *her*. Serena's face flooded my vision.

It all started when Serena had come to me one night. She'd never spoken to me before, but that night she asked me for a favor. Not your everyday request from a friend of your girlfriend's. *Could you get me a cab? Could you make me a reservation at that hot new restaurant I can't get into? Could you pick us up from the night-club because we've had too much to drink?* Those were normal requests. No, not Serena.

She asked me to get rid of a dead body in her apartment because she didn't want the police involved.

The moment she'd entered the restaurant where I was enjoying a glass of wine at the bar and her eyes locked on mine, I knew she needed *me*. I sensed it immediately—she was full of desperate hope, full of hopeless desperation. She had the keen, quiet determination of a lioness with the startling calmness of an ordinary cat, but for the first time, there was a scent of vulnerability about her that put the bouquet of my Cabernet to shame.

Something inside me flared awake, a slick of pleasure washing through me, unlike any I had ever known.

I agreed instantly to her request, eager to see the consequences of her wrath. At her trashed and blood-filled tiny apartment, I'd recognized the club tattoos on her victim's burly body. I knew there was a story there, not the bullshit one she told me. I would unwind the truth from her tightly fisted hands, loosen it from those sensual lips.

And I did.

I was like a dog with a barbecued pork bone. I chewed deeper, chasing the flavor, and got to the delicious marrow. Serena was Med McGuire's former "old lady." He'd kidnapped her as a teenager and kept her, abusing her for years, until she'd escaped and landed in Chicago.

Initially, I had fully intended on making her pay her debt to me for cleaning it all up in a number of satisfying, interesting ways, but an alternate plan had unfolded before me like a mathematical equation suddenly clarified. To have insider information from an intimate source on this mysterious legendary outlaw who worked with our rivals was a priceless opportunity.

The things I could do with that sort of information. I would do them all, and the Boss would be not only impressed, but grateful, so fucking grateful. As time went on, I'd realized, much to my surprise, that I had an ulterior motive in terrorizing Med and ruining his business—I wanted to make him suffer for what he'd done to Serena. Emotionally, physically, sexually. A compulsion to satisfy her with his torture overtook me. I would make him pay and make her smile. A dark mission from my dark heart. An unspeakable gift.

I'd promised her he'd pay, and I sensed her tense excitement. It was in her silence, in her tripping breath, the slow blink of those eyes, her stillness. I knew.

She agreed to rat on him.

By killing Med I'd gotten rid of a cockroach in the crap apartment of life and cut off a vital circuit on the motherboard of the Tantucci network. But what had given me the most pleasure was the simpler thing. It remained through the flames and the smoke —I'd done a good deed for a good woman. That actually *felt good*, and in a wholly new and different way. Surprising. Worthy of a grand statement kill, worthy of risking the fallout.

I'd ignored it at the time; that tug deep inside as I thrust the knife into her tormentor's neck that afternoon. It had been sharp, that tug. Made me blink, take a breath. Satisfaction. Justice. Full circle. Definitely a good deed.

I had his body trashed in the dumpster at the motel because I wanted the animal's ugly demise heralded on the news—I wanted *her* to know. Serena had left Chicago behind, but wherever she was, I wanted her to know that I'd done this for her. To know that beyond a doubt she was finally safe.

"What would you like me to do for you tonight?" my fake Serena whispered from the bed, snapping me back to reality.

Serena certainly hadn't said that to me that night on the floor. She'd been angry, angry in her pleasure, cold, distant, but I hadn't cared one damned bit. I was getting what I wanted, wasn't I?

I yanked on the zipper of the bag the girl had brought, yanking away those memories. "Get on your knees."

She folded herself into position immediately, and I found what I wanted in the bag.

"Is that for me?" she asked, plucking at her nipples.

What a quick learner.

She bit her lip, one hand slowly stroking the inside of a thigh. My cock stiffened at her words, at that soft pliant voice delighted for my direction, those eyes inviting more of whatever the fuck I wanted, those strokes preparing the way for me.

Sell the fantasy. Sell, I'm buying.

I tapped the side of her cheek with the leather crop, and her lips parted.

"Tonight, I want to break that fucking headboard." I swatted the side of her tit with the crop, and she let out a small gasp. I swatted her nipple. Again. Harder. I slid the crop between her legs. Back and forth, back and forth. She lifted her hips, planting her hands behind her on the mattress. Her breath shorted as her eyes followed the crop trailing up her torso, fluttering around her tits, skimming up her throat, across her lips. She took it in her mouth.

"Yeah."

We broke the fucking headboard.

7

TURO

"Excuse me. Hey."

Something tapped on my shoulder. I forced one eye open, blinking up at her.

The girl had settled on the edge of the bed. "Are we finished now?"

"What?" My eyes were bleary from sleep, my limbs aching from the alcohol and so much feral activity. "You have a date or something?" I said, turning over on my back, rubbing my face.

"Actually, yeah I do. With my boyfriend. I need to go home, clean up and get ready."

Everyone was in a relationship, for fuck's sake.

"I don't mean any disrespect by asking," she said, a finger rubbing the edges of her very swollen lips.

"None taken."

"I wasn't scheduled for tonight, but I'm glad it worked out."

Twisting over on the bed, I opened my night stand drawer and tossed her a tight, crisp roll of five one hundred dollar bills. "Here."

"Gosh, thank you, but Tricia's paying me for this. She said—"

"This is from me. You did well. Keep it up."

Her face brightened. "Okay, great. Thanks." She scooted off the mattress. "Have a good rest of your evening."

She dressed quickly in the living room where she'd taken off her clothes. Naked, I saw her to the door, pulling it open for her. Another figure stood in my private hallway, filling the shadows with his aroma of cigar smoke and anger.

The Boss. Mauro Guardino.

My breath throttled in my weary chest. I'd recognize that bulky form, that smell anywhere. I pushed the girl into the elevator and she squeaked out a yelp as the doors closed in her face.

"What do you want?" I asked.

"To interrupt you. Seems like I did."

"No, you didn't. Sorry to disappoint you."

He brushed past me, entering my apartment. "Get some clothes on, wash your hands, and pour me a drink."

Motherfucker.

I let out a sigh. "I'm going to take a shower."

I showered, put on a cotton robe, and returned to my living room where he waited for me on the sofa, his coat thrown sloppily on a nearby leather armchair.

"Whisky? Brandy? Cognac?" I asked.

"Brandy."

I poured the liquor into a snifter and handed it to him. Water for me, I'd had enough.

"You found another way to amuse yourself after what you did today?" he asked, gripping the crystal glass.

"Had to pour all that energy into someone else, didn't I?"

He threw the glass at me, I ducked, and it missed me, crashing on the floor at my side.

"That was Baccarat," I muttered.

"You trying to make some kind of point today?" he asked through gritted teeth.

"Your daughter has always had a crush on me, Mauro. I, for one, have always stayed away."

"Today you encouraged her. She's your sister!"

I let out a breath. "I apologize, it was stupid. I allowed all that shit with Val to get the best of me." I handed him a new glass with more liquor.

Mauro took it and dipped his head. "All right."

"Val's jealousy and resentment are a fucking problem, and you need to deal with it," I said. "He's starting to interfere with my business, the very successful business I run for you, and I don't like it."

He took a gulp of his drink. "I'll handle it. You watch yourself."

"There's something else I need to discuss with you. Something important."

"Other than that biker mess? I have to hand it to you, Turo. I'm glad you made that fucker tap dance all this time, making the Tantuccis scramble. Well done. Very well done."

My pulse thudded in my neck. He'd been impressed? It certainly hadn't seemed that way earlier in his office. Once again, he'd never acknowledge his approval and pleasure in front of Val and all the rest of them, would he?

Was this why he'd come over here? To pat me on the back as well as slap me upside the head for my confrontations with his children? I used to like it, love it, in fact, his special attention to me when I'd perform well; taking me aside and complimenting me with a quick slap on the back, a wink across the room, a quick call hours later. But I wasn't a kid eagerly climbing up the ladder anymore. I was stuck on the middle rung, and getting stepped on by assholes who were hustling to the top.

I said, "It's about my mother."

"Erin?" he narrowed his eyes as he took another swig of his brandy.

"Why are you fucking with her? I thought that was done the minute you got me over to the dark side."

His forehead buckled. "Did she come crying to you?"

"No." I put down my glass. "Erin doesn't cry or whine."

He licked his lips, shaking his head. "Her and her friends are making my life difficult. So I'm pushing back."

"Unpush."

The heaviness of his glare turned positively leaden, and the air sucked out of the room. "Why do you give a shit?"

"My mother is off limits to you. Let go of her liquor license. She's just as stubborn as you are. You don't think she'll come up with some way to expose you, get the law interested in you? They've laid off you for a long time now. You've been lucky. But if you make things contentious—"

"It's my neighborhood. She needs to show respect."

"What do you want? A hundred camels and ten pots of gold?"

"Don't be flip with me."

"Don't be an asshole when you don't have to be."

"You better watch your mouth." His lips stiffened, pressing together.

He was capable of anything, wasn't he? How many times had I seen it and been impressed? Whether it be bankrupting a small, family owned business in the blink of an eye because they were overdue on a loan, or beating a lackey to death because he'd spoken out of turn, I'd seen it all from Mauro Guardino. He could convince himself of anything to make himself feel better, to feel righteous.

What made me think he wouldn't turn that on my mother, a person who he'd transformed into an enemy?

"You better not hurt her in any way, do you understand?" I said.

"Or what?"

"Don't."

"You give a shit about the woman who turned her back on you?"

"That's between me and her."

"Well, this is between me and her. She's there, in my face, and I don't like it. I don't like her."

My chest tightened. "You know, I don't much like being your go-to boy on call, but I do it when you need me to. I never say no."

His upper lip curled into beginnings of a snarl. "You trying to tell me something?"

"I want a real cut of the business that I've been running for you. I made your crappy brothels streamlined moneymakers with a good reputation. You need the cash and the contacts I cultivate, the favors that business generates. And yet—"

"And yet, what? You get a percentage, a good one. I can't give you no more, how would it look?"

"You keep feeding me pieces here, pieces there, making promises...'Someday, Turo. Be patient, Turo.' I'm done being patient, Mauro. I get that I can't move up the Italian ladder, but I work hard for you. I lost out on having anything from my mother. She'll never trust me again. She's done with me."

"It's not my fault she's a cunt."

I ground my jaw. "*She* is my mother. Don't call her that. Not ever."

"What's gotten into you, huh?"

What had gotten into me? Seeing Erin today in her lair, how she'd continued to be a success without me. How I'd once been a part of that success. Of her life. I missed her. My ego had been keeping me company just fine all these years, but being in her presence again had brought back things I had pushed away... belonging, a sense of family, sharing the same taste, building something together.

With the Guardinos, I fought on my own for every inch, every cut. Erin's business was competitive and cutthroat too—well, not literally cutthroat like Mauro's. But there wasn't all this fucking drama I had to deal with here on a daily basis. The older I got, the more I was over it and the less I wanted to put up with it.

I raised my chin. "Did you threaten her?"

"I'm not going to let her and her pansy ass gentrification committee pals get the best of our neighborhood. They think they can just steamroll through when and how they want."

"You're going to have to make adjustments. This isn't anything new. Don't let your personal shit with her cloud your judgement."

His lips twisted. "Oh, I don't need your council on this particular matter."

"Obviously. That's why you've kept me out of it, right?"

He leaned back against the sofa. "As I said, none of your concern."

"My mother's safety and well being are my concern, Mauro. I'm asking you to pull back. If it's not her restaurant, it'll be someone else's. Then a bar, a café, a fucking Starbucks."

"None of your concern."

End of discussion? I ground my jaw. None of his family knew about me, and I'd accepted that. I'd accepted his conditions from the very beginning. He liked me working in his business, appreciated my talents. He needed to give me this much. "I've been your lackey, your bodyguard, your pimp, your secret messenger, your assassin, your accountant, your advisor. But I'm also your son, and I'm asking you to let this go."

Mauro sniffed in air, rubbing his fingers along his throat. "Pour me another drink."

I took his glass and poured him another, handing it back to him. He drank. "I need you, Turo."

"You need to need Val," I shot back.

He pointed a finger at me, eyes beaming. "You're right. Do one thing for me, and I'll give you what you want. I'll lay off your mother."

That phrase. It was always one thing, one more thing. Hang on, Turo, just do this *thing*. His exact words ten years ago, words

I'd sucked into my soul and fed on, thinking they'd feed my hunger.

"What is it?" I asked.

"Val was supposed to get hired by Gennaro Aliberti for his new hotel in Chicago," he said.

Aliberti was a hotelier from Miami who owned a popular hotel conglomerate which included high-end casinos in Vegas and trendy boutique hotels in New York City and Miami. Now, he was planning on opening a hotel in Chicago. Mauro wanted in on that prestige. He wanted the connections that such a working relationship with Gennaro might provide. And to top it all off, Gennaro came from mob royalty in Napoli. His brother was the head of one of the strongest and oldest families there.

"Right," I said. "You'd made a bid for construction, carting—"

"The whole thing. This was going to be the beginning of a new relationship."

"You and Aliberti have always been on good terms. I thought that was a go ahead," I said. Aliberti's resort in Vegas was Mauro's favorite vacation spot. Aliberti's *famiglia* back in Napoli were a major locus of crime in southern Europe. Getting this job would be a coup for the Guardino name among the other Chicago Outfits.

A pained look morphed his features as he put the empty glass down on the table in front of him. He wanted this so bad nothing else was filling that need. He wanted it so bad he'd come to me. "I let Val negotiate terms on his own, and he went a little overboard."

"How overboard?"

His lips twisted. "You know how he shoots his mouth off, gets started on a joke then takes it too damn far to get one more laugh? He must have insulted him. The deal broke down. I need you to fix it."

And there it was. He wanted this so bad, he was asking me behind his son's back to fix his fuck up.

"You're good with the smooth talk, Turo. Gennaro Aliberti is very old school, like you. He's got money and shows it off but in the right way. High end."

That was me, moneyed and high end, as opposed to the lowbrow lugs who worked for my father.

"I mean, I can't send Lou, can I?" Guardino let out a stiff laugh. "What kind of impression is my Underboss going to make in his For Members Only jacket?"

"They still make those?"

"I don't think so. But Lou loves them."

Lou. Major lug. And you could barely understand what he was saying through those fat lips of his, his swollen face. His brother owned a bakery and pizzeria chain, and that's where he spent most of his time when he wasn't tooling around in his old DeVille.

"I want this deal to go through," Mauro said. "I have to be a part of Gennaro's Chicago hotel. I need to get this sewn up before he goes to someone else. I know they're lining up outside his door, but I was first in that fucking line and I'm not about to get kicked to the curb. He knows how things work. He's a smart businessman, well known, respected. He doesn't put up with any kind of crap, why should he? I need to be back on Gennaro Aliberti's good side, Turo. You go impress him with your talk." The Boss's eyes lit up. He was being convincing, enthusiastic. "Your whole slick but firm thing. You never rush, you take your time—"

"Careful, Daddy, you sound like you actually admire me." I lit a cigarette and sucked deep on the smoke until my lungs hurt. His eyes positively gleamed. Was I simply a convenient tool for him like Val had said?

"Do the research, quote some numbers at him," Mauro said in his gruff commander voice. "Come off well-studied, and we'll get him back."

We.

Yeah. We.

He pointed that finger at me again. "You know how to handle these guys."

I knew. Oh, I knew.

"And then I'll give you what you want," he said.

I held his gaze through the smoke that rose between us from my cigarette. "Val is threatening to feed me to the Tantuccis—his words—for killing their biker pal," I said.

He waved a hand at me. "You do this for me that won't happen. But—" that hand went rigid, index finger pointing, a threat. "—you stay away from Francesca, and no matter what Val does or says, you don't lose control again. You even consider saying anything to my kids about us—"

"We've been over that a million times. I've kept my word."

"They can never know, Turo. It would kill them and their mother."

"We wouldn't want that now, would we?" I inhaled deeply on the cigarette.

"No." His low, jagged voice scraped up my spine.

"Then I guess you'd better work a little bit harder at keeping both your kids out of my way." I squashed my cigarette in the Baccarat ashtray at my side and rose from my seat. "I'll do the research tomorrow and head out to Miami."

"Miami? What the fuck for?" said Mauro getting up from the sofa, heading for the front door.

"Gennaro—"

"He's not in Miami right now. He just took off for an early summer vacation in Europe."

"Ah."

"His brother in Naples has this big yacht and he goes over every year for a cruise vacation. Last year they went to Malta, he'd told me. This year, I don't know." Mauro's bottom lip curled, he made a face. Was he envious? He scoffed. "Nice, huh?" He was envious.

I helped him with his coat. "Very, very nice."

"Find him. Find him now. You don't have time to waste." He pulled on the cuffs of the coat.

There was no slap on the back, squeeze of the arm, or wink as he left my apartment. There was only a stern glare as the elevator doors shut on him, separating us.

No, I had no time to waste at all.

I went to my laptop and started investigating the trails of Gennaro Aliberti in Miami, in Italy. His brother, his nephews.

Three hours later I had my answers, booked my flight, and went to my walk-in closet and packed my compact carry-on suitcase.

Mediterranean, here I come.

ATHENS

8

TURO

T<small>HIS WAS ANOTHER</small> R<small>IVIERA.</small>

A huge, blood orange sun hung heavily over the mountains in the sky across from the supper club. A thick breeze whipped around me on the grand veranda overlooking the pink blue sea. The Aegean Sea. The air had a fresh, salty yet sweet sharpness to it, laced with the fleeting rich intensity of the delicate jasmine vines I'd noticed in the courtyard earlier.

The burning sun dipped in the sky beginning its dramatic final bow, leaving us mere mortals with a sigh in our throats. Do we experience a *petit mort* in watching this spectacle over and over? A little taste of our mortality painted in rich pinks and reds before the sexy whisper of dusk emerged and darkness quickly swallowed it up. A good sunset was like an orgasm, an intense high for just a moment, that second that grabbed you by the throat and offered you heaven, but then you're slung back down to earth.

"Here's to you, Dionysus," I heralded the mythological god of wine and good times, taking a good swallow of my smooth dark red nectar. "Watch out for me, would you? I need to make this quick and get back home and unscrew my life." The god's drink of choice and mine bloomed warmly in my mouth, sinking into my bloodstream. The lights along the coastline grew brighter, and I let out a short breath.

Greece. I'd never been here before. Lucky me.

I'd found out that Gennaro Aliberti had gone to Naples and joined his nephews Alessio and Luca on the family yacht and they'd sailed to Greece. First stop, Athens. Probably only for a couple days in the city at best and then they'd be back on the yacht to island hop. The yacht was now moored in Glyfada, a swanky suburb south of Athens right on the water.

I hadn't been on a vacation since I started working for my father, and I'd quickly put the concept of taking recreational time for myself out of my head, except for trips to the gym. Vacations had been a way of life for my mother. Every year there was skiing in Aspen, relaxing in Saugatuck, trips to New York, Europe, Palm Beach in the winters to see my grandparents, the odd trip to the Caymans. That was our way of life. Standard. All of which I'd taken for granted. After I became a working boy, how quickly I realized that simply wasn't the case for the common man. I missed it, of course, but put the loss out of my head. I was good at that, wiping the slate.

Even though I had a trust fund, I guarded it ferociously. I liked having it, my one constant, I liked knowing it was there. I had a few solid investments in the stock market as well and monitored them carefully.

I was my mother's son, after all.

I never flaunted my money anyhow. It wasn't wise in my line of work. Petty resentments built up easily, and I avoided it. I had to.

I'd taken Ciara on weekend getaways a couple of times, but it had proved challenging, always being on call to the Boss, plus, surprisingly, I'd gotten bored quickly. She'd complain about trying to organize a trip to Mexico or the Caribbean and me not being available or always changing the dates on her. She'd eventually given up. Once I sent her on a vacation with a friend to St. Barts, and that had appeased her. For a little while at least.

Now, Guardino business had brought me to Greece. Greece in May for a few days at the most. Not fucking bad at all.

I made my way back to the bar through the growing throng of very well-dressed people. The club, aptly named "Island," had filled up quickly. A colorful variety of foreign languages flowed around me just like the long canopies of fabric billowing in the breeze over the grand terrace. Great boughs of deep fuchsia and purple bougainvillea climbed over the stone archways along the terrace of the nightclub where Aliberti had arrived an hour ago for drinks with a large group of people at a table overlooking the water. Really, every table here overlooked the water at this beach nightclub, a tony, chic spot in Varkiza on the outskirts of Athens on the Saronic Gulf. A steady stream of house music filled the air, but without being obtrusive.

Gennaro Aliberti laughed at something his nephew Alessio said. Gennaro was in his late-fifties, fit and lean, well-groomed, an elegant figure in a blue linen jacket over a snow white T-shirt and perfectly creased linen pants. A full head of salt and pepper hair, wavy, and thick. Where he was a refined classic, Alessio was the artsy, tattooed, boho hipster. Tall, built, dark hair and eyes, a fine Roman nose, a cut jaw, and tanned skin which he showed off with a couple of long, thin chains with crosses and charms falling against his bare chest at the opening of his unbuttoned dress shirt. He wore lots of rings, an earring. He was an up and coming jewelry designer after all.

His double A logo was synonymous in Europe with his rock and roll bohemian aesthetic. He had a shop in Milan and had recently opened a small outpost on the Greek island of Mykonos. Their entourage was heading to the island on their yacht as Alessio was hosting a party at a beach club to promote himself and his goods.

Next to Alessio sat his brother Luca. Lighter hair than his

brother and the same dark eyes, though his were leaden, heavy, not warm and electric like his brother's. And unlike his brother, Luca only sported one leather cord with a small simple gold medallion around his neck. He wore a loose fitting jacket over a thin V-neck T-shirt, and a tattoo swirled on his chest.

Alessio and Luca's father was a major drug kingpin in Naples. Luca was twenty-six, Alessio twenty-five, and on the outside, purely a civilian. From what I'd read online, since his jewelry line had taken off three years ago, he'd been focused on that, keeping his nose clean while his brother Luca had become more entrenched than ever in the family business, taking on more responsibility from Daddy. Was Luca like Val? Overly eager and overly arrogant, a hazard? Their father hadn't joined them on this trip as he usually kept himself low-key and out of sight for security reasons.

Gennaro Aliberti traveled with his own security man from Miami. A tall, very built, very tanned guy, all muscle and angles and finely cut suits. Alessio glanced around himself frequently, Luca was more relaxed. Relaxed but alert. The brothers traveled with their own two man security team. Luca's infrequent, subtle glances were check-ins with his two big, broad shouldered guards.

The Italians had a busy day. Shopping for designer Greek gold jewelry on Voukourestiou, lunch at the famous rooftop restaurant of the elegant Grand Bretagne Hotel in the center of Athens where I was staying. Visiting the Parthenon and its new museum, walking through the historic Plaka neighborhood, iced espressos and strawberry granita drinks in an outdoor café in the Thiseio area in the shadow of the Acropolis. I followed them, observing their interactions, the people they met up with, noted the behaviors of Gennaro's bodyguard, of Luca's.

At the café, they'd been joined by two fashionable young women, one of whom Alessio treated like a girlfriend—quick kisses, arm hung around her shoulders. Affectionate but low key.

She had her hair pulled back in a low ponytail and wore huge brown sunglasses she never took off. I'd bet Alessio had a girl in every port. A few paparazzi had hovered and took photos until the bodyguards talked them down and then the entire group had taken off in their cars.

Now at the club, Alessio was flirting with some tall blonde as his brother nursed a cocktail on his other side, a look of ennui on his face, but he was anything but. I knew that stance well. All vigilance. Gennaro rose from the table and took his time cutting an elegant swathe across the dining area. The mens room? His bodyguard stood in the inner dining room where Gennaro would have to pass through on his way to the men's room, his gaze on Gennaro.

I'd noticed a special rapport between them throughout the day. Alessio had his own car and driver which he shared with Luca sitting up front. That guard from Miami always got in the backseat with Gennaro in their own chauffeur driven car.

They shared a communication shaded with emotion and color that only the most closely acquainted could achieve. Intimacy. A nod of the head, a slight smile to the eyes, the lips, that delicate curl of anticipation. Of knowing. A protective hand on the back that was beyond the perfunctory guarding gesture. A gentleness and a fierceness. The way Gennaro had smiled at him when he bought him a bottle of cold water as the base of the Acropolis. A satisfied smile on his lips as he watched the guard greedily swallow and smile back at him as he wiped at his mouth. It was all there. And why not? I knew plenty of much older men who kept up with two or three very young mistresses in addition to a wife, and they weren't half as healthy looking or attractive as Gennaro.

These two were lovers. Gennaro Aliberti was gay which was why this was such a clusterfuck for Mauro and Val.

Paul had told me that when Val had met with Gennaro in Miami, he'd made his usual asinine, crude jokes which included a shit load of negative comments about homosexuals. That's what had pissed off Gennaro.

This would not be an easy fix. This was personal offense, an insult for Gennaro Aliberti.

Just like I was sure that Gennaro and his guard were not just taking a leak at the moment.

I rose from my chair, licking the last of the wine from the edge of my bottom lip. I had to see with my own eyes what these two were up to. Had to confirm.

"Oh!"

I rocketed to the side, a body plowing into mine. A woman's hands speared my chest, hair lashing my face, stinging.

"Hey!" My hands seized an arm, braced a curvy hip.

Our eyes locked.

And in that thunderous split second, my life as I knew it changed course forever.

9

TURO

I QUICKLY REGAINED my footing and steadied the woman in one move. Coppery brown waves settled around her face and down her shoulders. Gray blue eyes held mine, and the wind sucked out of me.

My eyes roved over her. The dark purple metallic color of her dress lit up her eyes. Silky bronzed skin, full, sensual lips, a long throat, and breasts that were threatening to spill from her very short shimmery dress with split sleeves. Golden skin peeked out from slits in the shoulders down to her elbows. She righted herself, found her balance, yet her fingers still clung to my arms, and I didn't let go of her hip and arm either.

A smile teased her lips and those large eyes widened at me. "Ach, *signómi!*" Greek. A breathy, rich voice.

"Are you all right?" I asked, my voice stern as I released her.

"Yes. I'm so sorry," she said. Her Greek accent was shaded by a slight British lilt. She was young, early twenties at most. A girl woman. "Forgive me, I did not mean to—" She smoothed long fingers over my shoulders and the hair on the back of my neck prickled. "—crash into you."

A strange warmth filtered through me at her slightly wicked intonation, that silky smile.

"Oh, I've annoyed you," she said, straightening her posture, sardonic amusement in her tone. "Pardon."

That once familiar burn flared in my chest, between my legs. I adjusted my jacket, my shoulders shifting. "No, not annoyed. I was supposed to meet with someone," I managed to say, smoothing down the side of my hair, "But..." My eyes darted around the space. Gennaro and his bodyguard were gone.

"Ah, she did not show up?" the girl asked.

"No, she was here," I replied.

"Oh, she left? Had you argued? You were about to chase her and I—"

My eyes narrowed at her, a smirk forming on my mouth. "Something like that."

"No. No." She shook her head slightly.

"No?"

Her hands fell down my upper arms, lightly squeezing the muscles. "You are much too handsome to be with a woman who does not recognize your worth."

"Do men always recognize your worth?" I quipped.

Her features tensed, an eyebrow arched high, and for just a moment she looked a decade older. "All men in Greece know my worth," she said.

What the hell did that mean? There was acid in those words. Not hauteur or arrogance, but a cocktail of bitterness and resignation.

Her features suddenly relaxed, her eyes glittered at me. "Must I be with a man?"

There was something familiar about the graceful slant of her head as she chuckled, that lift of her chin, but I couldn't place it.

She touched the edges of her shiny hair. "You are American, yes?"

"Yes."

"On vacation?"

"Yes, on vacation."

"Other than this evening's disappointment, you are enjoying your visit?"

"Very much."

"You've seen the sights?"

"All the usual."

"You don't sound impressed."

"It was all very impressive, I assure you—the Acropolis, the museum, the Agora, Monastiraki. Shopping on Voukourestiou."

She slanted her head. "Well, very nice."

"But I had my mind on other things."

"This woman?"

"Hmm. And you?"

"What about me?" she asked.

"Why were you in a rush just now? Were you escaping?"

"You could say that."

"I caught you," came out of my mouth which curved into a grin.

She raised a dark eyebrow, her lips parting. "I don't like being caught."

"I don't either."

Truth had met truth like the *clang* of two swords, the shock of first contact. That blue light in her eyes flared at me telling me I'd struck a nerve.

She slid onto the bar stool next to mine, and my pulse suddenly kicked up speed. "I was escaping from an ass."

I sat down next to her, gesturing to the bartender, bringing my wine glass closer. "Really? A donkey? Here?"

She let out a dry laugh. "He's the son of a man my father works with, and he always assumes that I should be infatuated with him."

"You must have a lot of admirers vying for your attention."

"I do." Her lips twisted and she released a small sigh. She said that without a hint of egotism. It was plain, simple fact, and somehow, not a pleasant one.

"The last time I saw him," she continued, "I slighted him and, obviously, he's still quite upset with me. We just had words, and I walked away a bit too enthusiastically. These new shoes I'm wearing are a bit too high." She reached down and tugged on a strap of a gladiator sandal with a very high, very slim heel.

My balls tightened at the sight of that webbing of straps climbing up those sexy as fuck legs, of her hand trailing up her sleek thigh.

"Would you like me to set him straight?" I asked.

"Oh, no." A hand wrapped in a stack of gold bangles touched my wrist, lighting my skin with a prickle of heat. "That's not necessary. I don't like scenes."

The bartender brought over a glass of wine, and I slid it closer to her. "I hope you like wine?"

"Very much, thank you." She sipped. "Hmm. Good choice."

I raised my glass. "What does one say here in Greece?"

"*Stin iyiá mas.*" She raised her glass to mine. "To our health."

"*Stin iyiá mas,*" I said, and we both drank.

"Your accent is very good." She licked her lip.

"Thank you."

"Ah, so polite. The ass in question has no manners. I went out to dinner with him once at my father's request, and it ended quite badly."

"Is he the type who behaves one way in front of parents, and another when you're alone?"

"Exactly. Are you that type?"

I only chuckled.

She drank, her eyes meeting mine. "You were right about the donkey."

"I'm sorry, I don't follow."

"The ass. I don't care for his looks either—thick brows, large ears, long face. Donkey."

I grinned. "Acerbic."

Her lips twisted just a bit. "Ah, I've heard women being called much, much worse."

"True."

"There he is, see for yourself." She raised her chin in the direction of a tall thin man with indeed a long face and large ears, his hand on the back of a short, dark haired woman being led to a corner table by a hostess.

"He's here with another woman and he came onto you?" I was more offended than she was.

"He's the type of Greek man who must always have the last word. Well, that rather describes most men, doesn't it?" A noise escaped her throat. "And you? Do you feel strongly about having the last word?"

"No, I have no such obsession. I make my points known in other ways. Ways that echo louder than words."

"Hmm." She drank, her eyes on me.

Our gazes locked and heat seeped through me; it wasn't only the wine having this sultry effect on my bloodstream.

"Are you here alone or with friends?" I asked.

"I'm here with a friend, but he's busy now," she gestured casually toward the tables outside, "and I don't want to intrude."

"Kill some time with me."

She laughed. A dirty, dark laugh which made me grin. "Oh, I don't wish to kill anything tonight." One long finger traced over the rim of her glass as she studied me, her lips quirking up. I wanted to taste those lips, discover her tongue, suck on that finger.

And then out of those perfect lips came the perfect reply.

"You are a lovely distraction I'm indulging in."

I let out a small breath, rubbing a hand along my jaw. "I've never been called 'lovely' before."

"Oh yes, you're quite lovely. Indecently lovely," she murmured on a soft laugh that was a sincere response, not a brazen come-hither.

A spill of heat flowed through my veins as I held her frank gaze. A gaze that flared into amusement at my surprised reaction.

"Have you never been called indecent before either?" she asked.

"Indecent, yes. Many times," I replied. "But never with so much finesse."

Her eyes sparked, narrowed, that slight smile widening. She didn't quite know what to make of me, but was enjoying this as much as I was.

"Well, then—" I traced my middle finger over her hand and up her arm, and her breath caught. "Let's indulge in some lovely indecency."

10

ADRIANA

"Now that's an original proposition," I said.

He laughed. A warm, rich baritone laugh, and my pulse quickened at the sound. Sexy, sly. *Yes, quite indecent.* A crooked grin flashed over his face giving him a sudden boyish look. Just for a second then it was gone, and the lethal returned.

Tonight, Cinderella had met a foreign prince. An indecent one. Very indecent.

Oh, but he was lovely, handsome in an austere way. His hazel eyes had a golden glimmer that shone in the muted lighting of the club. Gleaming with precision, pinning me to the spot. Their initial cold, savage irritation at my violent interruption had transformed into a vampiric-like interest.

I met his gaze full-on, and he only slanted his head at me. The chiseled angles of his jaw were ridiculously masculine. His slightly wavy, short hair was a light brown colour that he had perfectly slicked back with gel at the sides. He tended to every detail. Suddenly, that muscle along his jaw tensed as if something had changed, a thought had occurred to him.

Here we go.

I waited, but it didn't come. That familiar cocky look hadn't flickered across his face, that look that assumed, expected, antici-pated, relished.

None of that. I was so tired of all that.

My face heated under his brutally fastidious gaze. A gaze that was patient, a gaze that sizzled over my flesh, that searched for signs of worthiness of his attention. Certainly, what he deemed *unworthy* would be charred and discarded.

A few small lines marked the skin around his eyes, the corners of his mouth. He was older than me, but by how much? Certainly in his thirties, but he was as fit as any twenty something I knew. A defined chest, back, and shoulders were evident under that lean cut suit. A suit that was finely tailored, a very expensive suit—nothing off the rack, as they said in America. His gold wristwatch glinted in the lighting. Patek Philippe. One of the most expensive, prestigious Swiss watches, understated, lean, and classic in design, and not ostentatious in the least. Decadence packaged crisply and cleanly. Elegant sophistication with an edge.

Oh, that edge.

He moved closer to me and took my hand, bringing it to his lips. The barest of kisses on my skin, yet an electric charge jolted through my arm, charging any and all inanimate particles inside me into a furor. I could see him taking his time with every detail, savoring and enjoying himself, the world burning to cinders around him and he not being bothered. Not one bit.

"I've never been called an indulgence before, though." His fingertips lingered on the back of my hand and my breath caught in my throat, burning there. He lifted those eyes to mine once again and something jolted inside me.

Indecent, lethal, and merciless as well.

The room, the music, the chatter faded.

"Indulgences are necessary," I said. "After all, isn't life meant to be enjoyed?"

He slanted his head. "Is that a Greek philosophy?"

"Yes, it is."

A quick flash of his edgy, sly smile and my stomach caved, clenching, sending waves of heat washing through me. I squirmed on the barstool. "It's something you Americans need to learn."

He released my hand. "I think you're right."

I took another sip of wine to steady myself, the mellow flavors of berries and cocoa swirling through my mouth. The sleeve of his jacket rubbed against my bare arm, its texture more harsh and prickly than it actually was. What would his hands feel like on me? His body pressed against mine, demanding from mine?

Tonight I'd had plenty to drink already along with that one hit of coke, all of which had blessed me with a swell of fearlessness. Or was it recklessness? All the better. I hadn't been out to a club in a long time. Quiet restaurants and cafés with my mum and little brother or a girlfriend or two, a few shops, yes, but a full-on glam it up, loud music, party 'til you drop night like tonight? No, not in a very long time.

The moon had risen higher in the sky, its heaviness suddenly giving way into bright, shining prominence over us. One of my favorite songs throbbed through the room, and I swayed to the music, the beat swelling inside me.

"I love this song. Dance with me?" Touching his arm, I stood.

He cuffed my wrist tightly and my breath caught. "Ask nicely," he said.

I moved closer to him. "Please dance with me, you lovely, indecent man."

"Better." He took my hand in his and I led him to the dance floor. Winding his fingers in mine, we moved easily together with the pulsing beat. He pulled me in closer, his arm wrapping around my bare back, and a shiver raced over my flesh sparking through me. I pressed my fingers into the tightness of his shoulders. I didn't take my eyes off him. I couldn't. I had no choice. I didn't feel powerless under their spell, but exhilaration swept through me under their heat, a different kind of arousal. The intense kind. The kind I'd always craved.

"Do you like the song?" I said in his ear.

"What? Yes." His voice came out lower than usual.

I sang the lyrics as we moved, our hips meeting, sliding against each other. *Dear Lord.*

"What's the song saying?" he asked.

"Se thélo—it means, I want you."

"Hmm." His hand gripped mine tighter, his fingers spread out over my back.

"You're a game of the gods..."

"A game of the gods," he repeated. He stroked my back, just above the slope of my rear, making an ache unwind inside me.

"The way the current hits..." I continued translating, my voice rougher than usual. "I'm drowning, but I'm not leaving. That's how I want you. At the edge of my life's cliff, come and be the end. Finish me off."

Cliff indeed. That's exactly how I felt right now, that breathless rush at hurtling toward the edge of a cliff.

"Ah, poetry," he murmured.

"Welcome to Greece," I replied.

He glanced over my shoulder, something had caught his attention. Or someone. I slid my hand around his neck, and his head snapped to mine.

"Is she there?" I asked

A slight scowl crossed his features. A scowl sliding into that brittle, teasing grin. "Who?"

"The woman you were—"

"There's only you," he breathed against my ear.

My heartbeat skidded. His lips took mine. Warm, demanding. Possessive. He released me much too quickly, and clinging to him, I struggled to catch my breath, licked at my bottom lip where his heat had just been.

"What is your name?"

He rubbed a thumb across my burning lip. "Turo," he whispered.

"Turo?"

His focus remained on my mouth. "Short for Arturo."

"Ah." Italian, he didn't look Italian, yet—

He bent his head to mine and his citrusy, musky scent filled my senses. I knew that cologne. That was Italian. His lips stole up my throat like warm silk. He nipped at my earlobe, his breath fanning my face, the side of my neck.

"And your name?" His voice was suddenly urgent. A gentle command. As if my answer would give him the keys to a mystery that he needed to solve.

"Adriana."

He stilled. I let go of a tiny breath as his hands gently cradled my face, his jaw easing. "Adriana."

Our bodies moved to the music once more, as if on their own, in a hypnotic trance. But I wasn't in a trance, I was very, very aware of his keen attentiveness, his subtle yet firm touch. I felt like I was on the edge of that cliff Hatzigiannis was singing about, and Turo would push me off any second with that smile on his face. I was suspended there between wanting to run away and wanting to see over the edge of Turo's cliff.

The music gradually changed its beat from languorous and sensual to a more throbbing, tribal rhythm. The party gods were being summoned. People had seeped all over the terrace. Laughter and excited chatter floated in the air. We were in the thick of the throng. The DJ had begun his show, and the crowd was excited, moving to every beat he generated. Lights flashed, the wind blew at the blood colored canopies over us. The club was packed, more so than before. How hadn't I noticed?

Turo's eyes flashed at me, that quick, crooked grin making him look younger yet more jaded all at the same time. A stunning combination on his handsome features. He pulled me in closer once more and that thrill of risk made my heart pound harder.

Like skydiving. I was at the edge of the open plane door, taking my final breath before—

After tonight I'd never see Turo from America again, would I?

Stop thinking, just do. Do what you want. Jump off that plane.

I took his hand and led him to the inner lounge where it wasn't so crowded, darker and shadowy, the muted glow of candles in a number of wooden lanterns on the tables, larger ones hanging from the ceiling.

I wrapped my hands around his waist beneath his jacket and his lean torso tensed, his breath cut off. I pressed against him, and *yes, there*...evidence of his hard arousal for me.

"What are you doing?" he asked.

"Indulging."

I moved toward him, but he lifted my chin, holding it firmly in his grip. My breath burned in my lungs as I held his hard gaze. Was he offended? Not interested? Was he going to push me away?

A warm hand slid around my neck pulling me close, and he slanted his head over mine. His tongue flicked at my lips, and I opened up to him, my tongue reveling in its slide against his. He took my mouth. The taste of his wine filled me with unbearable heat—a sudden rush of desire, fiery and wild threaded through me and pulled tight in the very center of me, knotting, threatening to explode. Startling. Deliciously shocking.

Dangerous.

Yes, he was dangerous. And I was on the edge of that danger with just this kiss. This amazing kiss.

His other hand stole down my hip to my rear, pressing there. "Tell me, Adriana..."

That deep voice rolled out my name like a dare. The heat of his closeness overwhelmed me, the musk in the shadow of the citrus scent coming off his throat whipped my senses into a riot.

"Yes?" my voice shook.

"Did you like that?" he breathed.

Ach, I like it all. I kissed him in reply, and his eyes flared. He nipped at my already swollen lower lip, his forehead sinking against mine. A new rush of warmth enveloped me, cocooning us.

What would it be like to have sex with this man? Intense, animal-like. And something told me that if he gave a damn about the woman in his bed, his attentions would be exacting, blistering, soul squeezing. He was discerning. He would know precisely what to offer and take his time doing it, relishing it.

A shiver raced through me.

I'd never initiated anything with any man ever before. I'd never felt this sort of bold reaction to a man before. Even *him*. This was beyond the alcohol, the coke. It was Turo who intoxicated me. This stranger I'd just met.

He was a tourist on a short visit. Was that what was so appealing about this? All the more reason to—

A small, ominous noise unfurled in his throat, and his tongue commanded I deepen the kiss. I did, and he *fucked* my mouth. There was no other description for it. Carnal. Ruthless. The dynamite he'd set along my veins sparked and lit as he molded our bodies together with his hands, the press of his hard form against mine. I was all sensation. Need.

Yes. Yes. Yes.

A slight groan from his lips vibrated against mine. Was he surprised by his own response? Was he as overwhelmed as I was?

Give in, indecent Turo. Give in as I am.

"Adri." A familiar Italian accented voice sliced through our sensual fog, and I flinched.

Turo tore his lips from mine, his brow furrowed, his grip on my waist tightened possessively, his fingers digging into my flesh. He swung his head sharply to reprimand whoever had interrupted us. His body went rigid at the sight of Alessio.

Cinderella's midnight bell had tolled.

11

TURO

ALESSIO ALIBERTI STOOD THERE, shooting me a hard look. My fingers only dug deeper into Adriana's waist.

He sniffed in air, his chin lifting at Adriana. "*Tu viene?*" *Are you coming?* he asked her.

What. The. Fuck.

They were together?

No threats, no anger, no explosion. Only a muscle along his tightly set jaw ticked, his built shoulders rigid under his open to the waist dress shirt.

"*Si,*" she replied glancing at him, then back at me as casually as if her chauffeur were picking her up from a playdate.

A hand went to my chest and, leaning her cheek against the side of my face, she whispered, "*Adío,* Lovely." Her exotic accent laced with wistful regret drilled deep into my chest, burrowing there on a burn. Her eyes glimmered, she swept past me, and they were gone. They wove through the crowd. His arm around her. Adriana and Alessio Aliberti.

Alessio Aliberti.

My pulse heated. He was the "friend" who was busy and she hadn't wanted to intrude? Had she been trying to make him jealous all evening with me? What the fuck did I get myself into? Well, I'd gotten his attention, hadn't I?

I wiped the side of a thumb across my upper lip. Just a little girl looking for a good time. Just a girl looking to make a boyfriend jealous and she'd chosen me to *indulge* in a little quid pro quo. Drama.

Lovely, my ass.

I'd live, although my cock was really pissed off, not to mention my fucking ego. I hadn't flirted like that in fuck knows how long. Not just the same old suggestive bullshit and teasing looks back and forth, but something else. Something more. I'd actually enjoyed myself. Imagine that.

Her warm scent lingered, teasing me—cinnamon, nutmeg, barely sweet, something darker. My insides hardened. Just as well; that's not why I was here. Yeah, she was definitely different, but hell, I could get a flavor of the week any time of day or night back in Chicago.

Note to self: Ask Tricia if she has any Mediterranean goddesses with an accent on the payroll. If not, get on it immediately.

The happy couple hovered at the table with Gennaro Aliberti. Alessio brushed the side of her face with a quick kiss like a caring boyfriend would. Why hadn't he torn my head off, or hers for that matter, when he'd found us together?

Was Adriana one of the girls at the café with the Alibertis today? She looked different now with her hair down, glamorous short dress—not capri jeans, a loose blouse and sandals, sunglasses, a ponytail. Fuck, yes, it was her.

A blonde stepped in my eyesight and spoke to me in a torrent of Greek, blocking my view of Alessio and Adriana. The woman laughed, holding out an unlit cigarette.

"I don't smoke." I glared coldly at her, and she quickly turned off her tap of cloying words and fawning looks.

Gennaro crossed the club terrace followed by his bodyguard. Luca, along with Alessio holding Adriana by the hand, also left their table. Other members of their group trailed behind. They were leaving.

I paid my tab, which took forever, and quickly pushed through the crowd past the stone archway toward the main entrance. Outside, people stood waiting for their cars, waiting for taxis, talking, talking on their mobile phones. Flashing lights went off. Paparazzi stood in bunches to the left and right, on the other side of the road, yelling out names. People I assumed were Greek celebrities waved at them, posed, talked to the photographers. Others ignored them and hustled into cars, taking off.

Alessio stood with his arm around Adriana speaking to her and she nodded, her body somewhat stiff, lips pressed together. He kissed the top of her head once more, and she leaned into him. She was uneasy. I ground my teeth. Their intimacy pissed me off. He still didn't seem angry or annoyed with her though. He'd found his girlfriend kissing another man on their night out. Then again I'd only been her bit of fun while he'd been "busy" as she'd put it. I'd spotted him with another woman earlier.

Was this their entertainment when they went out? They'd arrive together but give each other the freedom to play over the course of the evening? And now they'd go back to his hotel room and swap tales as they fucked wildly.

The images exploded in my head, injecting their poisonous fumes into my lungs.

One

after

the other

after the other.

I had a healthy imagination, which was good, but often not. Like now.

My pulse sped, cold adrenaline surged up my chest and down to my fingertips, my blood icy, slewing through my veins. I swallowed hard against the urge to go bash that pretty boy face of his.

This isn't Chicago. Take a breath. She's just another girl.

Luca smoked a cigarette at Alessio's side, his eyes on a group of women being photographed. Alessio had let go of Adriana and was in deep discussion with his uncle.

"*Adri!*" someone shouted. Adriana pivoted quickly and lost her balance on those damned heels again. She rolled her eyes, grinning, wiping her hair back from her face.

Fuck, she's adorable. Hardly the pretentious beauty she could so easily be.

She steadied herself, the lines of her face relaxing as she approached the woman she obviously knew. They embraced, exchanged Greek double kisses, spoke, laughed, and the friend got into a waiting Lamborghini.

Adriana flinched at the shrill scream of a motorcycle on the bend of the narrow waterfront road. A hand went to her heaving chest. She turned away from the road, and her troubled gaze snagged on mine. Her eyes widened, and my pulse gained speed.

Remember me, baby?

Her lips parted, she shook her head at me. A slight movement, but I caught it. Was she calling Game Over or was she warning me off? Maybe she hadn't been some random girl bumping into me, flirting with me? Did the Alibertis know I was shadowing them and had sicced Adriana on me as a distraction?

Only one way to find out.

I strode toward her. Toward them. The traffic on the road behind her got thicker. A tourist bus, droning motor scooters with helmet-less teens, motorcycles with couples, cars.

Those blue gray eyes got huge. "Turo?" Adriana said, her voice low, stiff.

"Leaving so soon?" I asked.

Her long, elegant neck straightened. A swan preparing to take flight.

Not so fast, Lovely.

"Aren't you going to introduce me to your boyfriend?" I asked.

Alessio prowled over. Luca tossed his cigarette, tracking to the other side of Adriana. Alessio's dark eyes gleamed as he gave me a curt shake of his head. That Italian *"Who the fuck are you, what the fuck is this?"*

"Turo DeMarco." I stretched out my hand to Alessio.

Alessio stared at my hand, an eyebrow raised. His full lips twisted into a smirk. Luca's face was a mask.

"Adriana! Adrianaaaa!" shouted photographers from across the street. She immediately turned her back to them, pressing next to Alessio, her body bunching up. She was uncomfortable.

"Adriana!" the paps shouted. Her jaw set, her face tightened. Was she famous?

"Ignore them, Adri," muttered Alessio, a hand at her back.

Just over her shoulder, a few yards beyond us on the main road, a mud splashed motorcycle with two helmeted figures in long sleeved jackets slowed down at the curve approaching the club's entrance, weaving in front of the line of cars parked at the end of the walkway. They moved deftly, swiftly. They weren't paparazzi. They weren't club-goers. Not to this club.

Needles pricked the back of my neck.

The rider in the back raised his arm, a semi-automatic in his grip.

I lunged at Adriana.

Crack. Crack.

Twisting her into me, I rolled onto the ground with her in my arms. I covered her, our bodies pressed together into the pavement. She clung to me.

Rat-tat-clip-clip-crack.

A high-pitched scream ripped the air above us. Muffled moans. A tidal wave of shouts.

I pushed up, digging my fingers in her hair, cradling the side of her pale face. Anguish, terror. "Are you all right?" my voice as tense as my grip on her. "Adriana? Are you okay?"

"Yes! Yes—" She couldn't catch her breath, her eyes opened widened even more, flitting to the side of my face. A hand reached out, touching the side of my stinging face. Blood stained her shaking fingers.

I touched the side of my face and found torn, wet skin. Must have been from falling to the sidewalk.

Alessio, Luca over us. A flurry of Greek, Italian. I pulled her up and held on to her. Her arms were cold, so cold. Alessio, the bodyguard, an ashen Gennaro hanging behind him. Luca shouting, gesturing. My head reeled, was I swaying on my feet? I grabbed Alessio by the shirt.

"That motorcycle—" I gulped in air. "Did you see that motorcycle?"

"*Si.*" Alessio grabbed Adriana whose eyes stayed on me, not wanting to let go. Alessio took her and brushed past me, and I staggered.

"Turo!" shouted Adriana, looking over Alessio's shoulder, eyes wild. She fisted Alessio's shirt. "Don't leave him here! Don't!"

A thick arm wrapped around me like a stiff belt, a hand at my chest, holding me up. Luca steered me toward a black Porsche Cayenne manned by a security guard who held the back door open. Alessio and Adriana climbed inside.

"Come." Luca picked up his pace, leading me toward the car. "We have to get out of here. Now."

I shoved him off me. "What are you talking about?"

He grabbed my arm again. "You are coming with us."

12

TURO

THE HEAVY DOORS of the Porsche thudded closed, and the sudden stifling interior of the crowded SUV made me lightheaded. Alessio, Adri, and me in the back, the driver and Luca up front. Gennaro and his bodyguard were in another Cayenne in front of us. We tore out of the parking lane and zoomed down the road, police sirens blaring in our wake.

Luca tossed me a first aid kit from the front seat, and I got the box open, tore at gauze, an antiseptic wipe. I glanced down at Adriana who sat in between me and Alessio. Dull eyes brimming with water, pressing her lips together against their trembling. She was visibly upset, but not hysterical. No, she was clamping it down, holding it in. Trying to control it. Something told me this wasn't new to her.

Not even an hour ago she'd exuded a breezy self confidence, sexual allure, radiated glamour, but now, now she was a terrified and withdrawn girl. A girl whose body shuddered against mine. Had those bullets been meant for her?

Her hands curled into fists in her lap. My hand slid over hers, my thumb stroking over her cold flesh. She let out a ragged breath, her hand turning, clasping mine.

Alessio leaned forward toward his brother. "What the fuck was that?" he bit out in Italian.

I winced at his sharp tone. My skull ached, the blasts still echoing in my head. That pitched wave of screaming, everyone crouching, scattering like rodents played over and over again in my brain, in my bones.

Alessio and Luca argued, Luca spitting out a torrent of seething Italian at his brother and Alessio firing back. It was all too quick for me to understand, but I recognized the name of another Naples family. Did a rival family follow them to Greece?

Alessio slid back against the leather seat. "We weren't even supposed to be here tonight, but you insisted, Luca."

"I heard it was a great club, I wanted to see for myself," Luca replied, his voice colorless.

"This cannot be happening. Not now, dammit!" Alessio rubbed a hand down his face.

"Have you pissed someone off since you got to Greece?" I said.

"We piss people off all the time," replied Luca calmly, his gaze sliding to mine. "And you?"

"Me?" I asked.

Had Valerio told the Tantuccis about my killing Med? Were they out for me all the way here across the Atlantic? Slightly melodramatic? Not really. Nowadays, families were huge organizations that had multinational business relationships. Anything was possible.

Alessio's narrowed eyes darted to my and Adriana's hands clasped together. "Who the fuck are you to even open your mouth?" His sharp voice split the air. "Why is he here?"

"Alessio—"Adriana wiped at her face. "Turo saved my life and yours."

"Yes, so he did." Alessio focused on Adriana, his tone now considerably softer.

Her hold on my hand remained tight. "The gunshots, the sounds, the screaming...just like..."

"*No cara, no,*" Alessio murmured. "This was different."

She'd been through a gun assault before? Because of Aliberti? Who the hell was she, really? She clamped her eyes shut, her hand in mine remained cold, stiff. She was doing battle with memories of the past and sensations of the present. A grim twist remained on Alessio's mouth.

"I can't get *Papa* on the phone, and I really don't want to try again if someone is tracking us." Luca smacked his cell phone on his thigh, releasing a wave of Italian curses. "We must leave Athens. Now. Tonight." Luca's jaw muscles flexed, his hard gaze drilling holes into me. "You will come with us."

My pulse drummed. Adriana stiffened at my side.

"What? Why?" spit out Alessio.

"His response out there was quick, efficient. Professional," said Luca in that low, ominous Italian accented English of his. "I know who you are, Turo DeMarco, and I want you on this trip. You are of use to me."

Of use to him? To Luca Aliberti?

The back of my neck razored with a thousand spikes like it did with every confrontation, expected and unexpected. Part excitement, part tense twitchiness. I let go of Adriana's hand. "And what do I get out of this?"

"A few moments with my uncle. Isn't that why you're here?" Luca said, his lips curling at the edges.

Adriana sat up against the dense leather upholstery of the seat. "What are you talking about?"

Luca ignored her. "If you cooperate, Mr. DeMarco, my uncle may be open to discussion."

"Adriana," Alessio said, his voice just above a whisper, a hand on her leg. "You keep refusing to have security on you, even after everything that's happened, and I keep telling you, your father keeps telling you, but you are stubborn."

"Having security with me attracts more attention, Alessio. The kind of attention I've been trying to avoid," she replied.

"*No.* After tonight, you need professional protection."

"Now, you have Turo," Luca said.

"*Ti?*" she said. "What are you talking about?"

"Yeah, what the hell are you talking about?" my voice snapped.

A thick eyebrow rose up Alessio's forehead. "Don't tell me you two aren't pleased."

"I'm not for hire," I gritted out.

"Yes, you are." Luca's dark gaze slid to me. "For as long as we need you."

Pulsing against my aching skull, that tick went off in my head. My what-the-fuck tick. My this-isn't-everything-it-appears-to-be tick. My there's-something-behind-door-number-three tick.

I'd been recognized by my targets, hired by them, *and* I had no choice but to go off with them on their yacht. Glass half full or glass half empty? At least there would be Greek wine in that damned glass.

Adriana muttered something in Greek, folded her arms across her chest and stared straight ahead, legs pressed together. Her body no longer touched mine. What did she object to more —having a bodyguard or having me as that bodyguard?

I settled back in my seat. There were worse assignments than being a beautiful young woman's security detail on a yacht, Greek island hopping. Most definitely, incredibly fucking worse assignments and I'd had quite a few in my time.

Alessio rubbed a hand down his face. He was troubled by the shooting, by me, by plenty more. He sprang forward toward his brother. "Luca, everything this week in Mykonos must go perfectly. Cleanly. *Capisce?*"

Luca didn't even look at him, his attention remained on the road ahead.

"Kaspar is flying in from Norway or Berlin or wherever the hell he is now," Alessio continued. "All sorts of celebrities will be there, even the Mahmouds from Dubai. Tag is coming from Istanbul with friends from London and—"

"They are my friends too, Alessio," Luca muttered, cutting him off with his low, grim voice in Italian.

"Yes, they are. But this is a very special time for me and my company, Luca. Adri and I organized this party for almost a year, and it's fucking important. And you—" he shot his brother an even darker look, a snarl on his lips.

Luca's eyebrow arched, his jaw set, offering his own warning, his own ultimatum. Weapons drawn against a threat.

Alessio's shoulders rose, his teeth dragging on his lower lip as he took in a deep breath, maybe to help him rearrange his words, his argument, to get a grip on his temper. "You take care of what you need to do without the crazy, eh? If this gets fucked up for me —if you start—"

Luca's eyes flared at his little brother. *"Cosa?"* He challenged him with a big 'what are you gonna do about it' in that smoky, ominous voice of his. No challenges tolerated. Alessio clamped his mouth shut and slid back in his seat.

There was tension between the Aliberti brothers.

I knew Luca, unlike Alessio, worked directly with their father along with two older brothers of theirs. Alessio was the youngest of the four brothers. Obviously, Luca was on some sort of business trip here to Greece and not just vacationing with his brother and uncle, and Alessio wasn't happy about it.

"We are getting on the boat tonight," Luca said, his hard gaze landing on me. "All of us."

13

TURO

WE GOT into the heart of Athens where I picked up my small suitcase from my hotel and checked out. Now, we were headed to Adri's house in a northern suburb so she could grab her bag.

"It's about time they finished building this bloody highway," muttered Alessio as the Cayenne flew over the smooth asphalt.

We were headed north on the new *Attikí Othos* highway which ribboned through Athens connecting the city to the surrounding suburbs. An essential in preparing for the Olympics next summer.

We exited off the highway and a sign flashed by—*Ekáli*. Manicured, fenced off properties, tree lined streets and huge villas, some modern and new in their sleek, clean lines, others older with the aristocratic charm of a bygone age. We stopped at a huge, black iron gate decorated with griffins, and Alessio got out of the vehicle, letting Adriana out to tap in the key code. They got back in the Cayenne, and the gates opened. We passed through and up a slight hill of lush green lawn enclosed by a high stone wall. A contemporary Mediterranean mansion rose before us. Adriana took in a tight breath at my side.

The SUV came to a stop, and I immediately opened the door

and got out, holding out my hand to her. She took it, hers still cold, shaky. She quivered, her legs as unsteady as a young deer's.

I quickly gripped her waist, pulling her up against me. "Adriana?"

Her eyes skidded to mine. "I'm fine. Fine." Her voice trembled.

"Not fine enough. Why don't I come in with you?" I said.

She pulled away from me. "You take your new job quite seriously, don't you?"

Alessio lit a cigarette. "It's a good idea. Go with her. Don't be long."

I shut the door of the Porsche and slid Adriana's arm through mine. She stiffened in my hold. "I don't understand what's going on with you and Luca, but I know I don't like it," she whispered.

"Between you and me, I don't know if I like it either."

"What did he mean that he knows who you are? Who are you?"

The *whirr* of a motor cut her off. She stopped, her gaze trained down another driveway toward a large garage where one of the doors rolled down.

"*Gamóto,*" she said under her breath. The Greek equivalent for "fuck"?

"What's wrong?"

"My parents are home. They were at the opera tonight and then a dinner party after, but they're home early."

She unlocked an impressive coffered wooden door, and a grand foyer of gleaming marble swallowed us up. A house that seemed discreet and minimalist on the outside was anything but on the inside.

A Francis Bacon painting hung on the wall in all its ugly twisted splendor, marble sculptures, both ancient and modern, tiny and large were perched on pedestals. An enormous, colorful, perfectly designed flower arrangement lay in the center of a round marble table, and a series of small paintings in ornate gold frames which, at my passing glance, certainly seemed like authentic French Impressionist pieces, dotted the wall.

Adriana was not ordinary rich folk.

A well-dressed, attractive older couple stood in the living room drinking brandies. Their conversation ceased and they stared at us.

"Adri?" her mother said.

"You're home early, aren't you?" Adriana said, her voice suddenly casual and in control as she led me into the salon.

Her mother's head slanted, eyes narrowed. Was it because Adriana was speaking English or because she'd brought a man home? Straight blonde hair edged her mother's shoulders, perfect makeup. They both shared the same blue gray eye color. "Your father was quite tired, so we decided to cut this evening short. And you?" British lilt to her crisp, confident English and her sharp gaze had me standing taller despite the fading adrenaline in my system.

"*Mamá*, this is Turo. Turo, this is my mother, Liana Lavrentiou."

Liana, the Queen, tilted her head at me. Both her perfectly manicured hands were adorned with twenty-four carat gold rings, including a large diamond solitaire. "Hello," she said.

"Petros Lavrentios," said Adriana's father, stretching out his hand for me to shake, and shake I did.

"Turo DeMarco."

A pair of intense dark eyes held mine. Eyes that assessed and brewed with a blend of coldness and suspicion.

"Turo is a friend from America," Adriana said. "And he's coming with us to Mykonos tonight."

"Tonight? I thought you were leaving tomorrow?" asked Liana.

"We decided to leave tonight instead of in the morning. I just need to grab my bag."

A tall, teenage boy with mussed dark hair and his father's

large brown eyes tracked into the room. "Adri?" The boy darted at Adriana. Her brother? They embraced.

"We woke you, my love? I'm sorry," Adriana said.

"*Óxi*. I was reading and I heard *Mamá* and *Babá* come home. *Óla kalá*?"

"Yes, yes, everything's fine. Turns out we're leaving tonight for Mykonos," said Adriana. "Come meet my friend Turo. He's from America."

"Ah. Hello," Marko said, holding out his hand to me, his sister's arm around his shoulders. "I visited New York the Christmas before last."

"Ah. Great city." We shook hands.

"Where are you from?"

"Chicago."

A uniformed maid appeared, holding a silver tray with two crystal tumblers filled with an amber liquid. She offered me a glass.

"Thank you." I put a glass in Adriana's hands, steadying them in my own. She lifted tired eyes to mine and an ache spiraled in my chest. "Take it, Lovely," I whispered, and she did. I took the other glass for myself.

"To you, Turo, and your quick reflexes. To your skills," Adriana said, her voice suddenly shaky again.

"Skills?" Petros asked.

"Survival skills," Adriana said.

"Here's to enjoying life," I said, holding Adriana's heavy gaze. "To Greek philosophies."

Liana studied us as she swallowed her brandy. I'm sure she hadn't missed the fresh scratch on the side of my face.

The liquor slid down my throat and my muscles relaxed under its aromatic, syrupy heat. *Shit*, this was a Rémy Martin Louis XIII. I'd first tasted it at a special formal dinner for heavy hitters to which my mother had insisted I accompany her. The price of a single bottle was anywhere from two to ten thousand.

"Where is your *mafióso, agápi mou?*" Liana's voice had a sharp bite.

"Really, Mother." Adri's shoulders dropped. "Alessio is a jewelry designer, you know that. He can't help what his father does for a living."

"*Kalá*," her mother said, the venom of her ironic tone splattering at her daughter's feet. The Queen wasn't buying it. Liana obviously knew who Alessio's daddy was. "Why the change of plans? Did something happen this evening?" Liana asked as she handed Petros her glass to refill.

"Just the usual with the paparazzi." Adriana swallowed the rest of her brandy, pressing her lips together.

"Hadn't we agreed that all that was behind you?" Liana said.

"Liana, really. Not now," muttered Petros as he handed her more brandy.

Adriana gulped at her drink, wiping at her eyes, smearing her already smeared mascara. Some monster from her past was rearing its ugly head in her rear view mirror and she wasn't handling it very well.

"Gennaro's had enough of Athens," I said. "That's why we're leaving tonight. He's impatient to get back on board the yacht and get to Mykonos."

"When you come home from Mykonos, why don't you go back to London, my darling?" Petros said, his voice taking on a firmer tone. "I really think you should consider it more seriously. Then come back in August for the month and we'll go on holiday all together and relax and see how—"

"I don't want to go back to London." Adriana's tone was incisive, piercing Petros's goodwill balloon.

"Now would be a perfect time," Petros insisted gently. "They don't chase you there, and you have the office, the flat, your friends—"

"Not now," Adriana said, a hint of sadness in her voice. Whatever London offered, it wasn't enough for her, it wasn't right. "Not yet. Please." She put down her empty glass.

"*Télos pándon*," Petros huffed, gesturing in the air. Was that an "oh well"? He was resigned to his daughter's negative response.

Liana folded her arms across her chest, her elegant fingers stroking a gold medallion hanging from a long, thick chain at her neck. "Are you taking everyone to the house?"

"No, no. We're staying on the yacht," Adriana said.

"I know you don't want to hear it again, Adri, but I'm going to say it one more time—" Liana said.

"What is it, *Mamá*?"

"You must take a security man along to Mykonos with you," Liana said. "Your own man. You know better, you—"

"I am." Adriana touched my arm. "Turo is my new security guard."

Her parents and brother stared at me as if I'd suddenly transformed into a frog from a prince. "You are a security guard?" Liana's shoulders became rigid. The interview was underway. "Is this your line of work in America? You are an experienced professional?"

An experienced professional.

My chest tightened. Old photos I hid in a drawer, postcards I'd tucked in the pages of books I would never open, now they fluttered before me.

There was the time I'd smacked a gang member with the butt of my gun, breaking his jaw because he'd set fire to the trash cans at the back of the deli where Mauro was holding court.

Me killing Joey Caliccio, my first kill and unplanned. Joey had refused to pay his protection fee to the Boss, and my then Capo, Tony, had taken me along to confront him. But Joey had played it tough, refused to pay what he'd agreed to and threatened to go to the cops. He cursed at Tony, and I shot him in the back of the head at point blank range.

"What the hell you doing?" Tony had blinked at me, Joey's lifeless, crumpled body oozing blood between us on the cement floor.

"Disrespect, it's the tip of the iceberg," I'd replied, sliding the safety back into place, my shaking fingers pressing around the gun as I tucked it away.

I'm proving myself, I'm just doing what I need to do, I'd told myself over and over. It hadn't been difficult, I didn't think, I just did it. And I liked it. Was that what was making me shaky, the realization that this was easy for me?

Tony had shot me a grin. "True. Very true." He pointed a finger at me. "I like that."

I'd swallowed down the bile rising in the back of my throat at the sight of all that blood forming a puddle in the mottled floor. Ignoring the throbbing of my hand, I'd taken in a breath and held the door open for Tony to pass through as if we'd just been at the barber. Later, he told Mauro all about it. Mauro only nodded and gave me that small wink.

My professional experience was a resumé full of blood smeared faces and body parts in basements, foul smelling vans, silencers quickly fitted on guns. Hiding and holding my breath, counting, checking twice, three, four times. Plunging my knife into Med—

"Yes, I'm a professional," I replied to Liana's question, my voice firm, pushing back the loud memories and Liana's prickly suspicions like an arm sweeping across a set table, clearing the surface of every item. All that was visible was gleaming, polished wood. "I'm licensed to carry a weapon and I know how to use it. I run my own business in Chicago and have a background in security and defense."

"Alessio has his men," Adriana said, standing next to me. "Mr. Aliberti has his security man from Miami who always travels with him, and Turo will be with me." She held my gaze, her neck long.

Turo will be with me.

Yes, with her. And her lover, his mafia brother who's got it in for me, and the uncle who I need to impress. Perfect.

I took in a breath under Adriana's stare. Was I jealous? Irritated? Yes, dammit, yes, I was. I hoped it wouldn't take too long to get to Mykonos, because if I had to listen to her moaning loudly as she and Alessio fucked, I'd need a whole bottle of that Rémy Martin to myself.

Her mother's lips tightened, eyes narrowed. "I don't want you to be alone."

"Mother—"

"She won't be alone," I said.

Both women glanced at me. The mother's claws retreated and the daughter's eyes softened. "Surely, you must have other plans, Mr. DeMarco?" Liana said, swirling the liquor in her glass. "Can you possibly drop everything on your stay here in Greece to accompany my daughter?"

"Actually, I came to Greece to do research for a client," I said. "I've done what I can in Athens. Going to Mykonos fits perfectly into my plans, thank you."

"*Polí oréa*," Adriana said to her mother. She wanted this over just as much as I did.

"Yes, very nice," Liana replied, her verbal volleyball icy on contact.

Eyeing us both, Petros lit a cigarette, snapping a small, thin, gold case shut. Adriana's parents didn't much like her relationship with the Prince of *Napoli*, and yet she persisted, and on top of that, the girl wanted me along on the getaway. I needed to focus on the fact that I was going to get face time with Gennaro on a yacht and—bonus—in Mykonos, of all places. There was an airport on that island. I'd do what I needed to do and get back on a plane to Chicago.

Adriana led me to the staircase. "I fit into your plans, hmm?" she tossed over her shoulder as she climbed the stairs, a slight smile touching the edges of her beautiful lips, dissolving the worry and anxiety that had etched her face earlier. The little minx was baiting me.

I grinned.

You do. You fit into my hands, my mouth, and I'll fit into your every curve and hole, baby.

14

TURO

THE SIGHT of the Aliberti yacht cut off my breath.

The *Allegra* was magnificent. The sleek luxury vessel had to be about eighty feet long or so, dark navy blue with blackened glass windows stretching down the length of the boat which gleamed in the harbor lights. The whole damned thing gleamed. Seductive, ominous. Uniformed attendants scurried to take our luggage.

"What do you think?" Adri asked as we followed the others, tracking across the long plank to board.

"I'm not thinking right now," I replied, and she laughed.

And I was being completely sincere.

My feet touched onto the deck of the massive yacht, and Alessio eyed me as he spoke to a crew member. An icy chill razored over my skin. I had no fucking idea what I was getting myself into. Could it be some sort of trap that he and Adriana had set me up for? The fogginess of their relationship status was irritating, but I had to remain focused on getting a shot at talking to Gennaro Aliberti. Of course, all the while I'd be out in the middle of the water with these people and no chance of escape.

Well, except for drowning.

I was either a foolish idiot, or the luckiest bastard in Athens.

"I'm going to use the ladies room." Adriana glanced at Alessio and headed down the narrow staircase to the lower deck along with Uncle Gennaro and his Miami Vice bodyguard. Alessio lit a cigarette, his features an aristocratic snarl as he sucked on the smoke. The air between us suddenly thickened.

"Come," said Alessio. "Let's have a drink."

I followed the Aliberti brothers up two flights of stairs to the top deck where there was a bar and a long dining table and, a few feet over, a long banquette with a low table in front of it and two console chairs on either side. I sat down across from Alessio and Luca, and a uniformed waiter appeared and asked what we'd like. Alessio and Luca ordered whiskys on ice.

"Whisky, no ice," I said.

The engines gunned to life, their vibrations rattling in my gut. The water frothed and churned below us, and the engines whirled and hummed as we pulled out of the harbor. The humid wind lashed at our hair, our clothing.

Alessio eased back into his seat as the barman placed our drinks on the table before us. "*Salut,*" he said, raising his glass. Luca raised his.

"*Salut,*" I answered in perfectly accented Italian. We drank.

The harbor receded from us. The dark blue water frothed and foamed in our wake, hints of aqua in the lights. We were at sea. The very dark sea. Alessio continued to study me, Luca looked rather bored and shifted his gaze out to sea.

"Any news about the identity of the shooters?" I asked.

"Their motorbike was found, abandoned and burned outside the city. But no clues as to who they are or who hired them yet," Alessio replied.

"You have any ideas?" asked Luca.

"Do you think those bullets were meant for you?" I asked.

"Do you think we would discuss it with you?" Luca said.

"Why do I get the impression this is not the first time this has happened to Adriana?"

"Because it is not," said Alessio

"Was it recently? Another occasion with you?"

Alessio let out a rolling chuckle, a hand going down his middle. "*No.* Not with me. With her boyfriend."

Her boyfriend? *Wasn't he her boyfriend?* My grip on the glass tightened. Shit only seemed to get more interesting.

Alessio's head slanted at me. "You should be careful, eh?" He drank, his gaze returning to the choppy dark sea.

"How long do you plan on staying in Mykonos?" I asked.

"For about a week or more. Then going on to Santorini and a few smaller islands, depending on the weather and the winds. The winds are very eccentric here."

"And you think Adriana will be safe with you after tonight?"

"That's why you're here, Turo DeMarco. Will she be safe with you?" his voice snapped, his jaw clenching. He wasn't so sure.

Luca let out a dark laugh, stretching his arms over his head, muttering something about girl problems in Italian. One of Luca's bodyguards appeared on deck, sitting down in a low armchair farther up from where we sat, his arms spread wide over the top. His holster and gun visible.

A slight smile I couldn't quite figure out shimmied over Alessio's mouth. "You ever been to Greece before, Turo?"

"No."

"Nothing like the first time." He chuckled softly. "Your first time will be very memorable."

Luca made a noise in his throat, muttering an agreement in Italian.

"It's magical, quite different from other places." Alessio leaned back in his seat.

"It is," I said. "Very different."

Alessio inhaled long on his cigarette as he continued to stare at me, the red glow of the tip flaring brightly. A signal. *Enter at your own risk.*

"One thing, Turo DeMarco." Luca's eyes glinted as he released my name from his lips, the "R"s rolling exotically on his deep voice. "You fuck with my uncle, you fuck with Alessio or Adri, and I will fuck you right back."

I pushed my glass to the side. "I'm interested in talking to your uncle on behalf of my boss to offer an apology, an explanation for his son's unfortunate behavior."

"Hmm. I heard all about it." Luca licked his lips. "And did you arrange for all this to happen to Adri so that you could get an in with us? With her?"

"Frankly, I don't even know who Adri is. She literally bumped into me at Island tonight. I was annoyed, in fact, thinking she was probably a set up on your end."

Alessio's dark eyes narrowed into slits. "Adri is not some *puttana* I use for my own means."

"I'm glad to hear it," I replied.

A harsh smirk slashed Luca's features. "You may have saved Adri's life and ours, so I won't throw you overboard right now like I want to. But all it takes is one signal to Ciro here—" he gestured at Mr. Bodyguard. "—and he tips you over like a doll and you'd be in that cold water and gone, and no one would know."

I sat back in my upholstered seat. Looking relaxed was my modus operandi. Even the pretense helped me refocus. "You just hired me and now you want to kill me?"

"He's a Gemini, deal with it," said Alessio, rolling his eyes. "I do."

"Luca, I came to Greece to apologize to *Signor* Gennaro for my boss's son," I said. "His ill chosen words were most unfortunate and quite disrespectful."

"Ahhh." Luca slanted his head, a slight nod. "Very pretty words. I see why you were sent. That was wise, because that Valerio Guardino is a little shit."

"You've met him?"

Luca waved a hand to the side, a sour look crossing his face. "From what my uncle has told me."

"I, for one, don't care about all that, that's your business—" Alessio gestured between me and Luca. "I want you to look out for Adri, Turo. I have a lot going on this week, and I need to be sure that she's safe."

"You do that, I'll let you talk to my uncle," said Luca.

"I'll do it."

Gennaro Aliberti and Adriana came up the stairs arm in arm breaking the grim mood of our threesome. Alessio settled back in his chair, a tight grin on his face for Adriana, but the harsh set of his jaw remained as she sat next to me.

Gennaro took a seat and his and Adriana's orders were taken and quickly served: chamomile tea with honey for her, and a cognac for Gennaro.

"We'll stay here tonight," said Alessio. "And continue on in the morning for the island."

"Here?" I asked. The yacht had started slowing down, yet I'd only just noticed.

Adriana touched my arm. "Look up there, Turo. So beautiful at night."

I turned in my chair and there, perched high on a cliff, was a colonnaded temple lit with dramatic lighting. An ancient beacon in the dark.

"That's a sight," I murmured.

"Cape Sounio," Adriana said. "The Temple of Poseidon." The evening's strong moon shed its silvery light over the dark waters and the god of the sea's temple ruins high above us.

"Did you not get a chance to visit Sounio?" Gennaro asked me.

I reached for my drink. "No, not yet."

"Ah, you must," he said. "Especially at sunset. You know, the English Romantic poet Lord Byron came here several times, even scratched his name in the marble of a column." Gennaro pointed to the temple.

"Didn't he die in Greece?" I asked. "Fighting in their revolution?"

"He did," replied Gennaro, an odd smile crossing his face.

The rough sound of scraping, clanging, the rush of metal on metal broke the temple's spell. The anchor had dropped. We were stationed for the night. Our first night. Maybe I should shoot Poseidon a prayer to keep my sea travels safe?

"Mr. DeMarco, I believe I know you," said Gennaro sipping at his cognac. A cold yet relaxed smile laced his mouth.

"*Bella*, let me show you this new painting my father bought for the stateroom." Alessio rose from the table, taking Adriana's hand in his. "He found it a gallery in *Roma*. Absolutely pornographic."

Her gaze slid to me for a moment as she followed Alessio down the steps to the lower deck.

Gennaro and I were alone. With Luca.

"Go ahead, Turo," said Luca. "Introduce yourself. We like the formalities. Let my uncle know why you are here."

Gennaro took another sip of his liquor, his eyes narrowing.

"Mr. Aliberti, I would like to speak to you on behalf of Mauro Guardino," I said.

He raised his chin.

"I have no intention of interrupting your holiday."

Gennaro set his glass on the table. "But you have."

"Sir, this shooting has interrupted your holiday, not me. I merely hoped to have the opportunity to apologize for Valerio Guardino's rudeness to you. His father was quite troubled by it."

"He should be."

"Yes."

"Were you?"

I said, "It's certainly no way to conduct business."

"Oh? Why do you think so?"

"I believe respect counts."

"It does. Which is why I won't be working with Mauro. He wants to stick his imbecile son on me? I'm not having it." He gracefully shifted in his seat, facing me fully. "I won't be strong-armed either. So don't think you can come here and toss a threat at me and I'll tremble and give in. Do you understand?"

"I do, sir. I'm not here to threaten or bully you. You run a quality international corporation, I only—"

"And my name stands for that quality all across the board. Why would I do business with an arrogant boy like this junior, when there are so many others to choose from?"

"Mr. Guardino could make it difficult for you in the Chicago area."

"He can try all he wants, Mr. DeMarco."

"I'm sure we could all reach a mutually agreeable solution, Mr. Aliberti. One that will work to everyone's advantage. If you would speak with Mr. Guardino once you're back in the United States, I'm sure you would find him most agreeable to work with, most amenable to your needs. You could have a very positive working relationship."

A thick brow furrowed, he folded his hands.

I said, "Mr. Guardino knows—"

"Oh? What does he know?"

"He knows that his son should not have spoken to you that way, and he wishes to make it up to you. I'm here to ask you simply to meet with him, hear him out."

Gennaro fingered the delicate crystal glass. "Tell your boss to fuck off."

"I'm afraid I can't do that, Signor Gennaro."

He glanced quickly to my left. "But you will. Right now."

Cold metal shoved up against my temple. The bodyguard stood over me, his gun at my head. Luca remained still, relaxed.

I took in a deep breath. "This isn't necessary, sir."

"It is," Aliberti said in his Italian accented English. "I don't like being interrupted over nonsense. Your boss is a respected man, but his son is a shit which tells me a lot about the father. I don't like it. At all. You are his messenger, are you not? Relay your message or Ciro—" he flicked a hand in the bodyguard's direction— "will take care of you. Call him. Now."

"Very well." I took out my cell phone slowly and hit the Boss's number. It rang, and rang. Athens was eight hours ahead of Chicago. It must have been early evening there.

"What?" Mauro finally answered.

"Mr. Guardino, I'm here with Mr. Aliberti and he wishes me to tell you to fuck off."

Silence.

I held Mr. Aliberti's firm gaze. Ciro ground the gun's metal nuzzle into my skull. Mauro's laugh filled the line.

"Keep trying or don't bother coming home."

The line went dead.

I really, really loved being in the middle of disputes and conflicts. Of two grown men having a pissing contest. "I'll let him know, sir," I said, clicking off.

I put my cell phone on the table in front of me. Shooting my hand out, I twisted it around Ciro's neck and, using all my weight, shoved him back onto the table. Cuffing his neck, I raised up over him, grabbed his fist and slammed it on the hard surface, sending the gun flying. Gennaro popped up from his chair as the gun slid across the deck.

"Don't touch me, and don't threaten me again," I said through gritted teeth.

"Let him go," said Aliberti, his voice strained, staggering two steps on the suddenly bumpy boat. Luca watched, unperturbed, a grin playing on his lips.

I let go of Ciro, who cursed at me under his breath as he grabbed his gun and put it back in his holster, facing away from us. He retreated to the end of the deck. I'd humiliated him.

Gennaro cleared his throat. "It's been a very long night. I'm off to bed." He headed down the stairs.

"Maybe next time, eh?" Luca said, crossing his legs.

"There needs to be a next time," I said.

Adriana returned.

"Adri, your bodyguard is in cabin five." Luca rose from the small sofa taking his phone and packet of cigarettes with him.

"Okay," she said.

Luca shot me a final look, and he and his acridity were gone. Adriana's gaze returned to me. Intent, curious, guarded. The tension between us was palpable, and it wasn't only the sexual kind anymore. Her cell phone vibrated on the table breaking the heated charge between us. She glanced at the screen, her face tightening. She hit a button and the phone stopped making noise.

I sat down on the small sofa. "Don't want to answer that?"

"No, it's much too late." She gnawed at her lips as she sat down next to me.

"How was the painting?" I asked.

"Remarkable use of color, and definitely a triple X rating." She grinned. Sly, raunchy, yet sweet and disarming all in a subtle sweep of those lips.

I let out a jagged breath as a wave of heat spilled over me. "Triple X, huh?"

"Depends on your taste, I suppose. And your mood."

"Oh, baby, I'm always in the mood."

She laughed, a rippling sensual laugh, and the tension left-over from Gennaro's and Luca's presence was finally broken, replaced with hot electrical sparks ricocheting between us. She didn't seem to be in any rush to join her boyfriend in their cabin. And he hadn't returned to claim her.

I slid closer to her on the sofa "Tell me, are you some sort of princess?"

She let out another laugh, softer this time. "No."

"Movie star?"

"No." She wiped the hair from her face.

"Singer? Model?"

"No. And not really."

"Not really?"

"I have posed for photos in magazines, but nothing on a grand professional scale."

"Fashion shows?"

"Many, but as a viewer."

"Then, are your parents celebrities?" I asked.

"Something like that."

"Adri—"

"What is going on between you and Gennaro? I heard your voices from the lower deck. Both of you threatening, challenging the other. Was meeting me at Island tonight part of some plan to get to him? Have you been following us? Do you have something to do with whoever shot at us?"

"No, I don't."

Her eyes searched mine, and she pressed her lips together. After all the tense game playing of this endless evening I was more than tired, and Adriana looking at me like I was a con man she shouldn't trust had me ruffled. And something told me I wasn't the first con man she'd come up against.

Her tight gaze hung on mine, and my heart thudded in my chest. Her opinion of me mattered.

"It's been a very long night. I'm quite tired, and you must be too." She pushed back from the table.

I grabbed her wrist and pulled her close, and she let out a gasp. "I know Signor Gennaro. We've met before in the United States. He and my boss were about to work together and—"

"Your *boss*?"

"Yes."

"I see."

"Adri—"

"I'll show you to your cabin," she said, her tone clipped.

She was annoyed with me, but there was nothing I could do about it now. We were both exhausted. The adrenaline that had hauled us here, to this point, to this boat, had finally drained away, taking us with it.

I followed her down the stairs to an elegant long living room in metal, gray, and black tones complete with an electric fireplace, two sofas and fluffy area rugs and pillows. Quite different from other yacht interiors I'd seen in my time. No nautical prints or bright whites and blues here. It was elegant and sophisticated, uncluttered, calming. Down another dramatically lit hallway, Alessio and his brother stood talking in Italian. Adri stopped in front of a black door marked with a chrome number plate. "5"

She shifted her weight. "Here you are."

"Here I am," I murmured. I wanted to say something. Get rid of this tension between us. Explain. *Explain what, exactly?* "Good night," I said.

"Yes, good night." She strode away from me and went to Alessio who put an arm around her shoulders. Luca shot me one last heavy look and strode into his cabin. Alessio pushed open a door to his side, and he and Adri went through, disappearing from view.

Their door closed with a heavy thud.

15

ADRIANA

SUNLIGHT DRENCHED the vast wooden deck of the ship, the sea shimmering, a sparkling veil. The lapping of the waves, the slight rocking of the boat, a sea gull's *caw*. I took a last sip of my cappuccino and breathed in the damp morning air.

I loved the early morning, the quiet, the stirrings of life without the interference of human noise. After the insanity of last night, a night that began so beautifully, so glibly, then ended in horror.

My fingers toyed with my *máti* charms hanging from a leather cord necklace. It was good to be in comfortable clothes after last night. Yes, last night seemed to have lasted forever. Yet after the shooting, the running off, the keeping it from my parents, and taking off on the boat, something still gnawed at me.

Some*one*.

Even after I'd gone to bed, I couldn't stop thinking about Turo. Every time I closed my eyes, I saw his eyes, eyes filled with concern for me after he'd covered me with his body, shielding me from bullets. This American tourist who was working with the Alibertis in some way. A man I'd kissed shamelessly. A man I'd had an overwhelming attraction to. And not just physically, but attracted to his way of talking to me, the way he looked at me. It was playful, it was fierce, demanding and challenging. It was sodden with desire and burned a path through my middle. He was a man, not a boy.

"Good morning," Turo's deep, smooth voice made my chest constrict. "Sorry, did I startle you?"

He planted himself in the chair beside me, his piercing gaze scouring over me as if he'd never seen a woman dressed in jeans, a T-shirt, and trainers before. My skin heated, a furnace setting off in my veins. Even though I was wearing more clothes than last night, I suddenly felt exposed to him, naked. Vulnerable.

"*Kallí méra.*" I pulled up my legs on the seat, but the barrier did nothing to make me feel less vulnerable to this man.

"No one else up yet?" he asked, his gaze darting to the ancient ruins above us then returning to me.

"No. Just us," I said, gesturing to the waiter who stood to the side.

Turo ordered an espresso. It arrived quickly and we sipped our coffees in silence. The anchor chains ground and scraped loudly, the engines rumbled to life. We were off. A lane of aqua foam trailed behind us as the ship gained speed, leaving Cape Sounion behind us. Turo slid on his sunglasses and adjusted his chair toward the best view. His cologne wafted over me, and I ran a hand around my neck. His scent was brisk and bright, almost sharp. A crisp citrus that softened and became silky and warm at its depth, offering up a hint of mystery.

I stole a look at him. Like the man himself.

I knew that fragrance. It was elegant and modern, an expensive vintage Italian men's cologne. Most men I knew wore the heavier, spicy, arrogant big brand scents. Not Turo DeMarco. Turo DeMarco appreciated the subtler, finer things in life.

"You smell good," I said before I could stop myself. *Oh, for fuck's sake, why should I stop myself?*

"Do I?" His lips formed a crooked grin, appealing and

sardonic all at once. He liked that I'd noticed. Or maybe all the ladies noticed and he was pleased with himself?

"Shall I guess what it is?" I asked.

He chuckled. "Give it a go. No one's ever gotten it."

"Poor girls."

I leaned in closer to him, the edge of my nose gliding along that slice of jawline. His breath rumbled in his throat. "Acqua di Parma," I whispered to his skin.

His lips twitched. "Very good," he whispered back.

His mouth was a breath from mine, and I could feel its warmth on my lips once again. A thick, roll of desire unfurled inside me, and I let it. His head slanted slowly, a movement which brought him closer, closer.

"Lovely?" he said.

"Hmm?"

"Be careful."

My head jerked back. "Why? Do you Americans bite?"

"If you take advantage of us, yes, we do."

I sat up straight. "You'd better not take advantage of me, then."

"I'm not." The playful tone in his voice was gone, replaced with something quieter, firmer. "This security guard gig wasn't my idea, but I've been hired and I'll make good on that commitment." His jaw set. "Your safety is my concern now."

My insides tightened. I believed him. "All I ask of you, is that you don't ever lie to me or soften the truth," I said. "If you're connected to the Aliberti family in some way, do what they do, work with them, that's fine, that's not my business. But don't pretend you're something or someone else. Just don't lie to me."

He sat back in his chair, his focus riveted on me. "I work for an organization in Chicago, and I came to Greece on behalf of my boss in Chicago to speak to Gennaro—*speak* with him, nothing else—about a business deal that soured. That's the truth. That's as much as I can tell you."

"Thank you," I breathed.

He studied me, his features tense, as if he were waiting for a backlash. "You don't care that I'm...connected?" he asked.

"No. I care about the truth from you."

"Why?"

"It's easy for people to spin a tale, to tell you what you want to hear. Something pretty. I've seen it all my life. But the truth is the only dependable, unchangeable thing in this life and we rarely allow ourselves to face it. We sculpt our own versions of it, wrap it around us, gild it to make it prettier. But events remain one and only and unchanged. It doesn't matter to me anymore if it's ugly, it's just the truth. I need to depend on you, Turo. After the shooting..."

I took in a deep breath to push back the wave of emotion building in my chest, that wave that was sticking up my throat. I had to conquer this, I had to. I didn't want to run away from it anymore.

"Adri—" He covered my hand with his warm one, and my head shot up at his touch, at the sudden soft tone of his voice.

"I'm glad you're here with me, Turo."

He took my hand between both of his. "You're cold." He laid a kiss on my open palm. A gentle swipe of warmth which left behind a current of heat on my flesh. His thumb rubbed over the spot. "Only the truth, I promise."

"Thank you." I took my hand back. I pulled my legs up again and stared out at the sea.

"Greeks must take this weather, these views for granted, right?" Turo brushed a wisp of my long hair to the side, tugging on it. "How can you be moody on such a beautiful day?" His playful, ironical tone was back.

"I'm in mourning for my life," I replied.

"Oh, it's too early for Chekhov, Adri."

My head knocked back and laughter ripped from my chest. He laughed with me, and I liked it. "*Ach*, Turo, you're the only one who's ever understood that line." I clapped a hand on his leg.

His grin broadened, his taut thigh muscle tensing under my touch.

My phone pinged, and I checked the screen. *Mamá.* "Good morning, Mum."

"*Adriana.*" Whenever she used my full name, it was either for a formal social introduction or because she was terribly irritated. "I heard about a shooting on the news. You were there last night, weren't you? Why didn't you say anything? I knew something was off."

"We were there, yes, but we were already in the car leaving when it happened. There was so much confusion."

"Is your security with you?"

I knew her anxiousness for my safety would never die. Better she speak directly with the source. I handed the phone to Turo, and he took it, an eyebrow raised.

"Good morning, Mrs. Lavrentiou." His gaze remained on me as they spoke, his tone professional, calm. I squirmed in my seat. An utter turn on. Something must be wrong with me, a man who spoke with my mother while his eyes lasered over me and my body coiled in heat.

This unusual state of intense arousal had not subsided over the past twenty-four hours. More arousal than I'd felt over the past two years combined, and all because of Mr. Turo DeFuck-ingMarco.

He handed me back my phone with a lift of his chin. All taken care of.

"Mum, I'd best go. I've got a thousand things to do before the party," I told her.

"Are you sleeping with him?"

"What? With who?"

"Mr. DeMarco?"

"No, Mother."

She paused. Using the term "Mother" in English always made an impression on her. It was sharp, a warning she was treading into shaky territory. "I'm asking—" she continued, "—because it makes for confusion between a security man and yourself. You want him alert and focused on the environment, not dreamy-eyed over you."

Turo, dreamy eyed? I suppressed the laugh rising in my throat. "This concern is coming from experience?" I asked.

"Yes."

I always loved my mother's honesty. She was blunt, but that characterised her love for me and my brother, uncompromising and fierce. Unconditional.

"Don't worry, I'm saving that for when we get back to Athens," I replied, my gaze darting to Turo.

"*Entáxi.*" I could practically hear her grin at my flippant reply over the phone. Snark was always appreciated between the two of us.

And it was snark because we both knew I wasn't the wild and crazy type of girl that my mother had been, that my friends were. I'd once had an active social life—parties, clubs, restaurants, bars, holidays. But not anymore, not since *then*. And from the very first, I'd never tumbled easily into men's beds. I'd only slept with three men, not the twenty or thirty most of my girlfriends had.

My mother liked Alessio, but she wasn't a fan of his family's business, so our relationship did not get her official stamp of approval. She put up with it though. She knew what it was to sow your wild oats; she'd been a wild girl in her day. Everyone expected me to be the same, but I'd disappointed them.

Well, not completely.

"Have a good party, darling," Mum said. "And let Mr. DeMarco do his job."

"Oh, I will." I slid my phone back on the table.

"She's worried about you," Turo said.

"She's a mum. Isn't that what they do? Doesn't your mum worry about you?"

He took in a deep breath and shifted his gaze out to sea. "In her own way."

"Have I said something wrong?"

He turned back to me. "No, why?"

"You got a bit moody there. Like me."

His shoulders visibly relaxed, and he reached for his espresso. "What's really upsetting you, other than getting shot at? I know last night was frightening for you, of course it was, but you're much too young and gorgeous a girl to be mourning anything. Your life has just begun."

"Why are you talking like an old man? You're not that much older than I am."

"How old are you?"

I signaled for another cappuccino. "Twenty-three. You?"

"Thirty-three."

"Hmm." I'd been right.

"At your age—"

"Oh, for fuck's sake, don't you dare," I cut him off.

"At your age," he continued, "I felt I had the whole world in the palm of my hands. It was a joke though, I came to realize."

My cappuccino arrived. "*Grazie.*" I stirred in a spoonful of sugar. "Turo, you're too late. I already made that mistake and learned my lesson two years ago." My eyes pricked, and I swallowed my fresh coffee. My tongue blazed with the hot brew. "Last night was another reminder that I can't hold on to anything."

"You held on to me." His voice was low, intimate, but not in a tender way, and my stomach knotted, heat flaring through my system.

"Yes, I did."

"And I'm still here."

"Yes."

"And you got me out of there," he said.

"Luca did that."

"Because you insisted."

My ringtone went off, slicing through the magnetic pull of our words, the hypnotic lure of him. I glanced at my phone.

Him again.

Third time this morning. I still didn't want to listen to his concern and lame sentiments. And his incessant phone calls were pointing to what I suspected, weren't they? No, I didn't want to believe it could be true. I didn't want to hear it, not now, not yet. I hit the ignore button and flipped my phone over.

The boat thwomped on the water, making us sway back and forth with the movement. The wind was relentless, the sea had turned choppy.

"*Bongiorno.*" Alessio and Luca sat down at the table.

"Good morning," said Turo.

The Aliberti brothers gave their order to the steward, and their espressos arrived quickly along with an ashtray. Another steward brought *cornettos* and *sfogliatelle*—the Italian versions of a croissant—colorful sliced fruit artistically arranged on a huge white platter. Alessio munched on a cornetto, Luca on an apricot, Turo a few strawberries.

Alessio piled a dish with fruit and slid it toward me, his eyes boring into mine. Always watching out for me. I took a slice of melon and nibbled on it as he lit a cigarette.

"We have about five more hours to Mykonos," said Alessio, stacking his lighter on top of his pack of cigarettes. "What would you like to do today on the island, *cara*?"

"We both have a lot to do," I said. "You have to check in at the store and the beach club. I need to talk with—"

"Yes, but still, I want you to have a good day today. You need it. How about lunch at Nobu, and then—"

"Alessio, wherever we go there will be lots of people and photographers, and I don't think I can do crowds right now, especially not paparazzi. Not right now. I don't want you worrying about me when you have so much to deal with today. Please. I'd prefer to stay on the boat. I'll be calling and texting everyone from here."

His head jerked back. "You are coming to the party, aren't you? You set up the whole thing. You—I need you."

"Of course I'll be there. This is a very important night for both of us. I just need some time before the event starts."

"Okay," he said, his eyes darting to Turo. "Whatever you wish." Alessio swung me into his lap, pulling me close.

"*Grazie*." I stroked his tattooed arm. "I'll be at the party a few hours before it starts."

"Don't worry, bro, I'll hold your hand today," said Luca on a lazy laugh, diffusing the tension. Alessio only scowled at his brother and planted a quick kiss on my cheek.

Turo visibly stiffened. He eyed the waiter who stood like an obedient soldier at the edge of the deck, and the man scurried over. I imagined Turo had that effect on a great many people. Even though those eyes of his were now shielded by sunglasses, his glare was powerful, the set of his jaw sharp, the tightening of those sculpted lips adding to his sudden fierceness.

"Sir?"

"Another espresso," Turo said. "Make it a double."

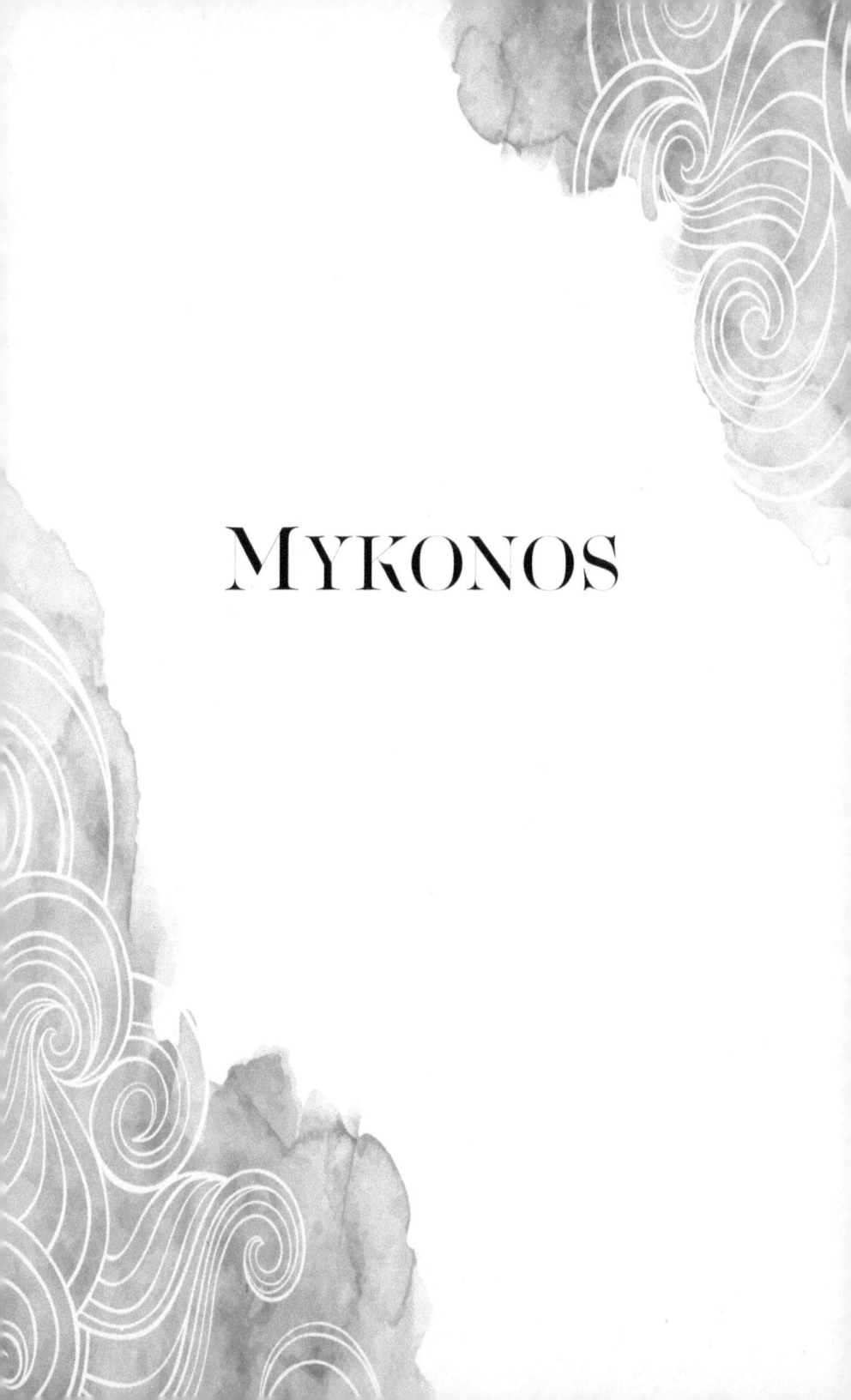

MYKONOS

16

TURO

P<small>SAROU</small> B<small>EACH WAS INSANE</small>.

We were anchored in the cove facing the shoreline where the party would be held tonight at a beach club. On the shore, tall straw umbrellas and loungers stretched back onto the beige sand, row after row after row. Frankly, I couldn't see much of that sand.

The party Alessio was throwing tonight at the Delfini Beach Club to promote his new collection was meant to kick off the summer season, but this place was already crowded with swimmers and cocktail drinkers, and quite a number of yachts, large and small, were moored all around us. What must this place be like at the height of the summer season?

"Look at that monstrosity, *tsk*," Gennaro said, his sharp gaze chewing on a massive beast of white metal anchored farther out from us. "Those Russians..."

"You don't like Evgeny's new yacht, *Zio* Genni?" Alessio asked.

Gennaro made a hissing sound. "No taste at all. Only *look at me and how big my cock is.*"

Alessio let out a dry laugh and muttered something under his breath as he scanned the huge ship with masts as tall as any city skyscraper.

Gennaro turned to me. "Alessio designed this boat for his father," he said, tapping his fingers on the table. "It's all about discretion. The *Allegra's* dark color reflects the sea. It does not show itself off from hundreds of miles away like—" he slanted his head toward the Russian giant, his hand swiping the air "—that monstrosity."

"These new Russian billionaires want to be noticed," Luca said. "Ev is enjoying himself."

"Yes, he likes to enjoy himself," muttered Gennaro.

"He's here with his daughter," Alessio said. "She'll be at my party."

Luca stretched out in his chair. "Which one?"

"Which one haven't you screwed yet?" Alessio shot back.

Luca smirked. "I don't remember."

"Behave tonight," Alessio said.

"I'll try my best." Luca headed for the stairs at the stern to board the launch that waited for them. Gennaro and Miguel, his bodyguard, followed.

Alessio took Adriana's hand and kissed her once on each cheek. "Join us by five o'clock, okay?"

"Five o'clock," she repeated.

Alessio lifted his chin at me and joined his family on the launch. They zoomed away on the water, heading for the beach club.

Ciao.

Standing at the railing, Adriana and I watched them until the launch docked at the shore. We turned to each other. My pulse thrummed, and it wasn't from the hot sun or the double espressos. The two of us. Alone.

"So," she said.

"So," I said.

She giggled, a throaty sort of laugh that only cranked up the tension in my muscles. Especially one particular muscle. I needed an outlet or I was going to do something I might regret.

"Is there a gym on this yacht?" I asked.

"Yes, small but fully equipped. Do you have gear with you or do you need—"

"I'm good. Show me the way?"

"I was going to head there too. Nothing like cardio to clear the head and refresh the body."

"Oh, I agree."

"There's a jacuzzi on the top deck we can go to right after if you like."

"Perfect."

Adriana and I hit the *Allegra*'s gym. Her on a spin bike, and me pounding it out on the treadmill. She'd turned on music from the built in stereo system and wasn't chatty but remained focused on her workout, like me. She finished before I did and got two sports drinks from the mini fridge. Our eyes met as she opened one and popped it into the drink clip of the treadmill for me.

"Thank you," I mouthed, and she grinned.

She stretched out her sweaty body on a mat, and I kept my eyes pinned out the window to the sea, as ideas on how to make her even more sweaty rioted through my mind.

Dionysus, you fucker.

We both finished and went back to our cabins, changed into swimsuits, and headed for the top sundeck. A jacuzzi was frothing in invitation, a number of padded lounge chairs stretched out over the beechwood decking. Our very own private beach club.

Adriana slid into the jacuzzi. "Perfect," she purred, her head falling back, her face bathed in sunlight.

"Certainly is." I got into the warm water next to her.

She was perfect. Her long, wet throat glistened in the sun, and all I wanted to do was lick that slick skin down to her full round breasts that now seemed to float in the bubbling water from within that pink bikini top. Watching her body work in the gym was enticing on one level, but this was enticing on a whole other. A prolonged feast for the eyes, the imagination.

I adjusted my sunglasses. "I'm really appreciating the... sudden quiet."

She glanced at me, squinting, a grin on her lips. "Yes, me too."

We stayed in the warm water another ten minutes then lazed on the loungers side by side. She took off her top and stretched out in the sun, her long, curvy body, slick and shiny from her spray of sunscreen oil.

Motherfuck.

I took in every line of her. Better than I'd imagined while kissing her the night before. In the bright light of day, my fantasy had been made reality—curvy hips, tight ass, long legs, those full tits. She turned over on her stomach.

My phone pinged. I blinked at the screen in the glare of the sun. *Jesus.* Two texts from Francesca.

Francesca: Turo! Sorry about Dad. He's such a bulldog

A bulldog? She had no fucking clue. Mauro was a bull with two swords stuck in his neck on a good day. When the going got tough, he bucked, roared, trampling anyone in his way. Stubborn, intractable to the very end. An end of his own making.

Francesca: I'll be at Crawfish tonight at 11. Let me make it up to U with a drink?

Crawfish. One of my and my mother's successes from my era with the company. A New Orleans style bar restaurant featuring craft beers from all over the country with a performance area for Zydeco artists. Crawfish had been my brainchild, my baby. And, obviously, it was still a hot spot.

That tight thread of concern for my mother that I hadn't been able to let go of since I saw her the other day ticked against my chest. I should check in with her.

I deleted the texts.

My gaze fell on Adri's relaxed body next to mine, and I let out a heavy breath. The desire to lose myself in her curves gripped me by the balls. My muscles tensed, and I tore my eyes away from her hot little body.

I needed to make sure that Gennaro was going to play ball with Mauro, and then I should be getting back to Chicago, shouldn't I? *Should. Should. Fucking should.*

"Bad news?" Adriana's eyes squinted at me.

"An interruption." I shut down my phone.

She turned over, her nipples hard and begging to be bitten. "Work or pleasure?" she asked putting on her sunglasses, her masked gaze directed at me.

I tossed my phone to the edge of the towel. "Right now, Miss Lavrentiou, you're my one and only work and pleasure."

"Lucky me."

"You are. Very lucky."

"Women must fawn all over you."

"They do, honey."

She laughed.

My hand itched to cup the round fullness of her breasts, to knead their soft firmness. I wanted to see her face morph with pleasure and shock at what I'd do to those ripe tits.

I cleared my throat. "I don't think I can have a conversation with you two inches away from me in a state of near nakedness."

She grabbed her bikini top and fastened it over herself as I watched. "Better?" she asked.

"Such a shame." I let out a lazy laugh, silently urging my cock to settle down.

"Was the text from a woman?" she asked, taking a sip of her iced coffee.

"Yes."

"Your lover?"

"She wishes."

"But you don't?"

"Absolutely not."

Her eyebrows popped up at my swift, sure reply. "You're already involved with someone, is that it?"

"With you."

"No, Turo, in America."

"Broke it off just before I came here."

"Oh, sorry."

"You don't have to be. It had gone on too long."

"You didn't love her?"

"No. I also didn't care enough, and not the way she wanted me to."

Her lips tipped up. "Well, aren't you in demand?"

I leaned over and brushed her upper arm with my lips, and she shivered. I grinned at her, enjoying her reaction. "Women see a certain thing in me they want and try to get it." My tongue traced a circle on her shoulder. "I offer things in return."

She eyed me. "You've designed that very well."

"Designed?"

"Your relations with women sound like an objective business transaction."

I released her arm. "I don't look at it like that."

"From how you've just described them, they have a non-organic quality—"

I let out a laugh. "Non-organic?"

Her lips pressed together. "More practical and pre-organized. Efficient. Rather like—"

I slanted my head. "Don't say it."

"—hiring a prostitute?" She licked at her upper lip. The satisfied cat.

"I do make sure terms are clear and understood, that certain expectations are exposed and deflated before proceeding."

"And if they're compliant with your terms, they get rewarded, I imagine? You seem to be a fair sort. An extravagant night out? The theatre? An expensive meal, jewelry on occasion? Good sex?"

"Yes."

"To all the above?"

"Yes, but most especially the good sex. Always the good sex."

"Very fair," she murmured, a grin stealing over her lips. "But you are a...Tefal."

"Excuse me?"

"Tefal—em, a frying pan that does not stick."

"You're comparing me to a non-stick frying pan? That's a first."

She let out a small laugh. "Nothing can attach to you. Everything slips over and around you with ease."

Her words blared their hard light on my winter of discontent. I ground my jaw. Why did that annoy me? Why did I give a fuck?

Because I gave a fuck about her opinion.

The waiter brought us a second round of whipped iced frappé coffees. Adriana's phone went off. "It all begins," she murmured, eyeing her screen.

"What's that?"

"I hired an official planner and PR person from Athens for Alessio's party tonight, and I've been the creative consultant, but ended up managing the entire affair."

"You know all the right people."

"I do. I've worked with my mother planning events before, but this is the first one on my own, and I feel responsible for Alessio's success. It was my idea that he open the boutique in Mykonos in the first place, and this party will go a long way in cementing his brand, and getting me back on the horse as it were."

"What do you mean by that?"

"I've been off the social racetrack for a while now. Tonight feels like my debut as well but on a different stage."

Her Blackberry buzzed. She answered and, for the next two hours, Adriana was on her phone in a flurry of non-stop Greek and English, answering questions, asking questions, confirming, reminding, disagreeing, re-confirming. Her emphatic tone had me at attention. She knew what she wanted, she knew what she was talking about. She was in charge.

My cock hardened at her firm demands, at the stream of Greek. What a language. It was round and curved and sensual; its sounds more suited to soft endearments and sentiments than orders. Greeks colored their speech with washes of emotion, up and down it went, round and round, so different from the angular practicality of English.

She clicked off her phone and made notes to herself on her keyboard. A steward approached her, and they spoke in Italian. "Turo, they'll be serving lunch in about fifteen minutes. Should we take a shower before or no?"

"Was that an invitation, darling?"

She grinned, putting down her phone. "For you, to shower in your cabin on your own, *darling*, and me in my cabin, on my own."

"Ah. Not if that means you won't be in a bikini for lunch."

"Are you objectifying me, Turo?"

"Forgive me, no. I'm admiring your work of art. Because, you, Adriana Lavrentiou, are a work of art for all the senses."

Her face reddened, her gaze deepened and that odd warmth flared up in me again. We both had our sunglasses on, but they did nothing to hide the crackling that zinged between us. There was something unpredictable about her. She could be soft or brittle, witty and ironic one moment, sad and lost the next.

"The things you say," she whispered.

"All true."

148

I surprised even myself. I was usually very careful and selective about the things I said to women. Not with Adriana. She inspired a fountain of verbiage, thoughts, feeling inside me. My insides tightened with the desire to run my fingers through that mane of long, unruly hair of hers and tug her mouth to mine.

What the hell was going on with my impulses around her? No control whatsoever.

I let out a breath. *She already has a lover.* Was she freshly fucked? She hadn't seemed too relaxed this morning.

She sat up straighter, chewing on her bottom lip. "I'll stay in my bikini for lunch, then. Shower after."

"How did I convince you?"

"Such a level of appreciation deserves rewarding."

I bowed my head to her and amusement flickered across her features as she slid on her designer flip-flops. I said, "I'm suddenly quite hungry."

Letting out a laugh, she rose. "Me too."

―――――

WE LEFT the sundeck and headed to the dining area where the long table had been set for two under the welcome shade of a thick canvas canopy that had been rolled out for us. A cold bottle of white wine was uncorked, a basket with different textured breads and rolls was placed to the side, and a dish of *ceviche* and a *caponata* of eggplant awaited us. We dug in. Oval plates of black risotto with calamari were placed before us.

"Is this calamari?" I asked.

"No, it's *soupiés*...em...a cousin of calamari. Ah—cuttlefish," Adri said. "Do you not like it? Black food is off-putting for many. Do you not like seafood?"

I slid my fork into the creamy black rice and ate. She watched me. "This is good," I said. "Excellent, in fact. Squid ink pasta and risottos are a favorite of mine. I've never had cuttlefish this way though."

Adriana blinked.

"I love seafood," I said. "Food, in general, is very much my thing. Good food."

"I love good food too."

"You're not eating though."

She only shrugged, pressing her lips together.

The steward brought over the bottle of *Vermentino* and refilled my glass with the white wine. Pale, liquid sunlight rising in my glass. I put my fork and knife down and leaned back in my chair. A simple thing, that I experienced on a daily basis in Chicago— fine food, a great glass of wine. But here, on the Aegean on a luxury yacht alone with Adri under a bright sun and a blue sky, a phenomenon. A little piece of perfection for us to share.

Adri raised her glass. *"Stin iyiá mas."*

"Stin iyiá mas," I murmured and drank. Light, crisp, and dry. Brightness in my mouth.

"Alessio's chef is a good friend of his from *Milano.* He always comes on the boat trips with him."

"He's very good. The risotto is cooked perfectly, the texture is just right, and the ink is that perfect salty contrast to the creaminess of the rice."

"Yes." She scooped up a bit of risotto on her fork. "I think I'll enjoy it more now after your precise analysis."

This sort of quality must have been routine for Adriana, standard. I was raised on a silver spoon too, but Adriana's spoon had been thicker, heavier with an intricate, baroque filigree. My mother had trained my palate from an early age, and I'd enjoyed the lessons just as much as she had enjoyed giving them. I'd been raised to appreciate unexpected tastes, and the ability to discern, not only between mediocre and good, but between fine and remarkable.

This was very fine.

I swallowed my wine, a refreshing flood washing away the sudden memories of satiny laughter, beaming amber eyes across small tables in hundreds of restaurants.

A platter of seared scallops arrived on a bed of mixed greens along with an aioli sauce for dipping. Using the silver spatula, I served a scallop into Adri's fresh plate and one onto my own.

Wine glass in hand, she watched me as I ate. "You know food?"

"I do. I grew up in the food industry in Chicago. My mother owns a company that develops and manages restaurants. She's done very well."

"Really? How interesting."

"It is. Over the years, Chicago has become quite a force in the restaurant business. A foodie capital, they call it." I drank the wine. "I used to work with her."

"Used to? You gave it up?"

I stabbed at the arugula. "It was time for a change."

Adriana squeezed lemon on her scallop. "You don't get along with your mother?"

"My mother and I are very much alike, actually." My gaze skittered to the sparkling surface of the water.

"Maybe that's why you needed time apart."

My eyes caught on hers. "Maybe."

"I've worked with my parents since I was a teenager, all through university."

"Are you finished with school now?"

"Yes, graduated and full of all sorts of degrees." She twisted her lips into a self-deprecating smirk. She wasn't impressed with herself.

"Your father wants you to go to London but you don't want to go?"

"It's quieter there for me, unlike here. But I'd rather be with my family right now, rather than be in England by myself." She went back to pushing her food around her plate. She'd been picking at her food, not eating. "I've been tagging along with Mum on her fundraising projects and the odd job at her real estate development company."

What Alessio had said about her boyfriend and a possible other violent incident in the past had me wondering if that was the cause for her wanting to stay put at home, instead of living the high life on her own in a big, flashy city like London after finishing college. She certainly had the financial means to do whatever she wanted, to go wherever she wanted.

"What's in London?" I asked.

"Our headquarters. The plan was for me to go to the London office after uni." Her fingers played with the stem of her wine glass.

"The weather would be very different, that's for sure."

Her lips tipped up and her face relaxed once more. That got a grin out of her. Something was troubling her, and I liked that I had pulled her out of it even for just a moment.

"Real estate is the family business?"

"No. My mother started that company on her own about a decade ago."

"What is the family business then?"

"Shipping," she said quietly, straightening her shoulders.

A word. A single word like any other.

"Shipping?"

"Hmm." She wiped at her mouth with the linen napkin, swallowing hard.

"Shipping as in Onassis, Niarchos—*that* kind of Greek shipping?"

"Yes, that kind."

I put my fork down. Adriana was a Greek shipowner's daughter. An heiress of massive proportions. Fuck millions—a few billion?

"Every man in Greece knows my worth," she'd remarked. She was right. A stunning, sexy, gorgeous, good girl heiress.

"My mother's family is the shipping piece actually," she said. "My father's family business is petroleum and refineries. Plus a football team, a bank, media. When they married, they combined the companies."

"Right. That explains the paparazzi liking you so much," I said.

"Hmm."

Which explained that house, the artwork, her casual familiarity with all things *primo classe*. "And it explains you needing a bodyguard," I added. "But why would someone shoot at you? If that was meant for you, of course."

Her gaze remained fixed on her dish as she pushed at the salad leaves with her fork. "I don't know."

I wanted to know.

Was her family embroiled in some kind of mess that had a gangsta style duo try to shoot at her in a public place? Why Adri and not her father or her mother? Still, I felt the shooting was most probably Aliberti related. Although, from what her mother had hinted at and Alessio, this hadn't been Adri's first experience with a violent assault. Maybe this was some crazy, obsessed celebrity stalker after her?

She drank more wine, staring out at the sea, the lines of her face taut. I didn't like that tension creeping into her beautiful eyes, tightening her body.

My legs found hers under the table, pressing against them. Her eyes darted to mine, her cheeks reddened.

"Do you work at the family business?" I asked.

"I'm spearheading a research project for my father. In between that, my mother has been ferrying me to photo opportunities at galas and fundraisers and opening ceremonies. She and I make a brilliant pair on a magazine cover and tasty fashion fodder for the gossip chat shows on TV. Good publicity for the brand, you know."

"And what do you want?"

She put the fork down. "Now, with the Olympics coming to Athens next summer, many new things are going on here, so I wanted to stay."

"And not go back to London."

"Right."

"What do you really want, Adri?"

"I used to know, I used to be so sure, but a couple of years ago everything screeched to a halt, and I felt like I didn't fit anymore. Didn't fit anywhere. That's something I'd never questioned before."

"Fuck fitting in. Fuck what everyone else thinks or expects from you."

"Turo—"

"You seem to be on top of things today for Alessio's party. I couldn't understand a word of what you were saying, but you were in full command of every conversation you had."

She made a face. "It's just something I know how to do. It's fun for me."

"No, Adri. It's more than that. I can tell."

"I believe in Alessio's jewelry, in his art. That makes it a passion project. I also convinced him to make it a fundraiser for my mother's charity, so it's important to me that tonight is a success."

"That's the best, to combine your interests like that. To be passionate about your work."

"Are you?" Those blue gray eyes of hers sharpened suddenly.

"I...certainly like the benefits of what I do." I tossed my napkin on the table. "You must have lots of experience as a party-goer."

She raised an eyebrow. "I do."

"What I mean is, you must know what works and what doesn't. What might excite a certain type of crowd and what won't."

"I know what I like at an event," she said. "For Alessio's party I envisioned the way I wanted the space to feel, what kind of emotions or responses I'd like to arouse, the colors, textures. A certain energy I wanted to create that is only enhanced by the people who are there. Every event has a distinct spirit or personality. And Alessio's work has a distinct character that I want this event to reflect and celebrate."

I raised my glass at her. "Well said."

A smile flickered across her lips at my honest compliment.

"What did you study in Switzerland?" I asked. "Something you had a passion for or something your parents made you study?"

Her chin lifted. "Something I wanted to study."

"Which was?" I waited to hear "Art History" or "French Literature" or "Decorative Arts and Design of the Early Twentieth Century."

She said, "Economics, with Chinese and Russian languages, and then a Masters Degree in Business."

A flash of adrenaline spiked through me.

She rolled her eyes. "And a lot of literature so my head wouldn't explode."

My fucking dream woman. I refilled her wine glass.

She sipped, her eyes on me. "So, now that you no longer work with your mother, you are a full-time security specialist or was that a little white lie for my parents?" she asked.

My white lies, and they are many, are for everyone and especially for me. I have them stacked up all nice and neat ready to deal them out like cards. I fingered the base of my glass. "I am a security specialist. Among other things."

"Oh? What other specialties?"

"Customer service, human resources. Public relations."

Our eyes met. There was no concern, worry, or panic. Only amusement. Intrigue.

I raised my wine glass at her. *"Stin iyiá mas."*

She raised her glass in return, a small smile brightening her features.

I poured out the last of the wine for us, and we took our glasses and stood at the railing taking in the busy seashore in the distance. Her shoulder brushed my arm, the scent of her perfume mixed with the suntan spray. A concoction of oranges and vanilla, a hint of coconut, maybe cinnamon too. Full of warmth and sunlight, enticing me to touch her, taste her. Be in that warmth with her.

I kept my eyes trained on the busy shoreline. "How long have you and Alessio been seeing each other?"

"Almost two years, off and on."

"How off? More off than on?" my voice demanded a little more harsher than I'd expected.

She glanced at me. "He lives in Italy, I don't." Her tone was casual, her voice drifted off. A verbal shrug.

I knew better, and I wasn't going to leave it there. "Why did you kiss me last night at the club, Adri?"

She raised herself up from the railing, arms long and stiff. "Should I apologize for it? Did I offend you?"

"No, you didn't. I liked it. Very much."

Her lips wavered under my silent scrutiny.

I said, "I don't want to offend Alessio."

"You didn't. You aren't."

"Why not?" I shot back.

"Why all the questions?"

"Because I want to fuck you," I clipped, leaning into her. "But I'd also like to keep my dick intact and all my other limbs. My head, too. That would be my priority no matter the insistence of my lust."

She burst out into laughter, wine shooting from her mouth, warm wet landing on my skin. I wiped at the side of my face.

"Oh, I'm so sorry!" Her fingers brushed at my cheek, my chest. I grabbed her hand and pulled her to me. A breath apart, a breath together. Her eyes flared, jaw tightening. She was steeling herself against *not* kissing me.

"Why did you laugh at me?" I asked.

"I've had many men tell me they want to fuck me in many different ways. But you? There's no art or artifice to your language, no pretentiousness. No bullshit, no pretty words, pretend emotions, or enchanting promises. Just your bloody intensity and that grim honesty of yours."

"Grim?"

"Oh yes. Then your dark sense of hum—"

I kissed her. She stiffened, pushed at me, a grunt rising in her throat. I tossed my wine glass into the sea, grabbed hers from her hand and threw it overboard.

My fingers gripped the sides of her face tightly. "Kiss. Me."

"Why?" she breathed against my lips.

"You liked my kisses last night, you begged for them. You—"

Her tongue lashed at my lips, breasts smashing into my chest, warm hands sliding around my neck.

Hell yes.

I took what she offered and took more. Wine, honey, heat, sea salt. Her tongue slid against mine, fueling my desire for her. I wrapped my hands around her bare waist, pressing into her sleek flesh, pulling her close against me.

The scream of an engine grew loud. Another roar and grind swerved past. I tore my lips from hers and shoved her behind me.

"Turo?" her voice breathless, her fingernails dug into my sides.

A jet ski roared past and another and another swiped through the dark blue water even closer to the *Allegra*. Two men on each jet ski, the ones seated in the rear with cameras in their hands focused on us.

"*Sto thiálo!*" Adriana spit out.

Pulling her back from the railing and into the dining room, I wrapped my arms around her and held her. "They were just taking pictures. It's okay," I murmured, brushing my lips against her temple.

She shivered. I held her tighter, rubbing her back, but her shivering wouldn't stop.

"Is it always like this?" I asked.

"Always."

17

ADRIANA

Turo ushered me inside the boat, his arm around me.

"You okay?" He searched my face.

"Fine." I pushed his hands away, and he released me. "I'm fine."

His jaw tightened even more. "Adri."

I brushed my hair behind my ears. "I'm going to take a shower and—"

"Get some rest." He glanced at his watch. "We have about three hours before we need to leave for the club."

"Right." I headed down the corridor toward my cabin, a hand trailing the wall.

"Adriana."

His heavy voice stopped me in my tracks, and I turned back toward him. Turo's brow was pulled together forming a stiff ridge over his eyes. "I'm sorry—I should have been more careful."

"It's not your fault, Turo. It's the way things are."

The way things had always been.

I went to my cabin and curled up on the bed. I didn't want another private moment stolen from me. I gave them enough, all the time, but it didn't matter, did it? Now they'd try to find out who Turo was and whip up some steamy "Adriana and her sexy bodyguard" story.

Something to look forward to.

I rolled over onto my back and replayed the memory of Turo's firm grip on my flesh—I could still feel it. His throwing our wine glasses into the sea, kissing me, demanding from me. His biting looks, his deep kisses. I curled up on the bed. I hadn't given myself over to *it* in a very long time. Giving myself over to Turo wouldn't be difficult. From the moment I met him I could feel the earth under me giving way. A wild landslide. A landslide I was powerless to stop.

His kiss had dared me to kiss him back, a kiss that said he wanted to consume me, conquer me. And a piece of me wanted to be his captive. Last night at the club, I'd given in to the over-whelming urge to experience that dare blazing in his eyes. For once, I'd taken the chance and leapt. This was no ordinary attrac-tion. A kind of high, a jolt, a shock that pulled my insides tight with a searing heat the moment he'd gripped me just now, his taste becoming mine.

My fingers went to my lips. I could still feel his possessive ferocity. 'Kiss' was such a sweet, charming, even simple word, but Turo's version was anything but. His kiss was a portal to a shrouded mystery that called to something brutal, something volatile inside me, inside both of us. This was no kiss perfor-mance to impress or dazzle me, win me over like it had been with so many others. There was a connection, I'd felt it shudder through me. I saw it in his eyes, a moment of surprise then it had darkened.

I slid a hand over a breast and stroked, kneaded. What would his hand on my body feel like? I closed my eyes and saw his face, felt the heavy heat of those eyes on me, his touch. It had been so long, so long since...

My nipples hardened, my skin heated. I ached. That loneli-ness coiled inside me.

My hand traveled down my middle to between my legs. *Bloody hell.* His burning mouth on mine had lit a fire in me only moments ago. A fire that still blazed, and I didn't want to let it die. My breathing deepened as my fingers slid under the waistband of my bikini bottom.

Yes, *there.* Like that. If he touched me here, would he be work-manlike or sensual and possessive? I was positive it was the latter; he would listen to my body, he would answer its call. My fingers moved faster. Was he hard right now? Was he relieving himself of that arousal in the shower at this very moment, water streaming over the muscles of his body?

His deep voice murmured in my ear, his eyes seared over me. His fingers dragged over my skin, his mouth. I stroked harder, a cry with his name on it escaped my lips, and I buried my face in the pillow.

———

TAKING A DEEP BREATH, I knocked on Turo's cabin door.

I tugged on the end of the short skirt of my dress as I shifted my weight on my damned heels. Why was I so nervous? Was it the party? Was it because I had fingered myself to an almost orgasm fantasizing about him less than two hours ago? Something I hadn't done in forever?

I hadn't felt this crazy combination of feelings and anticipation in a long time. No, not like this. This was exhilarating, a high.

I like him. A lot.

And I was fascinated by him too. Tonight we would be spending the evening together and I looked forward to it. Close together. With hundreds of other people, but still, close together.

"Come in."

My stomach dipped at the sound of his strong voice. The strong, sure voice that belonged to the strong, sure man who saved me from bullets, paparazzi, but he hadn't saved me from his tongue.

I pushed open the door. "Turo?"

He pivoted, and my breath caught in my chest. A towel was wrapped around his waist. Low, low on his waist. His skin shimmered with a sheen of water. He'd just gotten out of the shower. His shoulders, arms, chest were sculpted in hard lines and firm planes, a dusting of hair in all the right places. There was nothing overdone, trying too hard, imposing to impress; he was perfect. He took care of himself, and that was incredibly sexy.

Heat flooded my chest, swarming through my insides. "Oh, pardon, I—"

His eyes glittered in the beams of sunlight coming in through the small window of the cabin. He enjoyed my mental stutter as my eyes swallowed up his fine assets.

"No pardons necessary."

"They never are with you, I think." I grinned, my shoulders relaxing.

"Rarely." He unfastened the towel, tossing it on the bed in one quick move.

Amán.

I stilled, my eyes bolting to his. Two could play this game. My intense curiosity to see his—I was very certain—generous endowment gnawed at me. I couldn't help but notice it last night when he'd pressed against me during the first kiss. And earlier on the deck. My eyes remained locked on his.

He pulled on a pair of black boxer briefs that had been laying on the bed. He had all the time in the world. He stalked over to the closet, and my eyes fell on his sculpted rear. Those long, baggy American swim trunks had hidden a very fine bum. Muscular and round. The long muscles of his broad back moved as he pulled out a shirt and a dark suit from the closet.

"Wait. You're still wet," I said.

He stopped in his tracks as if I'd told him to freeze. I took the shirt and suit from his hands and laid them carefully on the tightly made bed. Picking up his damp towel, I patted the firm flesh of his back with it, rubbing it down his arms and over his shoulders under his heavy gaze. His breathing audibly quickened.

"Do you need anything...pressed?" I breathed in his ear, keeping my tone matter of fact as I continued to rub over his chest. "That can be taken care of."

"Could it?" he said, his voice husky.

"Oh, yes."

He grabbed the towel from me. "Please."

I went over to the side of his bed, picked up the telephone, and called the housekeeper, asking her to send someone to pick up Turo's clothes for a quick press. Turo watched me as he brushed a hand down his mouth.

I hung up the phone. "On their way."

Smirking, he tugged on the plush white *Allegra* bathrobe from the closet. He left the bloody robe open, and my gaze fell to his chest, down his firm, rippled muscles, chiseled one by one. My mouth dried, and a low noise growled in his throat, making my gaze return to his. He moved toward me. The gentleman beast.

A loud knock at the door and my body jerked at the sound. I opened it. The steward had arrived.

"*Signorina?*"

I gestured absently at the bed. The steward scooped up Turo's clothes and left, charging down the hallway.

Alone again.

His eyes still on me, Turo drank from a small bottle of water and wiped at his mouth. "You look beautiful," he said. "You always do, but you in that dress—" His eyes flicked downward and back up over me. He sucked in air as he twisted the cap back on the water bottle a bit too forcibly, and it cracked. "—spectacular." The word came out hushed but incisively articulated, and my flesh heated. I was on a stage in a vast, dark theatre, a spotlight shown over me. Turo's spotlight. All for him.

I cleared my throat. "Thank you. My cousin Silia is a fashion designer. This is from her new spring/summer couture collection."

"Turn around." He remained still, his voice coming out low and stern, cutting off my speech, my train of thought, my heartbeat.

I turned around, slowly, my heart pounding wildly under his fierce attention. Silia's creation was a very fine silvery chain mail draped over a gauzy, white sheath, dipping low down my front, just covering my breasts. The dress was short, the bottom portion, just past my hips, was a web of embroidered silver flowers embellished with Swarovski crystals. My high-heeled, silvery beige sandals with the crossed straps on my feet gave me extra height. I'd sprayed a perfumed oil on my arms, legs, and chest for a bit of sheen and had done my makeup quite simply except for smokey eyeliner and deep red glossy lips. Large diamond stud earrings and an Alessio-designed skull ring flecked with tiny diamonds were my only accessories.

"Spectacular," he murmured, his eyes finally resting on my legs. His shoulders moved under the thick bathrobe. "So, tell me what to expect at this party."

"This beach club just opened last summer and they do very well as a restaurant bar and nighttime club attracting an international crowd that is willing and eager to pay. They started as a small restaurant but they've expanded and have lots of plans to keep on doing so. Think posh St. Tropez meets Greek Island. Their prices certainly reflect that. They also put on several concerts with some big name Greek singers. Tonight, we start with a fashion show with a number of models, all very theatrical. After that, it will be a nightclub experience. Alessio has a good friend from Norway who's a famous DJ here in Europe coming to play. He's been a big draw."

Turo's gaze darted out the cabin window. "There are more and more yachts out here since lunch, aren't there?"

I followed his gaze outside. "Hmm. We've sold out."

"Big crowd then?"

"Big crowd."

"Are you up for that?"

"I have to be." I sucked in a breath and pushed my lips into a smile.

"It'll be crazy, but you'll be fine. I won't leave your side."

His words, the intensity of his eyes made my pulse race. "Okay."

He came closer. He didn't touch me, but the air between us was charged. I shifted my weight to combat the sudden weakness in my knees, a quiver rolling through my tummy.

"Unless you want me to keep my distance," he said.

"No, I want you to stay with me," I breathed, my heart beating faster and faster.

"And if you need to get out of there, we get out," he said. "I know you're used to being in the spotlight, have done it hundreds of times before—"

"I have."

"But after the shooting, tonight may be different."

"Are you trying to talk me out of going?"

"No." He shook his head slightly. "I only want you to be aware. It's important you don't push yourself too far. If you get uncomfortable in any way, you let me know. We leave or we just lay low in a quiet corner of the club. Whatever you need."

Somehow I knew that if I got the least bit uncomfortable, he'd notice. I wouldn't have to tell him.

"Okay."

"Tonight may be important to Alessio, but it's your night too," he continued.

My heart thudded in my chest at his words, at the fresh, clean scent of his skin. He'd used the green tea and mint shower gel, just like I had, but now that fragrance mingled with his, became his, and made my insides curl tightly.

He took my hand and stroked my fingers. "You've worked hard. You deserve to enjoy this party and see it be a huge success." His tenderness wrapped around my anxiety and dread like a velvet cloak. Easing them in softness and warmth, loosening their grip on me. My vision got blurry and I blinked the unshed tears away.

"Thank you," I said. "That means a lot to me."

He brought my hand to his lips. The featherlight brush of his mouth set off a rage of sparks on my skin.

"Well, Lovely, you're ready to conquer the world on looks alone." His fingers lazed a trail across my collarbone and those sparks exploded again.

That crooked grin of his was etched across his lips, but something softer flickered over his face for just a moment. "You're very good at conquering, baby."

18

ADRIANA

"THERE YOU ARE, BEAUTIFUL!"

Kaspar lifted me in his arms, brushing his lips against mine. I pulled back from his embrace. "Good to see you."

He placed me back down gently onto his narrow stage platform which had been set up over the shoreline of the beach club. Just beyond the stage, the sea sparkled with the lights from all the boats and yachts crowding the cove before us.

"Gorgeous as ever." His infectious grin widened.

Kaspar wasn't the most handsome man, but his outgoing personality and reckless enthusiasm for life were so charismatic and mesmerizing that he left you breathless; you wanted to be a part of his energy. We always flirted with each other, although he flirted with everyone. We'd snogged after a concert of his in Montenegro last summer, but that had been it. And that had been enough.

His bright blue eyes teased me as he raked a hand through that perpetually messy blond beach hair of his. "You never showed up in Abu Dhabi last September like you promised, sweetheart. You broke my heart."

Dip a toe in, use the Alessio card, run the other way. That

always worked for me, but then I'd met Turo. I'd dipped my customary toe in, but now, oh now, I craved a full bath.

"I know, Kaspar. I'm sorry," I said. "Bad timing, I couldn't make it happen. But I'm so glad you're here. Did the sound check go okay? You have everything you need?"

"Yah, it's good. All good." For the third time he shot a quick look at Turo who stood to my side, but he quickly re-focused his attention on me. I could feel the barbed prickle of heat that was Turo's glare. His annoyance was a force of nature.

Having security wasn't unusual, and security guards were everywhere here. Huge, tall, ruggedly attractive men every five feet kept a close eye on everyone and everything. Turo may not have been large and brawny like all these superhero types, but he was fit and sharply handsome, and he was my very own security superhero.

His dark tapered suit fit him perfectly, and every time our eyes met, my pulse raced and I found myself staring at him a bit longer than I should. And he, cocky devil that he was, always returned my looks with loaded ones of his own—part respectful appreciation, part protectiveness, part outright lust. That heady perfume still lingered in the air between us from the moment he'd taken my hand and guided me onto the launch earlier.

"You need a drink, love," Kaspar said, gesturing at the generous shots of vodka being served with ice cubes that had colorful flowers frozen inside. Alessio had partnered with a trendy new Polish vodka company for tonight's party. All organic ingredients and interesting flavors. Add the sculpted hand-painted glass bottle encrusted with Swarovski crystals and that was supposed to make it worth one thousand euros a bottle.

"I will, very soon. Too much to do just yet." I winked at him.

If I had a drink now, it would be too easy to keep drinking, and I'd convince myself I was more at ease than I actually was. I was working tonight. Tonight I had responsibilities and I would see them through.

The screaming tension that had tightened my every muscle to the point of a full-on, dizzying, chest-crushing, cold sweat panic on the launch coming over had evaporated bit by bit under his shadow, and I felt much more comfortable than I'd expected to be. From the moment Turo and I arrived at the club, I pushed back my panic and focused on Alessio's panic, the models' last minute snafus, the restaurant manager's thousand questions, the lighting designer's issues, Theo, the PR man's checklist. One by one, I answered questions, made decisions, insisted on changes, gave lots of hugs brimming with enthusiasm.

As the sun set and the club filled with people, my anxiety bit at the edges of my jagged pulse like a desperate wild dog wanting to get his way. But Turo's presence at my side, at my back, him watching me insistently with those bright hazel eyes of his made the few embers of confidence inside me blaze to life again and the dog receded. Turo was a consummate professional, a constant presence, unobtrusive, but always there, always within my reach. And that uneasy panic that had become so familiar had been slowly dissolving.

"Come on, love, wish me well—" Kaspar held out a glass of vodka to me as he grabbed one for himself.

Behind me, Turo cleared his throat.

"You will slay them all tonight." I grinned brilliantly as he tossed back his shot. "I have to check in with the restaurant. I'll see you later, okay?" I touched his arm. "Have a great show." We double kissed in goodbye and I moved back, leaving the stage. Kaspar was immediately swarmed by his staff and the entertainment coordinator from the beach club, fans hungry for him. He and his vodka were gone in a vortex of enthusiasm and cacophony.

I turned to Turo with a slight dip of my head, and he immediately leaned in closer. "I need to check in with Alessio and the models. It's almost time."

He glanced at his watch. "Right. Ten minutes."

His eyes scanned the crowd as he guided me toward the restaurant area. He held out his hand and I took it as we mounted the few steps to the restaurant and my insides fluttered. He knew, he knew exactly what I needed and when I needed it. Either for him to hover when a journalist began to ask me overtly personal questions, as one had earlier, or simply a hand reaching out for support as I made it up three deep steps.

And thank God because these bloody shoes were merciless. My feet were already killing me. They were good for taking a few steps to your table and sitting there for hours, then getting back in the car to go home. Not charging around like an army captain drilling his regiment, keeping close watch that every soldier was in form. And this battlefield was full of wooden steps, pebbled pathways, irregular stone tile.

That distinctive touch of Turo's settled on my bare back and my pulse skipped a beat once again. It didn't matter that we had spent the entire day together, that he'd been in close proximity all evening long. With his every touch, no matter how slight, my body reacted. I reacted.

Flanked by the hair and makeup artists, Alessio was going down the line of the ten models who wore his jewelry. The models, Athens's finest along with a few imports, had been strolling through the cocktail party wearing Alessio's creations for an hour already. It was now time for the grand finale.

"How's it going?" I asked Alessio who was arranging the leather bindings of a choker around a model's neck.

"*Bene.*" His fingers worked quickly, his focus on his task fierce. "Have you seen Kaspar? He was asking for you."

"Yes, he's all set up and ready. Doing last minute checks, but everything's set."

Alessio's dark eyes flashed as he pulled on the ends of the leather necklace, placing them down the model's chest. Eva, one of the latest Greek model stars that Silia had insisted we hire, wore a silk, dark pink bikini top and a long, mandarin orange silk skirt with two high slits up the sides and a bit of a train in the back that Silia had designed for us. Eva was barefoot and wearing colorful beaded leather and gold anklets on both her ankles and a larger one around a thigh. Wrapped around her head and nestled in her long, wavy, dark hair was a strip of leather with a hanging gold charm that Alessio had designed as part of his new summer beach collection.

I squeezed an arm around his waist. "This is it," I said to him.

"This is it," Alessio repeated.

"*Perfetto*, Alessio. It's all so perfect," I said, and he took in a deep breath.

He needed to hear it, and it was all true. I was very proud of him. I'd encouraged him to spend the outrageous amount of money to open his boutique here in Mykonos and I felt responsible for its success. It had done well, but I knew it could do better. This event had been an idea of mine from last year.

Alessio was a sexy character who was very personable. His jewelry being branded with exclusive Mykonos boho-chic worked. Putting him at the center of a party promoting his own exclusive Mykonos boho chic line *really* worked. Tonight we were making it all a visual in action. We were making it an experience.

"*Grazie, cara.*" Alessio planted a quick kiss on my mouth, and Eva slid her arm through his.

I gestured at the four other models who waited to proceed. "*Páme,* go on!" I said.

They grabbed their small, gourd-like baskets filled with flowers and descended the steps, moving through the crowd, tossing the red and purple petals and bay leaves everywhere to the *oohs* and *ahhs* of the guests. Topless young male musicians who waited on either side of the steps struck on their *touberlékia*, handheld goblet style drums which produced that rolling deep Middle Eastern bass beat that was very Greek. Their hands snapped, slapped, popped, and rolled on the small drums. Alessio and the models wove through the crowd and the palm trees and the candlelit tables like beach royalty to that ritual-like rhythm.

Photographers and news cameras rushed around them to capture their every move. Brightly colored Eastern rugs lined a pathway for the models and more topless male dancers who posed along the walkway with tribal hennaed tattoos all over their oiled skin. After Alessio and Eva passed, they joined in the parade, holding lit torches, dancing suggestively along with the Middle Eastern beat.

The crowd cheered, danced, and hooted. Kaspar's original music perfectly underscored the drumbeats, setting a dramatic, daring but fun rhythm to the goings-on. My heart swelled. This was everything I'd hoped for. More even.

Turo's hand touched my back as he leaned into me, his heat searing my side. "Adri, Theo's trying to get your attention," came his low voice in my ear, and heat pooled in my belly. "Nine o'clock." His warm hand fell away.

I turned my head in the direction he noted and found Theo, the Athenian PR specialist who was officially running the show, grinning. I waved at him, blowing him a kiss, and he blew me a kiss right back, giving me a thumbs up.

"She conquered," Turo whispered from slightly behind me, his low voice sending sparks through my bloodstream, his warm breath tickling my ear, fanning the side of my neck. His hand moved down my back.

I turned and touched his lapel, fingering the edge. "Thank you for being here. For helping me blast through it. It was just what I needed tonight."

"This is all you."

"It was a lot of people working together."

"You coordinated it all, and that's an amazing feat."

I shrugged, my face heating. "It's fun for me."

He leaned in even closer to me. "Adri, you hit all the right notes and you hit new ones. It's a gift."

My hand pressed over his tie. "I'm glad Alessio is pleased. He deserves this," I murmured.

A jubilant roar went off in the crowd, and we turned to see what the commotion was about. Alessio and his models had taken the stage, and with the mic in hand, Alessio welcomed everyone to the official beginning of summer. Cheers and champagne bottles popped madly. He introduced Kaspar and the crowd jumped up and down eager for his magic. Kaspar's synth music exploded over the speakers, beating a new, very loud, hard driving rhythm. The coloured lights strobed. The crowd danced and yelled for more.

"Alessio's on top of the world." Turo grinned.

"Agápi mou esí!" A voice I recognized had me turning. Turo's grip on my back deepened.

"Elektra!" I hugged my friend, and we kissed cheek to cheek. I introduced her to Turo. "Elektra is a legend here in Greece."

"A legend?" Turo's face lit up as he studied her.

A woman in her late forties, Elektra could easily be mistaken for a glamorous hipster in her early thirties. A formidable figure in the Greek music scene for over twenty-five years, Elektra was adored and respected both by the very young and the older generations. A powerful and unpredictable presence onstage, her voice was incredible, strong and operatic, her own distinctive musical instrument. She was an icon, continually setting trends with her changing looks and free spirit lifestyle.

"In America you have Stevie Nicks," I explained to Turo. "In Greece we have Elektra."

"Ah, the great Stevie is in a class by herself, *vre* Adri!" Elektra laughed.

"So are you, darling," I said.

"It's an honor to meet you, Elektra," Turo said as they shook hands, assessing one another.

A rush of photographers and journalists surged on us. "Elektra! Elektra! Adriana!"

I stiffened, my chest constricting at the onslaught of faces, cameras, flashing lights. Turo stepped away, yet remained a wall behind me. The heat of his body in defensive mode was palpable, and I steadied myself, throwing an arm around Elektra's waist and pulling her close.

She conquered.

"Here we are!" I declared, my lips curving. My legs instinctively angled out, my head slanting, an eyebrow raised, my smile just so. I didn't have to think about it. I'd grown up doing this, and it was an automatic reflex when needed. But tonight, tonight I was enjoying it. These moments were mine, I'd achieved something to be here.

Elektra pulled me close, striking her own pose, her newly coiled hair falling in her eyes the way she always liked. She greeted the photographers she knew, answering the questions they flung at her about her new hair color, her latest boy-toy. I laughed at her risqué responses, but she kept it oblique at the same time. Satisfying them, making them hungry for more.

"You're good," I murmured to her as we posed for another round of photos.

"I know," she replied, her hand squeezing my waist. "Live and learn." She certainly had. She'd started from a small country village in the north, but that voice and her determination had her striking gold at a young age. And as the years wore on, she kept her golden balls in play at all times, through the husband, the boyfriends, the world tours, platinum albums, style trends, and a bit of nip and tuck here and there.

Elektra showed off the Alessio jewelry she wore this evening, and I piped in about the pieces. We posed, showing off our Alessio rings. Weeks ago I'd sent her the four rings she wore tonight—gold and silver rings emblazoned in colored enamel with skulls, crosses, a broken heart. Around her neck hung Alessio's red skull pendant along with his jagged pink lightning bolt. Paired with her own mass of long, thin, gold chains and beads, her smoky eye makeup and thickly coiled and curly dirty blonde hair, flowing silk blouse with a torn hem and tattered skinny jeans with high-heeled sandals and a sequined vest she was perfection—the perfect personification of Alessio's brand. Authentic rock and roll and luxury bohemian chic in one.

Ten minutes later the paps scattered to the next celebrities who swept by, a pop star acquaintance and her footballer husband. "Thank you so much for coming, my love." I kissed Elektra on the cheek.

"Since you gave me that first necklace last year, I've fallen in love with Alessio's jewelry," she said. "And any excuse to come to Mykonos. These new pieces are fantastic."

"I love you." I hugged her.

"I know you do," said Elektra. "I brought Dimitri with me. Come meet him."

"Yes, I will. I'll come find you in a bit."

She hugged me and strode off into the throng.

"She's pretty incredible," said Turo.

"Isn't she? Having her wear the jewelry, be photographed wearing it, at this party is—"

"Perfect," he said, his beautiful lips curving into a smile. "You did that, Adri. You."

His smile filled me with a dancing heat. Turo's approval, his esteem lifted me somewhere higher, where normal breathing was difficult. The air was sharper, purer here.

"Who's Dimitri?" he asked, clipping my reverie.

"He's an actor she just started dating," I said. "He's younger than me." I winked at him.

"Oh yeah?"

I loved teasing him, ever since he'd made a point of our age difference. What was the eleven years between us? Not fifteen or twenty or thirty, but even if it was, if we got along, could communicate and have interesting conversations, and enjoyed each other in bed, really, where was the issue?

His eyes narrowed, their fierceness flashing at me for just a moment. "You like that don't you?"

"When I'm Elektra's age, I hope I can do the same."

"A husband and babies aren't in your future plan?"

"I don't have a future plan, Turo. I want to swallow what life has to offer as it comes."

Damn, you sound so good, Adri. If only you'd do as you want for a change. Yes, that's what I wanted, but I'd become a fearful creature the past two years, hadn't I? Hiding behind my parents, behind work, Alessio. Tonight felt different, though. *I* felt different.

Turo and I continued to weave through the crowd under the palm trees dancing with fairy lights. "Louder!" Kaspar's voice demanded over the speakers. "Everybody!" At his side, Alessio clapped, hands in the air. Two dancers in silver bikinis dripping with crystal tassels danced on a huge speaker, throwing flower petals and beaded bracelets to the crowd.

Turo's attention was captivated by something at the edge of the dance floor. He was perfectly still, his gaze intense, a predator tracking, keeping watch. My insides dipped at the sight. God, what was wrong with me? He could crack an egg into a bowl and I'd probably get turned on.

"Is something wrong?" I asked.

"Hmm. Not sure. Luca's arguing with someone. And that someone doesn't seem to belong here, by the looks of him."

"Do you need to go over there?"

"No." His gaze returned to me, and softened and my pulse raced, my lady parts thrummed. "I'm busy," he said, just above a whisper.

"Hmm, yes you are."

The mass of partiers danced and jumped to Kaspar's booming electronic beat, hands in the air, reveling in something primal and wild. I moved to the throbbing rhythm, dancing with friends. I drank the pink champagne. The moon beamed through the passing wisps of gray blue clouds, and delivered its silvery, shimmery approval over us. And Turo watched, and watched me.

I climbed up a stone step to where he stood leaning next to a wooden pillar. My hands slid up his firm chest. A sharp exhalation escaped him at my touch, and I blinked at the sound. Did he want me as much as I wanted him? Did my touch make him reel with desire as his did to me?

"I want to fuck you," he'd said. Abrupt. Brutal. A jolt.

And I want him to.

I pressed my lips to his, and his mouth immediately opened to mine. His arms wrapped around me and pulled me up the last step, behind the thick layers of sheer white drapery at the edge of the restaurant.

Lost in each other's heat, a heat that pounded out a rhythm of its own over my flesh, binding us together like a magnetic force of nature, his tongue slid against mine, no longer teasing but demanding, deepening the kiss. Our bodies pressed together, my every nerve ending tingled and erupted with thrilling possibility, with a tidal wave of raw desire. He pulled back suddenly and stared at me, his eyes piercing mine.

"Turo," I breathed. A plea of need, a plea of mercy.

"Indulging again?" his voice rasped; a dark query. Was he annoyed with me? Here I was throwing myself at him, and for all he knew I was with Alessio.

My fingers dug into his hair. "Kiss me, dammit."

He kissed me, he punished me. He delivered me.

We twisted in each other's arms. The gauzy white curtain fabric caught on the crystals of my dress and wrapped around us, binding us.

The two of us, wrapped in our own web of moonlight.

19

TURO

I TORE my mouth from Adri's delicious tongue.

Someone was in the back of the empty restaurant. I gripped her shoulders, tracking the shift in movement in the shadows beyond where we stood.

Adri's choppy, ragged breaths matched my own. Her wild eyes gleamed in the flickering light of the tall, flaming tiki torches around the porch.

The thin, dark haired man I'd noticed Luca arguing with earlier clocked us, turned, heading for the bathrooms. Was he a dealer? Did Luca know him? He'd seemed out of place at this party with the glitterati, and it wasn't just his ill-fitting suit—he'd been observing, not partying, slinking through the crowd, making small talk here and there, searching for an opportunity.

Luca stopped on the stairs, his eyes on us. *Speak of the devil.*

"I—I'm sorry," Adri sputtered. "Damn." Her fingers worked to untangle the wispy curtain that had wrapped around us. It wasn't working.

"I'm not sorry, baby," I said, my thumb rubbing a corner of her mouth. "But Luca is watching us, and I don't think that's a good thing, do you?"

She bit her lip, and I ripped the curtain away from us. Exposed to the night air again, to the world.

Luca tossed his cigarette and headed off in the direction of the men's room. His bodyguard draped himself over a railing at the other end of the porch steps from us talking up a blonde in a bikini.

Raising Adri's chin, I brushed her lips with mine—I just had to—and she let out a perfect little cry. *Fuck me.* "I want you to go to Gennaro's table."

"Is something wrong?" she asked.

"Not yet."

"Turo—"

"Go interrupt Luca's bodyguard over there and have him take you to Gennaro and Miguel. I need to talk to Luca. I'll come find you right after. I promise I won't be long. You stay with them until I get back to you."

She took in a tiny breath, teeth scraping that swollen bottom lip again. "Okay." She left me, her heels clacking on the restaurant veranda tile. She talked to Luca's bodyguard, and he raised his chin at me. I gestured toward the bathroom, and he nodded at me and led Adriana into the crowd.

I headed toward the back of the restaurant to find Luca. One loud voice. Luca growling in his rough English, his tone unmistakeable. He was livid. "Who do you think you are, you piece of shit?"

"Let go of me," came a heavily accented reply. "Eh! Stop!"

I darted into the men's room. Luca had the skinny dark guy in the cheap suit up against the wall by the sinks, a hand cuffing his throat. "You don't tell me what to do, I tell you what to do," Luca's voice sneered. "Where are you from? Albania? Moldavia? Georgia?"

"Athens!"

"Fuck off." He tightened his hold on the guy's neck, his hard gaze darting to me and back to his victim. "This is a private party. How did you get in, past the guards?"

"A friend of mine, he cleans here. He let me in."

Luca got in the guy's face, his brow a fierce ridge. "I warned you before to leave, but you didn't listen. You have no right to even lick my shoes."

"You—"

In a swift snap of movement, Luca shoved the guy down on the floor, his foot on his chest. Luca went off in Italian, yammering away, kicking him once, twice, three times, the blood gushing and spilling from the guy's face.

"Lick it, lick my shoe." Luca's foot hovered over the guy's face. Luca kicked him in the side and shoved his other foot over his face once more. "Lick!"

The guy raised his head, his tongue hanging out, inches from the sole of Luca's expensive leather shoes. A flash of black from the stalls had my hand going to my holster, but I wore no holster, had no gun.

Fuck.

"Behind you!" I yelled.

From his back, Luca brandished a gun, aiming at the man rushing toward him from the stalls.

"Move and you die," Luca spit out. He kicked the other's guy's face and lifted his chin at me. I jammed my foot into the guy's chest, keeping him down as he groaned, bled, his head lolling.

Luca shoved his gun into the head of the other guy, pushing him onto the floor to his knees next to his buddy. "You're lucky this is my brother's party and I don't want to fuck it up for him with your blood making a mess all over this fancy bathroom. Who sent you?"

"N-Nobody."

Luca's voice seethed. "Tell me who you work for."

"I don't work for nobody, okay? We heard about this party, we came to sell. Many people here—rich people."

"And did you sell anything?"

Two shaking fingers rose. "Two only."

"That's too bad." Luca took a step back and bashed the guy in black across the face with his gun, and the guy collapsed onto the tiled floor in a heap.

Luca sniffed in air and tilted his head, stretching his neck. He went to the bank of sinks, turned on the faucet, pumped out soap and washed his hands, inspecting his face in the mirror. "You left Adri for me? I'm touched."

"I spotted him earlier." I rifled through the pockets of both men, found baggies with packaged pills and powder and handed them to Luca. "Saw the two of you arguing, then saw him in here."

"Motherfucker was trying to sell his shit."

"Keeping your brother's party clean, Luca? Now I'm touched."

He held my gaze as he sniffed at the contents of the baggies and dumped them in the sink under running water, rinsing out the baggies, throwing them away. He washed his hands again, pulled at a towel and rubbed them dry. We went back out to the party which was in a full rage. The place was packed. "I'll let a security guard know we had some trouble in the men's room," I said. "I'm heading over to your uncle's table where I had your security guard bring Adriana."

Luca nodded as we wove through the crowd. Something told me to keep watch on our periphery. I scanned to my left and right as we were jostled by dancers and gawkers holding enormous cocktails. Enormous shiny pink and gold champagne bottles flew by. The music boomed, strobing lights flashed. I found a security guard and let him know about our trouble in the men's room. He scowled and immediately notified his *compadres* on his two way radio.

Luca and I made it to Gennaro's table, and the moment I spotted Adriana, I let out the breath I'd been holding onto. Photographers snapped her non-stop as celebrity friends, acquaintances, fans, and wannabe's posed with her, everyone showing off their Alessio jewelry for the cameras. After Alessio, Adriana was tonight's next best attraction and she was making the most of it. I caught her eye and winked, her lips tipped up at me and she seamlessly slid back into another photo op pose.

Theo, the publicist, was in a deep conversation with Gennaro, Miguel standing watch on the other side of them. Our eyes met as we both scanned the area repeatedly.

Luca danced with a girl in the press of the crowd before the stage. Alessio, with his arm slung around one of his models, came over and they sat in one of the small sofas by the table. Adri only glanced at them quickly and went back to being interviewed by a journalist without missing a beat.

These two, what the fuck?

I kept my eyes on Luca. He had moves, dancing slower than the girl, than the music, but somehow still in the beat. The music turned over into a new song, and he took the girl's hand and they pushed their way off the dance floor. She stopped to talk to someone and he kept going toward one of the bar areas. Movement in a diagonal headed straight for him entered my sightline. A prickle razored over my neck, my pulse ticked. A man headed right for Luca, his hand clenched in a fist—no, he was holding something. I charged toward him.

I pulled Luca by the arm out of the way, and his eyes flashed at me, jaw a tight blade. Turning, I shot out my knee into the man's stomach, and he doubled over on a grunt. Twisting his arm behind him, I pulled him off the dance floor, Luca and I dragging him into a grouping of palm trees, shoving him up against the spiky bark. He grunted, his grip loosening on the small knife in his hand and I grabbed it, pressing it into his throat.

Luca searched him for more weapons. "Are there any more of you?"

The guy's face curled into a creepy grin. I slashed at his flesh, and he jerked in my grip, letting out a loud, panicked hiss. His blood slicked over my fingers.

"Answer the man," my voice simmered as I twisted my fist in his gut.

His dark eyes flared. "No! No!"

Two of the club security guards surrounded me. "Deal with this piece of shit before we attract any more attention." I released the guy and he fell to the ground, clutching at his throat, gasping loudly. Luca's face remained set in grim lines but a smile curved his lips as the men hauled the bleeding guy off.

"You were right," I said.

Luca raised an eyebrow. "About what?"

"You need me."

His face suddenly relaxed and he let out a laugh, smacking a heavy hand on my back. "I have good instincts, Turo."

"You were out on the dance floor to attract more attention if there was more attention to attract, weren't you?" I said.

His lips curled.

"What's happened?" Adri stood before us. A vision from another world in shimmery white and silvery lilac under the strobe of the lights, and I blinked at her glittering diamond gorgeousness. Her face was stricken, anxiety marring her features.

"Luca doesn't know how to make friends," I said. "It's over."

Her gaze darted to Luca then back to me. To my hands stained with blood. Her eyes widened, her lips parting. I grabbed a towel from the hip of a passing waiter and wiped it off.

"What's happening? What aren't you telling me?" Her voice trembled.

I dumped the towel and grabbed her elbow, guiding her back to the table.

"What is going on?" Her face tightened as we tracked through the crowd.

"Someone wanted to get to Luca, but I got to him first."

"As I said, you have skills."

"Are you done for the night?" I asked her.

"Why?"

"Because I'd prefer to get you back on the boat."

Alessio stood by the table watching us with that same model on his arm. Adriana muttered something harsh in Greek under her breath and grabbed a flute of champagne from the fresh batch a waitress was setting on the table.

Up on the stage, Kaspar was in another zone, in sync with the crowd, with the music he was creating. The high priest conjuring magic at his altar. Showers of champagne spouted and sprayed from those huge bottles. Laughter and shouts, singing. Colored lights streaked over hundreds and hundreds of faces. The Lord Sorcerer had his subjects in his thrall.

I moved toward Alessio. "Alessio—I want her back on the yacht. Now."

He slanted his head. "What the hell was all that with my brother?"

"That was Luca's problem. My only concern is keeping Adri safe."

Alessio's ground his jaw. "Take my uncle and Miguel with you. I'll call the crew for the launch." He got on his cell phone.

I gestured at Miguel, and he hustled over. I let him know what happened and that he and I would be taking Gennaro and Adriana back to the yacht.

He smoothed a hand down his formidable chest. "Let's roll." He went over to Gennaro, interrupting his lively conversation with two young women, and spoke in his ear. Alessio and Luca argued in Italian in low tones.

I leaned into Adri. "We're going back to the boat. Say your goodbyes."

"I'm ready." Adri put down her empty glass, and we headed for the beach along with Miguel and Gennaro. She came to an abrupt halt and ripped off her high-heeled sandals, and we continued down the sandy shore to where the small boat waited. A busboy trailed behind us, holding a crate filled with bottles of pink and gold champagne.

Luca caught up with us. He was alone. Did Alessio tell him to leave?

The boat propelled us back to the *Allegra* over smooth dark waters, the music a thumping haze behind us. Finally, the launch came up against the yacht's bumpers, the two crew members on board pulling on her ropes, steadying her. Gennaro and Miguel got off first. I took Adri's hand and led her to the edge.

"*No, no,*" came Luca's gravelly voice. "You two are coming with me."

"*Ti?*" Adriana said. "What are you talking about?"

"I've been invited to a party on Evgeny's boat." He gestured at the white Russian mega ship anchored beyond the cove, not too far from us. "Special party. Very special."

"Have a great time," I bit out. "We're not interested."

Luca muttered in Italian to the crew, and the rope was immediately tossed back at the launch. "Sit. Down," he said, his voice low.

"Luca!" I gritted out.

"Don't you still want to make a deal for your boss, Turo? You will get that chance, *si, Zio* Gennaro?" he said loudly to his uncle who stood on the deck of the *Allegra* watching us.

"*Si.*" Gennaro eyed me. He gave us a slight wave and put a hand on Miguel's arm. They turned and disappeared into the yacht. My gut knotted.

"I'll come with you," I said. "But not Adri. Adri stays on the *Allegra*. I don't think Alessio would be happy to know you've taken her for a night out."

"I don't know how happy Alessio would be about the two of you so cozy together all day and all night, eh? It's just for a few hours. I want to enter Evgeny's party with more than just another pretty *fica* on my arm."

I ground my teeth at his use of the term "pussy" for Adri. "Watch what you say—"

"I want you with me, Turo. I need to re-negotiate a few terms with him. He's very stubborn though. You have a certain reputation in Chicago. The negotiator with the velvet tongue, yes? Tell me, Adri, is his tongue that remarkable?"

Adri let out a string of foul curses in Italian and Greek.

"Tsk tsk." Luca let out a soft rolling laugh. "Turo, you do this for me—with Adri—and I'll let you talk to my uncle again. And I won't say a word to my brother about the two of you." His tongue slid along his upper lip.

This fucking asshole.

"Let Adri go," I said.

"No." He gestured to the boat staff with a flick of his finger and leaned back in his seat.

The powerful twin motors kicked up, and I tugged Adri down on the seat next to mine, keeping my grip on her tight. Her breathing quickened, her legs pressed together.

We zoomed toward the Russian mega yacht. It loomed ahead, towering over us, this floating white fortress. My heart fisted in my chest.

Yes, it was a kingdom, a continent unto itself.

The question was, how mad was its king?

20

TURO

BEHEMOTH. Mammoth.

Insane.

Those were the first words that came to mind.

It was after three in the morning, but the party was going strong here on Evgeny's ship. We climbed a free floating spiral staircase to an upper deck, then an elevator to another deck. There were eight decks in all. Adriana stayed close to me as we walked behind Luca through this gold-plated universe.

"Have you been on this ship before, Luca?" I asked.

"Not this one, no. I've been on the old one. Much smaller. I've been hearing about this ship for a while now."

We paused at the entrance to a gambling hall. Roulette wheels, blackjack, poker. The mood was serious, the chatter a low hum edged with the *clack clack* of chips, the *thrip* of cards, the whistle of spinning wheels. Tall, long-haired beauties in plunging neckline dresses served drinks and manned the tables. The betting level in here had to be stratospheric.

We moved on to another room where flickering soft lights played in the darkness.

"Hmm." Luca's lips tipped up as we entered the room.

A staccato electric rhythm echoed in the room; a haunting soundtrack mimicking my thudding heartbeat. Adriana glanced at me as we moved farther into the space.

People were gathered around a stage where two performers were singled out by a spotlight. Moans hung heavy in the darkness. Adriana's hand skimmed mine, my insides tightening at the flash of her warmth over my skin.

A naked woman was bound to a thick, wooden table with large cuffs and a scarf binding her mouth. The man picked up a ladle and ceremoniously poured hot liquid over her middle. Her body arched as she cried out, and the onlookers let out moans of their own.

"W-What is that?" Adri whispered roughly, pressing into my side.

"Hot wax," I replied.

"Hmm," she whimpered, pressing her lips together. Adri's hand brushed mine, and my fingers searched for hers. Our fingers meshed and clung, heat igniting heat.

I'd been to sex clubs before, but on my own, not with a date. Not with a woman like Adri; a woman I gave a shit about. The desire to be her guide overwhelmed me. The need to protect her overwhelmed me.

Another man appeared on the stage flourishing a spiked, double-headed glass dildo as if it were an impressive weapon or instrument of magic his audience should be in awe of. He stroked it between her legs, and the girl moaned and writhed. Adriana's breathing deepened. With a dramatic groan, the man fucked the girl with his dildo. Adriana gasped, and I licked my lips at the raw, slippery sounds of sex filling the space. I squeezed Adriana's hand and she tightened her hold right back, the two of us pressed together, breathing together, watching the girl writhe, moan, twitch, jerk. Witnessing every moment of her body coming to orgasm.

The man raised his hands in the air, beckoning his witnesses, and they moved forward, taking turns using other, almost macabre, dildos on the girl, admiring. Touching her, touching themselves. Cum spewed on flesh. Satisfied, excited, exulted cries, and soft laughter shot around the circle.

"Oh my G—" Adri's voice was jagged, her body wavered.

I wrapped my arm around her, holding her close, steadying her, and she pressed against me, small, low noises escaping her lips. The heat of her body seeped into mine and my pulse jammed in my neck.

"Turo," she breathed.

My cock tightened in my trousers at the sound of my name on her lips, my heart thundered in my chest. That was what need sounded like. Raw, unapologetic, undisguised need.

I know, baby, I know.

My fuck switch had been turned on, but as I tightened my grip on Adri, I gripped my fierce arousal even harder, like a steering wheel in a race car I was commandeering. I wanted nothing more than to take her mouth, rip at her dress, feel her body shudder under my hands. But I had to stay sane. Anything could happen at any time on this crazy vessel in the middle of the sea, and it already had.

I ground my jaw, my gums aching, balls throbbing. Adriana's hand swept up my middle and stroked back and forth, back and forth, her breathing choppier than before. Our gazes locked in the half light, her blue gray eyes molten ink.

Luca turned to us and winked. *The fuck.*

The back of my throat burned. Luca had an endgame in mind here, I was sure of it, and we were his pawns. We were at the mercy of an Aliberti. I planted a tense kiss on Adriana's forehead, and she let out a low moan, her arms snaking around my waist. Most of all, I was at her mercy.

Other spotlights deeper in the room revealed women and men strung up on St. Andrew's crosses, ball gags in their mouths, being whipped dramatically. A woman was bound to a bench and being caned. Adri flinched at the sounds—the woman crying out, the thrash of the cane, at the harsh red marks blistering white flesh. The most popular seemed to be two women with masks over their eyes bound tightly, legs up, with small electrodes attached between their legs, on their nipples. Laughing, people took turns zapping, making them come repeatedly. Others only watched as they got serviced by their companions—given head, stroked. Evgeny Berezin knew how to put on an extravaganza, a three dimensional spectacle.

There were no rules, no good, no bad, no do or don't. Only one thing. Take. The only thing that mattered was the intensity of your satisfaction and the thrill of reaching for more.

Another softer light suddenly flickered on and illuminated a low cushioned leather platform in the shape of an X on which two naked couples danced. An erotic acrobatic ballet. Licking, rubbing, humping; a choreographed tangle of limbs and moans. A blur of sensation.

One of the female dancers rose from the pile of flesh and went to a man and danced before him, pulling him over to the cushions. Magnetized, the audience immediately followed to witness whatever would follow, to engage in more. A couple brushed past us, stumbled over to the sofa and started to screw, and another to kiss and clutch, and another.

Adri's hand squeezed mine. Her breath quickened. Was she panicked, upset, or was she turned on? Was she burning like I was? With her body pressed to mine, her curves splaying out of her dress, her perfume all over me, the taste of her tongue still on mine, raw desire swelled in my blood, tearing through my veins, ripping through my flesh. Her breasts crushed against my chest as she molded herself around me.

Turned on.

My hand slid down the back of her dress over her hot, bare flesh, and she trembled, letting out a cry. I found the swell of her ass and stroked her there, my heart pounding, my pulse going crazy.

A rush of heat blew through me. We were down some goddamn Russian rabbit hole and part of me just didn't care. The only thing that was real right now, the only thing that mattered was Adriana's touch on my body, her hands, her lips.

She stroked my chest. Skimming up, pressing down. Up and down. I wanted to rip off my shirt and feel her flesh against mine, the hard metal beads of her dress scraping down my skin as my tongue invaded her mouth, her hair in my fist. Her hand slid down my torso and palmed my erection.

My body seized, I stung. "Adri."

Her hand pulsed and stroked firmly over me. She turned into my chest and with her free hand, pulled my head down, and our lips finally touched. Warm and searching. Insistent and restless. We kissed to fuck. Need, spiraling need and raw desire bound us together. I clutched her ass and brought her in between my legs, nestling her right where my ache and hers demanded.

Taking her mouth, I swallowed Adri's cries and groans. The moans and whispers that had been lodged in my throat finally rose all around us. The *crack* of the cane, the *snap* of the whip made her body jerk in my hold and open to mine. Muffled grunts, excited giggles, greedy demands razored past us.

I wanted nothing more than to pound into her and make her body ripple with pleasure, and for her to tear me in two. But that would be giving into the Russian madness, to Luca's manipulation. To Gennaro's smug indifference.

My heart raced painfully, my stomach roiled. For the first time in a long time, I felt paralyzed, as if I needed someone to tell me what to do. My need for her skyrocketed as the friction we'd created threatened to combust.

I nuzzled her lips, kissing the edges of her mouth.

"Turo, Turo..." her ragged voice clawed at my flesh, her warm lush lips opening under mine.

What I needed to do was to protect her, keep her safe. At all costs.

"Shh." I brushed her lips with mine.

Stop. Stop.

"Lovely..." Was that my voice? Husky and choked. I nipped at her bottom lip to get my sanity back, to stay connected to her. To keep her alert with me.

My hands cradled her face. Her jaw was set, cheeks streaked with red, skin damp. "Not now, baby. Not here," I pleaded. Yes, I was pleading before I exploded and pushed her against the wall. Before I lost it. "Here they have us where they want us. And I'm not sure what that is yet."

She smashed her face in my chest and a breath heaved from me, my arms wrapping around her, holding her tight. Inhaling the flowery scent of her hair, digging my fingers into her silky waves, I shut my eyes and dragged in a deep breath.

"We need to get the fuck out of here," I muttered.

Before we went too far.

Before—

I pulled her out of the room, the two of us cemented to one another and moving fast. Fragrant, thick cigar smoke wafted in the hallway from the room opposite. Another party was in full swing inside—girls twisting around stripper poles, lap dancing to pop music, sucking cock.

How very ordinary.

"Where do you think you're going?" Luca's deep voice penetrated my skull. Adri skidded on her heeled sandals, and I steadied her.

"Aren't you done with the tour of this fun boat?" I spit out. "We are."

"*No*, there's more. There is always more." Luca gestured toward another stairwell. "Come."

We climbed the stairs to the upper deck. Adri and I both sucked in the cool, salty air. An enormous swimming pool was lit up with lights and four naked girls cavorting in it. Several ice sculptures stood guard over a huge buffet table laden with tiered platters of shrimp, crab legs, lobsters, and shellfish. Jumbo bottles of Armand de Brignac champagne were everywhere. Tens of thousands of dollars worth of bubbly. My muscles clenched together, my stomach twisted, my head swam.

"This way, please," said a man with a crisp British accent dressed as a classic butler. He led us to a huge banquette where a man held court at the center. That man being the one and only Evgeny Berezin.

Berezin and a few partners had jumped on the dissolution of communism in the Soviet Union by buying up government owned natural gas and oil refineries, a ton of formerly government owned real estate in Moscow, and here he sat, the king. He couldn't have been over forty-five. A slight paunch to his belly was the only thing that belied an indulgent lifestyle. Berezin was tall and clear eyed, well-dressed and well pleased with himself.

His blue eyes landed on Luca and he rose from his seat. "My friend, you have come!" He gave Luca a bear hug.

"You should have come to my brother's party. It was quite a scene," Luca said.

"Marina is there now. She's a big fan of that idiot DJ, Kaspar."

"Marina is his daughter," Adri whispered to me. "They say he's buying her her own yacht for her twentieth birthday."

"I don't like that electronic music shit. And I like my parties better." Evgeny laughed as he gestured toward the shoreline. "All night we hear that crazy music and we see the lights from here but no crowds for us. Come sit."

Room was made for us on the thickly upholstered sofa. The low, long table in front of us was decorated with white stripes and spirals—ribbons and mounds of cocaine.

I put my arm around Adri's shoulders and she nestled close to me. "Don't drink anything," I said, and she nodded.

I couldn't take any chance where Adriana was concerned. I

wouldn't put it past Evgeny's party people to drug women's drinks, and I didn't trust Luca either.

Luca leaned over the table and took a long hit of coke from one of the many spirals of powder. Leaning back again, sniffing in deep, his tongue swiping over his gums, he slid a hand down a thigh and crossed one leg over the other. A figure in satisfaction.

Luca had Evgeny talking yachts, how impressive his was, how tall his carbon masts were, what his summer plans were. I wanted this fucking over. As they talked, Adri's and my breathing got hooked in a rhythm. Intense, heavy. The heat from our bodies melded. Every moment that passed stretched us toward something unknown, kept our bodies tense. We were on edge, together.

I'd been in situations like this many times before on Mauro's behalf, this waiting for the ball to drop, the wire to be cut. But this was different. My chest tightened painfully, a cold sweat prickled over my skin, nausea rode me. I was literally feeling this situation. I sucked in a breath. I couldn't lower the volume or shut it off. This was a fucking first. Why?

Adri. That was why.

Protecting her wasn't simply a job. The thought of anyone taking advantage of her, of her in danger, had me ticking along with my watch to get us off this goddamn monstrosity of a cruise ship. She was better than all this. She was another world from this, my world.

Luca's hand landed on Adri's bare thigh and he stroked her skin as he spoke with Evgeny about Italian soccer teams and Ducatis. She let out a tiny yelp, her body stiffening at my side.

And there it was.

Evgeny's eyes darted to the movement of Luca's hand, his gaze traveling up Adriana's leg, resting on her face.

Tick, tick, tick.

Adri grabbed onto Luca's wrist, stopping him. He didn't miss a beat, though, continuing his discussion of Juventus versus Real

Madrid in an upcoming match as his thumb circled a spot on her thigh.

Bitter venom filled my mouth. "Luca—"

He ignored me.

Evgeny interrupted. "Who is this fantastic woman with you?" His eyes were lit. Appetizer served.

Luca released his hold on Adri's leg. "Adriana is a special friend of mine. I thought you might like to meet her." His voice was unusually silky and warm.

My pulse hammered in my head, my jaw ground together.

"Ah, a real Greek beauty, eh?" Evgeny shook a thick index finger at Luca. "How you know me, you motherfucker."

"I don't forget," replied Luca.

Berezin's gaze took in the three of us. He was turned on by our portrait of a *ménage*.

"*Gospodny Berezin—*"Adri said, and a chill stole up my spine. Luca and Evgeny's eyes narrowed at her while she spoke to Berezin in Russian. Evenly, confidently.

Go, baby.

"We've met before," she continued in English, her voice clear.

Evgeny's eyes grew larger. "Oh?" He was almost amused that she'd spoken to him. After all, pussy wasn't supposed to talk. Only giggle, moan, and open wide.

"My father introduced us. Petros Lavrentios. It was last year in Paris," she said.

Berezin's hard eyes darted at Luca for a beat then back to Adri. "Ah, yes." His arms stretched out in the air then came together on a *clap*. "I remember. That small restaurant by the Ritz. Terrible food." He made a clownish face.

Adri laughed softly. "Yes, it wasn't very good. Marina and I were at the same table. We talked about her plans for her birthday party in Greece. So full of ideas. It was wonderful to see her again tonight at the party. Is she coming back here tonight?"

Not a tremble in her clear, smooth voice. Only a feminine

strength in a gentle inquiry, an inquiry that held weight, had substance. Evgeny crossed his arms. Luca remained still. With one swoop, Adriana had defused the situation, put us all on a different game board.

Had Luca intended to offer her to Berezin as a sexual favor or to use her name and his association with her? Whatever it was, I hated him for it. Fucking hated him.

"No, she's staying at a resort on the island with her friends," Berezin said, sniffing in air. "Come. Dance with me," Evgeny said, standing up, adjusting his suit jacket.

"Adri—" I didn't get much further.

"It's all right," she murmured, letting go of me, rising from the sofa.

The loss of her heat beside me, the sight of her striding toward Evgeny made my chest crush together. She didn't take his outstretched hand but walked beside him to the dance floor by the pool talking, surely in Russian, as they went.

I moved next to Luca. "I'm going to cut your balls off the second we get off this boat, do I make myself clear?"

Luca met my hard gaze with one of his own.

"You need me and Adriana to grease his ass for you, is that it?" I asked.

Luca let out a breath, pressing back into the sofa. "My father has been buying petrol from Evgeny for years. Last New Year's he caught me with his daughter and he's never forgiven me. He wants her fucking aristocrats, not working class southern European men like me. I've got too much dirt under my finger-nails for him. He forgets where he came from."

"Ah, Luca."

"Oh, she's no innocent. The point is, I need to smooth things over with him."

We both focused on Adri and Evgeny talking as they danced. "How do you plan on doing that?" I asked, my voice tense watching Evgeny's arm around Adri's bare back.

"Offering him a cut of my new business venture. Counterfeit designer goods—handbags, sunglasses, wallets, belts, shoes. Used to be that shit was sold only on the streets in certain neighborhoods of big cities by African immigrants. But now with the internet exploding, that is all changing."

"Online shopping."

"Yes. People want bargains and they want the top brands from the privacy of their own home. Demand increases, and if you make it available, they will buy.

"And you can't tell the difference between a fake and a real piece on the computer screen."

"That's the best part. You have to be able to inspect the stitching, feel the material, smell it. Can't do that on a computer. Even so, fakes aren't as obviously shitty as they used to be. Now, it's hard to tell the difference between a real one and a *imitazione*."

"The products are coming from China?"

"Yes." He let out a dry chuckle as he lit a cigarette. "Sometimes from the same factories where the real goods are being made."

My gaze fell to the coke splayed out on the table. Gone was the pure narcotics trafficking of old. Luca and Alessio's father and grandfather had risen to power and notoriety on their cocaine and heroin distribution successes in southern Italy and Europe. Now Luca was taking the business into multinational corporate mode. That was vision for the future.

"Does Alessio know about this?" I asked.

His eyes slid to mine. "I don't involve my brother. He wanted out years ago, he got out."

"So, you only do business at his parties? Are you making copies of his jewelry too?"

"Of course not." Luca made a face at me as he took a long hit of his cigarette. "Only Cartier and Tiffany."

"What do you need Evgeny for?"

"Shipping. He'll make sure my product gets through to

Turkey where I pick it up. And he'll make sure they get seen in Russia and a few of the former Soviet countries in the region for a share of the profits."

"Does he sell you interesting weapons, too?"

"Only if I ask nice." Luca let out a long stream of smoke.

"Why do you have to get Adriana involved, an innocent civilian, especially when she's your brother's girlfriend?"

"I didn't know Adri knew Evgeny. She played the daddy card and the I'm-your-daughter's-friend card. No matter. He likes them young and glittery." He leaned over the table, dabbed a short line of coke into formation and sniffed. "He has no morals, so she's only made herself more attractive to him. Now she's a true trophy." He rubbed his tongue across his gums.

My heart thudded in my chest as Luca and I watched Evgeny insist on dancing a second song with Adri, holding her flush against his body, hand splayed on her back.

"Your moral compass is pretty fucking stellar too, Aliberti."

"I'm a businessman, DeMarco. Same as you."

"Keep Adriana out of this."

"The minute you boarded this boat with me, she was marked as mine to give," he breathed. "So were you."

My heart shot into overdrive, pummeling against my ribs, churning ice into my veins at his words, at what he implied. At his fucking easygoing tone. My body flinched as the man next to me on the sofa bumped into me as he and his friends snorted blow like college kids on spring break. Their loud laughter jarring, their wild chattering in Arabic intensifying the ache drilling through my skull.

Evgeny and Adri returned, and my lungs began to ease. She took a step toward me, but he gripped her hand, stopping her, and her face tightened. Evgeny slid a thick arm around Adri's middle, pressing her against his body, and she swallowed hard, her eyes finding mine. Spooked. Anxious. My heart collided with my ribcage, my pulse jamming.

"Let's play, Luca," said Evgeny, his tone decidedly different. "That's what you came here for, isn't it?" His dark gaze slid to mine then back to Luca. He knew I was on edge, he liked it.

"It is, yes." Luca put out his cigarette in an enormous gold plated ashtray with three naked cherubs humping each other along the rim. Luca rose from the sofa, his poker face firmly in place.

"Let's play."

21

TURO

BEREZIN LED Adri off the deck and through an archway, Luca and I behind them. My chest was heavy with lead.

"What the hell is going on, Luca?" I muttered under my breath.

"Obviously, he's still pissed at me. My father wants me to make it up to him. Any way I can. "

"Whatever way, you keep Adri out of this."

"You might have to work for that."

I grabbed the collar of his expensive T-shirt. "Do not involve her, you fuck. Use me if you want."

He patted my cheek as if I were his brother. *"Bene."* A dark grin flickered over his lips. That had been his plan all along, hadn't it?

We entered a dark room, smaller than the others, the odor of vodka thick, sweat and perfume streaking through the humidity. The walls were different here from the other rooms, textured. Soundproofed.

People were clustered in a circle, one spotlight beaming down harsh white light over a round table where a wide smear of blood was smudged on the surface. Evgeny held out his free hand, and another white-gloved butler placed a revolver in his palm. He released Adriana and took bullets from his pocket and loaded the revolver, spinning the chamber. His audience buzzed. Not anxious or agitated, they were fucking excited.

Evgeny's hand went to Adri's bottom and pulled her up against him. She visibly stiffened as he brushed his lips across her jaw.

A low growl ripped from my throat.

Berezin raised the revolver for all to see. Staring at Luca, still holding onto Adriana, he placed the gun ceremoniously on the center of the table.

Russian fucking roulette.

The raucous jabbering of the spectators grew louder at Evgeny's challenge. An excited, impatient babble of foreign languages.

"Prove yourself to me," Luca breathed, his voice steely, low. Just for me. "Prove yourself to *her*. Now is your time, DeMarco."

My heart slammed in my chest, my eyes jammed shut. *Do this one thing for me.*

"Luca. Time to play." Berezin's voice sliced through the air, silencing everyone. Everyone but me.

He'd unloosed the pin in the grenade.

Adriana's fierce gaze held me in its grip. She remained rigid. She needed me.

I needed to protect her. Save her.

I needed her.

Pushing through the tittering crowd, I stood in the light in front of the blood smeared table. Everyone's gaze devoured me. Their knotted expectations released and filled the air with the press of something more fervent than before. Something nauseating, bracing, galvanizing. Adriana twisted in Berezin's hold. Evgeny only took me in anew, dissecting me from head to toe as men in absolute power were want to do, men like my father, searching for the intriguing, useful pieces they needed, wanted to acquire.

The useful tool.

"Luca?" asked Evgeny, his eyes still on me.

Luca came up beside me and bowed his head slightly, a hand gesturing in the air. *With my compliments.*

"Sit," Evgeny said, slanting his head at me, his voice lighter. The courteous host.

Come out a winner, Luca got his chance at a contract with Evgeny and, hopefully, me and Adri would walk away. Come out a loser, Luca lost his contract, maybe a limb, and I lost my life. And fuck knew what would happen to Adri.

That wasn't going to happen.

I pulled out the chair and sat at the table, blowing out short breaths to steel myself. But there was no "steeling" anything. It was all an illusion right at this very moment. All of it. The spotlit table meant to blur my vision and thoughts, the excited betting and shuffling of money all around me.

I'd never done this before, played this particular game. I'd seen it once in a warehouse on the outskirts of Chicago. Both hapless victim and the speedy adrenaline rush it had left us with had been dismissed and forgotten almost the next second.

Now I was the victim, the bull in their arena, the dice, the wheel of chance providing the adrenaline rush.

The hushed tones of the men and women around me buzzed in my ear, the shuffling of their tense movements suddenly loud, their anticipation crackling in the air like lightning in a coming storm. A cold sweat prickled my skin and ran down my spine. I was the offering. The sacrifice to their party god, to their thirst for entertainment. To big business.

This ship must have a freezer full of dead bodies that got unloaded once they were out at sea.

"Turo, no." That beautiful, exotic voice uttered.

My eyes darted to Adriana's. Terror. Worry. Was she worried about me? There was something different, new. I let it wash over me, fill me. She lifted her chin and held my gaze, those memorable lips of hers pressed together. *That was one fucking great kiss. Was it my last?*

"Place your bets, everyone," Evgeny announced.

An eruption of activity and noise. Paper shuffling, shouts, clamoring voices. A man darted quickly around the room, collecting more money, jotting down final bets.

"Take the gun now," Evgeny said to me.

I lifted the gun, the cold, hard surface slippery in my hand, and my stomach dropped. I'd held a gun hundreds of thousands of times, now this one, a run of the mill revolver, felt heavy, unusual. My lungs crushed in my chest, my ability to breathe suddenly thwarted. Did that even matter? *Enjoy it*, this could all be over in a matter of minutes.

Don't look up. Don't look at her again. It will kill you. It will. Don't. Fucking. Do. It.

But I wanted to. Wanted to look in Adri's eyes once more, be held by them, by her. Would this really be it? My life to end here on an oligarch's floating empire in the middle of a foreign sea, halfway around the world from home? Home. Home. My parents would never know what happened to me. There'd be no body, no evidence of foul play. No traces.

No trace of me left in the world.

And why should there be? What have you accomplished so far, fucker? What is it you think you deserve?

Ciara's last words mocked me: *"I hope you die alone, you bastard, because that's what you deserve."*

"Prepare," Berezin's voice ordered.

I raised the gun to my temple, an almost silent moan escaping my mouth, my feet pressing into the floor, my thigh muscles pulsing, back rigid, neck straining. Excitement raced around the room, whipping around me like wildfire devouring dried weeds.

"Turo!" that voice cried out, a broken, muffled cry from somewhere far away followed by a stream of Russian, settling like a haze on that tense organ in my chest.

"The music will play," came Evgeny's voice. "My favorite piece of Bach's."

From the darkness, a young woman in a revealing black evening gown appeared at his side. She held a violin ready on her shoulder. Berezin was cultured even when playing his savage little games. This would be ridiculously insane if it wasn't really happening to me right now.

But it is.

It is.

"The music will play. And play," said Evgeny, his eyes lighting up. "And once it stops you must pull the trigger. If you don't, I will pull my own on you, and that wouldn't be much fun." He raised another pistol in his hand.

My elbows ground into the table. My shoulders straining, arms tense as iron, one hand gripping the edge of the table. Pulse raging.

The violin began, and my body lurched, my jaw ground together at the raw edginess of the abrupt chords. I loved Bach. I should be happy he'd be sending me to my final resting place.

The gun pressed against my temple, and I forced my finger to move to the trigger, to the commitment to unleash a bullet.

The bullet that might be there.

Might not be there.

To be or not to be.

The metal was cold. My arm shuddered, my neck.

I shuddered.

The violinist's bow and arm moved quickly, sawing out my summons, my eulogy.

My battlecry.

Every muscle wound tighter.

Ready. Ready. Ready. Ready. Ready.

I shut my eyes. My mind flew with the stabbing, strident notes of the violin.

My mother's elegant face, the press of her hand in mine that last morning in Chicago that had made me ache inside, her knowing laugh, the one I missed. Yes, yes, I fucking missed it. Her determined voice from a decade ago. *"Turo, you are better than this."*

Better than this.

Am I?

Everything, everything, everything was loaded on this trigger.

The note screeched, hung in the air.

A roar escaped my chest.

The gun pressed into my head. I tightened my finger.

Click.

A gasp of silence.

An exhale ripped from me, lungs gulping for air.

Everyone around us cheered and whooped, jeered and argued. Clapping filling my ears. My heavy eyes lifted and found Adriana's.

Victory.

Berezin had released her from his grip. She watched me, eyes gleaming, still, quiet, but not quiet. *I'm here, Turo. Here with you.*

"Ah!" Berezin clapped his hands loudly and I flinched. His face lit up in a huge smile. The master of ceremonies was pleased.

Now what, you fucker?

"However, this was two in a row, eh?" He looked around at his audience and they agreed in a cacophony of languages. "Tss, *nyet.*" He pressed his lips together. He wasn't truly fulfilled; he wanted drama, spectacle to have the last word.

Evgeny gestured to someone behind him. "Bring him again."

Two muscle men brought over a haggard man who wore glasses. In his forties, fifties? The drink in his hand was taken away. "No, no! Wait, no!" his voice slurred. "What are you doing? Why?"

Whatever he was high on, booze, drugs, or relief, it was now being driven off the road by a fresh, bitter gust of fear. He was shoved down in the other chair at the table opposite me.

Evgeny clapped a hand on his shoulder. "My friend here won a round before you," he said to me. "Let us raise the stakes now."

"Yes!" they shouted.

Evgeny said, "A duel."

"*Da*, like Pushkin and Lermontov!" shouted a Russian accented voice.

"Exactly," said Evgeny. "Those were men of fire."

First Bach and now nineteenth century Russian poets who'd dueled to their deaths.

"No!" said my opponent, jerking, twisting himself out of the security guards' hold. He'd already gone through his ring of fire. He'd been hijacked from his victory lap.

Poor asshole. This was far from over.

"Stand," ordered Evgeny.

I launched from the table, knocking back my chair.

"Move the table, everyone to the side," said Evgeny and the bettors scurried to one side of the room, servants quickly dispatched the table as I stood there waiting, heart thudding. Evgeny placed another revolver in my opponent's trembling hand, another gun was placed in mine. The butler brought my rival to the center, close to me. He stank of liquor, his eyes red, full of water. I looked away.

Adriana's determined, large, steady eyes found mine, her chest heaving with breaths, lips pale.

Determined to survive, to live.

Yes, live.

"Now turn around."

We did.

"Good. Ten paces only, just like Pushkin. Begin."

The audience emphatically counted to ten, enjoying their part in the grand entertainment. With each number, I took a step. New bets were taken, shouts, the fold and slap of paper bills so very loud, the din of rushed, heated voices. My insides tensed against the jitter of my flesh. Cold purpose filled my every vein. I took in a breath and held it tight. I was ready. Ready to kill.

And Evgeny and this idiot and Pushkin weren't about to take that away from me.

"We will close the lights," said Evgeny. "And when they come back on, that is your signal to fire. Lights!"

Engulfed in black darkness, my flesh prickled with ice, the gun a part of my hand. The crowd tittered and babbled. The air thick.

Pulse pounding, pounding, pounding.

Lights.

Fisting the gun, I swiveled in the bright white, everything a blur except for my target.

I fired.

He fell back on a yell, slamming into the floor. I banged the gun down on the table at my side. Cheering exploded, a pandemonium of laughter and whoops. I dragged in a painful breath.

Evgeny clapped, his applause thundering in my ears. "Bravo, Luca. Bravo."

My insides clenched. I didn't even get ownership of this fucking victory?

"Is he dead?" I asked.

"He is," Evgeny said on a laugh. "He is." Evgeny bowed his head at me. The clapping grew louder, the shuffle of bills louder still.

An arm slid around mine tugging me back, but I couldn't move. I was metal bones stuck together. Brittle. I would collapse. "Turo," Adri's hoarse whisper, the heat of her hand on my cold, numb flesh. "Turo, come."

Come where? Back to life? Back to functioning in this fucked up circus? How much more? How much more?

Luca brushed past us, a hand touching my arm. He strode off with Berezin.

Adri held on to me, and warm blood pushed through my

veins as the crowd jostled around us, leaving the game room. We moved. She murmured words in Greek. Not sweet, not kind, harsh words, brutal words.

Up on deck I gripped the railing, my back stiff, breathing in the damp air. Adriana still held on to me. My anchor.

Those voices echoing in that room ran through my brain, the violinist's bland face done up with so much makeup, Evgeny's excitement, the cold, hard metal slick in my sweaty hand. I'd faced myself in that moment, in the flickering, loud darkness, the violin ripping through me.

A stillness took hold of me. A big chasm opened before me. A chasm I'd never wanted to see before, but had always been there. A loneliness I had created, nurtured.

That's where I festered.

When the music had stopped and it was just me and the gun and the silence, I knew. I knew I had put all that bluster and nothingness there myself, and I stood alone and cold in the bitter wind as it bore down on me.

Adriana wrapped her hands around my arms. "Thank God—"

"Don't, Adri. Don't involve God," I said, my hands pressed into the sides of my pounding skull. "He has nothing to do with this. Nothing at all. Nothing."

22

ADRIANA

WE SAILED BACK to the *Allegra* in silence, the water sloshing against the launch, its engine humming confidently, normally as if it were any other night. But it wasn't. Turo had given me his suit jacket as we'd waited on deck. He wouldn't look at me as he'd tucked it around me. His warmth lingered on the fabric, his scent, and I breathed it in deeply. A scent of bright lemons and oranges and intriguing musk. A fragrance of yesterday, not now.

No, not now.

The sea was an iridescent pastel color, pale liquid hues of pink and lilac in the first haze of sunrise. Its delicate beauty was lost to me. Turo stared straight ahead toward the *Allegra*. Tight, closed off. I wanted to help him, but how?

The girl Luca had brought with him from Evgeny's boat was speaking to him in French accented English, but he was only pretending to listen. He caught my gaze, and I returned his hard look with a cold one. She was a dark-skinned beauty from Lebanon. Was she a model who'd come for the party? Or maybe a slave girl, his prize from Berezin for the night? Or...

Hell, I'm too tired to care.

We finally came up alongside the *Allegra*, where two crew

members waited for us. And Alessio. A furious Alessio, his hands gripping the railing, lips pressed together, the line of his jaw sharp and tight. Turo sat up immediately and held out his hand to help me board, a cold hand. The girl followed and then he climbed on.

Alessio stalked toward me, taking in Turo's dark suit jacket hanging on me. "Are you all right? Why the hell were you on Berezin's boat?"

"Your brother insisted we go along with him," I replied.

He let out a hail of curses.

Luca hopped on deck, and Turo grabbed his arm. "You make sure I get that agreement from your uncle, you hear me?"

Another agreement. Another business deal. All of them with terms and clauses, and no guarantees. Luca only lifted his chin in a silent reply. Was that good enough for Turo? Why would he trust Luca after tonight? I knew I wouldn't.

Alessio charged toward Luca. "You took her to that boat? What the fuck were you thinking?"

"*Rilassati!* Relax. She's a big girl. And she had her bodyguard with her." Luca gestured at Turo.

"I told you, I made myself very clear," said Alessio. "You do not get the rest of us involved in your shit."

"My shit is what keeps you afloat when you're in need, little brother," Luca's voice seethed.

Alessio ground his jaw. "You could have seen him tomorrow. Tonight was—"

"It had to be tonight." Luca patted Alessio on the side of his face. "*Tutto bene.* Is good." His insouciant gaze bounced over me and Turo like an errant ping pong ball. "You all enjoy the rest of your evening." That ping pong ball became a barbed weapon, meant to sting. It only dropped to the floor at my feet and rolled away.

The girl laughed. "It is morning now."

Luca tugged her arm and they both entered the bowels of the

ship, their footfalls thudding in the distance.

"You look like shit," Alessio said to Turo. "What the hell happened?"

Turo only closed his eyes and opened them again, staring out at sea. I took off his suit jacket and put it over his shoulders. A sharp intake of breath tore from him at my touch, and my heart ached at the sound.

"I can't thank you enough, Turo. I don't know what to say. Which words. You risked your life again, you—"

"Don't say anything. Don't thank me." His voice was terse, bitter and my stomach dipped at the roughness, at his trying to control whatever he was feeling right at this moment.

Once again, he'd stepped in for me. A mercenary taking the dive, risking it all.

My mercenary.

"*Cara*—" Alessio took my hand in his and I let him. We left the deck. Left Turo alone staring out at the sea.

"Have you ever been on that Russian's boat?" I asked.

"No, but Luca's told me stories about Berezin's parties." He kissed the top of my head and held me close. "I'm sorry. I'm sorry I wasn't here to stop him. What happened?"

"I'll tell you tomorrow." I squeezed his arm. "I'm so tired."

"Of course you are. So am I."

"How did the party finish?" I asked.

"Crazy. But good crazy. You did an amazing job, Adri. Pure magic. It was everything I wanted it to be and more."

"I'm glad, Alessio." I gave him a kiss on the cheek as he opened the door to our cabin.

Alessio headed for the bathroom, and I kicked off my shoes and stared into the mirror where my makeup lay scattered on the dresser.

What I saw tonight.

What Turo did.

I wouldn't be Luca's toy again. Anyone's toy. And I hated

seeing Turo forced into doing such horrible things. He'd killed a man tonight. But there was no mourning that tragedy, because otherwise I would be mourning Turo.

Everything was different.

Alessio turned the faucet on in the bathroom, and the sound of him brushing his teeth through the door made me grab onto the edge of the dresser. Nothing was ordinary anymore. I couldn't just go to sleep and wake up tomorrow, have a *frappé* and a laugh, stroll through Mykonos and shop and swim as if it were any other day.

All I could hear were those gunshots, feel the pull of Berezin's hand on mine, imprisoning it, the close of my throat as he grabbed at my bum. His filthy insinuations that were his arrogant way of flirting. His too spicy cologne nauseating me as we watched Turo play his sick game of death.

All I could see was Turo's haunted face, his cold, hard stare, just now on deck.

Alessio came out of the bathroom and my body jerked up from the dresser. "Come to bed." He ripped off all his clothes and, dumping them on the floor, threw himself onto the bed, groaning, burying his face in his pillow. His breathing deepened immediately, a low snore rising from him. He was asleep.

I knew what I wanted to do. Needed to do. And it wasn't sleep.

I took off my jewelry and tucked it into my cosmetics bag along with my makeup, went into the bathroom and quickly washed my face. As quietly as possible I took off my dress and rolled it up, tucking it in my small suitcase along with my hair brush and cosmetics bag. I changed into jeans and a T-shirt, my denim jacket, my Nikes, and then wrote a note to Alessio on an *Allegra* stationery pad and propped it up in front of the mirror so he'd be sure to see it.

Holding in my breath, I grabbed my Vuitton backpack and suitcase and silently slid out of the room. I needed to find Turo. Now.

High-pitched cries and moans filled the hallway. Luca was working out his evening his way. I lifted up my suitcase so it wouldn't make any noise on the wood flooring and made it to the outside deck, finally gulping in the fresh sea air. Opening up my Blackberry, I made the call, whispering my request.

"*Kanéna próvlema. Se déka leptá eíme'ki,*" came the much hoped for reply.

Ten more minutes.

Glass crashed from the upper deck. Tucking my phone in my back pocket, securing my bags in a corner, I ran down the other end of the ship. A figure stood in the shadows behind the bar opening a bottle of liquor, broken glassware littered the counter. He brought the bottle to his lips and drank, drank. A thirst like no other. A thirst to erase, to numb. But the booze wouldn't fill that hole. That I knew all too well.

He slammed the bottle down on the bar, swiping a hand across his mouth. He was still wired from the Russian extravaganza.

Two fierce, light-colored eyes bore into mine, his ragged breathing the only sound to accompany the sloshing of the water against the boat.

"Turo."

"My bartending skills aren't great, so I can't make you a fancy cocktail. But I can open any bottle you like. He swept the broken glass with an arm and the pieces crashed to the floor. He planted his hands on the bar top. "What'll it be, Miss Lavrentiou?"

I went to the bar. "I don't want anything."

"Your boyfriend have any coke on him in your room?" He slugged back the bottle again. Whisky.

"I don't know."

"You don't know." He made a sour face. "What the hell do you know?" His voice was an acidic mix of brittle and bitter, and he poured and served that cocktail with grim delight.

"I can't begin to comprehend what you went through, but

drinking or doing coke isn't going to help."

"It's helping, baby." Turo let out a dark laugh. "I brought some coke back from the Russian bathtub, but I finished it. Very nice quality. Of course, I expected nothing less. Luca must have a stash of something on board. You want to help me? Go get it."

I went behind the bar. "I have something better."

His eyes blazed and he prowled toward me. "That stash between your legs? Yeah, that I could definitely use."

He fisted a hand in my hair and devoured my mouth. The warm caramel flavor of the whisky still on his tongue flared over mine. His teeth nipped and bit, his tongue demanded and burned a path through my mouth, my being.

His fingers dug into the sides of my face, his breath hot on my lips. "What's the matter, sweetheart? Your boyfriend too tired to get it up for you tonight? Is that why you came looking for me?"

He waited for me to react, to strike back. I only held his fierce gaze. The desperate clawing, the frenzied scratching. I knew it so well.

"We're leaving," I said. "You and me."

A cruel, cold smirk lashed his weary features. "You and me, huh?"

I put a hand against his cold cheek, and his eyes narrowed, a muscle ticking under my touch. "I called a friend who owns a small restaurant on the island, a fisherman with his own boat. He's out on the water now and coming here."

His eyes searched mine.

"I'm getting off this boat. Come with me," I whispered, my fingers curling in his shirt.

"To shack up at some hotel?"

"To leave Mykonos. He'll take us to the port and we'll get on the first ferry. There's always a ferry by seven or eight in the morning."

"And go back to Athens?"

"No. Not Athens. I don't want anyone to know where we are."

"Not even your man?"

"Come with me," I repeated.

"Why?"

"Because I won't be toyed with and used, not by Luca Aliberti, not by Evgeny Berezin. Not by anyone."

"Good answer."

"This once, let me do something for you," I said.

His eyes narrowed at me, his movements stopped. Had he never heard that before?

For the first time in a very long time, I was going to trust my instinct. And that instinct had been right about Turo from the beginning. He'd been a rock, a rock where everything else around me felt like quicksand. Always felt like quicksand.

He was different from anyone I'd ever met. A brisk intelligence, a dry wit I really enjoyed. He treated me like a human being he actually liked and wanted to get to know. I could see it in his eyes, the way they lingered, in the words he used, the way he listened, the questions he asked me. It wasn't only lust or desire or fascination or wanting to score entry into my realm. It was real interest, enjoyment, curiosity. In that piercing amber gaze of his I wasn't Adriana Lavrentiou, I was a woman.

My own woman.

In the gold and lilac haze of dawn, that harsh gaze now softened, and that tide of heat that was us together washed through me afresh.

"Where to?" he breathed.

"Another island. We passed it on the way here. It's quiet, not touristy or crowded like Mykonos. It takes a little over two hours from here on the ferry. "

"And how will your boyfriend take the news when he discovers we're gone together?" The angle of his jaw tightened again. "Won't he come after us?"

"No, Alessio and I have an understanding."

He let out a harsh laugh. "Isn't that convenient?"

"He has a lot going on here this week, the store, dinner parties —he can't leave Mykonos."

Turo's fingers dug into my neck, a thumb at my throat. "Doesn't he need you for that?"

"No."

He shoved me up against the glass wall of the bar, letting out a guttural noise. Pain radiated through my back, it hurt, but I welcomed the pain. We were alive.

Alive.

And I wanted to feel.

My gaze fell to his lips, tense lips, hostile, cruel, and I wanted them on me delivering their brand of punishment. I kissed him, and a groan heaved from his throat. He claimed my mouth in return with a crushing press of his heat. Warm whisky filled my senses, his taste, that unique blend of masculine perfection that I couldn't define. A taste which my body recognized as *right*. The painful grip of his fingers on my neck, the press of the hard wall of his chest against mine—the world whirled, and I soared in the twist.

His fingers dug in my hair and fisted there, forehead sliding to mine, our damp lips a breath apart. "Don't expect an apology for that." He nipped at my lower lip with his teeth, sucking on the edge, and I gasped at the sting, the rawness.

"I don't want one," I breathed.

Sharp grunts rose from the lower deck. Luca was taking and getting what he wanted, celebrating his victory. Wincing, Turo stiffened in my hold and pulled away from me, a hand brushing down his face.

I wanted more than grappling in the dark amongst thieves. I wanted more from Turo DeMarco from America.

I said, "You have two minutes to pack your bag."

That crooked grin slashed across those devastating lips. His head slanted, eyes burning. A conspirator.

"Sweetheart, I never unpacked."

ANDROS

23

TURO

We'd gotten on the first ferry out of Mykonos. Next stop, Andros.

Adri and I sat on the deck of the ship drinking espressos and smoking cigarettes in the harsh wind, barely speaking, but we didn't have to speak. For the first time ever, I didn't want to plan anything, I didn't want to know the details and analyze them. I trusted her.

We kept close, sitting on a wooden bench, watching the deep blue water churn in the huge ship's wake. I bought us a third round of espressos and stirred a packet of the dark sugar she favored in her cup then handed it to her. Her eyes gleamed at me, her leg pressing against mine as she sipped on the sweet, stiff brew. A little, simple thing, and it made her happy. Made me happy too.

She lit another cigarette for me, and it took her four tries because of the wind. We leaned in close together, our heads touching, our grins corroborating. I took her cold hand in mine and rubbed it, keeping it tucked between my side and my arm.

A curious sense of intimacy, wordless and gentle and quiet, had easily risen between us since we'd gotten off the *Allegra* and onto her friend's fishing boat. Once on the ferry, the thick fog in my head lifted, the ache crushing my skull, the heaviness in my chest dissipating. We leaned back on the hard bench, taking in the slosh and slice of the big ship through the rough sea, moving us toward another island. She'd given this to me, this relief, this escape, and it was ours.

Two hours plus later, the ferry slowed its pace and backed into a small cove of a harbor surrounded by mountains.

This was Andros.

We made our way to the lower deck, got our bags, and disembarked from the bowels of the massive ship along with a line of cars and a small crowd of pedestrians.

"Our caretaker is meeting us with the car." Adri scanned the people waiting in the harbor.

"Caretaker?"

"Of the family property here."

"You own property here?"

"We have a house. My mother's family is from Andros originally."

The sight of the great white ferry heading off into the distance made me take in a deep breath. A deep breath of fresh sea air. We were here, just the two of us on this island in the Aegean, and nobody knew. Nobody.

I rubbed a hand down my chest the sunlight warming me. A huge grin broke her face. "Ah, there he is." She waved.

An elderly grizzled man greeted us in a rush of Greek. They hugged. "Turo, this is Orésti. He's been with the family ever since I can remember."

We greeted one another, and he took our small rolling suitcases. Orésti led us to a rugged yet sleek black little Land Rover Defender SVX jeep where he loaded our bags. He headed for the driver's seat.

"*Stásou,*" Adriana said, and he stopped. She gnawed on her lips and said something to him in Greek.

Orésti nodded, agreeing with her in a rush of Greek. He handed Adriana the keys, tilting his head at us. *"Adío, despinís. Kírie."*

"Efxaristó, Kírie Orésti," said Adri. A wistful thank you.

Orésti gave us a wave and strode off toward one of the many outdoor cafés at the port. Adriana stared at the keys in her hand.

I came up next to her. "What's up, Lovely?"

"I haven't driven in a long time." She took in a small breath. "I have my own car in Athens, but I haven't felt comfortable driving, being in a car by myself, moving through traffic, dealing with photographers who are on my trail. So I stopped, talked myself out of it. Got anxious about it."

"Well, there's no paparazzi or traffic here," I said.

Her gaze found mine and a small smile grew on her face. "No, there isn't."

"Go for it."

She flipped the car keys in her hand. "You don't mind being driven by a woman?"

"Make it worth my while, baby." I shot her my ladykiller grin.

"Hmm." She grinned back, a blast of sexy hotter than the sun. "Are you hungry?" she asked.

"Starved."

"Me too. I know just the place. Let's go."

She climbed into the driver's seat of the jeep, and I got into the passenger side, and we took off. The cold air battered my face as we sped down the curvy shore road. Barely half an hour later, the road twisted and rose over a harbor town, the village of Batsí. Whitewashed homes with blue trim were stacked over the curved mountainside of the village. A postcard of a classic Greek island town—picturesque, charming, and all real.

The road descended through the town, and Adri parked in the port. Old-fashioned, black, wrought iron lamp posts dotted the crescent walkway along the water. A number of small fishing boats, sailboats, and catamarans were docked in the harbor which was lined with cafés, restaurants, and souvenir shops which were opening for the day. A hotel with a long strip of sandy beach complete with loungers and umbrellas filled the other side of the harbor.

Adri slid her arm in mine and led the way to a restaurant, Mastello. We sat on a raised veranda at a high, wooden table and bench, offering a sweeping view of the marina. Seashells, brightly colored walls, thick boat ropes and large cans as light fixtures worked together creating a fresh, rustic nautical feel. Small bottles of ouzo lined four shelves on top of the entrance to the interior of the restaurant. That was a selection I'd never seen before.

"It's a little early, but I know the owner," she said.

A tall man with curly hair pulled back in a ponytail came out. *"Then to pistévo!"*

"Believe it, it's me." Adri laughed. They hugged and kissed on both cheeks, Greek style. They spoke in a bustle of Greek and he nodded and gestured, agreeing to whatever she was saying.

She introduced us and asked, "Turo, do you have any aversions to seafood at this hour?"

"None whatsoever. No rules, no schedules for us."

"I like that, yes. No rules, no schedules." A small smile perked up her lips. "And ouzo?"

"Educate me."

"I like you more and more, Mr. DeMarco."

Under the table, my legs found hers and rubbed up against them. That urge to continually touch her wasn't dying down anytime soon. Her tongue lashed at her bottom lip as she glanced at me then glanced back at the colorful tabletop, her face reddening.

No menus were needed, of course. A waitress came over with a pad and a pen and scribbled along to Adri's long order in a vivid tumble of Greek. Something special was about to begin. Like when a very rare and fine bottle of wine was finally opened and

I'd been offered the cork to smell; the scent extraordinary, the promise of the ruby liquid elating me, transporting me. Or when the curtain is about to rise on the stage of a play you've been dying to see.

My pulse kicked up, my mouth watered as she continued to order in that enthusiastic, colorful waterfall of words. Adri handed me a fork and knife from the bread basket the waitress had deposited on the table.

"You're happy to be here, aren't you?" I asked.

"Am I that obvious?"

"You're relaxed, not tense, a smile on your face."

"You too," she said. "And it's good to see." She blushed again.

Fuck, she's beautiful.

I could imagine her in high summer, skin bronzed and sleek, wet and salty from the sea, laughing as she ran over to me where I waited for her with a towel and a deep kiss. An incredible combination of girl and woman, naive yet wise. Innocent heart with the soul of a vixen.

Dangerous. A dangerous I'd never known before.

"I'm taking your advice seriously," she said. "I'm determined to stop being moody and glum."

"You be any way you want, Adri. I'll be right here."

Her gaze caught mine. Truth, my words, not offhand bullshitting.

Twisting off the cap on the large icy bottle of spring water, I filled our glasses and drank like the thirsty traveler I was. Water, relief flowed through me.

"When was the last time you were here?" I asked.

"A long time ago," she murmured. "The past few years we've only been going to Mykonos where we have a vacation home. But Mykonos is so very different. All of the world goes to Mykonos for a holiday, to party, to shop, to be seen. It's fun, but—"

"Not much of a getaway if it's the same people you see in Athens."

"Exactly. Andros is not that. Here, things are not pretentious, extravagant, or flashy. Here, it's simple and not so loud." She bit off a piece of bread. "I like it very much."

The Eurotrash heiress preferred simple and not so loud?

"You said that your mother's family is from Andros?" I asked.

"Yes. I was very close to my grandfather. He lived here all year round the last ten years of his life. I would come here on my own as a child and stay with him all summer. I lived with him here for a while too." Her lips twisted slightly. "He passed away four years ago. I suppose that's when we stopped coming regularly. For me and my mother it was much too painful." Her gaze darted to the sea.

The bright blue, wooden, louvered doors that led to the kitchen swung open on a squeal and two waiters brought out dish after dish for us. Butterflied roast sardines in a pool of olive oil, wine vinegar, and oregano, two long octopus tentacles on a bed of black lentil puree, a Greek salad like no other I'd seen before—a high mound of tomatoes, cucumbers, green bell pepper, and thinly sliced red onions topped with a creamy white cheese and a thick swirl of olive paste and oregano. Serious Mediterranean *meze*.

Adri dug into each platter with her fork and filled my plate. No serving spoons, no turn taking, just indulging and sharing that indulgence. Rich, simple flavors filled my mouth; my palate whirled on a Greek pinwheel. The sun shone brightly over our table warming us, glinting in the gold-green olive oil lacing the dishes.

She filled our small, slim glasses with ice cubes and poured a measure of ouzo and a dash of water in each. The liquid clouded immediately, the glass frosting. "This was my grandfather's favorite."

"I've had it once or twice before, but I must admit, I didn't care for it much."

"Well, ouzo in Chicago in some restaurant or this—" She

waved her glass over the glistening-in-olive-oil colorful platters of fresh seafood and salads, and raised it toward the calm, blue bay before us, the mountains on the opposite shore. "This is how it should be enjoyed. Keep all this in your heart right this very second, so that every time you take a sip of ouzo after this, wherever else you may be, you'll enjoy it the proper way."

"All right." I raised my glass at her.

She held her cloudy ouzo glass before mine, those blue gray eyes full of light. *"Yiá mas."*

"Yiá mas," I repeated. We clinked glasses.

We sipped, her gaze on me. Anise, aromatic and icy, flooded my mouth.

She licked at her upper lip, sliding on her sunglasses. "What do you think?"

"Refreshing. Crisp. Provocative even."

"Provocative?"

"Yes, makes me want to devour all this amazing food. And you."

She only laughed. We ate, we drank. We ordered more—mussels steamed in a garlic ouzo broth, boiled wild greens in a lemon and olive oil dressing. Perfectly fried calamari—not crusty and thick like the ones I was accustomed to in the Italian American restaurants I'd frequented, but crispy on the outside and delicate, tender, sweet on the inside. The small dishes of delights kept coming.

She ripped a sesame-seeded crust of bread apart, dipped it in the creamy remains of the Greek salad and offered it to me. "Go on, you must, consider this a rite of passage."

I bit into the bread from her hands and closed my eyes enjoying the chew of the freshly baked bread bathed in oregano and the caper-perfumed lushness of the oil. The rich cheese.

"That's not feta cheese, is it?"

"No, it's a local cheese that's made only on the island."

"It reminds me of French goat cheese but milder."

"Yes, you're right," she said.

"Our lunch yesterday on the *Allegra* was good, very good, but this food has soul. It's a rich experience we're moving through. We're not just consuming a fine meal."

Letting out a small laugh, she leaned over the table and clinked my ouzo glass with hers. "You really are a foodie, aren't you, Turo?"

"I am," I admitted. "My mother raised me with a finer palate than most."

"More hidden talents." She raised her ouzo glass, and a prick of disappointment hit me that sunglasses hid her expressive eyes.

"What more is there to be discovered?" she murmured.

"You'll have to find out for yourself."

"Hmm."

We talked more, we drank another bottle of spring water. I hailed the waiter for the bill. She reached across the table and touched my arm. "This is my treat, Turo. Please. Your first meal on the island, and I'll bet your best yet in Greece. Let it be my treat for you."

My chest filled with heat.

It had been perfect. But it was something more than good food.

This meal had been a sort of ritual ceremony. A colorful washing away of the gray and black of the past couple of days and nights. Of the hundred prickly tensions and strains from every direction. This had been both a cleansing and a celebration we'd shared.

Having her all to myself the past few hours had been a balm and a treat. Exciting and relaxing. This getaway of ours was suddenly precious and vital to me. Her gift of this bite of paradise to kick it all off was pleasing in a way that I couldn't quite figure out. But I knew that I wanted to swallow the experience—whatever happened between us and for however long it lasted.

Swallow it whole.

She took off her sunglasses and those eyes glimmered at me, her lips swept up in a confident smile. A pact, a deal, a grabbing of hands and jumping off the cliff. She wanted this, just like I did.

Fate sealed.

"Your treat, Lovely."

Her smile deepened and she sat up straighter. I surrendered to her pleasure. I surrendered to her smile, I surrendered to her simple joy in a simple gesture of generosity. I took an easy breath right there in her genuine smile, in the affability of her tone as she asked for the bill. She'd created this moment for us and she'd truly enjoyed giving it to me. She'd enjoyed my appreciation. Something curled inside me, wanting more moments like this. Needing them.

A new craving had taken hold of me.

She took care of the bill, and as we rose from the table, I took her hand, kissing the back of it. "Thank you."

"My pleasure," she said quietly, sliding her arm through mine as we strode along the harbor toward the jeep.

Just another couple on a vacation. But this couple had two of the most powerful crime families trying to figure out where they were right about now. Would they try to find us? An ache raced over my skull, the hard glare of the sun pricking my eyes even though I was wearing my sunglasses, and I raked a hand through my hair, my scalp tingling.

"Roman emperors used to banish people to Andros and other islands as punishment," she said. "I imagine it must have been devastating to be banished back then, separated from everything and everyone you knew."

"Definitely."

"You and I, on the other hand, have chosen to be here. To banish the madness of so-called civilisation from our minds and spirits." Her playful voice had taken on a more serious tone.

Was that where we'd been the past couple of days? In a well-mannered, high-powered, enlightened, educated, cultured society?

"A man was killed last night," she murmured.

And there was the giant troll tracking behind us all day long, his heavy footsteps, his thick smell. Neither of us had said a word about it. Neither dared. I didn't want to see any signs of hate in her eyes, or disgust. I hadn't. Not yet.

"And I killed him," I said.

"You had no choice, and you almost killed yourself, Turo. And for what? For the sadistic whim of a madman?"

"It's men like Berezin who rule the world, Adri."

She stopped, her eyes leveling with mine. "I don't know how long this will last, us being alone here in Andros."

"Until they find us? Because I'm sure they're looking."

"I'm sure they are." The wind whipped her hair around, and she swept it away from her face. "But there's nowhere I'd rather be at this moment than right here with you. Nowhere on this earth."

My heart ticked to a quicker rhythm at the firm tone of her conviction, her words. Was she running away from something other than the shooting? Or was it from someone? Maybe it was my exhaustion from the deluge of last night's sewage waters, but I really didn't fucking care. We were on this island, me and Adri, together.

A shimmer of sunlight created kinetic sparkles on the surface of the sea before us, like tiny, golden, magic fairies dancing on the water. Yeah, I wanted this exile with her, here, now.

"Me too," I held her gaze. "Nowhere else I'd rather be."

Adri beamed that grin at me, part sly, part sexy, part girl having fun. All woman. The most beautiful woman.

The jeep waited behind us and she unlocked it. "Let's get on with our exile, shall we?"

24

TURO

ADRI SHIFTED GEARS like a seasoned race car driver. Her jaw tense, eyes riveted to the road, hair flying. My Formula I Lady Godiva.

Ah, if only she were naked.

The Land Rover skillfully ate up the twisting, winding roads we climbed in this thorny mountain scape once we left Batsí. I glanced down past the edge of the road and my stomach shoved up my throat. The edge of the road was truly the edge to the immediate sheer drop of a cliff. Everywhere cliffs. But there were rewards. With every twist and turn of the road a glorious sweep of blue flashed in the distance, glinting in the sunlight like a fantasy promised land. A prize revealing itself bit by bit. A treasure to wait for.

"And where are we going?" I asked over the roar of the engine, the brunt of the wind.

She glanced at me and smiled.

"Eyes on the road, Lovely."

She let out a dark laugh. She was enjoying my angst. "Don't worry, Turo. My father taught me to drive and he was a top rally race car driver in his youth."

"Great. I'm not sure rally and cliff roads jive though."

She laughed again. "I'm taking you to a very special beach."

"That sounds so very benign. Yet this is the furthest thing from it."

"These are the Cyclades islands. For the most part, they are barren mountain rock. The roads that do exist are cut from that rock. Villages were tucked away in these high, remote spots to make things difficult for all the pirates who came hunting for treasures."

"Pirates, really?"

"Many, many pirates over the centuries."

We were on the historic trail of marauding pirates. Somehow that seemed fitting. The deep valleys and steep mountainsides were laced with miles of stone walls. Constructed of wedged and piled flat stones, the handmade walls outlined an endless pattern of loping terraces of land. Unusual flat crags of jagged stone jutted out of the cliff sides giving the landscape an otherworldly quality.

"The stone here, it's different," I said. "The rock shimmers, like it's been scrubbed with gold. It actually glitters."

"Yes, the stone here has layers of different minerals and can be split into thin plates."

"And that's why they build walls and small buildings out of them."

"Right. There's lots of marble and quartz everywhere as well. I used to go hiking with my grandfather. He knew these things."

My ears popped with the height. A series of medieval oblong towers dotted the steep mountains. "Are those dovecotes?"

"Yes, the Venetians left them behind."

"The Venetians were here too?" I sat up in my seat.

She nodded, eyes focused on the road. "They came here for a holiday after a Crusade in the 1200's and stayed awhile."

"And they left their love of pigeon poop behind."

She laughed. "Great fertilizer."

Adri powered the jeep around yet another tight curve, and I

said a silent prayer of thanks to Dionysus for the perfect choice of vehicle. It gripped the road and easily managed the steep turns. A small black goat perched on a sliver of rock glared at us as we rounded the bend.

"The asphalt is good here," Adri said, shifting. "But it ends in about fifteen minutes."

So much for that prayer.

Soon enough the asphalt vanished before us and we were left with a dirt road strewn with all kinds of stones and rocks. Adri downshifted and cut her speed, as my feet pressed against the floor of the jeep, my one hand gripping the bar above me. Twisting around a cove—the sheer drop steep as hell—we passed around a huge, round tower planted on the side of the mountain, a vestige of medieval construction.

"Watch now," she slanted her head to the right as we swerved to the left, Adri gripping the steering wheel, her lips pressing together, forehead lined. Focused as fuck.

I shifted in my seat, and there it was in the distance, a perfect cove, turquoise water glittering in the sunlight edged with a pale halo of shore. Something out of a travel magazine or a postcard but it was no glossy ten-cent photo. It was real, and we were heading there together.

"Isn't it beautiful?" her voice soared. "Andros has many, many amazing beaches, but this one, Vitáli, is my favorite."

"Are they all as challenging to get to as this?"

"Many, yes. We'll get there, Turo. Don't worry."

"I have no doubts."

Her cheeks reddened, a small smile lit up her face and that flare of heat went off in my chest. She enjoyed my compliment. And it wasn't bullshit, it was the truth. Ordinarily I'd hate being driven around by a female. Especially a female I wanted to bed, but this girl driving this jeep was the take charge tigress I'd seen at the party in Mykonos, on the Russian's boat, and I fucking liked it. She hid the tiger more than let it out of its golden cage. Her quiet roar had my blood racing in my veins.

"Eyes on the road, Lovely. Eyes on me later," I said.

She let out a low, sly laugh. The tigress wanted to come out and play.

The road descended, and that insane, impossibly perfect beach grew closer, nearer. A surprising clearing of emerald-green grass spread out before us and opposite, stood a small building with a covered veranda filled with tables and chairs and a donkey in the yard.

Adri slowed down. "That's a *tavérna*, a restaurant. We'll eat there later."

"Of course we will."

Just past the field on the edge of the shore, Adri pulled in to a wide patch of rocky dirt and parked alongside three other vehicles. We'd made it.

We got out of the jeep, and I stretched out. Vitáli Beach was a hidden cove surrounded by a rise of low mountains.

She stilled, staring at the sea.

Oh, this sea. Aqua blue blended with turquoise. Pure and clear, calling to something thirsty in my soul. Waves swelled in a relaxed rhythm, beckoning us to enter their soothing swirl. A sensual seduction of a different kind. Smooth, round, white stones were scattered over pale gold sand. We were on the edge of the world. A different world from everything I'd ever known.

Perfect.

Unbelievable.

And yet, here I was. Here *we* were. Me and Adri together.

I went up behind her and leaned into her. "Nowhere else I'd rather be."

Her hand reached out and fell back into my chest, and I took it and rubbed it there, liquid warmth spreading through me. Our fingers entwined, and we breathed in and out. Breathed in the pure salty-sweet air blowing over us, capturing it in our lungs.

She turned to me, her fingers squeezing mine, and my heart stopped. Eyes a brighter blue than ever before locked on mine, smile huge and relaxed, hair floating in the breeze. The magnificence of this beach wasn't enough. No, it was Adri herself.

"Nowhere else I'd rather be," she whispered.

We got our bathing suits out of our suitcases and took turns changing in the jeep. We headed toward the pairs of loungers stretched out underneath straw umbrellas over the sand. She chose one up front by the water, smack in the center. "I have plenty of sunscreen, so don't worry. I won't let you get burnt."

"You've thought of everything."

"I'm thorough, Mr. DeMarco. Now, onto important matters. What would you like to drink? A juice? An iced coffee? Soda?"

A waitress in a bikini top and shorts holding a pad and pen marched over to us in the sand.

"Whatever you're having," I said. Yes, how very unlike me, but I wanted to experience Adriana's island, Adriana's way.

A feathery eyebrow lifted. "*Freddo* espresso it is then. How do you like your sugar?"

"On your skin so I can lick it off you."

Her teeth grazed her lip. "And in your coffee?"

"I'm a purist. No sugar in my coffee, no milk."

Her gaze lingered on me as the waitress waited. Adri ordered our coffees and bottles of *neró,* water. Sitting on the edge of the lounger, I buried my toes in the small, smooth, warm stones that filled the beach. She removed her tunic and my eyes burned at the sight of her fantastic body in a pink bikini with a strapless top, and a high waisted bottom that had ties at each hip. My hands itched to pull on those ties, pull her hips to my face and—

She said, "Shall we go in? I can't wait."

Baby, neither can I.

I placed my sunglasses next to hers on the small, round table between our loungers. "Why should we wait?"

We entered the chilly water, both of us moving through the

full rolling waves that never broke or got very high. Crystal aqua-marine. I could see straight down to the smooth, sandy bottom. I dove in, the cool water sheathing me. I broke the surface as Adri swam to the other end of the shore where the beach bar was, and I followed her.

At the end of the shoreline rose a high wall of concave rock which towered over the water, the sides jutting out into the sea where a lone snorkeler swam. The water was darker and wilder here, slamming and smacking swiftly into the rocks of the small cave. Adri emerged from the sea and clambered up over the slippery slabs of that shimmering mica, and grinned like a kid who'd been given the birthday present she'd been coveting for a long time.

But she was no kid.

She was Aphrodite rising from her seashell, water sluicing over her skin, wet hair in a long tangle down her body, eyes huge and bright, ready to greet her ardent lover.

The compulsion to drop to my knees and worship her as any ordinary mortal would overwhelmed me. But she was no ethereal goddess. She was real, and she had chosen to run away to this hidden paradise with me. To share this special place in her heart with me.

"Isn't it wonderful?" she asked, sniffing in air, hands wiping the water from her face.

"Fantastic." I smoothed my hair back, a hand down my middle, catching my breath. The cave, the wind, the loud smack of the waves.

The girl.

"In the summer, it gets crowded," she said, "so being here now, having it all to ourselves is wonderful." Her eyes glimmered as her attentive gaze darted around the small yet high cave, taking in every detail. True, satisfied joy as she moved deeper into the small cave.

I caught up with her and grabbed her, planting a kiss on her wet, cool lips.

Her eyes popped open. "What was that for?"

"You're so damn happy right now and I wanted a taste of it."

"The things you say."

"They're true." *For you.*

I hadn't had to dissemble with her. I didn't have to look over my shoulder or over hers or double guess. And I think she didn't either. It felt odd, liberating.

"Do you mind if we stay here all day?" she asked.

"Is there somewhere else we need to be?"

"We don't *need* to do anything, Turo. "

"There's a thought." I laughed.

"This is our secret getaway. Ours."

"It is."

Our eyes melded into each others, and she averted her gaze as she wiped tiny pebbles from her hands. "I ask because not everyone is a beach person," she said. "And I don't want this to be tedious for you."

"There's nothing tedious about being here with you, Adri. Nothing at all."

And there wasn't.

What would I be doing back in Chicago about now?

Grinning and bearing it.

Extinguishing a string of fires.

Agreeing to shit I didn't want to agree to.

Keeping my head in the game, as I listened to endless bullshit and observed posturing and took mental notes on any weaknesses on display that I could use later.

Putting up with old men who thought they knew better, and young assholes who thought they knew even better.

Standing on street corners waiting for red lights and green lights to change, over-thinking about where else I needed to be and how I had to get there, and where was Ciara.

Ciara?

Nope. Not one thought. Not one. I was in Greece, in Andros. With Adriana.

There was no *it's enough, it's not enough. Fine.* None of that. There was only being here right now with her, sun in our eyes, brisk sea at our feet, cool air nipping over our wet skin, Adri holding up a glossy, long, slim white stone, and me saying, "Can I have it?"

She placed the stone in my hand, and my thumb rubbed over it. Firm silk. Smooth, simple, soothing. I tucked my souvenir of this moment into my small swimsuit pocket.

We howled in the small cave and laughed at our echoes. Lunging back into the water, we let the wild waves swish and swing us around like a crazy amusement park ride. A heavy wave smacked Adri, shoving her to the other end of the shore, and I dove toward her and grabbed her hand. We paddled away from the mouth of the small cave where the brisk sapphire currents collided in a persistent fury.

We swam a few yards farther out where the sea was calmer, and I brought her closer to me. Laughing, she splashed my face and slipped from my hold, and I followed her back to shore where our *freddo* espressos waited for us under the straw-thatched umbrella. The icy brew slid down my dry throat as she sat on her knees on my lounger and rubbed a sunscreen onto my back and shoulders.

I closed my eyes, her firm touch burning into my flesh in the cool breeze, easing the knots of tension I'd probably been holding onto since Chicago. Or was it Evgeny's boat? Fuck, I always held on to tension.

My dueling partner's haggard, pale face flashed before me, his wails echoed in my ears, and I took in air, pressed my hands to my eyes, willing him away. Away, dammit. *I'm the one who made it out of that room alive. That's what fucking counts.*

"Turo? Are you all right?"

"Yeah, just a headache. Too much coffee."

Her hand pulsed at the back of my neck. "Do you want to leave? Go to a hotel so you can rest? Is the sun too much—"

"No, baby." The back of my throat burned the second that endearment spilled from me. "I just need to unwind. This is perfect. Really."

"You must tell me if—"

"I'm good."

"Lay down. I'll rub your back."

"You don't have to—"

"Turn over."

The pointed tone in her tigress voice ticked at me, nudging at my pulse. I turned over, chest down in the lounger. She kneeled in the sand next to me and rubbed ribbons of cool sunscreen into my muscles, her thumbs kneading my lower back. Heat radiated from her intense touch, dissolving the bunching, the aches.

"Damn yes. Right there," I muttered, my body surrendering to her skilled hands.

"Hmm." She slid her hands just under my waistband above my ass, and I clenched my muscles on reflex.

She let out a soft laugh. "Don't worry, I won't do anything inappropriate."

I really wish you would.

She worked my shoulders, my back, and my suddenly heavy eyes closed, bidding farewell to the sight of her tits straining in that bikini top. Her fingers raked through my hair, my scalp tingling in their wake, and I drifted. Drifted on the scent of brine and the swish of the sea and the tigress's warm, insistent touch.

———

I BLINKED.

"Hello." A pretty face filled my vision. *Adriana.* Turquoise water, foamy waves, smooth round white rocks. Pink and orange flip-flops.

I sat up. "Was I asleep?"

"You were. Is it so unusual?"

"I never take naps."

"You're not in Chicago, Turo."

No, I wasn't. I took in a breath, scanning the impossibly beautiful shoreline. Greece, island, gorgeous girl.

Adriana slid a purple paisley tunic over her bathing suit. "Are you hungry? I thought we'd go to the *tavérna* to eat."

"Yeah, starving actually." I tugged my T-shirt on.

Adri filled a small purse with her car keys, wallet, and cell phone, and we headed for the restaurant where a young man greeted us. She chose a table by the railing facing the sea, and he spread a paper tablecloth over the cloth one, clipping it in place, leaving a menu behind which Adri ignored. Did anyone ever look at a menu in this country?

Another, older man rushed out and greeted her loudly. He was thrilled to see her. The Greek double kisses were exchanged.

"Turo this is Thanási. Thanási, Turo."

Thanási's wavy dark hair fell in his bright blue eyes. "Welcome to Vitáli."

"Thank you."

Thanási and Adri had an animated discussion, and within moments a waiter brought out a small copper carafe of white wine along with two small glasses, crusty bread, and cutlery. Thanási and the waiter left us to it.

"You know everyone," I said, pouring the wine for us.

"Not everyone. But there was a time when we came to Andros consistently. Not just for a summer holiday, but for long weekends, every Easter. But after my grandfather passed away, my mother finally completed construction on her dream villa in Mykonos and we went there instead."

"So Andros is a special place for you?"

"Very special. I'm only beginning to realize how much I've missed it." Her lips pressed together.

"What did you order?" I asked, gently nudging her foot with mine.

Her lips tipped up. "You'll see."

"I don't think I've ever felt this hungry before."

"Fresh sea air, swimming. Stress on the road. No sleep the night before..." Her hand touched my wrist.

It was a gentle weight, a momentary contact, yet an odd sliver of heat and comfort rose up my arm and filled my chest. I swallowed it down along with the cold white wine, savoring them both.

A Greek salad with that creamy local cheese and lots of capers made its appearance on our table, along with fried zucchini flowers filled with melting cheese, grilled sardines, a heap of tiny fried fish. A dish of roast meat in a light lemon and oil sauce.

"What kind of meat is that?"

"Goat, what the island is known for."

"You mean the cute creatures we passed on the road through the mountains?"

"Yes, they roam free in their natural habitat. You won't taste any finer. Rather like lamb, only not as fatty."

I pulled the plate in front of me and dug in. Delicious, melt in my mouth, flavorful meat, the lemon adding the perfect acidic balance and pop of bright to the mellow rich sauce.

Adri's fork stabbed at a corner of the roast. "You like it?"

"Yes." I liked that she ate from my dish without asking, shared the feast. I moved the plate in between us and we both ate. The moody girl who picked at her food had thankfully left the building.

She dabbed a crust of bread in the salad dressing in the nearly empty bowl. "Tell me, how did you meet Gennaro Aliberti or is that secret?"

"No secret. Mr. Aliberti is a hotelier who wants to open a new hotel in Chicago. Recently the company I'm associated with tried to sign a deal with him, but my colleague was rude and Mr. Aliberti changed his mind about the collaboration. So they asked me to find him and apologize on their behalf, to find a way to make it right."

She chewed on the oil and tomato soaked bread, her forehead pulled in.

"What is it?"

"Gennaro is quite stubborn. All the Alibertis are."

"I know."

"So that's what Luca meant when we came back to the *Allegra*? That he would take care of that for you since...Evgeny's boat?"

"Yes. Let's see if he comes through."

"Honor among thieves?"

"You think I'm a thief?"

"Aren't you?"

I grinned. "Yes." No simple thief, though. A thief of identities, self-respect, honor. I'd brought many people to their knees often enough.

Adri's gaze went to her empty wine glass, but she didn't look distressed by my admission. She really did appreciate my frankness, and I was giving it to her. No editing with wit or charm. For the first time in a long time, I was being frank with someone.

I poured her the last of the wine and she drank. "I'm going to use the ladies room."

"I'll take care of the bill."

"Okay." She rose from the table.

I was a murderer in her eyes now, wasn't I?

She brushed past me, and I grabbed her arm. "Adri, I didn't just do it for Luca. I did it for you. To keep you safe."

"I know," she breathed. "I wish you hadn't had to." I released my hold on her arm, and she strode away toward the end of the restaurant.

I caught the waiter's attention and scribbled in the air—the universal sign for *bill please*. He raised his chin and brought over a slip of paper and I paid. Adri's cell phone rang out with a synthesized song for a ringtone. I flicked a finger at her phone and it swerved toward me giving me a better view of the screen.

Alessio.

I let out a huff of air. *What are you up to, amico mio? Searching your love boat high and low for your girlfriend? She ran off with the hired help.*

Adriana had said she and Alessio were in a fake relationship. Surely he would be collecting a posse of pussy this week like some rockstar. He was certainly doing it at his party, and Adriana hadn't seemed disturbed by it at all. Only Luca had pointed out to her that she was "straying" with me. Would running off hurt my case with Luca and Gennaro? Maybe sting Alessio more than he or Adri realized and he'd be after us, after her? Or maybe she was lying to me?

No, she couldn't be.

I slid the phone back to its original position. Adri returned to the table. "Shall we go?"

"You got a phone call."

She picked up her cell and her small beach bag, and meandered through the tables and chairs, her gaze focused on her screen. Stepping out into the sun, she put the phone to her ear, then looked at her screen again. "It's no use. Service comes and goes out here."

"That's too bad."

"No, it's good. I don't want to talk to anybody, even Alessio. I texted him earlier. He worries, and I wanted to make sure he knows I'm fine and not mad at him for some reason. Leaving the yacht was not about him."

"It's not?"

"No." She pivoted around in the sand, her brow furrowing. "Coming here is about me standing on my own two feet. Not hiding behind my work, my name, a relationship. Just me and what I want."

"And what is it you want, Adri?"

A grin curved her lips. "You and me on this beach."

25

TURO

THE SUN HAD SHIFTED POSITION, and she pulled her lounger to the other side of mine so she'd be full in the sun and not in the shade. Kicking off her flip-flops, she took off her tunic and unfastened her bikini top, and her breasts—fucking perfect breasts—bounced free of the material. She twisted up her hair, the movement making her tits reach high, her nipples hard in the bracing wind. I chewed on my lip, my mouth dried.

Dionysus, you're killing me.

She flattened out her chaise and laid down. Both of us stretched out side by side.

"Do you need me to help you with suntan lotion?" I asked.

Her lips twisted into a slight grin, her eyes hidden behind her sunglasses. "Yes, please."

"Always ask for what you want, Adri."

She handed me the tube of sunscreen and turned over on her stomach, turning her head to the side, sweeping away her hair. Her bare back was temptation in itself. I squeezed a line of the scented cream on her skin and rubbed the lotion over her sleek planes of firm flesh. She took in a deep breath and let out a low noise, her body squirming under my vigorous attentions. My fingers stroked down a curve so steep, just to the top of a slope so round—

A little boy screamed with laughter, his father throwing him in the shallow water, his yell piercing through me, and I let out the breath I'd been wringing in my chest like a wet towel I needed to dry. My fingers trailed down her spine and I snapped the cap back on the sunscreen.

"All done."

"Thank you," came her muffled, melted response. I grinned and tossed the tube back in her tote bag and fell back into my lounger, focusing my attention on the white gulls, their broad wings outstretched soaring and dipping in the sea. Adriana slept and I listened to her breathing, to the water welling and swishing on the sand, the occasional conversations the wind brought me.

Adri turned over again, her tits greeting me once more. I stretched my legs out, crossing one over the other. I felt like a fucking schoolboy struggling with a hard-on under my desk. But there was no desk and I was only wearing a bathing suit.

She let out a satisfied sigh. "This is perfect, isn't it?"

Fuck yes it is.

I wanted every goddamn inch of her under me, in my hands, every inch pulsing with my body. I grabbed a water bottle from the table at my side and ripped the top off, chugging what was left it. Hot water, dull and viscous.

"Did you sleep?" she asked, her voice mellow.

"Are you serious?" I clipped.

"Yes, why?"

I lay back down, closer to her this time. "With this view? And I'm not talking about the sea, Lovely."

She smiled. She was pleased with herself.

In one quick move I slid a hand around her thigh and pulled her against me. She let out a tiny yelp, formally summoning the carnal beast in me. Leaning over, I planted a kiss on her damp torso. Sun-kissed and scented with salt, her sweat, the lotion.

"Adri—"

She let out a small laugh. "Yes?"

"You evoke the strongest sensations in me and you know it."

Unexpectedly, she remained relaxed in my grip which only excited me. Dared me.

Kiss along her tummy.

Kiss on her navel.

Lick of my tongue *in* that navel.

Another lick along the edge of her bikini bottom. Always pushing boundaries until I'm told no.

She hissed in air, eyebrows doing a dance over the rim of her sunglasses, and she tried to twist away. I tightened my hold on her.

She brushed a thumb across my jaw. "Taking what you want?" she asked.

My head jerked, a muffled laugh escaping my mouth. "Always taking, that's me," I muttered. "How did you know?"

"I had you pegged from the very first, but I like that about you, Turo."

And with those words she wiped that automatic bitter grin from my mouth. My teeth tugged on the elastic trim of her bikini bottom and her eyes flared.

"Have you ever brought Alessio here?"

She shook her head. "He's never been to Andros."

"But he's been in you?"

An eyebrow twitched. "Yes, many times."

I liked her immediate, non-dramatic reply. Not a giggle, not a blush.

"Yet here you are with me," I continued. "There he is in Mykonos. And my tongue is enjoying itself immensely. And I'll bet his is too."

"I'm sure it is, I hope so." Her fingertips rubbed at my scalp. "Alessio and I are not in a relationship. Not a typical one."

"Then what is it?"

"Are you jealous?"

"I need to know if I should be expecting an assassin from *Napoli* to come for me in the night."

"He's not jealous," she said. "He may be—em—territorial?"

"Right."

"But not jealous."

"Why not?" I pushed up, taking her body with me. "If you're lovers, why isn't he jealous? And what are we doing here?"

"This bothers you?"

"Adri, if you were my lover, I'd never let you go off with another man. Never let you touch another man the way we were together in front of him. The way I'm touching you now."

She brushed a hand against my jawline, right by the scab from the night she'd got shot at.

My fingertips dug into her flesh. "Answer me."

"Alessio and I are good friends who have sex. Nothing more."

My muscles relaxed just a little. "Does Luca know that?"

"No."

"How long has this been going on?"

She raised her sunglasses over her head. "I met him in *Milano* almost two years ago when I went with friends to Fashion Week. We went out, had a good time, we slept together one night, and stayed in touch. That summer he came to Greece with a girl-friend, but they had a terrible falling out, she left, and we had sex again. Since then, he comes to Greece when he can or I go to Italy. The press likes us as a couple, and we realized that us together keeps the hangers-on and the questions away. There are many hangers-on for Alessio. He detests it and trusts no one."

"Because of his own notoriety and his father's?"

"Yes, exactly. But if he does find a woman he wants, I fade into the background, then re-emerge once it's over if he likes. Same goes for me."

"Is that what was going on the night we met in Athens?'

"Yes."

"Has he had other relationships?"

"Two or three."

"And you?"

"No, none."

"Why not? What's in it for you then, Adri?"

"With every man they have seen me with, the press hounds me with the same questions— *'Is he the one, Adriana? When are you getting married, Adriana? How many babies will you have, Adriana?'* Since Alessio they've gotten bored with me. Now they only remark *'Adriana Lavrentiou and her long-time boyfriend, Alessio Aliberti...'* It's worked out well for me." Her gaze leveled on mine as her thumb brushed the edge of my lip. "So far."

I cuffed her wrist. "So you don't think he'll be jealous or angry over us spending time together? Us being here alone?"

"No. Other than he doesn't trust you," she replied.

"That's good."

"Is it?"

"It shows he's a good judge of character. And he gives a fuck." I kissed her hand.

She sucked in air. "And what do you give a fuck about?"

"That you trust me." My pulse thrummed. I wanted her to trust me. "Do you trust me?"

Her foot rubbed down the length of my calf. "I feel safe with you, and you intrigue me."

"Intrigue you?"

"You have an icy cool about you, so icy it could cut, and at the same time a brilliant temper that is always simmering just beneath it—" She touched my bare chest and a ripple of heat went through me. "—just there. But you control it, and you use your temper constructively. It's quite a sight in action. You think quickly as everyone is busy trying to figure you out. I like it." Her fingers trailed along my skin, inciting a riot in my balls. "It's exciting."

"I excite you?"

"That's not what I said." She laughed.

"Do I excite you?"

"Yes," she whispered. "I like that indecency about you, beneath that clean polish."

"You like that?"

"I never thought so before."

"Lovely, you intrigue and excite me too," I whispered roughly, my eyes going to her parted lips, her quickening breaths reflecting the ticked up tempo of my pulse. "Now, put your top back on, because if you don't—"

She rolled her eyes. "You Americans are so prudish."

"If you don't put it back on, I'll be taking action."

"And what does that mean?"

"I will be sucking on those beautiful nipples. Making them hard and wet. Nibbling on the underside of those perfect round tits, palming them softly then very, very hard. Licking them like mounds of the finest ice cream I've ever tasted—"

Her lips parted, eyes widened.

"—taking them whole in my mouth like the greedy fucker I am."

Her eyes pinned to mine, she raised her arms over her head leaning them against the lounger, making her breasts even fuller, declaring loudly their stand-up-at-attention-perfection. She wanted to hear more.

Oh, baby, baby, baby.

I complied.

The warm scent of her suntan oil and sweat intoxicated me further the closer I leaned into her. "I'd squeeze your nipples, graze them with my teeth, nuzzle them with my mouth, then I'd lick a long, long trail down your tummy to your bathing suit and pull it down with my teeth, then I'd—"

She touched her fingers to my mouth and I bit them. A small moan escaped her lips, her cheeks visibly reddening under her sun-kissed skin.

Are you hooked?

"H-hand me my top?" Clearing her throat, she gestured toward the beach bag.

"Don't think you could take anymore?"

"There are children present. If I hear anymore, I can't be held responsible for my actions."

I spotted the pink band in the beach bag, grabbed at the fabric and dangled it in front of her. "For a kiss."

Taking in a breath like she was prepping for a dare, she sat up and pressed her bare tits against my chest, her tongue sliding past my lips. A part of me rose from that lounger and floated above that straw beach umbrella, that perfect shore. Cool and soft, slithering and hot. My every wet dream fantasy of her had been fulfilled.

Fuck, fuck, fuck.

My fingers released the bikini top; I was powerless before her. She'd rendered me so.

Adri nabbed the top from me and pushed away like she was done for the time being. She held my gaze as she quickly and efficiently smoothed the top back on her chest, my cock hardening fiercely. Men are such suckers.

I rose from the lounger and dove into the cold, clear sea. I came up for air, and Adriana was sitting still, gnawing at her lip, staring at me, eyes intent.

Fuck you, Alessio Aliberti. She's mine.

26

ADRIANA

AFTER OUR DAY swimming at Vitáli, Turo and I had gone back to Batsí where we'd checked in to a boutique hotel on the outskirts of the village. The villa which looked like an old Andrian stone fortress rose impossibly from a high cliff that towered above the sea.

Turo had already showered and dressed and showed up at my room, his body seizing at the sight of me wrapped in a bath towel fresh from my shower. My skin got a lashing from those light-coloured eyes, but I couldn't pay the prickles along my flesh any mind.

"Yes, *Mamá*, I heard what you said," I replied to my mother who'd called me. I only shook my head at Turo as a grin overtook his features. He headed out to the terrace of my room.

I'd told Mum how Turo and I had come to Andros and she'd been pleased. I knew this because she didn't barrage me with questions, only uttered an "Ah" in her sharp tone which implied approval on reserve, will ask questions at a later date.

"I need to go now."

"Mmm. *Prósexe, agápi mou*," she signed off.

Why was everyone telling me to be careful? I was the Queen of Careful and Hesitant, and they knew it.

"Love you," I said and clicked off.

I towel-dried my hair. My handful of moisturizer skimmed over my scar. The scar that wouldn't heal.

You won't let it.

I pulled on a short sleeved cropped blouse, and my copper and teal colored harem trousers with slits up the sides; my favorite kind of warm weather casual clothes. Rubbing a few drops of conditioning oil in my hair, I peeked out the terrace door.

Purple bougainvillea wrapped up and over the stone archways and the columns of the veranda. Flowery plants burst in a frenzy of fuchsia from bulbous pottery urns on the edges of the terrace overlooking the sea. Iron and glass lanterns with small candles dotted the marble table and larger ones stood on the patio floor. In the corner was a large divan upon which Turo was now stretched out.

His eyes closed, the thickness of his long, full eyelashes obvious. His chest rose and fell with the shallow breathing of sleep, an arm folded under his head. He'd given in to the insistent music of the waves slapping against the rocks down below, the cool mountain breeze brushing his skin, and his own fatigue—or was it the shock of sudden relaxation?

Something curled inside me at the sight of him at rest. The plains of his handsome face which were usually pulled tight in thought—his brand of grim thought and brittle wit—were relaxed for once. More often than not he looked tense, ready to spring, his mind constantly working, rapid firing, charging.

My gaze trailed over his dark trousers and his long sleeved, pale blue cotton shirt with the cuffs rolled up; the city boy's concession to the warm weather? Turo wasn't a T-shirt kind of man. That was only for sport and the beach.

I brushed on a bit of bronzer, then a smudge of eye pencil, a dash of mascara. I was a far cry from the glam, expensively dressed girl Turo had first met in Athens. I stared at the woman looking back at me in the mirror. I liked this Adri much better. This was me.

Sliding on my beaded leather sandals, I went back out onto the terrace and perched on the edge of the divan so as not to disturb Turo. I'd finally told him the truth about me and Alessio. A fake relationship that served a purpose; casual fun with a close, trusted friend which was also a form of self-protection since the horror of that day two years ago.

Taking in a breath, I leaned back against the stiff bolster pillow of the sofa. Back then the press had had a field day with me and my first love, tore us apart and built us back together like a Lego castle. But they hadn't gotten the parts right. Their castle was crooked and ugly, pieces missing. And it had taken me a long, long time to simply sail past the hideous structure and not let it rip at me. You could ignore it all you wanted, but you always knew it was there.

Being with Alessio helped. He'd been good to me, but I couldn't see out of our little aquarium any longer. The glass was cloudy and smudged and I'd curled up in a corner. Not Alessio though. Alessio dove out into the sea then dove right back into our glass haven when he was done. He'd been in several relationships since our arrangement had begun. It was easy for him.

A noise unfurled in Turo's throat and I glanced down at him. When I met Turo it was as if a flash of lightning had gone off, blinding me for a second. Startling, thrilling. A whip lashing me. A shock I couldn't ignore, a shock that jump-started a new rhythm to my sluggish heartbeat. His firm grip on me, his initial arrogant perusal which then transformed into a rush of desire. We talked, we laughed and danced, and that fierce and mesmerising arousal he incited in me was both scary and exciting.

Why did it scare me? Because Turo's brand of arousal was

intense and jolting, it shook me from my uncomfortable comfort zone. A comfort zone I'd created and bound with wire fencing because I'd made so many wrong choices in the past. One extreme to the other. And the one time I was sure I'd found it with the very wrong and very right person, it blew up in my face.

Literally.

I'd been playing it safe with Alessio. And in the process I'd gotten lazy, frightened, full of self doubt, and I hated myself for it, hated my restlessness, my dissatisfaction with everything. The shooting made me realize that there was no hiding, that I was only wasting my time. Those gunshots had pierced my fog, penetrating it.

And in the clearing of the haze, there was Turo DeMarco.

Escaping to Andros with Turo was like gulping down a cocktail in one swallow on a dare. But I'd dared myself. Heady, sweet yet sour, steadying, overwhelming. Today we'd made each other laugh, relaxed in each other's company. Flirted. Yet frosted over his flirting was not the pleasant white dusting of sweet icing sugar. His was a firm coating of something not so sweet, something darker, sharper. Underneath the shadow of that tense bravado of his, I recognized the glowing smoulder of grief and anger.

I knew it well.

I didn't know how much time we'd have here in Andros, and I didn't want to think about it in terms of days or even hours. Coming here was about escaping the world's demands, danger, and just bloody *being*. No noise. Andros was special to me, and I'd never shared it with anyone before in all the Greek island holidays of my youth. Turo's obvious enjoyment of it today had made my heart swell. It meant something to me, his enjoyment of this place.

I slid my knuckles against his sharp jaw. He stiffened, his eyes opened. Those eyes bunched then relaxed. That mouth curved into a smile for me.

Stunning.

That was the word he'd used earlier to describe the view from the veranda of the hotel, but he was stunning. Him. His scent of fresh lemon and musk floated over me, and a liquid calm spread through my veins after the tense morning, the blustery ferry ride, the driving and the swimming. I didn't want to move, to speak. To break the spell unwinding between us.

"Did I fall asleep?" he asked, his voice throaty.

"You did."

He raised his head. "That's two naps today."

"The Mediterranean agrees with you."

Taking in a breath, he stretched out a hand and gently touched the side of my cheek. "You agree with me."

My face heated. "I thought we'd walk into town and have a drink, decide on what to eat."

He sat up. "A drink would be good."

"I know just the place."

"I'm sure you do."

I got up and applied a quick swipe of shimmery lip gloss as Turo took me in from head to toe, and my insides hummed under his keen observation. He had a discerning palate and a discerning eye. His admiration was suddenly very important to me; I wanted it.

We strolled into town along the shoreline, Turo scanning the crowd as we went. A motorcycle howled past, and I flinched, brushing against him. He took my hand in his, his warm fingers enfolding mine, and the pressure in my chest eased.

"Here we are," I said, leading him up a broad set of white-washed stone steps to Capriccio, a bar café with a small terrace on the second floor. Whitewashed stone banquettes dotted with pale blue pillows lined the veranda, with high tables and matching chairs in the center. We settled into one of the high tables which offered an unobstructed view of the sea. Large straw lanterns hung over us, swaying in the damp breeze blowing off the water.

I ordered a mojito.

"Grey Goose on ice with a lot of lemon and lime," Turo told the waitress.

Our gazes hung on a sky smudged with thick swathes of bright pink and deep red, pale cerulean blue and indigo. In the distance, on the other side of the bay, a buttery yellow illuminated the edges of the mountains. The colors of the calm sea kept transforming. Ashy blue, deep pink.

The waitress brought us our drinks.

"To that glorious sunset," I said, raising my icy cocktail stuffed with mint leaves.

Turo clinked my glass with his. *"Yiá mas."* He swallowed and the muscle along his jaw ticked, eyes narrowed for a moment. Something wasn't right.

"Excuse me—" His curt tone stopped the waitress. "This needs more lemon."

"Oh. Of course." She took his drink.

"Needs to be just right?" I asked.

"Always. Why bother?"

Yes, why bother indeed. Why put up with less than what you know is the best. It displeased him and he did something about it without dramatics. A smile tugged on my lips.

An eyebrow flared as he fiddled with the edge of a napkin. "What is it?"

"I like that you demand quality. Of the right thing in the right way."

The drink returned and he sipped as the waitress waited. Somehow she knew better than to take off. "That's good. Thank you." He visibly relaxed and she took off.

The jazzy music was low and we talked easily as the place filled up. "Do your parents think that you and Alessio are in a relationship?" he asked.

"Only that we see each other whenever he's in town or I'm in Italy. My mother doesn't approve. She always says, '*You're wasting your time, Adri.*' Or '*He's a dangerous man, Adri.*'

"I think I like Liana."

"She's probably had you looked into already."

"She won't approve of me either then."

I sipped my drink. "And what will she find?"

He licked his generous upper lip, his thumb toying with the rim of his glass. "Rich boy. Illegitimate son. Honor Society. Championship athlete. Young executive. Rising figure in the criminal underworld."

"He's a dangerous man, Adri," I quoted my mother.

He let out a dark laugh, his gaze settling on the sea once again. I wanted his attention. I wanted him to let go of last night. I'd pushed those images in the sea today. Swimming at Vitáli with Turo, his skin against mine, the sun licking our flesh. I thought he had too. But now, with the setting of the sun, he seemed to have lapsed into a bitter introspection, and I wanted him to stop. I wanted to make him smile, laugh again.

"So, I thought maybe you'd like to try authentic street food tonight," I said.

His stern gaze remained on the sea as he drank. "Sounds good."

"We call it 'dirty' here."

His eyes darted to mine. Troubled eyes, shielded. "Dirty?"

Success. "I see that entices you?" I asked.

His fingers slid up and down his glass. "Lovely, my thoughts have been very, very dirty all day." He took a long swallow of vodka and rolled a piece of ice around in his mouth, crunching down on it. Those teeth nipped at me. "Tell me about this dirty," he said.

"You call it junk food in America. Something messy to eat, not exactly healthy for you—dirty."

His lips tipped up. "Yeah, let's do dirty tonight." He drained his glass with his eyes on me and hailed the waitress for another round of drinks.

Darkness had now settled over the seaport, and the twinkling lights from the shops, the boats, and the stars lit up the thick sky. We left the bar and walked down the port to Avra, a *souvláki* restaurant filled with families, boisterous kids at tables stretching all the way to the waterfront. An ache scrambled over my skull. After the perfect cocktail experience the last thing I wanted was a noisy crowd.

"Shall we get the food and bring it back to our hotel and sit on my veranda and eat?"

He stroked my back, bringing me in to his side. The tumult of the crowd was affecting him too. "Good idea."

"I'll order." I stepped up into the restaurant's kitchen which was blazing hot with live grills, roasting meats twisting on spits, oily pita breads being flipped over at a rapid pace, and a frenetic staff shouting directions and wrapping food tightly in paper and foil. I ordered, and once we got the selection of *souvláki* and *gyro* and two Fix beers, Turo paid at the register on the other end of the long counter. I grabbed an extra wad of napkins and shoved them into the food bag.

He took my hand firmly in his, and we made our way through the crowded high street where the shops were lit up. I stopped at a jewelry store and loitered over a glass cabinet filled with blue eye charm necklaces and bracelets.

"I've noticed these everywhere," Turo said. "In Athens too."

"The eye or the *máti* is a very powerful superstition in Greece. An eye combats evil in all its forms—unintentional, with intent to harm, and the hidden."

His features darkened. "Every form of evil. Huh. I like that. These eye charms help?"

"The eye reflects the evil back onto whomever is directing it at you because of their envy, jealousy, or hatred. They're also said to attract good luck." I shifted my weight. "I love them. I

262

have quite a collection, but I can't say I've had much good luck lately."

His eyes met mine. "You were wearing one the night we met. With a tiny diamond in the center."

My hand flew to my throat where there now lay a different necklace. "You remember?"

He held my eyes with his burning ones. "I remember everything about that night."

My mouth dried. "If we hadn't met—"

"Ah—if you hadn't crashed into me." He winked at me and sparks went off in my chest.

"If I hadn't *crashed* into you and liked you right off—"

"Were you drunk?"

"I was not."

"You were," he said, "or I doubt you would've come on to me the way you did."

"I came on to you?"

"Be honest."

My gaze held his. "There were several glasses of wine and one hit of cocaine, but I wouldn't call that crazy wild."

"Then the *máti* works," he said his voice low, his eyes flaring with warmth in the light of the streetlamp over us. "It protected you from the attackers' intent to harm." He leaned in close to me, his whisper tickling my ear. "It attracted good luck too, didn't it?"

"Yes." The word burned in my throat.

His lips hovered over mine, a breath away, that heat churning, churning between us. I glanced back at the display case and touched his arm. "Wait one moment."

Darting into the small shop, I spoke with the salesman. He pulled a tray of bracelets for me, and I quickly chose the perfect one and paid for it. I joined Turo on the sidewalk with a small gift bag in my hand.

"This is for you. A souvenir that I hope you'll wear in America and it will make you think of Andros, of me, and our stolen escape. Our luck together." An ache twisted inside me at the thought of us having to leave Andros. Never seeing him again.

His jaw tensed for a moment, and something clutched at my chest as he took the gift bag from me. Parting was inevitable, wasn't it? All of this was merely a bit of stolen fun, a frivolity. Not reality, not everyday life.

But it is real. It's real to me.

"I don't think I'll ever forget you or Andros, Lovely," he breathed.

My heart stumbled.

I took the food bag from his hand, and he opened the small pouch and pulled out a black leather strand with a single small *máti* charm in dark blue.

I bit at my bottom lip. "Will you wear it or is it too—"

"I like it very much." He held out his wrist and I widened the bracelet and slid it over his hand, tightening the leather ends over his wrist.

"Thank you." He touched his lips to mine. Soft warmth, an unexpected gentle caress.

"You're very welcome."

———

BACK AT THE HOTEL, we ate at the table on my veranda overlooking the inky dark sea. A fluffy, steamy, pita bread stuffed with grilled spicy meat and creamy, garlicky *tzatzíki* yogurt sauce, along with paper thin slices of red onion, tomato, grated carrot, parsley, and a few french fries. Just what we needed.

"This is good dirty," he said.

"It's very good. I'm glad you like it." I let out a laugh, swiping a napkin along the edge of my mouth.

"What's so funny?" he asked, chewing.

I tightened the juicy pita roll in preparation for my next bite. "Because I'm sure about now Alessio, Luca, and Gennaro are consuming a three hundred euro lobster and pasta dish along with a few bottles of Cristal. Throw in dessert platters—"

"With one of everything," he added.

"Of course. Add their favorite Cuban cigars, more liquor— their bill will probably be upwards of ten thousand. This cost us about ten euros and it's so much more satisfying to me right now." I took the final bite of my luscious *souvláki*.

"You're aware of the prices?" he said, drinking his beer.

I crumpled my napkin and tucked it in the bag. "I may come from money, Turo, but I've always been acutely aware of the difference between outrageous indulgence and mere expensive, for one." My voice came out sharper than I wanted it to and he looked up at me.

"Dammit, woman, now I'm truly impressed with you."

"It's not impressive, Turo. It's reality." I drained my beer bottle.

"It is."

We cleaned up, washed up, and returned to the veranda where he'd lit all the candles in the lanterns. I kicked off my sandals, and Turo his shoes, both of us laying down on the divan, looking up at the dark sparkling sky, listening to the waves sloshing and crashing on the rock below us. His heat, the traces of his scent, vied for my attention along with the jasmine from the blooming vine around a column of the villa. These were the scents of our island night.

I fingered his thin bracelet, and his warm hand closed over mine. Curling into him, I dragged my fingers through his hair, behind an ear. I didn't want him to go. I wanted to fall asleep here under the stars in his arms, my head on his chest.

"Don't go back to your room," I whispered. "Let's sleep out here together."

He wiped the hair from my face, his hand moving down to my chin, and he kissed me.

Oh, that was a good reply.

He pulled back, his eyes on my lips. My hands slid down his

chest and around his warm torso, pulling him closer, and I kissed him right back, my mouth opening fully to his, inviting. I twisted a leg around his, pulling him against my body.

His fingers crept under my top, caressing my skin, and I let out a sigh, my lips trailing down his warm throat. I licked at the throb of his pulse, and an animal-like growl escaped his throat. He pushed up the fabric and raw molten need surged inside me, the urge to feel his skin against mine making me lightheaded. I gasped for air as his mouth planted searing kisses down my flesh to the wide waistband of my trousers, edging them down slowly.

Do this, yes, do this. You want this. You want him.

I raised my hips to help him, and he easily tugged them off.

His eyes caught mine, eyes that glimmered in the flickering candlelight, and my breath burned in my chest. I had no idea what he'd do next, but I knew that Turo would take me on a journey only he could.

Leaning over me, he stroked my center with the hard edge of his nose, and I cried out, my back arching. He sucked on the damp fabric of my knickers taking in my most sensitive flesh over the silk and a low moan escaped me, my body shuddering in his tight grip.

He tugged the fabric down my legs, hands stroking the inside of my thighs, spreading them open. I was bare to him, to the stars, to the night, to this raging desire that brewed between us. Brewed from the first moment we'd laid eyes on each other.

"Adri," his voice a raw whisper that simmered in my veins.

His hands swept up my body, and his fingertips found my scar, lingering there in its discovery. My pulse jolted and I twisted, taking that hand in mine, away from my scar. Away from all *that*.

Those fingers slid between my legs. I moaned out at the flare of pleasure, my hips arching off the cushion. A hand cuffed both my wrists, pinning me down. He had me where he wanted me.

"Turo..."

Those lips brushed my mouth, and my tongue met his in a

languid dance. He took his time, savoring me, us. We had all the time in the world, didn't we? And he was going to take it.

His thumb grazed my clit, and he murmured something against my throat which I didn't understand. His touch grew insistent, his breathing louder. Heat flushed my skin, and his mouth crushed mine again, our kiss turning fierce. The hunger between us roared. Wild, deep, streaked with red, red and dark blues. We were underwater in our own sea, the current powerful.

Turo released his hold on my wrists and his mouth sank between my legs. Another growl escaped his throat, vibrating against my flesh. My one leg hitched around his shoulder, my other foot pushing against the divan as I ground myself against his mouth shamelessly.

His tongue lavished over me, his mouth ripping pleasure from me. He was the pirate looting. He was the crusader conquering. My body trembled and twisted on the thick cushions, and his hand fastened tightly on my hip, keeping me still as two fingers dipped inside me. He blew a small breath in a tiny, careful circle over my wetness.

Burning eyes met mine. "You feel that, Adri?"

I couldn't answer, I couldn't think.

He fluttered his tongue over me, around the center of me, and I cried out sharply, my fingers tugging on his hair. He nuzzled and licked and kissed me with a focused, determined abandon. If only *I* could abandon everything, everything but *this*, this moment, these sensations and feelings he'd summoned.

Turo. My conjurer, my conqueror.

The wall towered over me. The one I knew so well. The wall that separated me from receiving, from taking. The wall closing me in, threatening. The wall I had carefully built for myself. That familiar tightness filled my chest, my throat, choking me. I stiffened, I pushed back, pushed everything back.

"Stop. Turo, stop!"

I twisted away from him.

Lost his mouth, his touch. Lost him.

Lost.

Everything was a blur.

"Adri?" Turo's hoarse voice cut through the loud, dull thud of my pulse.

I pressed my bare legs together, feeling the emptiness, the loss of him. A new kind of hollow. He cupped my bare rear, kissing the curve of my hip.

"Adriana..."

I shivered under the tender caress of his touch, his voice. I didn't deserve them.

"Did I hurt you, baby? Did I do something wrong?"

I folded up my body. "No, no, it's me. Please...please."

"I'm sorry," he whispered roughly. Water on my ashes.

"You have nothing to be sorry for. Please. Don't. Don't be nice to me."

"What are you talking about? I only want to make you feel good, Adri, and I wanted to feel that on me."

My skin heated. I'd never ever heard anything like that from any man. "It felt good. So good." I swallowed hard. "Too good."

"What does that mean? Why did you stop me?"

I sat up, grabbing the thin throw blanket from the arm of the divan, covering myself with it, mortification sloshing through me. "I'm sorry."

He took my hand in his. "There's no sorry if you're not comfortable. I went too far. I couldn't help myself. I'm the one who's sorry if I—"

I took my hand back. "It's me, Turo. I'm the problem."

"What? What problem? You're upset. Why?"

My attempt at a smile curled my lips, but it was a shaky, unsteady smile.

"Don't be embarrassed with me, Adri. You don't have to be." He planted a kiss on my knee. "I wanted you to come, to feel good, feel good with my mouth and hands on you."

I chewed on my lip. "The things you say."

"I mean them or I wouldn't say them."

I believed him.

He wiped a hand down the side of my face. "It's all right. Let me get you some water." Turo got up and went back into the room, to the small fridge. I pulled my trousers back on and he returned with a small bottle of water he'd uncapped, and I drank.

He fingered the ends of my hair, smoothing it over my shoulder. "I don't ever want you to be uncomfortable. Especially because of me."

I brought up my hand. "I wanted you to go far. I did. I like you very much. Very, very much." I took in a deep breath to release the tension, the heat of embarrassment, but it didn't work. His tender thoughtfulness was making me tense again, because I felt awful. Because I was twisted with regrets at not being able to embrace what he'd offered me after I'd invited him to it. To embrace him.

"Is it Alessio?" His eyes hardened like gleaming gemstones. "Have you talked to him? Has he threatened you or done something to make you afraid? Is there something you're not telling me about the two of you?"

Turo, the problem solver. He wanted an immediate analysis, black and white data, so he could find the solution and resolve the issue. He knew a piece was missing. He knew, and he cared.

But I couldn't tell him now. Not now.

I shook my head. "No, it's not Alessio. Nothing like that. I've told you everything about him and me." I chugged another mouthful of the cold water down my burning throat. Wiping at my lips, I squeezed a hand on his thigh. "Let me make it up to you—"

His jaw tightened, his eyes narrowed. "I don't want you to service me. Not like that."

Service. The word cut straight through me.

"When you're ready—" He put my hand over his bulging, stiff

269

erection and rubbed. My eyes fluttered, my insides clenched with liquid heat. "—he'll be ready for you. I want you on me because you can't get enough of me, not because of some sense of polite obligation."

He brushed my lips with his, a quick kiss on my forehead. "We both need sleep." He tucked the blanket around my body. "And you have to drive us all over the island again tomorrow, my lovely Räikkönen."

"You follow Formula 1?"

"Yes, why?"

"Not typical for an American, that's all."

"That's me, not typical."

"No, Turo, you're not."

He rubbed my leg over the blanket. "Can I hold you?"

My heart dipped. That he would say that to me after my having stopped him.

"Can I hold you?" fell from my mouth.

We stared at each other, neither of us sure what to say next. He took the water bottle and drank, draining it, tossing it on the table. Taking me in his arms, he lay next to me, curving his body around mine. I sank into his solid warmth, grateful for it, for him. My eyes closed, his steady heartbeat under my ear, setting my breath to its strong rhythm.

"The stars are so bright," he murmured. "So many stars."

Sleep sunk its teeth into me. Like Turo DeMarco had.

Silken fangs.

27

TURO

AN ICY HARDNESS had me in its grip.

I gulped in air, but there was none to be had.

Laughter down a dark tunnel. Loud and shrill. What direction? Where?

I ran but my feet were caught in muck. I fought to raise my leg higher but it was stuck. My mouth opened to yell. Nothing came out.

A violin screeched in the distance, shoving at me.

"Do this for me. Do this for me," Mauro's voice filled my ears.

"Do this for me. Do this for me," Luca's voice took over.

My mother's cool almost imperceptible smile flickered before me. My arm was too heavy to reach out to her, my limbs pushed through muck. I opened my mouth to speak, but my vocal chords wouldn't work. I strained, but only a grunt came out. She vanished.

The violin charged ahead. That laughter. Berezin touching Adri.

"Turo—Turo—"

I pushed my eyes open. Adri leaned over me, her hair a

curtain around us. My hands were clamped on her arms. My heart pounded like one of those goblet drums.

"A dream. Only a dream," she said.

I released her. "Sorry."

All of that inexplicable yearning I'd wrung dry and stuffed down deep inside me since forever had floated up to the surface, taunting me with its screeching as it always had like some loud, evil cartoon character I wanted to throttle. What I'd had to do on Berezin's boat had agitated the sediment I'd let settle inside me all these years. That dark, foul residue had come up from the bottom. It brewed, it loomed.

I rubbed at my eyes and glanced at my watch. I'd slept for two hours. The breeze was now cooler and damper, the quarter moon still hovering over us, a cut out in the sky. Adri's cold body was plastered against mine. Her spicy floral scent poked at my senses.

"You're cold," I said.

"So are you."

I embraced her, and she snuggled against my chest. My grip on her tightened, my pulse doing double time.

What the hell is that?

Quickly, I brought her inside to the bed and laid her on it, covering her with the quilt. She took my hand, her eyes holding mine.

And then it occurred to me.

There was only one explanation for my unusual reactions toward this woman. Heart pounding, pulse racing, cock at attention at all times. It wasn't just some hard attraction, the fierce desire to fuck her and be done with it, or the instinct to protect a young woman who was vulnerable and in danger. With her there were no mazes to figure out, no strategies to come up with, just her and me and—

She reached out and pulled me down on the bed with her and, fitting the quilt over us both, curled her body around mine.

I pressed my lips against her forehead, a swirl of heat filling me. This wasn't a passing impulse. I knew, because I had many, all the time.

There was only one reason.

Only one.

I was completely in her thrall. How the hell was I ever going to let her go?

My phone vibrated in my pocket, signaling a message. I got it out, flipped it open, my eyes squinting at the bright screen.

Where did you go, Romeo? You better bring Giulietta back if you know what's good for you - Luca

Luca.

I let out a heavy breath. I didn't get a message from the jilted lover, but from his brother. Although Luca had given me his guarantee for his uncle's word, although I had put my life on the line for the good of his business and reputation, I still needed to make nice with that asshole. Running off with his brother's pseudo-girlfriend wasn't the greatest idea. Was Adri my Helen of Troy?

The warmth and weight of her sleeping body pressed against mine. I wasn't bringing her back to that yacht unless she wanted to go. And she didn't want to go.

Luca Aliberti could go fuck himself.

28

TURO

Räikkönen was at it again.

First thing in the morning, behind the thick leather steering wheel of the Land Rover, Adri powered over a narrow and very high mountain road. The land was positively lush with green once we entered *Paleópolis* or "old city" as she'd translated as the mountain village's blue road sign whipped past us.

"This town was the capital of the island in the days of Alexander the Great," she said. "There's been years of excavation going on here and they've found homes, drainage systems, a marketplace. Look down."

My gaze darted down the steep cliff to a tiny cove of vivid, turquoise water.

"You see the strip of stone under the water?" she asked.

"Yes."

"That's the old harbor from before Alexander's time. It's sunk now, but it remains."

"Incredible." I craned my head once more to scan the steep mountainside dotted with ruins.

The wind whipped her hair around her face as she focused

on the sudden sharp curve in the road, her mouth tensing for a moment, her hand on the stick shift. "Still amazes me every time I see it. There was a temple built there for Apollo the sun god, and they say there may have been one for Dionysus as well."

"Really?" It was meant to be, my god idol was here.

The sharpness in my tone made her head turn. "You're familiar with Greek mythology?"

"Standard part of my schooling. I'm certainly appreciating it now," I replied. "Dionysus has always been a particular favorite of mine."

We passed through several villages, each separated by miles of road and rock and dry brush. The routes through the small towns were narrow, twisting lanes probably only meant for donkeys and carts in previous eras. Whenever another car approached, one of us would slow down or stop altogether to let the other pass. We sped through groves of olive trees, their small silvery green leaves shimmering in the hard sun. How many centuries, millennia had these groves survived?

Adriana turned off the main road, and we entered the village of Meníltes built up and over the side of a mountain.

"I thought we were headed for Chóra?" I asked.

A grin brightened her face. "There's something special in this village that I'd like to show you. I thought you'd enjoy seeing it, since you like mythology. To give you a hint, the name Meníltes is derived from the name "Maenads," the female followers of Dionysus."

"The groupies who'd be carried away by a religious ecstasy during those blow out parties of his?"

She laughed. "Yes, them."

Trees with thick leaves, abundant green, green, green was everywhere here. The lushness of the area was astounding after all the stony dry and rocky terrain of the rest of the island.

She said, "Here, there are lots of natural springs and waterfalls which is why it's so green. Very popular with hikers."

We parked by a church and got out of the jeep. "They say this church may have been built on top of the ruins of a temple dedicated to Dionysus," she said.

"Have archaeologists found the temple here?"

"No. But the legend is strong."

We descended low steps to one side of the church which opened to an elegant cobblestoned square. A row of ancient stone lion heads was embedded in a great stone wall, their maws fountains of spring water.

Adri's fingers played in the water running from a lion's head. "Legend has it that Dionysus would turn these spring waters into wine."

"Of course he did."

"He was world famous in his day. There's documentation of this ritual in ancient Roman history. Pliny, I think it was, wrote about it."

"Dionysus was the son of the almighty Zeus and a mortal girlfriend, right?"

"Yes, he was half god, half man. Zeus's jealous wife engineered a brutal attack on him by the Titans and they killed him. They tore him up and ate him, but his heart survived and he was resurrected somehow. I don't remember the details."

"Half god, half man," I murmured, running my fingers across the smooth ancient stone, hot under the sun's glare. "He experienced death and came back to party hard. Who doesn't admire the god of wine and good times?" I cupped my hand under the cold water and drank.

"He was a vicious god as well, you know," she said. "It wasn't all wine and carnal delights. With such indulgences come the consequences."

"Drunkenness."

"Which leads to criminal behavior, atrocities."

"True, but the pleasures and intense experiences his wine

provided—that euphoria offers a momentary sense of rapture, power even. It's freeing, inspiring."

"Yes, a piece of the divine for us mere mortals," she agreed. "A gift of fearlessness, confidence, joy. He wandered the world teaching the art of wine making. His ceremonies and celebrations were controversial even then. Wild celebrations in the mountains, the forests, reveling in the beauty of the world."

The cold spring water poured over my palm like a tiny waterfall. "He's the Liberator," I said.

"He is the Benefactor and Destroyer. He offers ecstasy as well as madness." Her gaze darted to me once more. "The ancient Greeks understood that duality very well, in all their gods."

"Dangerous, if you don't understand."

"Absolutely," she agreed.

I took her wet hand in mine. "Thank you for showing this to me."

"You're welcome." She smiled, a sweet smile full of satisfaction in having given me pleasure. A small gift she'd given me, and I wanted to save the ribbon and the ripped wrapping paper. I squeezed her hand.

We got back into the jeep and headed for Chóra on the opposite shore of the island, not too far from where we were. After fifteen minutes, we entered the town, the capital of Andros, and we slowed down in the sudden stream of traffic.

"We'll park here and walk," Adri said, backing into a tight space. "The main road is closed off to vehicles, and that's where the house is."

I took our two small suitcases out of the back, and we followed the wide lane of smooth, curved cobblestones. Adri's pace was quick, her body rigid, focused. She wanted to get to the house.

Adri explained that the town was built on a bluff of a long, thin peninsula with two coves on either side. From in between whitewashed buildings on either side of the commercial main street, pieces of bright blue sea flashed at me as we walked.

This was no ordinary island village. Some buildings were the traditional, simple whitewashed stucco with blue trim, others were neoclassical mansions of old with archways, terra-cotta roof tiles, massive coffered wooden doors with vintage brass knockers in the form of a hand or a lion's head. We passed a museum library housed in one mansion. Small white balconies with curled wrought iron banisters peered over us as we walked farther down the main road. The blue painted shutters and doors on almost every building reflected that rich Aegean sapphire, but a good number had a more turquoise color or a pale grayish blue tone as well.

The color of Adri's eyes.

Colorful potted flowers punctuated doorways on the whitened curbs. Old fashioned black iron street lamps, much like gas lamps of a bygone age were on every corner. Shop after shop with their old fashioned signage beckoned. Bakeries, pastry shops, cafés, souvenirs, jewelry, handmade ceramics. Outdoor cafés were everywhere.

Welcome to the Mediterranean.

She stopped at a tall, neoclassical mansion on a corner. Italian Renaissance style archways and columned terraces wrapped around the second floor. A carved marble lintel above the main entrance heralded another age. The wood shutters on all the windows were painted that beautiful pale ultramarine, and worn terra-cotta tiles shaped as great acanthus leaves dotted the eaves of the roof. The stucco covering the house was peeling in spots.

"This is my grandparents' house," she said. "The original house was farther down almost to the end of the town on the water by the castle."

"Castle?"

"Yes. The Venetian Lord who came and conquered built

himself a castle fort on the end of the peninsula, but the Germans blew it up during the war. The family salvaged whatever it could and bought this house and restored it."

Adri put a key in the lock, turned several times and pushed open the double main doors which looked like they belonged to a medieval estate. We stepped inside and entered another age. A Victorian style ornate brass lamp hung from a high ceiling. A delicate hand-painted mural of acanthus leaves swirled over the walls of the foyer. Black and white patterned ceramic tile brought us into the house, and a tall, stately, wood credenza with white marble details towered before us in the foyer.

Adri dropped the keys to the jeep and the house on the credenza, and I brought in our bags, pulling the heavy door closed behind us. She pushed open two tall, wood paneled doors painted in that same pale blue revealing a living room with antique upholstered chairs, settees, and carved heavy wooden chairs. Draperies hung over floor to ceiling windows, a large terra-cotta and blue antique rug lay in the center of the tiled floor.

The shutters had been opened and the light poured through the room revealing faded painted leaf motifs on the walls and along the ceiling. Although worn by time, time had stopped here in this house, and we were the gentle intruders.

A wooden model of a clipper ship in a glass case took pride of place on a small pedestal table in the center of the room. A very old portrait painting of an eighteenth or nineteenth century mustachioed man with an attitude hung on the pale yellow walls.

Adri stood motionless in the room, held captive by memories, by sounds, a grandfather's embrace, conversations. Meaningful and heartfelt words, castoff sentiments uttered years and years ago. Were they whispering to her now?

I came up behind her, a hairbreadth from her back. "Your home is beautiful," I said, nudging at the spell that bound her, not wanting to break it.

She blinked. "It is." She unlatched a vintage window pane. A flower-filled garden lay beyond. Stalks of lavender swayed in the hard breeze, sending us their fragrance.

Adri let out a breath. "I haven't been here—spent the night here—in ages."

A flare of heat sheared through me. We'd be spending the night here tonight and a few more. How would we be "spending the night," I wanted to know? After last night, I'd be treading gently.

As gently as I possibly could.

"Let's get changed and go for a swim at the castle. It will probably be quite chilly." Those eyes of hers glimmered with more blue than gray now, casting their magic—a mixture of shy, excited, and passionate—on me.

"Whatever you want," I said, my voice husky. "Let's do it." But I wasn't only referring to swimming. I meant *everything*.

She smiled, a vulnerable, truly happy smile. And here in this house, in that smile, I knew that I didn't care if she was hung up on Alessio. I didn't care that I didn't get the chance to confirm that Gennaro would talk to Mauro and play ball. I didn't care that Mauro was waiting to hear back from me. I didn't care that Luca and Alessio were probably furious. I didn't care that I hadn't decided on a return date for my airplane ticket.

For the first time in a long fucking time, I didn't care about any of the things I *had* to be caring about. There was only *now*. There was only this beautiful island, this incredible house, this gorgeous girl.

Girl. Yes, she was a girl, but also a wildly alluring woman. A woman whom I did not, could not, would not resist. She had resisted me last night, but something was troubling her, and I would find out what that was and exorcise it.

I drew her chin close to mine and planted a soft kiss on that remarkable mouth. She kissed me back, gently. My tongue slid against hers and she let out a small moan, her body relaxing into mine, mouth opening fully.

Yes, just where I want you. Wanting more, ready and waiting for me.

"Tell me," I breathed against her lips, lips that were damp, swollen, lips that wanted more of mine.

"Hmm?" Her eyelids fluttered, her tongue licking the seam of my mouth.

"The model ship. Tell me about it."

Her head pulled back, face reddening, and she let out that rich, rolling laugh. I loved surprising her. Did she think that I'd try to get down her panties again so quickly? *No, baby, not just yet.*

"My great-great-grandfather—well, I suppose four or five times back really—made this model with his father. That's him in the painting, by the way. Stefanos." She gestured at the portrait hanging on the wall. "He fought in the Greek War of Independence which started in 1821. And this is a model of a cutlass that one of his brothers commandeered in a naval battle in 1825 during the revolution. He fought alongside him on this ship."

"These facts must be seared in your brain."

"They are, and in my heart." She touched the edge of the model's glass case. "The Greeks were greatly outnumbered, but they triumphed, and what was left of the Ottoman fleet scattered south. There was another battle here earlier, in 1790, and another ancestor, an uncle of Stefanos's, was a captain in that battle for a famous Greek privateer who had a fleet of small ships."

"Privateer as in pirate?"

She shrugged in that nonchalant way of hers. "Merchant, pirate..."

"Entrepreneurs all. My kind of men."

"Yes." She smiled, her shoulders dropping, our eyes meeting. "Mine too."

I cleared my throat. "What happened in the 1790 battle?"

"The Greeks were outnumbered almost two to one, but still

managed to defeat the Pasha's ships." She tapped the edge of the glass case. "Andros has a colorful history. The island went from Venetian rule, to Ottoman Turk, to Russian. The islanders were able to manage treaties that gave them naval privileges. They exploited what little freedoms they had and created a small merchant fleet."

"So Andros did well on its own before the revolution was even over?"

"It did, even before the revolution. Greece endured almost five hundred years of Ottoman rule until they finally fought for their independence, and the island persevered, always producing and exporting a lot of goods—olives and olive oil, honey, even silk."

"Silk? Really?"

"Yes. But then the silk worms were hit by a disease that wiped them out in the late eighteen hundreds. After that it was all about the boats. Bigger ships were built, more routes opened up when other nations were busy fighting wars. The Andriots got organized and built a shipyard on another island nearby, whereas in other Greek islands the sailing industry died a slow death. After the Revolution, ships from Andros were traveling across the Mediterranean, the Black Sea, even reaching India, and later on, Latin America. That's when they began registering the majority of their fleets in England, to benefit from the global maritime market."

"And thus a dynasty was born."

"Many dynasties." She let out a breath, her teeth scraping over her lip. "Sorry."

"For what?"

"I must be boring you."

"I like your tales of history and adventure."

One would have assumed she only told tales of fashion shows in Paris and night clubs in Cape d'Antibes and Mykonos. Not this heiress. Not Adriana Lavrentiou.

A small smile curved her lips. "Some children get read fairy tales about princesses and knights, but I got told naval legends of sailors and captains and cannon fire and sword fights." Her eyes were bright, alive, consuming, her voice soft, low as if she were sharing a deep secret. "My grandfather would tell me all sorts of stories about the glory days of sailors in our family and all their brutal sacrifices along the way."

"I'd like to hear those stories."

Her gaze returned to the model ship. "It was my great-great-grandfather Stefanos and his brothers who realized that the future of shipping was in steam. They were one of the first to build large steam passenger and commercial cargo ships when sailing came to an end by the turn of the century. They did very well. And so did Andros."

"They had vision and stuck to it, and created a huge economic boom for one small island."

"Yes, for generations. Charities were created, hospitals, a nursing home, and schools. Of course there were major losses too, but the shipowners kept on and became what they are today. My grandfather was the first to have carriers and tankers built in Japan."

"Ah yes, oil." The easy distribution of oil was the backbone of modern shipping and a huge global business.

"Always oil," she said, letting out a breath, her face tightening.

I didn't like that coldness and anxiety seeping into her beautiful eyes, stiffening her voice. I took her hand. "Let's go for that swim. Show me the castle."

The niggling question of why Adri would be the target of a gangsta style assassination in public burrowed deeper in my brain. Had her father and his company pissed off a criminal organization or a corporate rival? Such a vulgar and cruel act, yet maybe not beneath someone who wanted to make a very clear and very public point.

Alessio's remark came back to me. That Adri had been

through a violent attack with her boyfriend. Maybe this shooting was connected to him? Maybe this boyfriend was the one she was hung up on?

One thing I was sure of, I wanted to know who the hell this guy was.

29

TURO

Two minutes down the cobblestone road, we were at the end of the peninsula that was Chóra. Her mother's family name was everywhere—in the tiny church a few steps from the house where she'd lit several thin tapers and kissed an icon, doing the sign of the cross, and in the small Naval Museum, another neoclassical mansion that was the very last building in town right on the water.

We wandered around the small, crowded galleries of the museum. Models of the family's first carriers and tankers, sailors' diaries, old compasses and knotted ropes, certificates and maps all documenting the rise of shipping in Andros. The views of the blue sea through each of the paneled windows on the second floor of the museum were nothing short of magnificent. A huge stone terrace spread out below with a large bronze statue at its center, a memorial honoring lost sailors.

"Our original house used to be just behind this one, but both were ruined by the Nazi bombings. This one was rebuilt and donated for the museum by another shipping family."

"And that's what's left of the Venetian castle?" I pointed towards the stone ruins set on a high rock which jutted out into the churning sea. The only way to reach it was over a single high and very round-arched stone bridge that remained.

"Yes, that's all that's left of it. We'll swim just below."

We left the museum, passed the grand terrace with the huge statue of the lost sailor, and trekked down steps chiseled from the rock to the small lagoon where waves splashed on slabs of that unusual mica stone glittering in the sunlight. An elderly man and a young boy swam there under the shadow of the arched medieval stone bridge which led to a high promontory of red rock—an islet actually—where the castle ruins towered above us.

Adri greeted the old man and his grandson, I presumed, as they got out of the water, and he smiled and chatted with her. He was pleased to see her. The man dried off the little boy and himself with a towel, put on their flip-flops, and holding the boy's hand, they climbed the stone steps, leaving us all alone in this lagoon of shimmering rock and choppy blue green sea.

Adri dropped her colorful canvas tote bag with our towels and water bottles, stripped off her short, burnt orange tunic as her long hair was swept up by the wind. A strapless, one piece, lime colored swimsuit with big gold hoops at each hip was tightly fastened over her long, curvy body.

I wanted my hands and mouth fastened on her just as tightly as that lucky lycra over her flesh. Images of the bound women from the Russian ship flashed in front of my eyes. Adri's body bound and waiting for me. Anticipating my touch. Needing my—

Dionysus, you're fucking killing me.

Don't let up, you bastard.

Adri's phone rang and she picked it up and read her screen. She texted back quickly and tucked the phone in the tote bag. She picked her way over the flat, slippery stones and slid into the swirling blue waters. I followed her, and the ice-cold water shorted my brain, my lungs crushed together. Sucking in air, I plowed through the surface. My skin prickled in the cool wind blowing over us. It was bracing and refreshing, better than a cup of Jamaican Blue coffee on a cold Chicago morning. I could see clear down to the bottom, to layers of rock and sand, schools of tiny fish darting past us. We plunged down below the surface. We swam in liquid sapphire.

Adri came up next to me, wiping the water from her face. "When I was a little girl, just like that boy, every morning my grandfather would wake me up early and we'd come down here for a quick swim then start our day. Right here, first thing, was always a must."

"I can see why."

"I hated having to wake up early, but it was well worth it."

I dove underwater and swam through her legs coming up on her other side. My hands went to her sexy ass and pulled her in to me.

She rubbed at the goose bumped skin of my shoulders. "You're cold?" Her legs encircled my middle, and my eager fingers crept under her bathing suit bottom, gripping flesh. Her eyes widened, fingernails digging into my neck.

"Not now." I grinned, planting a kiss on the top of a breast, her cool skin wet, salty. "You?"

"No," her throaty voice, just above a whisper. She adjusted herself in my hold, pulling herself closer to me, her hold tighter. If she'd shown one shred of discomfort I'd have let her go.

I don't want to let go.

The winds blew over us as we bobbed in the water, nestled against each other. Her hand absently rubbed the back of my neck, her serious gaze holding mine.

"Was that Alessio who texted you before?" I asked, breaking the silence.

"Yes. He asked how you were."

"Oh yeah? What did he say exactly?"

"What he always says, 'Be careful, *cara mia.*'"

I pulled her in against my cock, and she let out a tiny gasp. I rubbed her body up and down mine, and her eyelids dropped, her lips parted.

"Are you being careful, Lovely?" I asked.

Her breaths grew ragged, a moan escaping her as my hand cupped an ass cheek, a finger trailing along her crack. Her eyes flared. "Not especially."

"Neither am I. And I fucking like it."

I bit the trim of her bathing suit top and suckled a curve of her soft flesh. She hissed out air, her body flexing, pressing into mine. My hand slid up her body—it needed that tit. Her eyes glinted at me all the while, and she plunged us underwater. I only tugged her close once more and we kissed, breaking through the surface of the cold blue water. The warmth of the bright sun poured over us, making our cool sapphire bath turquoise.

I released her and she pushed back from me, eyes dancing as she wiped back her slick, wet hair. Our eyes locked as we circled one another in the water. I wasn't being careful, I didn't want to be careful. I liked her, I wanted her. I'd have her. But a tight coil spiraling in my veins told me this was different.

She was different.

"Come, let me show you the castle." She lifted up out of the water, and I groaned at the sight of that delicious body of hers streaming with water, smooth skin gleaming in the sun. I'd never tire of the sight. We dried off with her thick towels.

As I tied my sneakers, I eyed the high arch of the stone bridge connecting the edge of the rocks where we stood to the islet jutting out into the sea. "Adri—"

"Yes?" She shoved her feet in sneakers she'd pulled out of her tote bag. "What is it? Are you afraid of heights? My mother is and would always refuse to watch us climb the bridge. Even watching makes her dizzy."

"No."

I didn't have a fear of heights. But suddenly a fear of something had me in its icy tentacles. The fear of something happening to her. One slip off that bridge. One—*Jesus Christ, shut the hell up. Stop. What the fuck is wrong with you?*

"Don't worry." Her face softened as she slid on her dark brown sunglasses. "I've done it many times before. Since I was a little girl."

"Have you brought many boys up there?" I asked.

"My brother."

"Men?"

Her lips tilted up. "My grandfather, my father."

A sudden brisk wind kicked up, groaning through the stones, whipping her hair between us. The Aegean winds wanted their sea goddess on their cliff rocks.

"Please, Turo, I want to show it to you."

That coil of warmth unspooled in my chest at the gentle yet urgent tone in her voice. "I want to see it," I said, and her face split into a grin. A red hot little ping pong ball shuffled through my insides at the sight.

She went on ahead of me, making her way up the steps made of stacked long, flat island stones. Her fingers gripped the smaller rocks that made up the base of the arch as she dug the toes of her feet in and pulled herself up. I followed her.

Up, up, up.

The bridge was small, the arch very steep, and there were no railings. I imagined there had to have been other bridges here to serve the Venetian Lord and his army who'd built this castle fortress, but only this one had survived.

We made it to the top, gulping in deep breaths as we straightened our bodies, which almost felt awkward and unstable there up high, the winds blowing, the bridge narrow. I took in the immensity of the sea. Everything seemed grander from up here.

"Quickly now," Adri said as she stepped lightly going down the other side of the arch. She reached the stone platform at the base and held a hand out to me, and my pulse skittered. I took her in like a breath of sea air—hair flying, muscles of her legs flexed, shoulders tense, eagerness stamped on her face, and that long arm stretched out to take me with her.

Our escape, our adventure. Together.

I clapped my hand in hers and she firmly pulled me toward her. "Ready?"

Yes, yes, yes.

"Ready," I replied.

We climbed up a steeper series of rock piles that were the fragments of the old castle wall and reached a tall metal pole where the Greek flag flapped persistently in the violent wind. Ambling over patches of thorny bushes and stones, we finally made it to the castle ruins. I took her hand in mine and we went inside. I wanted to feel her excitement, the urge to be connected to it physically, to her, was overwhelming.

Blasted high in one wall was a huge hole, an open window to the sky. We climbed up to a ledge just under it and swallowed in the view of the entire town laid out before us in one long expanse of whitewashed houses, accents of blue and terra-cotta, domed churches, the whitecaps of the turbulent water on either side.

Adri scrambled down off the ledge and up to another on the opposite wall. A tiny white lighthouse stood proudly on a slim chunk of broken rock, looking as if a huge axe had fallen upon it and sliced off large hunks of its foundation, narrowly missing the lighthouse itself.

"Another family donated the money to have it rebuilt after it was destroyed in the war. The rock was much larger before, this big chip was all that was left."

"It's a humble little thing, but noble."

"And it does its job very well."

I turned toward the horizon. The infinite Aegean stretched out before us, a never-ending sweep of churning cerulean blue filled my vision. The ancient sea of fables and epic tales.

"Must have been something to live up here all year round," I said.

"The Venetians built three castles on the island. This one was built by the governing Lord, the Doge's nephew."

"If the Doge of Venice gave it to his own nephew, Andros was important to him."

"Marino Dandolo," she said in a perfect Italian accent.

"There's a colorful name."

"He was a colorful character. Mean. Didn't last long. Decades of infighting followed his demise."

"Fool."

The wind howled softly through the stones. We sat down next to each other in the ruins. The ruins of so many battles and wars. Now, for us, this castle was a refuge of raw tranquility. A temple.

We sat close, our arms pressed against each other's, our legs. Like children spellbound by the sea. Up here, I was a million miles away from everything I'd built around me over the years. Like this castle fort, all my twisted truths, my white lies, the blood staining my hands, were stones piled high, creating walls. Walls with gaps, holes, the wind tearing through. Walls that were subject to assault, walls that crumbled, walls that had not withstood the truths of time and the ravages of war. So many wars.

"Turo?"

"Hmm?"

"What are you thinking?"

I let out a breath. "How I love listening to your stories."

And I did. That elegant, exotic voice, the way all her features —eyes, mouth, hands would engage in the telling. Was it Adri's way? Was it a Greek thing? From what I'd experienced so far, they were a dramatic people, very expressive. But it was obvious how connected she felt to the stories. They were important to her.

"I love that you enjoy them," she said quietly.

I leaned into her. "Tell me another."

"I'll tell you my favorite."

"Shame we don't have wine."

"But then how would we ever climb down?" A soft giggle

escaped her lips. Those lips. I wanted to drink wine from those lips.

My mouth touched hers. A brief, soft kiss. Salt and sweet air and humid earth.

Her hand wrapped around my arm. "We'll have a lot of wine this evening, I promise."

"Good. Now, tell me your favorite story."

She turned back to the sea again. "My great-great-grandfather, Stefanos, had fallen in love with a girl here in town. She came from a fine family in the silk worm trade. Natalia was her name. She had Venetian blood in her family and was quite wealthy. Stefanos's family had several small merchant boats, but they weren't as wealthy or as cosmopolitan. Natalia's family worked with the Ottomans, so they enjoyed many privileges. Stefanos's family did not. Furthermore, Stefanos was a bastard son. But none of that stopped him from asking for her hand in marriage.

"Her father refused him, so the two lovers met in secret. The night before he left on his ship she gave him a special gift to use in battle and to remember her by because he might get killed, might never come back."

"What was the gift?"

"A dagger."

"A dagger?"

"A two hundred year old family heirloom from Venice. A simple thing, it's been said. No jewels or fancy sheath, only an engraved silver handle on a sharp blade. Stefanos took it and wore it in his great wide belt along with his pistols and sword."

"And he took the dagger with him to war?"

"Yes, and the naval battle was a success—out here in the straights between Andros and Tinos. He survived that battle and many more with that dagger. But in the meantime, Natalia had been married off to another man. A much older man who was a very wealthy silk worm farmer and exporter like her father.

When Stefanos finally came home, Natalia had just given birth to her second child and was dying. He wasn't allowed to see her, of course, but he did anyway. The legend goes that he climbed up into her room and she died in his arms.

"They loved each other, and yet they hadn't been allowed to be together, and now death separated them forever." She heaved a sigh. "Eventually, after the war, Stefanos went on and married another girl, but Natalia's family realized the dagger was missing. They accused him of stealing it. He denied it and kept it hidden. It was his precious treasure, his connection to his great love. But they threatened him, his life, his business, his new family.

"The day his wife gave birth to their first child, a son, he came here to this cliff with the dagger. It didn't belong to anyone but him and Natalia, and he wasn't going to give it back, wasn't going to give in. That dagger had symbolized all his hopes and dreams for a future in a free, united Greece with the woman he loved. So he came here to that spot—" she pointed to the edge of the cliff down below. "— and threw that dagger in the sea."

Her voice caught. Her words, the vivid images she'd painted drifted into the wind, to the wild blue water below us, beyond. I squeezed her hand in mine and she squeezed back.

Adri said, "For me, throwing that dagger in the sea was his declaration of love for her, but also for life itself. He was a realist. He marked an end to that past and also marked a new beginning. When I was little, I always imagined that he must have wanted to keep it, to hang on to that part of himself that was Natalia, even though he would never have her. But he knew he needed to let go of that broken dream, that lost future, and move forward."

"Jesus said, 'Let the dead bury the dead.'"

"Yes, you must carry on, and not dwell on that which is no more," she said. "At funerals, Greeks say to each other '*Zoí se mas*'—'To us, Life'. We're reminding each other that our grief becomes remembrance as we carry on. Life doesn't stop for the living, and the dead are beyond us, elsewhere. Stefanos knew that clinging to the past was useless. He was alive, and he had to live that life.

"The dagger had brought him victories but now it also symbolized his greatest tragedy. To return it to her family would have been a form of defeat and would have exposed them both and potentially harmed Natalia's children. No good would have come of it. Now he had a new wife and his own child he needed to honour. He had a future to build."

"He let the dagger go on his terms," I said.

"You understand, don't you?" Her eyes softened.

"I do."

"I like to think Stefanos was a terribly soulful romantic, and this was his way of keeping her close. I always imagined him coming out here late at night or at sunrise, and standing just down there at the edge, pleased that his beloved Aegean was preserving their dagger, keeping it safe, right here, by his home. That was comforting, satisfying. That was enough."

"That was a different kind of victory."

Her eyes glimmered, filling with water. "Yes," she breathed.

"And then he was all in with his new life?" I asked.

"By all accounts he was a loyal husband, good father, and obviously a very astute businessman."

"Good man." I sniffed in air. "Did a vendetta begin between the two families after that?"

"How very Greek of you."

"It's the Italian in me. It comes out once in a while after the Irish has its say."

"Ah, the Irish are soulful poets and musicians just like the Greeks." She wiped her fingers through the side of my hair and my scalp prickled at the contact. "There was no vendetta, but there was a lot of hostility for years between the families. But that stopped when the silk trade was destroyed and Stefanos encouraged them to start over by investing whatever they had left into their own shipping business. The island was making a name for itself, and it was now or never for them."

"He had vision."

"He did."

"And did Natalia's family do it? Did they succeed?"

"They ended up becoming a strong merchant marine company, but not strong enough. Years later, Stefanos's sons bought them out."

I laughed. "Good for them." I stroked her hand.

"Yes, good for them."

"And how did Stefanos do in the end?"

"He lived a very long and healthy life. He had four sons and two daughters. He and his brother created a very successful maritime company, employing islanders, traveling the world." She fingered a pile of small stones at her feet. "He threw that dagger into the sea and went on to create something new and vitally important for his family and his island. His country even."

"Which still prospers today."

"Yes."

"And the dagger? Was it ever found?" I asked.

"Never. Men in the family have always dove down to try to find it, it's a secret tradition, a rite of passage. But the waters here at this cliff are deceptively clear, yet deep and moody blue. Calm, then wild. Lots of underwater rocks and caves. It's never been found." She grinned, a pleasant memory flickering across her face.

"What is it?"

"I tried, once."

"Of course you did." I rubbed her hand in both of mine.

Her eyes flared. "But I hope it's never found."

"Why? Wouldn't you like to have it?"

"No. It belongs to the sea that he loved so much, to the island they both loved. It belongs right here, here where they would meet in secret. Not behind a glass case, with people staring at it, a monetary value slapped on it. I know of its existence, and I know it lies here undisturbed, and I'm glad. I want Natalia and Stefanos's lost love, their unfulfilled hopes and dreams respected, their broken hearts healed and united in another time, another place beyond here. I sometimes wish there is such a place, an alternate universe where broken dreams are at peace."

"I don't think there is, baby."

Her face lifted and watery eyes met mine.

Something pinched in my chest, and I brushed the tears off her heated face. "Hey, what is it?"

"I worry that if the dagger's ever found and disturbed from its resting place, it will be our downfall. I used to imagine there was a sea nymph down there who kept the dagger safe for Stefanos and Natalia and cursed those who tried to take it."

"Is there a curse attached to it?"

"There is. First loves go unfulfilled for us or lost by some tragedy." She pressed her lips together. "They don't last. And it's been true from Stefanos on down through to my mother and me."

"For you?" I asked.

She wiped at an eye that was brimming with tears. "And for me."

There it was. I wanted to know, I wanted to take that pain from her and toss it in that sea. "Do you think many first loves stay together in our modern times?" I asked. "I think it's rare. The world now is a much busier place, a crazy interconnected place. So many distractions, so many choices unlike in Stefanos's time."

"It's a shame."

"Ah, who's the soulful romantic now?"

Her face was streaked with red. "Did you have a first love?"

"I thought I did, but I don't think it was."

"You *thought*?"

"She played me for a fool, I got over it quickly. A sour experience all around."

"Sorry."

"I let my loneliness and my hormones get the best of me." I cleared my throat.

She only nodded, her gaze sliding back to the sea as she grew still. Was her pain still fresh? I wanted to know. I wanted to wipe his memory from her so she could see only me, feel only me, my hands on her flesh, my cock thrusting inside her.

Selfish bastard. Yeah, that's right.

"How about you?" I asked.

"I've never told anyone," she said, her voice almost eerie. "Not everything. Not the whole truth."

30

ADRIANA

"TELL ME ABOUT HIM." Turo rubbed a hand down my back.

We'd only known each other a handful of days, but we'd spent them all together. I knew Turo would listen and not judge.

I took in a deep breath. "His name was Grigori." *There, you said his name out loud for the first time since forever and you survived.* "He was a graffiti artist and a musician. A rap singer. An anti-fascist, politically active demonstrator against government corruption."

Turo's head slanted. "How did you meet him?"

"At a rave party he was DJ'ing in Athens. Very talented. Very attractive."

"What did your parents think?"

"My parents were not amused. Especially my mother. But I didn't care. They initially didn't take much notice, hoping it was a fling. But I couldn't get enough of him. He was everything I wasn't, and everything I wanted. Outspoken, did what he believed in. He lived by his own rules, there were no rules. I liked that.

"His friends didn't like me. I was the spoilt rich girl slumming it. The high society party girl dipping low. His family was very uncomfortable with me. Many of his friends said I ruined his street credibility, his image. But Grigori didn't care about all that. He was anti all that to begin with."

"The press must have found it all incredibly scintillating and juicy," Turo said.

"God yes. My mother was convinced I was destroying my life." Our endless shouting matches, the stinging accusations, fiery eyes, demands, slamming of doors all replayed themselves behind my eyes.

"Do you two not get along?" Turo asked.

"No, we do. It's a long, complicated story."

"It usually is," he said, his gaze returning to the sea.

"I wasn't rebelling against her. My being with Grigori wasn't about her."

"It wasn't any kind of rebellion?"

"A rebellion over rigid expectations and a rigid way of thinking, but at the core of it was my love for him. I left university in Switzerland to live with him in Athens. We lived in his small apartment in one of the most dangerous neighborhoods in the city. I didn't have access to any of my money at the time, so I found a job in a bar, which I hated, but we needed the money. He usually performed in that bar, in that neighborhood. We were together and that's what mattered to me. I wasn't thinking about tomorrow or the next day."

"You did all that? Turned your back on—"

"I did. Being with Grigori was never romantic nights in fancy hotels, sex on high thread count sheets, fancy gifts or trendy cocktails and gourmet dinners. We were on his dirty sofa in his shitty apartment, on the beach on insufferably hot nights drinking cheap beer, at underground clubs. It was fun at first, liberating."

"What happened?"

My mouth was dry, I licked my lips to prepare the way for the words that had to come. "He was always out. Either with his mates composing music, practicing, working to make money, or running political meetings. I thought us living together would bring us closer, make things easier, but it didn't. I had to fit in to his schedule, his world, and I tried. That week, he'd been preparing for a performance and he was never home. I got upset, we fought. I insisted that we spend one night together, and he finally agreed.

"I took him to a nice neighborhood, to one of my favorite bars for a drink. Just one drink. He didn't like it, he didn't complain but it was written all over his face. He endured it, just wanted it over with. I felt like an idiot, but I kept trying to tell myself it was fine. It was just one night.

"We left the bar and were walking to where he'd parked his motorcycle, when I saw a friend of mine and I went over to say hello. It was so good to see a friendly face. But Grigori continued walking. He'd started his bike, waiting for me. Suddenly a group of men surrounded him, yelling and cursing. They were members of the new ultra right-wing party. Neo-nazis in black hoodies. They'd followed us there. I found out later that they'd been watching him for weeks and had been tracking us all night."

"What happened?"

"They argued and attacked Grigori with knives. All of them. He bled to death right there on the sidewalk in front of all these fancy bars and restaurants. A river of blood. His blood, everywhere. Terrible shouting and screaming, cars, motorcycles. I tried to go to him, but I couldn't even see him in the crowd. People were on a rampage, setting fires in the street, breaking shop windows, looting. Someone threw a molotov cocktail, and it exploded next to me."

"Is that how you got that scar?"

"Yes." *The scar I hadn't wanted him to touch.* "His blood stained those fancy streets, bringing a rebellion to an unsuspecting part of the city. Demonstrations and protests broke out all over Athens, the entire country," I continued. "It was an awful time. They turned him into a political martyr. But Grigori wasn't affiliated with any political party. He simply told the truth about what people went through in their daily lives. He held a cracked mirror up to the waste and the exploitation."

"And in the end, he was the one exploited."

"In the worst way, and it's my fault. If I hadn't picked a fight with him, made him go out, taken him there, he might still be alive. If I hadn't—"

"Adriana, stop."

"I played a part in Grigori's death. I made him more notorious than he already was, made him a target. Him going to that neighborhood, where he wasn't protected by his own—and they turned that beautiful neighborhood into a war zone, and it's all because of me."

"Adri, you didn't make those extremist hoodlums murder him and go on a rampage."

"They viciously slaughtered him right there in public, on the street, like an animal."

"Because they're animals."

"And I'm a fool, a selfish, self-centered fool."

"No, you're not. Stop." He tugged on my hand, willing me to listen to him. "What happened after?"

"The funeral was a horror, more like a political rally. His family was in pieces, I was booed. The press was rabid for me. The day after the funeral, my parents sent me back to Geneva. That was two years ago. I finished uni, worked in London in between and after for a bit, and I came home this past Christmas, and stayed on. For the media I'm the country's tragic little rich girl who wears a black tiara."

"Black?"

"The 'Bad Luck Princess,' they call me—'bad fate' is the literal translation. They put me in a comic book like that. Black raccoon eyes, black crown, black heart spray-painted on a long red dress. One magazine did a full list of every man I'd ever dated in the past comparing them to Grigori. It was awful. I stopped going out and agreed to this arrangement with Alessio."

"So you gave up?"

My back stiffened. Yes, I'd given up. "I made a choice."

His jaw set. "You're too young for that, Lovely."

"I don't feel young, Turo. I feel worn out."

"Adri—"

I touched his beautiful lips with my fingers. "This is why last night was difficult for me."

"But what about you and Alessio?"

"That's different. At first it was fun, and I was usually drunk when we had sex. He never pushed me, he's very protective. It's always been casual and comfortable with us."

"The sex?"

"I—" My tongue stumbled, my face heated.

"Say it."

"I don't completely let go and enjoy it."

"You've been faking it with Alessio?" his voice was calm, controlled. A scientist gathering information and data.

"Not always. Sometimes. He gets hurt if I don't enjoy myself, and I hate disappointing him. He's good to me. He's a very good friend. I try, but then I get caught up in my head, and I pull back."

"You pull back?"

"My heart's not in it."

"Neither is your body." His sharp gaze chewed on me, the weight of those words, his tone burned over my flesh. "He hasn't realized?"

"Maybe, but he's never pressured me or pushed."

His eyes flashed, his mind whirred and clicked with this information. "Huh."

"Was that irony?" my voice snapped.

"That was re-assessment." His penetrating gaze bored through me, and my heartbeat skidded at its fierceness.

"And you?" I asked.

"What about me?"

"How did being lied to by your girlfriend, cheated on, I imagine, change you? Did it make you want to find someone new and start fresh? Fall in love again?" My voice came out sharper than I expected, and I regretted it instantly.

"No," he ignored my defensive tone. "It made me never want to trust another female. To never let a woman interfere with my work. With who I am. I didn't want to make that mistake again."

"So you raised a fine mesh screen around yourself."

"Exactly. My criteria for females became convenience and indulgence."

"Have you ever admitted that before? Said it out loud?" I asked.

"No," he said.

"Your convenience, my comfort," I declared. Our white-washed truth.

"Adri—"

"I did all this with Alessio for relief, self-preservation, but instead, it's become another gold cage with another fluffy pillow inside for me to lay on. Another way to hide. But I feel trapped. I don't think I want to be there any longer."

"Have you ever said that out loud before?" he asked.

I shook my head.

"Get out of that cage, Adri," he whispered, squeezing my hand. "Get out."

Our gazes locked, our breaths, thoughts. We'd crossed a line together, that thick line we'd both so carefully drawn around ourselves. And it was there, in that moment, that I knew Turo DeMarco and I would keep crossing lines, keep daring each other, and I'd keep feeling this breathlessness, this terrifying and marvelous storm of risk and possibility coursing through my blood, bumping up my heartbeat.

And I was right.

31

TURO

THAT AFTERNOON we shared a pizza and too many beers in town and then went to bed early. The fatigue had finally caught up with us.

"Why don't we wake up early tomorrow morning and see the sun rise up at the castle? Start our day off right."

"Are you sure?" Her voice had that tentative quality, but I could tell she was excited. Pleased. And that pleased me.

"Yes."

"I'd like that." Her shoulders bunched together for a moment, as if she were squeezing herself. She touched my arm. *"Kálli níxta."*

"Goodnight," I murmured as she made her way to her bedroom, and I headed to mine.

Adri woke me up in the morning, a hand on my shoulder. "Turo, do you still want to go?" she whispered.

"Yes," I replied in the dark. "When we get back, you make the Greek coffee."

"Deal."

We made our way through the narrow, quiet cobblestoned streets, the day's possibilities lacing through the chilly air. Stray cats silently watched us as we strode toward the end of the town. We climbed the stone bridge, the water slapping against the rocks below us.

Once inside the castle, Adriana and I sat together, facing the sea, the lighthouse outlined by a sky aglow in burnt yellow, powdery blues, and an impossibly innocent pink. Rising to the surface, flaring all around us. It was ours, we were alone on top of the Aegean Sea.

"So beautiful," she murmured.

The wind was gentler this morning, but when it kicked up, a light howl sounded through the ruins, making me look over my shoulder as if someone else was here with us. Ghosts of the past. Maybe our intrusion before the first light of dawn had unsettled them.

An icy chill crawled over me, and I wrapped an arm around Adri, pulling her close. Her warmth settled against me as the heavy, blood red orange ball of the sun rose steadily, swiftly in the sky, blazing the pale sea with colored light.

"Are we supposed to make a wish or something as the sun rises or is that when the sun sets?" I whispered.

"I don't know."

"Screw it. Make a wish anyway."

"All right. I want to take control of myself again. Be that person I used to be. I don't know how to get her back."

"Maybe you shouldn't go back, Adri. Maybe you're someone else now, and you should find *her*. Embrace her."

Her gaze slid to mine, the yellow pink light flooding her face.

"Is that a new idea, Lovely?" I whispered.

"Yes."

I rubbed her arm. "Make something that's yours. Make your own luck. Like your ancestor Stefanos did."

"Have you done that?" she asked.

My head jerked.

"No answer?" she asked.

"We're talking about you now. And you need to stop functioning and live. Live big."

"Live big," she repeated as if it was something only crazy
Americans said.

"Yeah, live big. And you have it in you. First of all, you turned
your back on school, your family's expectations, and the high life
to be with a man you were in love with. That's pretty fucking fearless from where I'm standing. You were all in on all levels. No
shame, no regrets, no doubts. Look at what you accomplished
with Alessio's party."

The rosy pink and orange light shimmered over her as she
shrugged.

"No, no. Don't do that. It was designing, planning, organizing
every detail, the chemistry of it. You excel at it. That wasn't just
some good time. It was a business venture, a remarkable publicity
event. It was theater, and it was a success because of you. I know,
I've been to a long line of these events. You brought something
special to the table, Adriana, and you left your mark. You know
what else? You used your fame and notoriety for a purpose. Your
own purpose. You did that. That's powerful. That's power. Think
about that."

I'd rendered her speechless.

"Own that, baby." My lips brushed the side of her face. "No
matter what you choose to do, Adriana, you will be glorious."

"Glorious?" She said the word as if it were comical.

My fingers dug into her neck and she winced. "Yes, glorious.
You are very, very capable of doing whatever you put your mind
to. You just have to want it badly enough." I wanted to inspire her.
Wake her up. I could start with my fingers, my mouth, my cock.

"Ah, beautiful," she said.

I followed her gaze. The sun shone in the sky now. No more
pinks, and rich oranges. Bright gold light. The day had begun,
and it was no longer ours alone. No longer our quiet secret.

I kissed her, her eyes widening at my slow assault. Tasting, exploring. She opened to me, making little sounds that I drew into my mouth and swallowed whole.

"Turo," her voice came out low and hoarse.

I slid my forehead against hers. *Say it, you know you want it.* "Go farther with me, Adri."

The blue in her eyes flared for just a second. "What do you—"

"Are you attracted to me?" I asked.

"You know I am."

"Say it."

"I'm attracted to you."

"How attracted?"

"Very," she breathed.

"How?" I demanded. I needed to hear it, wanted to hear her say it, her words.

Her fingers gripped the back of my neck. "I can't stop thinking about you. About how I feel when you touch me, when you look at me. Your looks burn right through me."

"How do I make you feel?"

"Naked." She let out a nervous laugh. "Spellbound to you, to something I've never known before. Yet at the same time utterly clear-headed. I can't explain it in words. I even touched myself thinking of you."

Fuck yes. "When?"

"On the boat before we left for the party."

A noise rumbled in my throat. "Did you come?"

She nodded. "A little."

"A little?"

"I stopped it."

Hell no. She needed to be coming and screaming and writhing with the force of it. The force of me.

I tugged on her hair. "You wanted me to kiss you that night in Athens. You made that happen. Why? Because you thought you'd never see the tourist from America again?"

"That's right. A risk without consequence."

I lifted her chin. "I'm your consequence, baby." I licked the seam of her mouth and she let out a moan. "Do you like my kisses?" I breathed against her lips.

Her eyes flared. "I love your kisses."

"How do I kiss you?"

"Like you want all of me right the hell now. Like we don't have tomorrow."

"On this island, there is no tomorrow, only now."

Since those hours on Evgeny's boat, the adrenaline constantly outraced the blood in my veins, but my blood just caught up. Heat filled me, driving through me; a euphoric calm. I brought her in front of my body, my arms circling her, and pressed her back against my chest.

"The night of the shooting, when we spent the night on the boat—" I nuzzled her neck and she shuddered in my hold. "Did you and Alessio fuck?" The evil me wanted to know.

"No, I took half a sleeping pill and slept."

My fingers lazed a trail around a breast, around a nipple which was already hard as a pebble. My lips skimmed her throat, a finger following down the warm slope and back up again, tracing her lips. "You want me to kiss you now?"

"Yes..."

She slanted her head to mine, and my teeth nipped at the delicate skin at the base of her neck. She shivered again, and I pulled her closer. Adri was a wine spiced with passion, laced with vulnerability and a very slight hit of shy, and I breathed in that aroma, tasted that full-bodied richness. It mesmerized me, filling my senses with delicious possibilities.

When I'd first laid eyes on her, I'd assumed she was the jaded, wealthy Euro party girl, an easy pick, a fun diversion. She wasn't that, she was so much more. An unexpected *other*. I wanted her more than anything or anyone I'd ever wanted before.

She'd stopped time by bringing us here, and Andros had enclosed us in its veil. Had stopped the clanging of swords in my head, the *poff* of gunpowder, the rip of that violin, that horrible cheering of a greedy, bored mob intent on blood.

I'd been inside that fear, I'd ridden it, and it had stripped me, stripped pieces of me I'd always taken for granted, had cultivated. But here, now, right now with Adriana, that fell away, didn't gnaw on me, drain me. It was me and her on this rock. That was it, and that was all that mattered.

"Go farther with me, Adri," I whispered, my voice rough. "For however long we have."

"You are willing to get uncomfortable with me?" she breathed.

"Yes."

She turned in my arms and our eyes met. We held on to each other on that cliff in a rich silence, the seagulls cawing and dipping over the choppy Aegean. She took my fingers and put them in her mouth and sucked on them.

My fucking heart stopped.

She brought my hand down between her legs, inside her shorts, past her panties. My fingertips grazed wet.

I let out a groan. "Are you sure?"

"Touch me."

"Don't fake with me. Don't. I'll know."

"I want this with you," she breathed. "I want you. For real."

Her breathing got heavier, her eyes darker. Heat spiraled in my chest.

"Say it, say it again, dammit."

She took in a breath on a hiss. "I want you."

"Again."

"I wa—"

I claimed her lips, my pulse spiked as my fingers dove in her hot silk, claiming *her*.

Her hips rocked into my touch. I touched her secret hollows, and her molten eyes burned into mine; we met in that sliver between raw truth and madness. A fever rose inside me, and I wanted more of it. Craved it. Her cries echoed in the stone ruins around us. Clutching my arms, she ground into my hand, her low moans stirring a foreign ache inside me. I would give her whatever she needed. And she needed. Oh, she needed.

"Yes," I whispered against her skin. Her jaw slackened, her eyes gleamed and their fierce light heated my skin. "Stay with me, baby. Feel it. Take it as it comes at you. A wave in the sea, a turn in the road." I nipped at the delicate skin under her jaw. "Take it."

She trembled in my hold, inside and out, and with a sharp cry and eyes clenching shut, she burst on my fingers, my face buried in her warm throat. My Aphrodite had come, had danced in the rhythms of the pleasure I'd composed for her, and she soared in my arms and took me with her. I had given that to her, given it *back* to her. She'd tasted the wine again after so long.

My wine.

We held each other, my heart careening wildly in my chest.

I wanted to drink more wine from her.

My hand cupped her pulsing wet pussy. Claiming, treasuring. Owning it. Yes, this pussy was mine now, this glorious body. *Adri.*

She took my mouth, and we sealed that pact.

That morning on that rocky bluff, high above ancient blue waters, in the stony ruins of conquerors' ambitions and pirates' bloodlust, we held each other, breathing in the salty sweet sea air, and listened to our hearts whisper of what had been, and hum with what could be.

32

TURO

As PROMISED, Adri made us Greek coffee once we got back to the house. "You like it?" she asked, sipping from her small cup as she sat down with me at the kitchen table.

"Hmm." I took another long sip of the sweet coffee and held her gaze, my tongue swiping at my lip from a trace of the thick *crema*.

"Mind you, don't drink it to the very end. The coffee settles at the bottom of the cup into a mud," she said.

Her blue gray eyes were filled with a tense kind of vulnerability. The knowledge of our intimacy, my touch on her, her sharing that part of herself with me—that part she hadn't shared in so long with anyone. She didn't seem embarrassed or awkward, but pleased.

That unabashed look in those eyes told me something else. Those eyes lingered on me, swimming with warmth and fascination, and I'd put that there. Heat circled through my chest and it had nothing to do with the hot coffee I was drinking. This was intimacy, wasn't it? Delicate and intense, shared, private.

I wanted more.

"What's the plan for today?" I asked.

"Beach."

"Ah." I took another sip. "And maybe after...beach?"

"Yes, good idea." Her lips formed that sexy grin. "And then we could...beach."

We finished our coffee, changed, and stopped at a bakery for sesame seeded goodies and bottles of water to bring with us. My eyes moved around the small store, the open doorway as she placed our order. A man in jeans and a brown leather jacket stood across the street smoking and watching the bakery. His gaze suddenly shifted down the road. I'd noticed him earlier a few blocks from the house.

"We're going to hire a boat to take us to a remote beach just north of Chóra," Adri said as we left the bakery.

Áxla, she told me, was probably the finest beach on the island and not too far away. Driving there was next to impossible as the dirt road that led there was even more insane than the road to Vitáli. Fantastic.

We got on board the small boat which would take us to the beach. I turned to watch the harbor receding from view. And there was that man in the brown leather jacket on his phone, turning his back to the sea.

"This way you get to see the island by water, Turo," Adri's excited voice brought my attention to the rocky shoreline, the hidden coves as the fishing boat cut through the dark blue water. Truly spectacular raw beauty. Luckily, only two other couples were on opposite ends of the beach when we arrived by our hired water taxi. This was a remote location. If that man was following us, tracking us, there'd be no way he'd come here without it being obvious. My pulse ticked. For the time being we were good. For now.

The small, smooth pebbles on Áxla's shore shone in the sun, creating a blanket of unbelievable glimmering pale gold beach. As we neared the shore, the crystal clear, aqua water took my breath away all over again. I'd never tire of the sight of it, I knew.

Here, there were no loungers with thatched umbrellas, no café bar filling iced frappé orders. Just a sweep of clean shore in a low-lying cove which cut the velocity of the winds, and a rolling hill of green in the valley beyond.

"There's a river back there and a hiking trail." She pointed beyond the shore.

Taking her hand in mine, we made our way down the small plank, and onto the shore. We dropped our bags in the center of the beach, and I pitched the umbrella she'd brought along this time. Adri laid out a bamboo mat on our patch of sand with our towels spread out over it, and I set the big tote bag on top along with larger rocks in case the wind kicked up. We were efficient vacationers.

She tossed her sunglasses on the towel and ripped off her blousy caftan with the wide winged sleeves, a short, see-through number of burgundy and pink, and ran into the water. I tore off my T-shirt and chased my island nymph and her sculpted ass into the rolling waves.

We swam up and down the shore, collapsed on our towels relishing the warmth of the sun's rays. She applied sunscreen all over my chest and back. My pulse picked up. My erection knew no bounds and I didn't give a damn. Neither did she. She put the cap on the white bottle, her tits squeezing out of her tight bandeau top, and I leered at her, ogling like a hormonal boy.

We ate our sesame-covered *kouloúria,* the thin Greek version of a bagel. She took her bikini top off and, lying down on her tummy, fell asleep. I fell asleep too, if only for about fifteen minutes according to my watch, but it felt luxurious and indulgent. My body enjoyed being stretched out under the sun in the clean, clean wind, the refreshing sea swirling a few feet away. In fact, I was more relaxed than I'd ever been in recent memory on this remote beach. Chicago may as well have been in another fucking galaxy. Alessio's boat. The Russian's playground. All of it.

Adriana turned over and stretched out like a satisfied cat.

Jesus.

I straddled her, hands planting on either side of her head.

She blinked. "Hello."

I kissed her, nipping at her upper lip, and her hips curved up to meet mine. Her hand swept up my side to my pec, rubbing the hard muscle there, and my stomach tightened. I stroked the edge of a silky breast, my hand itching to cup the round fulness, to knead its soft firmness. I wanted to see her face morph with pleasure and pain at what I'd do to that ripe tit.

I leaned over her, whispering in her ear, "I want to bite you, suck on you, lick you."

Grinning, she dug her fingers into my sides as her hips raised against mine, searching for more friction, but I pulled away and went back to my side of the towel. I liked teasing her, keeping her guessing. She sucked in a deep breath and put her top back on, fiddling with the fabric.

I opened up our water bottles, and handed her one. Crossing her legs tightly, she gulped at her water. Her teeth scraped along her bottom lip. "Your sense of control, that's your strength. That's where you're comfortable, isn't it?"

I screwed the cap back on my water bottle. "It keeps things clear. Confusion sucks, in plain English."

"I agree, it does. But do you not think it keeps you stuck at the same place somehow?"

"What are you trying to say, Adri?"

She pressed her lips together.

"Say it."

"I don't want to be your *convenient.*"

"My *what*?"

"Or your something that *works.*" Her lips twisted.

"What are you talking about?"

"You want authentic from me? I want authentic from you. After this—" she waved her hand in the air in one of those throw-away Greek gestures "—you can go back to your controlled convenience."

My breath knotted in my chest.

She wanted my *authentic*. My erection felt pretty damned authentic. My pulse heating every time I touched her, kissed her. My thoughts, all of them, were shadowed by her.

And that *after*? Me leaving Greece and going back to Chicago was *after*. Her in Athens or London or wherever the fuck, stepping back into a sea swarming with men was her *after*.

After.

Fuck after.

"*Adriana? Vre, Adri, ti káneis ethó?*" a loud male voice bellowed, blowing our discussion to bits before it got a chance to meld.

A towering figure cast a shadow over us. A young guy, Adri's age, with messy, wind-tossed hair almost to his shoulders wearing a T-shirt, board shorts, and expensive Brazilian flip-flops gazed down at her, his dark eyes clocking every detail of her oiled up, sun-kissed body, his grin wide and eager. My spine straightened.

"Niko?" Adri jumped up and hugged the beach dude, and they chattered wildly in Greek. She grabbed onto my arm and introduced us.

"Turo, this is Niko Randopoulos. His family owns a huge plot of land he's developing just behind the fields and the river over there." She pointed to the green valley behind us.

Seriously? How the hell do you own a huge plot of land like that on this beach?

"I've brought the architect and the engineer to go over final details," said Niko in English following Adri's lead. "Construction begins next week."

"So it's finally been approved?" she asked.

"Approved enough." He winked at her.

Adri jumped up on a squeal and gave Niko another hug.

"Congratulations! I'm so happy for you! It's been such a long wait for this to go through."

The jerk slid his arm around her waist and she turned to face me. "Niko is building a new type of resort based on sound ecological practices with a small organic farm, a restaurant, and a number of private bungalows."

"Very exciting," I said.

"I'd love for you to see. Do you have time?" His gleeful delight was focused on Adri like a super laser and made my pulse tick, tick, tick.

"Would you like to, Turo?" Adri asked. Niko brushed a hand through his wavy locks, his eyes on Adri, his grin growing again.

"Sure, we have at least another two hours before our boat is due back," I replied, shooting him a brittle grin.

We picked up our towels and closed the umbrella, filled the tote bag, and piled it all in a mound on the mat. I put my tee on, Adri her coverup, and we followed Niko through the green brush on a short hike up past the narrow river to an expanse of land, where four men discussed and took photographs and noted measurements, planted small marker flags.

Niko explained his design plan, his hope for his resort to offer an alternate luxury vacation experience. Down to earth, but deluxe all the way. Adri told me that Niko's family owned the most popular yoghurt company in Greece. So that was how you bought a huge plot of primo land on a beach on a Greek island and developed it into a luxury resort.

"I've always wanted to combine my passion for ecologically responsible living with a business," Niko said. "My father is still trying to talk me out of it, mostly because he's worried. Things are changing in Greece, he says. He's even thinking of moving the company's headquarters out of the country."

"Really?" Adri said.

His gaze wandered over his expanse of green land. "But I don't want to leave. This place to me is so special, the island, Áxla.

Always has been. It's always been my dream to do something here. I want to see this through. I have to."

"Absolutely," said Adri, her voice suddenly as firm and quiet as Niko's as she scanned the valley.

I had to admit Niko's vision was impressive, his dedication to create outside the box, to build on what his family had, to stick it out and do it on his own. "You should see it through," I said. "Very impressive."

Niko grinned. "Thank you."

I glanced at my watch. "Adri, we should get back to the beach. The boat will be here in fifteen minutes."

"Ah, already?" She let out a sigh and put her arm through Niko's. They walked ahead of me on the trail back to the beach.

I ground my jaw at the sight of them arm in arm, talking and laughing easily. They were in sync. The perfect couple. My eyes fell to her sashaying hips and ass, and I tried my damnedest not to let that sight make me even crazier.

I lost that struggle.

33

TURO

ON THE BOAT back to town Adri talked non-stop about how the island had been a hotspot for hikers and eco-tourists for years now, and how she admired Niko for doing what he really wanted, how it would benefit the island. We never picked up that tense conversation of ours from earlier.

Back in town, we picked up sausage from a butcher shop, and headed for the house. No sign of our friend in brown leather. At the house, Adri headed straight for the kitchen and got right to work. She wanted to make me the island specialty for lunch. A frittata with spicy sausage and fried potatoes.

"My grandmother taught me how to make *fourtália* right here in this kitchen," Adri said, scooping up fried potatoes from the pan of bubbling olive oil.

The slices of locally made fennel sausage sizzled in the pan, filling the kitchen with their sweet, smoky fragrance. She handed me a wire whisk, and I whipped the eggs, an unusual rich orange color in the white ceramic bowl. This is what farm fresh looked like. She took the bowl from me and slid the contents into the pan and the eggs bubbled furiously. She added the fried potatoes, lowered the heat, and covered the skillet.

I poured the wine.

She wiped her hands on a towel. "Now we wait."

I took our wine glasses to the round table in the center of the kitchen as she cleaned up the counter. I'd barely said a word the past hour. Seeing her and Niko together stuck in my throat like a fishbone. The perfect pair. Easygoing friendship between peers, both ridiculously attractive, practically finishing each other's sentences.

Adri folded a kitchen towel and dropped it by the sink. I held out my hand to her. She came forward, reached out and took my hand. I said nothing. No funny remarks this time, no witty observations. She stood still before me, a quizzical, uneasy look crossing her face.

I was about to be very clear.

"Get on your knees."

Her eyes widened.

I squeezed her hand hard. "Do it."

She got on her knees between my legs and I pressed a thumb along the edge of those fucking glorious lips.

"Suck my cock, Lovely."

The taut lines of her face relaxed, and my pulse kicked up at the sight. She wanted this. She liked my frankness. She pulled on the drawstring of my bathing suit trunks and tugged them down. My hard dick sprang out of the fabric, and she took in an audible breath.

I did too.

I was exposed to her, and she took me in. My ab muscles tightened, my balls stiffened under her study of my cock. Admiring, deciding, planning, designing. Chest heaving.

Her lips parted as she curled a hand around my shaft and rubbed from base to tip. Her grip was firm, sure, rough. She brought my aching hardness to her mouth and her tongue laid a hot trail around the tip.

Ah fuck.

Around and around. Impatient, I fisted a hand in her hair, the other on top of her head and brought my pelvis up. My dick slid deeper in her wet mouth, and she immediately took me down her throat. Challenge taken.

Well done, baby.

"Yes." A hiss escaped my tense mouth.

She was smooth. Her pressure just right, taking me down a whirlpool of explosive feeling, all of it burning in my spine, bunching in my balls, feeding my lust and feeding her with it. She knew what she was doing.

She sucked faster, a hand cupping me firmly, stroking with a twisting motion. She worked me, her eyes lifting to mine, her tits squeezing out of her bikini top under the tunic. I reached down her back under the blousy tunic and snapped open the clasp of her bikini top, and it fell from her body. I filled my hand with a breast, kneading it roughly. Her taking me in hand was everything right this fucking second. Everything raw, everything slick.

I pumped harder into her mouth. A moan escaped her full lips which stretched around my dick, streaming with her saliva. "Fuck me with that mouth, Adri. Fuck me good," I said, my voice harsh, low, insistent. I stroked her other tit hard.

All of her would be mine soon enough.

My eyes jammed shut and the blood simmered through my veins. My hands cradled her face, keeping her there, and I exploded. She sucked, sucked, sucked it all fucking down. I released my grip on her, and she slowed her pace, still licking, still—

She kissed the glistening tip of my dick and a smile danced across her wet lips.

"So good," I managed, mesmerized.

She kneeled back on her haunches, her hands stroking my thighs. I handed her a glass of wine and she drank. "The *fourtália* must be ready," she murmured, handing me back the wine glass.

I let out a chuckle, my thumb wiping at her wet lower lip. "Suddenly I'm starving."

Her lips tipped up as she rose and went back to the frying pan. I pulled my bathing suit back up as she emptied the fluffy, thick frittata onto one large dish and brought two forks with her and set them on the table.

I grabbed her waist and hoisted her on my lap. An instant of silence. The game had changed, and she knew it.

I said, "We'll eat together."

Her already flushed face streaked with more red. She bit her lip as she cut into the omelet and offered me the forkful. I took it and ate. The spicy sausage, the mellow potato, and egg melted in my mouth.

"I like that. That's good."

"Hmm."

I steadied her with a hand wrapped around a thigh, keeping her close. A hand that rubbed right at the apex between her legs. She wriggled on my lap and my grip on her thigh tightened.

She fed me.

I traced circles over the fabric of her bathing suit right over her pussy.

She fed herself.

My fingers slid past the bikini bottom and into her wet slickness as her thigh muscles tightened over me.

Clang. Her fork clattered onto the dish. She fed me with her fingers.

I fingered her slit.

She fed herself.

She fed me.

I sucked on her fingers.

My thumb circled her stiff nub.

Her breaths came fast and short, louder, desperate.

The wooden curtain rod hoops clattered together on the rod with the warm breeze blowing through the gauzy white curtains on the window over the sink. A wind chime tinkled languidly from the garden leaving its elegant music in the air for us. I pushed the plate away.

Picking up her wine glass, I tipped it before her mouth and she drank, her throat moving carefully with each long swallow. Taking the glass away, I cupped the back of her head and quickly brought her lips to mine. I took her mouth, and she released wine onto my tongue. Warm, mellow, sweet.

A little river of understanding, of shared culpability. Of enticement.

Adri twisted in my hold and straddled me, rocking over me as her need for friction dictated. My girl was hungry and it wasn't for fucking omelets and wine and delicate caresses. I grabbed her ass and slowed her down, our humid breaths heavy between us. I suckled a nipple through the fabric of her gauzy tunic and she panted, her hands fisting my T-shirt at my shoulders. Her head knocked back and she groaned loudly.

My fingers slid down the rear of her bikini bottom, gripping her bare ass. She yanked at the ties at each hip and the bikini fell away and a groan ripped from my chest. I took out the condom I'd stashed in my pocket when she started cooking and we both pulled at my bathing suit trunks. My cock sprang free, and I pulled her over me again. She slid back and forth, back and forth making me harder than hard, making my dick slippery with her wetness.

"Fuck yes," I muttered in agony.

I squeezed those fantastic tits together, brushed her nipples with my teeth over the fabric of her tunic. She cried out, her back stiffening, arching.

"I want my cock inside you," I breathed against her skin. "Now." I gestured at the condom, and she snapped it up from the table, opened it with her teeth, and expertly fitted my hard length, her breath choppy. Her careful smoothing of the rubber over my aching shaft, so thorough, so conscientious; the blood rushed to my cock and brain in a crazy whirlpool.

Her gaze snagged on mine. She seemed unsure of what to do next. I lifted her up and she settled over me, my hand guiding my hard dick just inside her wet heat.

"Yes," came out of my lips on a long groan as I nudged and slid inside her inch by fucking inch. Slick and tight. Sheer fucking perfection.

"Bloody hell," she muttered. "Oh, Turo..." She stilled.

She was nervous.

I kissed her neck. "Baby, you're in the driver's seat. You shift the gears. One at a time. You know what's up ahead on the road. Hit the clutch, release. Do it."

She let go of a heavy breath and rocked her hips. She moved. She moved over me like a slithering snake, long and slow in a curving motion, slowly, slowly, quicker. She wanted more of me inside her. Buried inside her. Her rhythm became steady and harder. A creature gaining on her prey, her eyes on fire.

I tore my gaze away from hers and focused on her gorgeous tits jiggling and hopping with her rough movements. I brought them to my mouth, sucking hard on her hard nipples. The wet fabric, her sweat and the scent of her soft skin rising from her throat ignited me. They were the beach, the sun, the sea. My hips jacked up into hers and I quickened the pace. She blinked, her head dropping back, her jaw dropping.

Fifth gear.

Look at you, baby. On fucking fire.

That mountain of pleasure loomed ahead, and I was gaining on it. I would take her there with me.

She's taking me there.

"Turo!" she cried out.

And my heart flew up my throat.

I held on to her ass, my fingers digging into her generous cheek, the thumb of my other hand going between her legs, strumming her clit. A low moan escaped her lips, her fingertips digging into my shoulders as she fucked me. My eyes collided with hers. I couldn't not look. I couldn't not get there without her.

That's where I wanted to be. With her. We were doing this together. She was giving me this—

Her flaming gaze mirrored the sensations overwhelming me, and those sensations rose to dance with hers.

Hunger. Recklessness. Impulsiveness. Relentlessness. Single mindedness.

All of it. *Us.*

Her insides squeezed me in further, and I let out a harsh breath, my lungs crushing.

Fuck, yes, yes, yes.

"Hold on to me," I gritted out.

She clutched at me and, grabbing her hips, I lifted her and planted her ass on the table.

Crash. The wine glasses flew. Forks clattered on the floor, the sharp noises making her eyes flash. I pushed her back on the surface and cuffing her neck with one hand, gripping her waist with the other. Her legs spread wide and bent at my side, and I plowed inside her, pumping fast and vicious.

All of her, all of her, right the fuck now.

Her body jostled on the table, the table jostled with our bodies sliding and colliding into one another. Raw, nasty, loud. She cried out sharply and we both crashed, twisted, soared in our frenzy. A thousand pieces of us flew around the kitchen. My yell entwined with hers, and she melted back onto the table. Slowly, two of my fingers massaged up and down on either side of her clit.

She gasped sharply, her hips twisting, head knocking back, a hand swatting at mine. Greek words tumbled from her mouth. *"Oxi!"*

I slapped her hand away. "I decide," I gritted out in her ear on a thrust. "I decide—" *thrust* "— what's enough"—*thrust*—"when it's enough." *Thrust.*

Yes, I'm keeping that orgasm coming, baby, my wild, untamed Maenad.

Her legs hitched on my hips, her heels digging into my ass. I ripped the flimsy tunic down her chest and licked long, thick strokes around her hard nipples, grinding inside her. I licked her sweaty throat, up her chin as my hand cuffed her neck stiffly applying just the right amount of pressure. She blinked, her features tightening, my fingers pressed against her clit and I claimed her mouth in a deep, hard kiss. She shuddered in my hold.

"Turo!"

Releasing her, I smoothed her hair back from her damp face. Her breaths were fast and hard, her face flushed and sweaty, her stare dazed. I pinched the hood of her pussy and she whimpered, her head falling back again.

I hadn't come yet, but I couldn't tear my eyes away from her.

I wanted to kiss her, feel her arms wrap around me, feel her wonder at all the sensations she was experiencing sink into me and I'd soak it all up. Every drop. I wanted her fingertips pressing into my back, her sexy voice whispering something in Greek as she bit my ear. Her tongue searing my flesh with licks and kisses.

I took in a breath. Steadied myself, swallowed hard against the jolt rattling my insides. What the fuck? Maybe I'd gotten too much sun today and the wine had gone to my head?

And my blood...

And my cock...

And my heart.

Heat spiraled in my chest, unwinding through me. My mouth was suddenly dry, my shoulders stiffening. This was meant to be an escape from reality, wasn't it? An indulgence, not—

I sucked in air, my jaw set.

She'd propped her elbows up on the table, her eyes narrowing, face hardening. Nothing escaped her scrutiny. "What's wrong? Did that not qualify as a successful transaction?" she asked, her voice unusually taut, her tone positively flippant. "You didn't finish. Have you gone beyond your prescribed limits?"

I blinked away the sweat in my eyes. *Smartass.*

I expected to hear something else after having successfully plowed through her years of faking it, not getting it right, not getting any. Of denying herself. My jaw hardened. She was right, wasn't she? That was me—Impersonal Hard Fucks R Us. And now she'd caught me unable to deal with the other side of that.

With feeling it.

She'd felt it too, I know she had. That powerful tremor between us, an exchange of current. She was pleased, almost smug that she'd gotten me here, to the edge.

I tore her legs open wide with one hand and slammed inside her once more, my other hand jamming down on her chest. Her sharp gasp made my heart race—was it a shock? Painful?

I hope so.

I thrust and thrust until I finally came. I bit down on a grunt as I held myself balls deep against her. "Did *you* get what you wanted?"

She pressed her lips together, her chin lifting. Defiant to the last. "*Né*," she muttered, her voice ragged, unrecognizable. "Yes, I got what I wanted."

I slid out of her, snapping the rubber off, tying it up. "So did I."

34

TURO

After our sextravaganza in the kitchen ended on a strained, sour note, we both cleaned up the kitchen in silence and receded to our rooms.

I took a hot shower, and with the window wide open, sprawled naked on the bed and hoped that a Mediterranean *siesta* would claim me. The Greek afternoon nap when the heat was high in high summer was a tradition. It wasn't that hot yet, but hot enough.

Today, right now, I was plenty hot. The breeze danced on my bare skin and I drifted, battling Berezin's laugh, the feel of his gun in my hand, Mauro's glare at my front door.

Fuck off, all of you fuck off.

Forty minutes later I woke up with one thing on my mind. One person. One woman. I wasn't going to let anything get between us. Not defensiveness, not petty jealousy, not anything. I grabbed two condoms, and went to Adri's room.

Time to wake her up.

In more ways than one.

She was curled up on her bed in a tank top which was twisted on her torso revealing the swell of a breast and the valley of her belly. My cock hardened even more than it had on the short walk down the hallway to her room. I kneeled on the bed and licked a trail from her foot up to her thigh. Her body uncurled, stretched out on a moan. Stroking the silk of an inner thigh, I licked up and down her slit, my tongue swirling in her heat. Fuck yes. Yes. Yes. Slow and firm, round and around.

A loud gasp, legs tensing, a hand digging in my hair. Eyes blinking. "Turo!"

Her eyes wide and blazing locked on mine as I ate her, her taste racing through my blood. Her lips parted, jaw slackened, her body relaxed in my tight grip and she spread her legs wider for me, her hips rocking up to meet my mouth, a foot on my shoulder. Tugging her flimsy panty out of my way, two of my fingers slid inside her pussy and worked her inner wall and I sank my mouth over her clit and suckled. She moaned loudly, her back arching, heel digging in my back.

Yes, desperation, I loved its primal call.

I ripped the tank top off her and brought her face down to the floor so her tits would rub against the rough reedy rug on the wood floor. Her ass was up in the air, and I pulled on her panty, and it snapped off in my hand. I bit into that gorgeous ass and lavished the bite with a tender kiss. Moans rose from the rug.

Suiting up, I pulled her arms back and thrust inside her quickly, her tiny cries filling the room. She throbbed on me, and it took everything I had to not blow, to maintain my rapid, hard pace. Her loud moans fed my determination. She exploded, her face falling into the rug. I released her arms and, ripping the condom off my dick, I took my cock in hand and—*ah fuck*— came on that beautiful ass.

She lay sprawled on the floor, her breaths coming hard and heavy, my cum pooling on her flesh, marking her. More moans rose from the rug. Leaning back on my haunches, I wiped at the sweat on my chest.

Adri reached for my hand and I leaned over and gave it to her. Bringing it to her mouth, she kissed my fingers, and that warm curl in my chest sprang to life again. I lay down on the floor and took her in my arms, wiping my cum over her hips and middle, up her tits. She hooked a leg over my waist, her breaths easing.

"I really like siesta time," I whispered, nipping at her throat.

"I must say, I've never truly appreciated it until now." She kissed me, licked my throat like a cat desperate for every last drop of milk in its bowl. "I'm taking the pill, but do you have any more condoms or do we need to go to the chemist's?"

Oh yeah, we were definitely over the bullshit tension.

"Only one more," I replied, twisting a nipple.

A grin tipped her lips, and she pushed me over and straddled me. "We need to go shopping this afternoon."

"We do," I said, flicking a thumb over her swollen clit. "Now get that pussy on my mouth."

―――――

PEOPLE FILLED THE STREETS. The stores had reopened for the early evening and the cafés had filled up. We were entering the second phase of our day, and a long evening stretched out before us.

Adri stopped at a kiosk and lingered over a rack of magazines, not the fashion, beauty, or health variety. The gossip kind. I scanned the crowd. No sign of brown leather jacket guy.

I wrapped an arm around Adri's waist, and her forehead creased, her gaze riveted on the magazines.

"What is it?" I asked.

"Everyone's guessing who the target of the shooting was."

"From what happened at the party in Mykonos, my bet is it's Luca related. He doesn't make friends wherever he goes."

"Hmm," was her only reply as she scanned more headlines.

"Here's the party—" I pointed out a magazine cover featuring

Alessio laughing with Elektra, and an inset photo of Adri with Kaspar. Another gossip magazine, and there were so damned many for such a small country, had a photo of Adri's mother, elegantly decked out in a form-fitting suit, holding a plaque.

"Here's Liana," I said.

"Yes," Adri let out a breath. "Last week she opened the new wing at the children's cancer hospital."

"Were you there?"

"Of course." Adri pointed to another gossip mag on the lower rack, and there she was on the cover looking radiant, beaming in a pale pink suit, her hair pulled up, standing next to her mother and another woman. "Me, Mum, and the Prime Minister's wife."

This was the European heiress.

"Impressive, Lovely," I murmured.

"My mother's done a lot to get that hospital open and running. Used to be you'd have to send your child to America or the UK to get proper treatment. And if you didn't have the money…well. The state pediatric hospital for cancer treatment has excellent doctors, but the facilities? Quite behind modern standards. It was a labour of love for Mum. She had another child after me, before Marko. A girl. Leukemia took my sister's life before she was even two years old."

"That's awful, I'm sorry," I said.

"This project is very important to our family."

"Well done, Mum."

"Yes, I admire her tenacity very much. She certainly didn't let the impossible get her down. Bureaucracy is a fierce monster in Greece, unfortunately."

"Hey, isn't this Niko?" I pointed to another gossip rag. He'd been snapped rushing down a street with an older platinum blonde woman at his side, his cute boyish features tightened into harsh lines.

"Yes." Adrian rolled her eyes. "He's been seeing a married chat show hostess."

"Really?"

"Well, she's separated but not yet divorced from her husband, and it's quite the controversy. I guess their dirty little secret has finally been revealed."

I let out a sharp laugh.

"You didn't like him, did you?" she asked.

"I didn't like his arm around you, or the way he looked at you—"

"I've known him since kindergarten. We went to the same private school until we were eighteen."

"No touching in all that time?"

Her eyes lit up. "No."

"No tongue tangoing? No exchange of bodily fluids?" I persisted.

She pressed her lips to mine, her grin teasing my scowl. "Not even once. We should've though. He would've been a perfect first kiss, first sexual experience."

"And what makes you say that?" I said, my tone acidic.

She let out a laugh. "He's a good bloke. Truly a kind, thoughtful person. Unlike my first who was a right arsehole."

"Who is this bastard and what did he do to my Lovely?"

"Tsk tsk, not a bastard. A prince."

"A real royal prince?"

"Very real, quite royal—a cross of Hapsburg, some Bavarian, a bit of Dane..."

"What did this bastard, mutt of a prince do?"

"Lavished me with attention, gifts, whispered words of desire and obsession in French, seduced me and laughed that it was my first time, and then got irritated that he had to deal with my virginity. More extravagant words of desire and obsession followed over the next few days, and then he got back on his plane and flew north never to be heard from again. I didn't expect a full out relationship, but not a vanishing act. He'd gotten what he wanted or rather what suited him at the time, and he was done."

"Bastard."

She shrugged, lingering at a tiny grocery store with local goods.

"Hey," I brushed her shoulder with my lips and her gaze darted up at me. "You deserved so much more. So much better."

Her mouth curved in a shy, small smile, her teeth tugging on her bottom lip. A warmth seeped through me, the desire to make it better for her pulling on me like some primal mating call. Adri was easy to please in bed, a pleasure to surprise, and she appreciated everything I did for her. From the very first, she'd let me guide her, and then she flew. She wanted to experience, and she knew I could take her there. Had any man ever taken his time with her? Been unselfish with her? Stupid, stupid bastards.

I kissed her softly. Yeah, I wanted to make it really good for her. I liked having goals.

The thick fragrance of green botanicals and piquant spices, dried teas filled air. Hand labeled jars of oregano, thyme, jams, raw honey, bundled dried bouquets of bay leaves, mint, and mountain tea lined shelves outside and in.

"My favorite." Adri held up a glass jar of astonishingly huge capers. "Freshly harvested."

"Amazing." I picked up a jar filled with chunky white flakes trimmed with a thick blue ribbon. "Is this salt?"

"Sea salt."

"Huh. Of course, it is."

"It's good."

"I'll bet. My mother would get a kick out of this," I murmured. I bought two jars.

"Do you need a gift for your father too?"

"The only thing my father wants me to bring home is Gennaro Aliberti's consent."

"Ah, yes."

We continued walking through town.

"Do you like working with your father?" she asked.

"More like *for* him. It's complicated between us."

"I understand complicated," she said. "Is he fatherly at least?"

"No. No, he's not."

"That's too bad. I'm sorry."

I shook off her sympathy. "It is what it is."

Again, that brittle grin that understood what I was saying. "So you've been patient and responsible, proving yourself—"

"Over and over again."

"But something is lacking for you?"

"Yes, I suppose."

"And you came to Greece in order to score points?"

"I came to fix his Gennaro problem."

"You're good at fixing, aren't you?" she asked.

"Very."

"I wouldn't want to cross any of the Alibertis."

"You're aware of what the Alibertis do for a living back in Napoli?" I asked her.

"Of course I know who they are. Who doesn't? But Alessio is not a part of their organization. He's put a lot of hard work into his own business, and he's created something unique and sought after. He's his own success."

His *own* success.

A Fortinbras to my Hamlet.

I'd read how Alessio had taken his mother's hole in the wall fashion accessories store in a shitty neighborhood in Naples and turned it into a chic, trendy, and very tony brand of his own. Granted, most probably with his father's drug money to start and Luca's ongoing protection, but he made it a success. With his own good looks, swagger, and playboy reputation, Alessio had only pushed his exclusive jewelry further, embodying the brand himself—tough, tattooed, raw street Italo-masculinity all wrapped up in Gucci and Prada and Dolce & Gabbana. The party in Mykonos had just made that very clear for all to see and taste.

"Even if you do bring home Gennaro's acceptance, do you think your father will be grateful or will he belittle your success, just to spite you? Just because he can?" she asked.

"You sound like you've had experience with a difficult daddy."

"Hmm. Alessio's is, so's mine."

I put my arm around her shoulders and brought her close. "Yeah, mine too."

We ordered two *freddo* espressos at the Hermes Café. Sitting under a grove of thick trees in the center of the cobblestone paved town, watching the locals greet one another as they went to the bakery, the butcher, the shops. A modern, square, white building to our left with a large bronze plaque caught my attention. I read the bronze sign.

"The island has an archeological museum?" I gestured at the building.

"Yes, there are several museums here in fact." Adri nibbled on the thin cinnamon cookie that came with the coffees. "Would you like to go?"

"Yes, actually. I would. You?"

Her eyes brightened as she wiped the crumbs from her fingers. "I'd love to. I haven't been since I was in high school. Quite shameful."

"Shameful?"

She only grinned at me. Something was up.

I paid our bill at the café, and we went to the museum. As I paid our admission fee, I did a double take at the plaque over the attendant's desk. Adri's family name hung on the wall. I raised an eyebrow at her, tilting my head.

"My parents' foundation donated the money for the museum and renovated the building," she said.

I took her hand, and we entered the galleries. Sculptures from the Archaic period all the way to the Roman era filled the exhibition space. Small painted earthenware bowls and vases from over thousands of years ago with the early geometric patterns up through the more graceful design elements of later periods. And all of it found right here, on this island.

"Different from a big city museum?" she asked.

"Very satisfying on another level," I murmured. Erin would really enjoy this.

"There's also a contemporary art museum here."

"Let's go."

We walked on to the Contemporary Art Museum. A special exhibition of Georges Braque, a buddy of Picasso's and fellow Cubism creator, was on display—"Georges Braque: Order & Emotion."

Jesus, first I had Dionysus at my heels, now Braque.

We lingered in the last gallery in front of a painting of a pair of birds floating in a white space. Flat and simple. There was something delightful yet sad about it all at once. The birds soared free side by side in the flat space, but they seemed separate. Alone.

An ache creeped up my insides and curled tightly there. I wasn't going to think about how me and Adri would have to leave the island soon. We'd been here three days now, and I knew I had to get back to my reality and get her back to hers. *Not yet. Not yet.* I threaded my fingers in Adri's and she squeezed my hand, pressing against my side, and my chest eased.

We left the museum, both of us immediately adjusting our sunglasses over our eyes. The Greek sun was intense. We joined the flow of the afternoon crowd on the cobblestone main road, my gaze darting left and right.

There he is.

Brown leather jacket man, now wearing a denim jacket sat at a café at three o'clock texting on his phone.

I threw an arm over Adri's shoulders pulling her in close. "Is it too late for the beach now? I want to get wet with you."

"Of course not," she said, her tone bright. "On an island, beach-ing happens any time of day or night. Like drinking and eating."

And fucking, Lovely. And fucking. Day and night. Night and day.

35

ADRIANA

TWO MORE DAYS PASSED. Two glorious days.

And in that time we'd gotten into a routine. Our rituals of the day. A day that wasn't marked by time's necessities, but by our wants, our appetites. Our moods. And our moods focused on each other.

When he had demanded of me in the kitchen that afternoon my skin had set on fire, my lungs crushed together at the hard tone in his voice. I'd gotten on my knees before him gladly. It hadn't only been a submission to him, but to this deep attraction and need between us. I wanted to explore it. I wanted to experience, live it. I wanted him so badly. More than anything I'd ever wanted before.

He was methodical and studious and that only made my response that much more intense. He was always mindful of how hard to push and when, and encouraging. I trusted him. The more I trusted, the more I enjoyed what we had. His sensuality knew no bounds, his focus, his care, and it was thrilling. There was no dissembling between us. That glint in his eye when we fucked provoked me, was adamant that I ask for what I wanted, that I remain present with him and what we were doing. That I feel.

And I felt. Oh how I felt.

What I didn't feel was my old friend shame, and that alone was a revelation, a first. I stopped second guessing myself. There was no sense of tomorrow and no time to waste, and we both knew this. It made us greedy, voracious.

But I knew it wasn't just our chemistry or his technical mastery. Alessio was a very skilled and caring lover, but this, with Turo, was another dimension, another level. He and I had a need to reach each other, to soothe, to instigate, to challenge each other. All of it twisted and shaped with unrelenting desire and delicate trust.

An explosive molotov cocktail of our very own.

This one didn't destroy or scar, it fed me, energized me. Satisfied me in a new way.

We'd start each day early with a quick, cold swim at the base of the castle, then have a Greek coffee at Hermes, stop off at the bakery for my favorite cinnamon spiced cookies and *pastéli*, a sesame seed, nut, and honey bar I'd made Turo try and had become his favorite on the go snack. We'd get in the jeep and hit different beaches. Zorgos, Copper, Korthi. Each beach had a different personality. One had strong high waves and wind, another was a sheltered cove with easy rolling waters and caves in the rocks. One was quiet, the other had a crowded beach bar. At Korthi we swam out to the huge rock formation which stood upright in the water, a towering natural sculpture of stone in the middle of the cove.

The island's artwork.

"This is crazy," Turo said, shielding his eyes from the sun as he looked up at the huge geological formation which resembled a giant figure in motion pushing through the water.

"They called it the *Píthima tis Griás,* or the 'Old Lady's Leap',"

I explained. "Legend has it that an old woman jumped from the cliffs and was preserved in stone by the gods."

"Greece." He pulled me in his arms and kissed me as we floated in the water.

In the afternoons, we'd choose a *tavérna* and eat our main meal of the day—seafood or roast meat depending on our mood, along with boiled greens soaked in lemon juice and olive oil, a salad or roast vegetables with a side of the local cheese Turo loved. And wine. Always wine.

The simplicity of the flavors, yet their richness astonished him over and over again. And through his curiosity and enjoyment and articulation of that appreciation, I found mine again. For food, for my island homeland. For the finer details of my every day. I'd been spending holidays on Greek islands all my life. Yet this time, this trip, here now with Turo, had set me spinning like a child's top.

I was the spinning top, I was the delighted child laughing and applauding. Wanting more, wanting it to never end.

Insatiable.

———

HE LIKED SURPRISING ME. A tactic, I think, to keep me off my guard, shock my system.

We got back from lunch at Korthi, and I'd hung our beach towels on the terrace, emptied the beach bag, and took a shower. I wrapped a thick, white towel around me and inhaled the scent of my favorite fig and orange shower gel in the steam. I grabbed my tub of body cream.

And that's when I saw him.

He stood there naked by the bed, and I stilled. He'd been waiting, and he was hard and ready to fuck, his jaw set in that brittle way that sent a shiver straight through me. His face an unreadable mask of cool, of patience, and that heavy feeling settled in my tummy, pulling on me. As inevitable as gravity, as powerful. I believed that if Turo really wanted something, his patience was relentless and endless, and I loved that. It made me breathless, made my heart gallop in my chest, made me, thankfully, stop thinking.

Like right now.

"Turo?" I breathed.

He ripped the towel from me and pushed me back against the wall, his eyes flaring into mine. Wanting, yet revealing nothing.

A moment. Another. My flesh heated. Deep breaths. I licked my lips.

Kiss me, kiss me.

His hand passed over my collarbone, around my neck, and he bent, his lips touching mine in a wholly unexpected tender kiss, shocking my system. I melted rapidly in his hold, my body plastering itself against his warmth, a hard, hard wall of warmth that pressed me against the cold wall. The kiss was almost delicate, a hot, silky touch brushing, nuzzling. Gentle.

Ha. Gentle for now.

His tongue invaded my mouth and grew demanding, and I gave in. I loved giving in to him. He grabbed a condom packet, ripped it with his teeth, that flash of white ripping at me, and he suited up quickly. I hitched my legs one at a time over his hips with his support and slid a hand between us, taking his hard length in hand, stroking him, guiding him inside me.

He nudged in, and that high octane fuel that was Turo lit every particle of my being on fire.

He slid in slowly.

Dragged his hard length out, slowly.

Rocked in. Slowly.

Out.

Oh, here it comes.

He rammed his cock inside me in one swift move, and I cried out sharply, my head knocking back. He bit my upper chest in reply, and I hissed on the sting. Holding me in his excruciating grip, he thrust and thrust and thrust. Harder and swifter with my every cry.

Every day, every night. In the middle of the night. First thing in the morning. The afternoon, like now. Whenever Mr. DeMarco pleased, and however he liked. And he pleased and I liked, very, very much.

Turo's guerrilla fucking tactics were a strategic success on my battlefield. He was determined to overwhelm me, to obliterate any trace left of the 'fake it' response from my very bones after two years of my having perfected it, hiding behind it. In his conquest of me, I was compelled to feel every blast, every sting, every burn. No shame, no analyzing, or deciding. No morning after regrets or doubts. Only us feeding off each other. Pure sensation.

He moved us to the bed, but my limbs were no better than rubber. Lifting me up by the hips and sliding one arm between my breasts, he cuffed my neck, holding me up and thrust in quick, harsh movements. The old iron bed squeaked and jerked in complaint. I wanted to look at him very badly, but I couldn't squirm or turn my head even a fraction. Instead, I squeezed him inside me and slammed back against him, meeting him thrust for thrust.

He let out a low, long grunt, and my heart jumped in my chest. He liked that, and I liked that he did. I liked that he wanted me over and over again, that his desire for me seemed bottomless. A hunger I never knew I possessed had taken hold of me. A hunger he knew how to satisfy. He'd made that happen, my conjurer, my conqueror.

"Turo!" I hurtled over the edge he'd brought us to.

He kept at me, and I kept my hold on his cock until he finished. My arse cheeks burned from the odd bite he'd delivered. He stroked me and the burn transformed to molten heat. We both dropped onto the bed, and I curled into his chest, his arms

347

sliding around me, keeping me close. I breathed in the warmth of his skin. He never spoke during or after. Unlike me, where a constant ramble of his name flowed from my mouth as he watched me, maneuvered me.

I nestled against him, his heart beating steady and strong in his chest, and I focused on that powerful rhythm. My lips brushed his damp skin; a sweet thank you, a gentle connection I craved whenever we were done.

Done?

Oh, I didn't want to be done with Turo DeMarco.

36

TURO

ANOTHER DAY.

Another fantastic day, and I'd stopped looking at my watch to assess priorities. My prized Patek Philippe that my grandfather had given me on my twenty-first birthday was no longer a necessary tool to navigate my time.

A sundial better suited my needs.

This evening we'd caught the sunset drinking iced coffees as we strolled along the beach barefoot under a pink and orange streaked sky. Once darkness settled, we headed back to the house to get dressed for a night out. The second we'd entered the house, she'd pushed me onto the sofa, zipped down my pants, and swallowed my cock. Just before I'd come, I had her open her mouth and I sprayed her outstretched tongue with my cum. Right after, she swallowed me in once more, sucking me as I came down. I relented to her insistence, and it had been so fucking good, so fucking beautiful to experience that insistence and feel her drain me.

Her rough tenderness. What violins had once been. Gut deep, soul-rending music. My mind blanked and we'd lain there half on the sofa, on the floor, limbs tangled, sticky and sweaty.

Tonight we were going to a local bar. We'd showered and changed, and I strode down the steps to the foyer where she was applying dark red lipstick in front of the mirror in the credenza. She wore a long, royal blue dress with slits up the sides, and around her neck lay a mass of thin chains with colored crystals and the Greek evil eye charms.

She shot me a grin in the mirror as she twisted the cap back on her lipstick. I stood behind her dragging a hand through my hair, smoothing it back once again with what little hair gel I had left. She turned to me, her gaze traveling up and down my body.

"What? Is this all right?" I asked.

"Gorgeous." She winked at me, untucking the white linen shirt from my jeans.

"Well, now it's not."

"What do you mean?" She smoothed the ends of the shirt down.

"Now it's wrinkled."

She ignored my clipped tone. "It's linen, Turo. And it looks better this way. It's summer on an island."

"It's not summer, Adri. It's May."

Her eyes glittered at me. "Turo, this is not Chicago. This is Greece."

I caught my reflection in the mirror once again. "Hmm."

"You're pouting."

"I am not."

She tilted her head. "Men are such divas. And, by the way, you take forever to get ready."

"I do not."

"Sometimes, yes, you do." She got in between me and the mirror and holding my gaze, she smoothed her hands down my shoulders, down my chest, sending zings of heat through my flesh, the thin gold bracelets on her wrist clinking delicately. "But it's worth the wait."

My balls tightened at her words, at the spicy warm scent of

her perfume enveloping us. Goddammit, I was at her mercy. She could do anything she wanted to me at this very second, and I'd let her.

I'd fucking love it.

"Look at you, white linen on sun-tanned skin," she murmured.

"Hardly a tan."

"Golden." Her gaze tripped south. "Dark indigo jeans. Very nice." My muscles coiled at her long, slow, appreciative attention, at the low, intimate tone of her voice. It was almost unbearable.

"Are you admiring the goods or finding something lacking, sweetheart?"

"Do you own a pair of faded jeans? Or only these crisp, dark ones?" she asked, a hand on my thigh.

"I don't do faded or distressed. Ever."

She laughed. "I'll have to buy you a pair. They'd look amazing on you." Her fingers went to the buttons at my shirt. She unbuttoned the second, the third. The fourth.

I lifted an eyebrow. "Have you changed your mind about going out? Are we going for another round?"

Her eyebrows raised. "Your look needs styling. You need a more relaxed, Mediterranean feel about you." She opened the shirt revealing more of my chest. "All that's missing is a long gold chain and a medallion." She drew her nails down my torso.

"Adri," my voice warned.

"I'm teasing." She laughed, her fingers circling, burning through my skin. "That was the seventies." She buttoned the fourth button, leaving open the top three, her eyes holding mine, daring me to protest, her tongue darting over her scarlet lips. Who knew being dressed could be just as much a turn on as getting undressed?

"There." Her tongue lashed at my chest, and warmth shot through my veins. "That's indecent enough for you. Otherwise you'd be overwhelming." Her fingers brushed my jaw. "I like that you didn't shave today."

Indecent. Overwhelming. My heart pumped liters of flammable lust and desire through my veins at an insane speed. I put a hand over those fingers, crushing them in mine.

"Scruff."

She blinked. "Pardon?"

I rubbed her hand against my face and her lips parted. "The stubble, we call it scruff." I brought her hand to my mouth and kissed and nipped at her flesh.

"Hmm. Is that unusual for you as well, not shaving every day and having this...scruff?" She growled out the word.

I grinned, brushing my nose with hers, rubbing my jaw against her cheek. "Yes. I'll show you how good scruff can be between your thighs tonight. How does that sound?"

Her face reddened. "You know, I like that you have specific likes and dislikes."

"It comes with age, baby."

"Maybe. But it shows your confidence in your tastes and preferences, and I like that."

"Do you?"

"Very much. It's distinctive." She stepped back from me, and I physically felt the absence of her warmth. My slackened muscles tightened once again.

"Shall we go?"

At the crowded bar, Greek music thumping loudly, Adri ordered a Bombay gin and tonic with lime, and I had the same. She recognized a friend and then another. The two girls didn't seem like the jet set type. Local girls, one of whom had a boyfriend with her. Introductions were made, and I got us all another round of drinks. The music went from Greek pop and dance to a more Middle Eastern beat. The women got excited, and Adri brushed my cheek with her lips as she and her friends jostled to the packed dance floor.

352

With their hands twisting in the air, their hips gyrating, they flowed to the eastern rhythm. Suggestive, sensual, exotic. The boyfriend, a cigarette hanging from his mouth, left our table and got on one knee before them and clapped to the beat. Was this the Greek way to declare your admiration for a dancer's expression of her mood? Of her spirit?

Adri's sensual movements were right under that beat, stroking it, feeling it, flipping it. Her lips moved with the words of the song as she pivoted her gorgeous body. My heart jammed in my chest.

She was so beautiful. No, beautiful wasn't even the right word. Alluring. She had attitude and elegance in one. A free spirit singing, dancing, laughing. Completely uninhibited. No photographers to pose for, no paparazzi to dodge. No fashion police to impress. Only genuine joy. A tiny part of me, the selfish, egotistical part, hoped that I'd had something to do with freeing her spirit, tapping that joy in her.

Her eyes hooked on mine from the dance floor.

Joy for me.

Beguiling. Bewitching. That magnum of pink champagne had blown and the spray stung my skin. I had seduced her yet she was seducing me on a whole other level hour after hour, day after day, orgasm after orgasm, gentle kiss after hard suck. Adri was a creature of the bright sun and the velvet night. She evoked a new desire I never thought I had in me.

To bond and not let go.

It would end, though, it had to. And soon.

My eyes closed, and I soaked myself in that image of her, that feeling coming off her, off her soul's pleasure entwining herself in that exotic sensual music. I willed myself to never forget it, searing it on my soul.

I tugged a hand through my hair and took in a breath. The dance floor was filled with gyrating bodies, seats had emptied. The bar was jammed. And at the end of it, reality crashed on my private party. Standing at the bar, brown leather jacket guy sipped on a drink, watching Adri.

A flash went off behind my eyes, adrenaline bursting in my veins, and I charged over to him, cutting through the boisterous crowd. I slid in behind him, wrenching an arm around his neck, pulling him back against me.

"Who the fuck are you?"

His head twisted, eyes flaring, fingers digging into my arm, Greek curses flaring.

"Who sent you?"

"Turo!"

I blinked. Adri stood before us, breathless, hair flying. "Let him go."

"What? Why?" I gritted out. "He's been following us for days now."

"He's on my mother's security team. She must have sent him. Eh, Stavro?"

The man muttered in Greek. She put a hand on my arm. "Turo, please."

I released him from my chokehold and he sputtered, rubbing a hand around his throat, eyes blazing. She spoke to him in Greek, this Stavro of Liana's, as she wrapped an arm through mine. I tried to catch my breath, I didn't realize I was out of breath. My skull banged in my head. Adri took my hand in hers, another hand stroked the side of my burning face, and Stavro faded into the din of voices, the pounding music, the smoke.

"It's all right. It's all right." Adri's arms snaked around my middle and up my back, bringing our bodies together. Her steady heat silenced the drums beating in my head, the violins shrieking, the lights flashing. Those blue gray eyes gleamed back at me, and there was only her. Only her.

I took that beautiful face in my hands and touched my lips to hers.

"Oh, Turo..."

Her voice mirrored my ache, and I deepened the kiss wanting to obliterate it, be consumed by it, by her. She opened her mouth to mine, and we drank. We drank the wine.

————

BACK AT THE house we settled on the divan on the stone terrace at the back which overlooked the peninsula of the town with the castle ruins at its tip, the small lighthouse beyond in the vast blackness of the sea.

The lit whitewashed surfaces of the houses with their terra-cotta tiled roofs spread out around us like white building blocks. The deftly lit huge arbor of fuchsia bougainvillea, a thick wall of pine and cypress trees, and several lemon trees made this small garden very private. The jasmine had awoken as it did every night and shimmered through the thick air. The heady fragrance of the night flower bush was even more intense. The candle flames flickered pale yellow light from their large lanterns over the gray stone flooring, and the lights we'd switched on in the narrow lap pool, created a liquid aquamarine jewel at our feet.

"I have something special for us tonight." Adri went into the house and returned moments later with a vintage glass wine decanter filled with a pink red liquor and two glasses. She set the tray down and poured for us.

"What's this?" I asked.

"Taste," she said, an eyebrow quirking, her tone silky.

Heat filled my chest. My siren offered a gift to tantalize. I took the delicate glass. An intense flowery fragrance filled my nostrils, and I took a sip. Sweet rose filled my mouth.

"Rose liqueur?"

"Yes. A great aunt of mine makes it herself and there is always a bottle here. I like to keep it cold in the refrigerator. Do you like it?" She sucked on a fingertip where the wine had left a drop behind as she'd poured.

"You want me to like it," I said swirling the liqueur in my glass, mesmerized by its impossible color.

She took a sip of hers. "Hmmm. I do."

I drank again. "It's incredible."

Her face broke into a huge grin.

We were drinking roses. Roses. "Very pure flavor," I continued, still admiring its color. "Not that I've tasted a rose before. I like that it's not syrupy."

"I thought you might enjoy it. You've not tried anything like it before?"

"No," I breathed.

No, I've never had rose liqueur before.

No, I've never been with a woman like you before.

No, I've never felt my heart knocking against my ribs the way it is right now, the way it does whenever I'm with you.

No, I've never ached this way before. Ached for something else. Like a piece of me, the hard metal part, had melted and the heat turned my blood to liquid fire and that fire had leapt over the high walls of my castle that I'd so proudly built, just like your Venetian conqueror.

I drained the glass and held it out to her and she poured me more, that pleased smile dancing on her lips. We drank, the taste slightly sweet and very elegant, its warmth seeping through me, mellowing my insides.

Mellowing everything.

"Would you prefer it with ice maybe?" she asked.

"What I'd prefer is you without clothes," I whispered roughly.

She swallowed her drink, put down her empty glass, and slowly slid her dress off, her bare body offering itself to me to do with what I pleased. The blood pounded in my veins.

I kissed her soft, full lips gently and laid her down on the divan. Tilting my glass, I poured a thin stream of rose liqueur over her belly, and she let out a long hiss as we both watched it spill over her skin. I licked the sweet pink liquor from her navel up to the soft, firm swell of her tits, and her hips twisted under me. The rose was a heady perfume on her silky skin.

My tongue chased the liqueur and lavished her scar. A scar that still seemed fresh and irritated like the first time I'd noticed it. Her breath shorted, body tensing, gaze snagging on mine.

"Baby—" I planted a kiss on that wound that I was sure she continued to cut, keeping her guilt alive. "Oh, baby, let it heal. Leave it be and let it finally heal," I whispered over her skin, my tongue licking over it one last time, and her eyes filled with water.

I surged over her and took her mouth. She let out a gasp, eyes widening.

"What is it?"

"Your shirt, it's soiled."

I followed her gaze. Pink stains soaked the white linen. A growl heaved from my throat and I kissed her roughly.

She undid one button after the other, tugging the shirt off me. The cool air prickled my heated skin. Her fingers pressed into the sensitive flesh of my abs, up my sides, searching, her touch searing.

"Sit up on your knees," I breathed. "Face the sea."

She scrambled up on her knees, and laying down on the divan, I slid between her legs, wrapping an arm around her waist, bracing her and pulling her down to my mouth. I wanted all of her on me.

Sweet, sweet roses. Secret musk.

"Turo! Oh...*né*...*né*..."

Greek, English, her saying *yes* to me with her body and her mind was everything.

Leaning back, she gripped my raised knees and shuddered, crying out as my mouth possessed her. In a blur I pulled her off me and fitted myself with the goddamn rubber. I brought her body down on top of mine, her back to my chest, the two of us facing the stars, and angling my hips, I entered her.

If there is a heaven, this, this is it.

Panting, she let out a low cry, her face turning into my throat, her lips on my skin.

"Turo, Turo..."

"Look at the sky, baby. Send your moans up to the stars. Make them brighter for us."

Her fingernails dug into my arms.

Her insides so slick, so firm all around me. Our sweaty, sticky bodies molded together. My face pressed against hers and I found her lips once more. The taste of the rose liqueur stained them still.

She raised herself up, and my cock slid out of her. Pushing me back, she straddled me, her hair a curtain over us. Her hand went between us and fitted me inside her once more.

A slice of velvet in the dark.

"Yes," heaved from my throat. "Adriana."

She rocked over me, taking me deeper inside her, her body drawing me in and in and in. We kissed and tumbled in that kiss. I pulled her hair from her face. I had to see her in the candlelight. See that abandon satisfied along with mine.

"Adri—"

Our eyes locked, and her fingernails dug into my arms. She moved faster, her body creating poetry I couldn't quite decipher. We moved in the rhythm of her verses, their foreign words magic. We were the words, and she strung us together the way she wanted.

She came, grinding over me, and I chased my own end with her body holding me tight. Planting her hands in the cushion on either side of me, her eyes flared, her lips parted with the effort.

My hands slid up her back, a silent pleading. Heart pounding, pulse skidding. Everything hung on a teetering hinge. I needed her mouth, I needed her tongue on mine.

I needed her.

"Kiss me, baby," I whispered, my voice raw.

She dug her fingers into my hair and devoured my mouth, and I flew.

Not immune.

Not an outsider looking in.

I couldn't block it, fight it, stop it. Didn't want to.

I wanted to give in to her, and I had. I wanted more of her, and I got it.

I got *her*.

All the previous experiences I'd had with women had been characterized by a dual you-get-yours and-I-get-mine self-sufficiency. This with Adri, *this* was not that. This was messy, this was clear, this was layers of need, connection, raw hunger, sweet heat.

The cool breeze skimmed our hot skin, and she curled into my chest. I held her in my arms, our heavy breaths slowing. Spent, full. Tingling. I gulped in the perfumed air around us as her lips nuzzled my throat.

A vast, black, starry sky filled my vision. "So many stars," I murmured.

Her fingertips traced over my chest. "You know, your god Dionysus fell madly in love with a princess."

"Did he? I don't remember."

"Ariadne. Her Athenian prince boyfriend dumped her on an island and took off."

"Ass."

She let out a soft laugh. "And she'd just saved his life too. Anyway, Dionysus found her, rescued her, and they fell in love. Years later when she died, he took a crown he had given her and placed it in the sky with the stars."

"He was a soulful lover," I said, kissing her forehead, and she snuggled against me.

My gaze returned heavenward. Yes, my and Adri's pleasure was up there in that Greek sky—a crown of bright stars. Bright, bright, and so damn fierce.

37

TURO

FLUTTER, flap, flutter, flap invaded my sleep, and my arm curled tighter over Adri. *Flutter, flap.* My eyes peeled open. The light wind was making something snap close to us.

My shirt.

My linen shirt, perfectly clean from the rose liqueur was stretched out end to end on a small laundry line to the side of the garden terrace. The fabric puffed and filled with air. Bright, white in the morning sun. Teasing me.

Last thing I remembered was her ripping it off me, and us losing ourselves in each other. Adri smiled, her eyes still shut.

"What did you do?" I asked her.

"I woke up to get a glass of water and washed it for you," she replied, her voice lazy and warm. "I didn't want it to be stained."

"I liked that stain," I murmured.

She kissed my throat and nestled back into the blanket.

"Thank you, Lovely."

"Hmm. You're quite welcome." A smile rose over those lips— damn, I loved those lips—and I kissed them.

I reached up and snapped a soft branch of small jasmine flowers and traced them down her back, her arm. She hummed. I dropped the jasmine at her side on the pillow. "Sleep, baby." I pulled the hand knit blanket higher over her bare shoulders. The awning of woven ribbons of canvas flapped in the wind overhead as if we were on a great sailboat. Our very own cutting through our own blue, blue sea.

"Let's be lazy today," I whispered. "I'll go get us breakfast and bring it back."

"Hmm," and a slight grin were her only responses.

I moved the blanket out of the way and planted kisses on her bare ass. She buried her face in the pillow and giggled softly.

"You stay here, I'll be right back." I put on my jeans, took the washed shirt off the line and put it on. Sea air and bright sun had suffused the material with a fragrance unlike any other. The fabric was rough on my skin, and I grinned as I buttoned it.

I left the veranda but turned to grab another look at her. A greedy man, a thief. On a garden bed lay my ravaged sleeping beauty. My satisfied siren. I took her house keys and left.

———

THE CROISSANTS WERE warm and steamy in the bag, and I inhaled their yeasty, buttery sweetness as I left the bakery. I stopped in at Hermes and placed an order for two freshly squeezed orange juices. I'd make the Greek coffee myself this morning. I paid for the juices and headed back up the cobbled main street to the house. The bells of the clocktower in the main square bonged. Ten a.m. Shop owners were unlocking their doors, taking out their display stands, getting their coffees and small cheese pies, *tirópites*—the national breakfast on the go —delivered.

I passed the shop where Adri had stopped one afternoon and tried on a pair of flat leather sandals. It was a high end jewelry and accessory boutique, and the owner was just opening the display window's deep blue shutters.

"*Kallí méra*," she greeted me as I stopped and took in her well designed display.

"Good morning," I replied.

A variety of vintage and modern necklaces and bracelets had been posed around a number of painted seashells and starfish. Many pieces were on leather cords, others on silver and gold chains and a few on a variety of delicate blue cords, the same blues like the painted doors all over town. I found one that was perfect for my girl, and I went in and bought the necklace.

"Is it a gift?" she asked.

"Yes. Very special one."

Smiling, she nodded and wrapped the necklace for me in azure blue tissue paper and I tucked it in my pocket. "Thank you."

I made it back to the house and heard Adri speaking in terse Greek in the kitchen. She wore a short, white cotton robe, her hair a mess of long waves down her back. A tray with two white demitasse cups was on the counter. Her face was drawn, and she chewed on her lips as she listened to her caller, the teaspoon rigid in her fist.

I took our breakfast from the bags and placed her orange juice next to her, but her hand curled into another fist. With a steady hiss, the lava-like coffee bubbled quickly, flooding over the sides of the tiny pot. Adri barely noticed.

I shut off the stove.

"*Entáxi. Né, né, áde. Yia.*" She signed off in a tense barrage of Greek and tossed her phone on the table, a muscle along her jaw pulsing. She cursed under her breath, shutting off the stove, letting out a ragged sigh at the sight of the pooling lake of coffee.

"Hey." I picked up a sponge cloth and wiped it up. "What's going on?"

"Everything I've been trying to avoid."

"Who was that?"

She only took in a deep breath, her eyes watering.

"Adri." My sharp tone made her eyes lift to mine. "Who was that?" I asked.

She touched the orange juice cup carefully as if it were burning hot and not icy cold. "My father."

I took a sip of juice. "What did he say? Is there news?"

"Plenty. Always plenty of news from him. He always wants something."

Her bitter tone had me set my cup on the table. "And what is it that Petros wants?"

She let out a short dark laugh. "Not Petros."

"I'm not following, baby. You said your father—"

She took in and let out a deep breath, her eyes hard, lifeless. She looked years older than her twenty-three. "Petros is not my biological father."

"Okay. And who is?"

"My mother's first husband." She got up from the table and opened a drawer, taking out a pack of Camels. She lit one and inhaled deeply. "Yianni was a former Olympic water polo player who was her windsurfing instructor at this fancy beach resort all upper crust Athenians go to in the summer. Torrid first love. But he wasn't a somebody. He was a penniless nobody with a perfect tanned muscular body, and an enticing smile. Her parents forbid her seeing him, but she spent time with him secretly, got pregnant, and got her way. Marriage. It was a scandal, but a sexy one that people liked. My grandmother never forgave her for it."

"How long did it last?"

"Barely two years."

"But you have Petros's name?"

"He adopted me about five years after he married Mum."

"And you and your real father, obviously you know him—"

"Oh yes, I know him." Her eyes lit up, but the gleam in them was cynical. "Liar, philanderer, dreamer, gambler, egotist, narcissist. That's my father." She took a deep inhale on the cigarette.

Huh. That did sum it up nicely for me too, didn't it? "Why did he call now?" I asked.

"He's been calling since the shooting in Athens, but I've been ignoring his calls. Being in a particularly good mood, I answered today. Shouldn't have. Same old story. Only worse this time."

I pulled out a chair and sat at the table across from her. "What's going on?"

She blew out a long, thick plume of smoke like an experienced smoker. "He's in debt to the wrong people. First of all, he's always in debt. But this time was supposed to be different. He's always asking me for money. I used to give him here and there when he couldn't make his rent or he needed a new car, a new motorcycle, a vacation with a girlfriend. I always felt bad for him. He's never had what I have, and I wasn't a real part of his life. His reality is quite different from mine. But I always felt that as his daughter, why shouldn't I share some of what I have with him?"

"That's good of you. Generous," I proceeded carefully.

"My mother caught on and told me to stop, that I was only feeding the monster."

"She's right."

"But then he started owing money to the wrong sort of people."

"A lot of money?"

"Yes. He had this great idea to start a sailboat rental company with two other friends. He needed startup money and asked me for it. It was a lot but I thought yes, it's a good idea, this is perfect for him. The tourist trade is what he's good at, talking with people, teaching sailing, water sports. Perfect fit. And his own business.

"But then Grigori got killed and I was a mess and went back to Geneva and kept to myself. He was impatient, very impatient. And annoyed with me. He borrowed the money from a loan shark. There are many, many loan sharks here in Greece. And he knows a few personally from his days at the hotel and the nightclubs he frequents. The point being he owes money." She sucked on her cigarette, the end burned brightly.

"How much?"

Her hand gripped the plastic cup tightly as she sucked on the straw, swallowing juice. The sum must have danced a polka in her head.

I wrapped my fingers around her wrist. "Baby, how much?"

She swallowed hard. "I'm not sure. He wouldn't say. But it's got to be over eighty-thousand euros at least, *gamóto*."

Fuck, was right.

And it all made sense.

I lifted her chin. "They're after you now, aren't they? You think they're the ones that shot at you, don't you?"

She nodded slowly, putting out her cigarette. "I think so, yes." Her eyes widened. "It's not a secret that he's my father. Now he tells me they've been threatening him and used my name last week. They called him again just after the shooting." Her voice was hushed, strained. Her face pale.

Saying it out loud, sharing it, had finally made it real.

"Didn't he warn you?" I asked.

"I haven't been answering his calls lately," she said. "I was busy with Alessio's party, and I just wanted to avoid him and his mess for a little while longer." She made a face and took another hit of smoke. "This is where my hiding got me. Foolish girl."

"Stop. Do your mother and Petros know?"

"No. But my mother always suspects him whenever anything goes wrong."

"Smart woman. So what did he say now? How does he feel about you almost getting killed on his account?"

She squashed the cigarette butt in a small ceramic ashtray. "He was upset." She didn't sound convinced.

"Adri, did he ask you for money?"

"Of course he did, but I don't have that much cash available at the touch of a button. Maybe half if I liquidate my...but even then—"

"Don't panic."

Her head knocked back and she laughed. "All I do is panic. I panic on a constant basis, but I'm good at covering it up. Now, my mother will be livid, and Petros will be hurt and disappointed in me."

"I doubt that. You have a good heart, Adri. You were trying to help your father."

"Reporters will find out soon and make a mockery of all of us. And the men he owes money to will be pissed off with the publicity."

"Does Alessio know about this?"

"No. I've never told anyone. It's my dirty little secret." She lit another cigarette.

We all had dirty little secrets, didn't we? Even the most golden among us.

"I need to go back to Athens. I'm sorry," she said, her voice low.

"Call Alessio. Tell him you need him."

"What? Why? We can take the ferry back. I don't want to bother him now that he's—"

"Partying? Getting laid? Drinking champagne? Bother him. If he's the man I think he is, this won't be a bother. He'd sprout wings and fly to you himself if he could. We're going to need him."

She blinked. "We? We are?"

"This isn't Chicago. I can't take care of this on my own. "

She threw the lighter on the table. "Who are you really?"

"My father is a con artist and a liar and a thief too, Adri. Only mine is smart and mean and built an empire on those virtues. He's one of the most powerful men in America."

"And you...you don't save lives, like you did mine, do you? You take them, don't you?" A bitter laugh ripped from her throat. She threw the lighter on the table. "This is crazy, I can't—"

She fled the kitchen on a torrent of Greek epithets. I darted up the marble staircase after her, grabbing her arm, twisting her around. "Adri! I saved your life and I'd do it over and over again. I want to help you now. Let me help you."

"Turo..." A warning, a plea. Her face was wet.

I took her in my arms, and she pushed against my shoulders. "Everything will be all right, baby. We'll deal with it together. I want to help you. I'm going to help you."

"Everything's a mess. A mess. Like it always is."

"Shh. It's all right."

"Don't tell me it's all right when it's not, when it never will be!" Her fists battered at my chest.

I opened her robe, and her breathing sharpened. I ripped it off her body and it fell back onto the steps. "You trust me with your body, don't you? With your pleasure? Your body knows me."

She grunted, pushing at my chest, a punch, kicked out a knee, but I grabbed her thigh and steadied her on the steps with an arm around her waist. Nipping and sucking on her throat like a fucking vampire, sliding down her torso, pulling her to the steps with me. My fingers slid between her legs, stroking, and she gasped.

"You're wet for me."

She grit her teeth. "I'm always wet for you."

"Yes. But do you trust me?"

Her eyes bored into mine. "What is it, Turo? Our little self-imposed exile's over. You want my soul now? You want to claim me for your dark underworld like some Persephone?"

I did. I fucking did.

I replied by going down on her, and she let out a curse in Greek, her back arching, legs falling open and hitching around my shoulders, her fingers clawing at my hair. I scrubbed her smooth inner thigh with my scruff and clenched her ass, holding her against me, my tongue, my lips devouring.

My tongue, my lips were her slaves.

There on the stairs I devoured her until she stopped crying. Only moaning loudly, only repeating my name over and over and over.

Fuck, I loved that.

I kneaded her tits harshly, scraping her nipples with my teeth. I wanted her attention. She tensed, her eyes widening, fingers digging into my hair. *There's my girl.*

"Let me help you, Adri. We'll go back to Athens together and resolve this." A promise from the bottom of my dark soul. A soul that had made many threats, ultimatums, vows, but never a promise like this.

"I'm not leaving you," I said.

But that was a promise I wouldn't be able to fulfill.

38

TURO

ALESSIO INSISTED on leaving Mykonos and picking us up in Chóra on his yacht. We got off the launch, climbed up onto the boat, and he took Adri in his arms, murmuring in her ear, wiping a hand down her hair. I ground my jaw at the tenderness in his face, the soft waves of his Italian. Intimacy level ten, the motherfucker.

Staff appeared and took our luggage, setting the table with iced teas and coffees, a platter of crimson strawberries.

"Is Gennaro here?" asked Adri.

"No, he and Miguel stayed on at Cavo Tagoo. It's his favorite hotel. He doesn't need to be involved. He sends you his love, *cara*."

A smile brightened her mouth for a moment but her tense gaze darted at me. She wanted me and Gennaro to come to terms, for me to get what I wanted. *My Lovely.* She curled her legs underneath her body on the banquette next to me and slid her sunglasses over her eyes, a cigarette at her lips as we both watched Andros receding from us. Getting smaller. Farther and farther away. A speck.

Goodbye, beautiful, magical island.

I tugged on a piece of Adri's hair. Her chin wobbled and something scraped at the edge of my heart. Our secret escape was over. Our idyllic banishment in paradise had to come to an abrupt end. From the very beginning we both had known it wouldn't last, but there was still something shocking about it now which sent a prickly chill right through me, made my chest heavy. I didn't want anything to change between us. But everything was changing.

"Baby," I breathed as I entwined her cold hand in mine, our fingers meshing tightly. I brushed her cool cheek with my lips and she leaned into me, and my breath came easier.

Alessio left us and got on his cell phone at the railing.

"Remember I told you about my baby sister who'd gotten sick?" she said, her voice raw.

"Yes."

"She died in September. The summer before, my mother had sent me to Andros to stay with my grandparents while they took Anna-Maria to London for treatment. I hadn't wanted to go, to leave them and my sister. Of course, my grandfather and I had a wonderful time together, it was the idyllic summer holiday, but behind it all was so much grief and worry.

"Anna-Maria died and they brought her home to bury her. Everyone thought the funeral would be too traumatic for me, so my grandparents and I stayed on the island. I felt banished, left behind, not less sad. I wanted to be with my parents, to hug them. I wanted to say goodbye to Anna-Maria, to see her one last time. I wanted—" She swallowed hard. "A week later my mother sent her assistant to bring me back to Athens, and when we got on the boat, this was how I felt crossing the sea—" She clutched at her chest. "How I feel right now. Sad and homesick at leaving Andros, and full of dread as to what I'd find at home."

"I know you're worried, baby, but you're not that scared little girl anymore."

"No," she shook her head. "No, I'm not."

"And you've got me, Lovely. You've got me."

And she did. Oh, she did.

She nestled her face in my neck and breathed in. I held her tight, kissing the top of her head, a hand in her hair. This girl and her bleeding heart. She only wanted to love and be loved. But had been cut off over and over again.

Luca came up on deck and sat down next to his brother, lifting his chin at me. Adri stiffened at my side, keeping her attention on the sea.

"Tell us everything," Alessio said.

I told them what I knew about Adri's father and the money. A dark scowl morphed Alessio's features. He was pissed. About daddy or that he hadn't known before?

Luca sat back, stretching out his long legs. "*Che cretíno,*" he muttered, brushing a hand down a thigh.

Yeah, Daddy sounded like a real fucking prizewinning idiot.

"Can you find out who exactly these assholes are?" I asked Luca. "If they're local only, small time, or have a wider net? And then we can figure out a plan."

Alessio gestured at me and Luca to move our conversation away from Adri. We got up and followed him to the railing. Adri only lit another cigarette.

"I'm sure the asshole promised to pay off the loan using Adri's name as a guarantee," said Alessio. "Made him a sure thing in their eyes, eh?" he said.

"I'm positive he did," I replied.

"I'll find out what I can about these fuckers," said Luca.

"We have four hours until we get to port," said Alessio, his gaze darting at Adri then back to me. "I haven't seen her upset like this in a long time. I don't like it."

"I don't either," I said.

Alessio's eyes held mine, and I returned the hard look. He lifted his chin a degree and turned away. He knew she was no longer his.

Luca took his phone out of his jeans and went back inside the yacht along with Alessio.

Settling next to Adri, I pulled the strawberry dish toward us. "Have one."

"I don't want it. Don't want anything, thank you."

I bit into a berry. Sweet, luscious. Their season was upon us. "All those fucking cigarettes today. It's good vitamin C, and you need your strength. "

"I said I don't want anything." Her voice was sharp, jaw lean angles.

"Adri."

"No."

"No?" I chose another strawberry and sucked on it, chewing. "If we were alone, I'd take this strawberry, nestle it in your pussy and eat it from between your legs. All these little barbs on its flesh would make an excellent tool to make your clit pulse for me, don't you think? Your ass pucker? Make your nipples harden? Then you'd suck my fingers, all red and sticky from you and the strawberry, and I'd fuck you senseless until all you'd be saying is yes, yes, yes."

"My indecent gentleman." She dropped her head forward, her body shaking. She was laughing.

"My question for you is, do you want to sit here like this, mourning for your life for the next few hours, like that first morning we were together on this boat, or would you rather—"

She kissed me, licking the strawberry from my mouth. "Feed me."

"You say the most indecent things, baby." I chose a perfect berry. Holding my gaze, she bit into the fruit, and my dick pulsed against my jeans as the juice glistened on those lips.

"Sex isn't going to change things, Turo."

I slid my hand around her cold neck, my thumb stroking her drumming pulse there. "We have four hours before we land back in rotten civilization. You need to be relaxed and focused when

we get there, not frazzled. So, no more caffeine, no more cigarettes. Only strawberries and Turo for you—" My tongue swiped
over her lips. "Strawberries and Adri for me." I chewed the berry
from her fingers, and she let out a hiss.

She stood up and grabbed the shallow white bowl of red fruit.
"*Andiamo.*"

Fuck yes.

She led the way below deck to a cabin and locked the door
behind us. "Take my clothes off me."

I tilted back her chin, kissed her throat, and my hands moved
down her body, stripping her naked, leaving kisses behind on her
skin, breathing her in. Her bareness was a gift just for me. I held
her shining eyes in that moment when I'd tugged her panty off
her feet, and my heart swelled.

Afterward, the scent of sweat, musk, and sweet, sweet strawberry filling the cabin, she let out a long sigh which made me
raise my head. I wasn't sure if it was a sign of satisfaction or
unsatisfied longing.

And we couldn't have that.

Her head hung back over the bed, her long throat glazed with
sweat. Her hand lingered over a breast marked in bruises, bite
marks, and streaks of red. "You know, you've spoilt me completely
for any other man."

I wasn't sure what we'd find in Athens, but we had this
between us. This and more. And that piece of me that was on
high alert, ready for anything, was now not some professional
obligation but a roaring need that would not be quenched until
the enemy had been slain. Destroyed, and my goddess would
walk over the burning ashes with a triumphant smile on her face.

I pushed her hand away and my tongue flicked over a wet,
sweet, very hard nipple. "Oh, I know, baby. I know."

ATHENS

39

ADRIANA

PLACING a firm hand on my back, Turo glanced at the two security guards who stood by the Porsche Cayenne and got a nod in return. He guided me to the entryway of my father's apartment building in Vouliagmeni, an upscale beach and café neighborhood on the southeast outskirts of Athens where the hotel my father had always worked was located.

I took in a breath as we walked through the small gated courtyard and climbed the steps to the heavy wooden front door.

The first time I'd been to this flat was when he'd just moved in. I was nine years old. We'd spent the day together and ended up back here with a box of our favorite *profiteroles* in hand and a film I'd picked out at the video rental shop. He went to have a cigarette in the kitchen and got on the phone. He spoke loudly, and maybe he thought I was too young to understand the art of innuendo or maybe he just didn't care, but I realized he was speaking with a woman, a girlfriend. I'd understood every insinuation, every filthy suggestion that had come out of his mouth. I'd lost my appetite for the chocolate sauce soaked cream puffs, and he'd gotten annoyed with me and called me a spoilt brat.

The last time I'd seen my father was several months ago. We'd met at a café down the road from here. I'd laughed as I listened to his tales. He was a great entertainer, the ultimate storyteller—he reveled in the buildup, the cast of characters, the drama. Then there'd been a pause, and he'd launched into how things were "fine" but he had that restless look about him. That look that said, *"everything would be so much better, if only..."*

He'd told me about a new business idea and how excited he was about it. He'd need fifty thousand euros, however, to get it off the ground with his business partners. My father had many friends and "business partners" many of whom were figures of "the night", as they were called—nightclub, beach café, and bar owners. A shady lot who constantly opened and closed businesses.

I'd promised to consider giving him the money. I wanted to see him thrive, and I'd given him a great deal of cash for the last idea, a sailboat charter company. The company was doing well, or so he'd said, and I hoped it was true, and that his infatuation with the business had not waned.

I'd wanted to please him, like I always did, and I ended up giving him half of what he'd asked, twenty-five thousand. He'd been disappointed, but pleased all the same. That was the last time we met. We'd spoken on the phone, but he didn't share any news about how the new business was shaping up, and I hadn't asked.

The shooting that night at Island had shaken me to the core because I knew. I *knew* it had to be related to my father.

Now, I wanted answers. And no story of his would soften my resolve for the truth.

I hit the button with his name on it, and a loud *buzz click*, unlocked the door, Turo pushing it open for us. We took the small elevator to the third floor where I rang the bell at his flat. Footsteps became louder on the other side, and I shifted my weight, strangling the leather handles of my handbag.

The door pulled open.

My father.

Tall with more strands of gray in his thick, coppery brown hair than I remembered, and the bulky muscles from decades of water sports obvious through the thin fabric of his T-shirt. His lined and darkly bronzed skin spoke of a life lived outside, under the sun. His hair was messy, and his brown caramel eyes, although glassy and fatigued, suddenly leapt into tense lines. The worn tiger.

"Adriana?" my father said.

"Babá."

We kissed on both cheeks, hugged but my back stiffened under the pat of his hand. I pulled back from him, and his eyes narrowed at Turo and darted back to me.

"This is Turo, my security guard. Turo, this is my father, Yianni Karantis."

My father's face furrowed at my use of English, and he shot Turo a dark glower. A rush of Greek erupted from him, demanding to know why I was at his home with a stranger in tow at this ungodly hour of the morning.

"In English, please," I said. "Turo's American."

That got me a darker, deeper scowl.

"I trust Turo with my life," I said. "In fact, he saved my life that night I got shot at. I trust him with whatever you have to tell me about this...situation."

Yianni crossed his long, formidable arms across his chest, his jaw jutting out. "Okay."

The apartment was small but well furnished with the same modernistic chrome and glass and wood furniture he'd always had, a style that I'd always found cold and lifeless. A wide, sun-soaked veranda opened up before us and made the apartment seem bigger and warmer than it actually was.

We sat in the small living room. *"Kafé?"* Yianni asked, taking a quick sip of his frappé, lighting a hand-rolled cigarette.

I only shook my head, my gaze falling to the large glass ashtray full of butts and ash on the table between us.

"No, thank you," Turo replied, his eyes darting over the room, landing on a framed photo of little girl me in a red bathing suit, my father's arm slung around my shoulders, both of us smiling after windsurfing on the beach at the hotel.

"When was the last time they contacted you?" I asked.

"Two weeks ago," he said, sipping his coffee. "Two men came to this bar where I was with a few friends and told me that their boss had lost all patience with me and expected a payment." He made a face, that particular Greek expression of the *"what could I do? What did he expect me to say?"* variety.

"Who are they?" asked Turo.

"Here, it is very common to loan money to businessmen. Many want to expand—make their restaurant or store bigger, more fancy. Or open another one. It is normal."

"Normal," I repeated. "Going to the bank and applying for a loan is normal."

"*Élla moré tóra*," Yianni scoffed, his tone cutting, and my insides twisted at the familiar dismissiveness. "The banks don't cooperate, they take forever. You don't understand these things, Adri."

"No, I couldn't possibly understand," I muttered.

I couldn't understand because I was a girl. I couldn't understand because I was a very rich girl. I was only good for providing some of that "rich" to him. That ages old disdain of his pricked at me like thorns ripping at my skin. Turo pressed the side of his thigh into mine.

"And what kind of business were you getting your loan for, Yianni?" Turo asked.

"We found a yacht to buy. My partners and I planned on making it a nightclub for private parties."

"And what happened to the sailboats you were skippering

tourists to the islands for weeks at a time?" I asked. "Are you still doing that?"

"*Eh.* The rentals have been okay."

"What kind of rentals?" Turo asked.

"Many French and German families, Scandinavians rent the sailboat and hire me to be captain. I take them to different islands depending on the weather. They love it."

"It's still going well, isn't it?" I asked.

He shrugged. "I'm tired of it."

Of course he was. It wasn't bright enough, spotlight enough. Sexy enough.

"Anyway, it's only in the spring and summer," he continued. "The club yacht would be all year round. The Olympics are coming next year, so many foreigners will be here. There will be a demand for this sort of nightclub."

"Sounds like a good idea," Turo said.

"It is a great idea." Yianni lifted his shoulders, straightened his back. "The party yacht is for another kind of client—the rich Greek, Greek companies having parties, foreign companies, the celebrities having parties. The time is now for this sort of thing. Soon there will be great demand with all the foreign sponsors coming here. With the people I know—the athletes, the singers, the businessmen, the politicians. *Phhh.* They all always want something unique, and they all want to show off Greece."

My father and his business vision.

"You went to them for money for this idea?" Turo asked.

"*Ne.*" Yianni was exasperated with our questions. "My other two partners had bought the boat, and I would put in the money needed to fix it up. That was my part, that was our agreement. Adri gave me some money, and I borrowed the rest from these friends."

"I thought you'd said that married girlfriend of yours would give you—"

"*Eh kalá.*" His hand whipped in the air once more, swatting at my impertinent flies. "She gave me some money, not all of it. I got the rest from him. He knows me." He lit another cigarette and dragged deeply, his eyes boring into mine, making his point. "But this, this now is much more money. It's...impossible."

Impossible.

Impossible? Suddenly beyond his sphere of control? Therefore, not his problem?

I ground my teeth. He was well aware how serious all this was, how insane the sum was. They'd come after me to make sure he understood how serious. He'd been all emotional and penitent on the phone with me, but now? Now he was making his pitch, defiant, vehement to the last.

"How could you have agreed to borrowing so much money?" I asked. "Did you not wonder how you would pay back this bloody huge sum?" my voice sharpened.

My father only smoked in silence, seemingly unfazed, not frazzled. Consequences were a messy afterthought for him, like litter on the beach. You ignore it, walk by it, it's not your responsibility, not your problem. That is, until you wanted to go swimming and the reality of wading through all that trash in the water was disgusting.

How could he not be in a panic over this fiasco he'd gotten himself into?

Because he was sure I would take care of it for him.

When my mother and Petros had sent me back to Geneva, it hadn't mattered to Yianni that I'd been caught up in a horrible tragedy. He'd called once, we'd spoken. Rather, he'd done all the talking, I could barely form words. I'd been floundering, on the verge of an emotional breakdown.

"I thought we'd be making money by this time, and I would be able to pay something here and there," my father said. "But then the yacht purchase got caught up in paperwork and taxes and new taxes. My partners asked me for money to pay these fucking taxes."

"And did you?"

"Yes. But still, no boat. This government, *re gamóto, ti malak-izméni*—" He petered off into a string of curses and sour complaints about the current ruling political party.

Whenever possible, blame the government for your woes yet always expect a government handout to cure your ills. My father's generation had made that an art form.

"Babá," my voice snapped and he lifted his eyes to me. He was annoyed, annoyed with me, and for the first time, I didn't care. He wasn't going to derail yet another conversation his way. "Do you have any of the money left?" I asked him.

"A few thousand. I offered to give this back, they laughed at me."

Christé mou.

"And who is this man who lent you the money?" Turo asked.

"Efstathi Fokas."

The blood drained from my head, my mouth dried. "Fokas? You are friends with Fokas? You borrowed money from Fokas?"

"Who is this Fokas?" Turo asked calmly as if we were having an ordinary conversation on an ordinary topic.

Fokas was not ordinary. "The King of the Night, they call him. Athens's biggest crime lord," I said. "He's quite famous. Not only for lending money, but also for terrorizing judges and prosecutors with bomb attacks at their homes, hand grenades thrown at their cars. He works with drug lords, too."

My father's eyes blazed. "I have known him since we both started out. He was a kick-boxer who'd work as muscle at the nightclubs, just like I did when I stopped playing water polo. He even got me a job a few times in the winters, when I had no work, before I started at the hotel."

"And now Fokas has an empire," I said, my heart galloping in my chest, my head swirling in dizziness. "It's rumoured that Fokas is quite friendly with the remaining members of this notorious Greek terrorist group that was active in the seventies and the eighties. They've been experiencing a revival lately, made possible with Fokas's money. That anarchist group that killed Grigori is an offshoot of that group," my voice sharpened.

"I don't care about his political views. To each his own," Yanni said on a sneer.

"He sponsors terrorism and kills innocent people who are only trying to do the right thing," I said.

My father made a face. "Fokas has no control over what those extremists do."

"They killed Grigori!" I said.

"That was a terrible thing, Adriana. That boy did not deserve that, but this is not related."

"Not related?" said Turo, the deep boom of his voice sliced the tension and created more. "How about your daughter getting shot at to send you a message?"

No reply.

An icy tremor shuddered through me and I gripped my hands together in a fist. Turo's hand went to my leg, and I sucked in a breath. "I've helped you whenever you needed help. But this, this..."

"If I pay them the money, all this will be over, of course," said Yianni.

Was he implying that my getting shot at was a result of not having come through for him when he'd wanted me to? All this would just go away once I came up with the cash for him? Life would go on, and he would go on as he did before.

"Did Fokas ask you for special favors on your new party boat?" Turo asked.

Yianni scowled at Turo again. "What?"

"That he'd have a presence at your parties, be able to sell his drugs there? Prostitutes?"

Yianni only flicked his ash in the ashtray, and let out a thick stream of smoke, rubbing what was left of his hand rolled cigarette between his fingers.

"Of course," I murmured.

"*Adri mou.*" Yianni's tone lowered, softened. The tone of the caring father who had a simple solution to every problem. The tone he'd used with me for years. "If we pay them the money, this will be finished. I know this is asking a great deal, but it is simple."

I'd been shot at, my life was on the table, and this was *simple*?

"*Yia pes, Babá,*" I threw at him. "Tell me, will he send kidnappers after me next? A car bomb?"

Yianni's eyes flared, his fingers thumping on the table. I was being the difficult, disruptive child. "If we pay the money—"

"You promised them that Adri would pay, didn't you?" Turo said. "So when that didn't happen, they shot at her. Now what? Did you assure them that she got their message? Did you make a new arrangement with him? He'll do you a favor and set you up somewhere else if you pay them back everything in one go?"

Yianni took in a breath and held it, his face simmering.

"*Póso?*" I asked. "How much do you owe them?"

My father leaned back in the sofa. "One hundred fifty-thousand euro."

Turo made a rough noise in the back of his throat.

Sour bile swirled in my stomach, a cold creature slithering through my intestines, buckling there, stinging up my throat. I shot up from the sofa and went to the open veranda door, gulping in air. How could he be so stupid? How?

Because he only thinks about what he wants and how he must have it immediately.

Turo was right. God had nothing to do with this perverse folly of men like Evgeny, Fokas, and my father. Selfish, greedy choices over and over again. Wasn't that what evil was? The absence of God?

I was at the center of this horror show my father had created. If my money would keep my family safe, I would do it.

I turned to face Yianni. To face my years long denial of my

reality, my adversary, my own father. "I'll pay. But I want you to know I'm not doing this for you, to get you out of your mess. I'm doing this for my family—my mother and Petros, my brother, because Fokas just might go after them too, and they don't deserve that. You don't know the meaning of the word family. You don't."

"You are my family!" he spit out and my heart clutched. "You forget, you were taken away from me."

"You didn't fight for me. You didn't tell my mother no, I won't sign your papers, I won't take your money."

"*Ach*, none of that mattered, Adri, not really."

"It mattered to me!" I said, my own words stinging.

Yianni pressed his lips together, his eyes darkening, a long finger pointing at me. "You will always be my daughter, Adriana. It is my blood that runs through your veins, and nothing can change that, nothing. That new last name of yours is just another word."

"You really don't understand, do you?" My shoulders dropped. "It's always about you, what you want, what you think you deserve. What you could get out of it for the least amount of effort. Ah, and your *luck*." The word came out of my mouth like a spear cracking glass. My spear. Mine.

"Don't you dare talk to me like that," Yianni hissed. "You have no idea how the real world works."

Turo cleared his throat, his eyes darting between us. "Yianni, your friends and business partners—did they just swallow the money and move on?"

He slanted his head. "Yes."

"Did Fokas give you a deadline for payment?" Turo asked.

"Thursday."

"It's Tuesday today," I said.

"You weren't answering my calls!" Yianni's voice flared. "You were in Mykonos having your good time. I saw the pictures in a magazine yesterday." A hand flicked at Turo. "Kissing this one on the deck of your boyfriend's fancy yacht."

My face heated.

"You like your good time too, don't you, *agápi mou?*" my father threw at me. "Just like me, and just like your mother."

His icy spatter stung my skin.

"Don't you ever talk to her like that," Turo cut him off.

"This is none of your business, eh?" Yianni shot back.

"Oh, it is," Turo replied, and a chill stole over me at the cold simplicity of his hiss. Surgical steel. "You're the one who has no say in any of this any longer. The moment Adriana's life was put in danger by you, she became my business. Mine to keep safe."

The air went out of the room, and my heart stumbled in my chest. Turo's fierce tone shred my father's acrimony and shoved it back in his face, making him smell his own foul stench. His biting words were fangs that sank in and delivered their poison with clear cut precision.

The snake had trounced the tiger.

Perhaps it should have frightened me, his cold threatening stance, his obvious satisfaction in his victim's withdrawal. But it didn't. Every cell in my being tensed and pulled and cried out for him.

He's mine. And he was standing up for my worth, for my voice. For me.

I pulled myself up to that place that was new, steadied myself, there, where I needed to be. "My mother paid your price once," I said. "Now I will pay, and there will be no more. No more."

Yianni only ran a hand through his unruly hair, his lips twisting. No words, no more of his words.

"How does Fokas contact you, Yianni?" Turo continued.

"On my mobile. There can be no police. He's very connected to the police. He can find out very easily if we are working with them. No police."

"There is no 'we', Yianni." Taking my hand in his, Turo rose from the sofa. "You let us know the moment they contact you. Time, location. All of it. You leave anything out, I'll know. I'm not forgiving like your daughter. I don't give a fuck about forgiveness."

————

I WHISPERED in Turo's ear, "I don't feel forgiving right now."

He laid a hand on my leg in the backseat of the Porsche. "I'm sure you don't. You have every right not to, and that's okay, no obligation."

"He's scraped out what's left of it in me. I used to think him misunderstood. A larger than life man who just could never get the right break. So handsome, charismatic, strong. But that doesn't count for much when the going gets tough. It's under-neath that veneer that counts. He's had lots of opportunities, lots of shining moments, but no follow through. No sense of personal responsibility. It's as if he cannot compute those things. They simply do not occur to him naturally."

"It doesn't for some people. You can't expect it to."

"It's difficult when it's your father."

"Fathers aren't Supermen." A heavy breath heaved from Turo's lips, his jaw set. "They're just another guy."

I squeezed his hand on my leg. "Before Petros adopted me, I would stay with my father on the occasional weekend. One night he was going to take me out for pizza at one of the new American chain restaurants that had just opened in Glyfada. I was so excited. But Yianni didn't take me to the pizzeria. We went to a café bar on the beach where a woman was waiting at a table for him. He put me at a table next to theirs, ordered me a toasted cheese sandwich, and the two of them had lots to drink and lots to laugh about. I was so disappointed, but I swallowed it. It wasn't anything new, this crushed anticipation. We were there a while, it was late, and I fell asleep.

"When he woke me up, the lady had left, and we got back on his motorcycle to go home. I was so tired, he was drunk and driving fast, weaving around in the traffic. I still remember that feeling of hanging on to him so tightly, my legs squeezing so hard around the bike that they hurt. I couldn't breathe the entire fifteen minutes. When we finally got home, he asked me if I'd enjoyed the ride, because I was his little *"mánga"*—slang for 'tough guy.' I didn't want to show any fear or disappointment. He never liked that. He was all about spontaneous adrenaline rush living. So I said, "It was the best. You're the best."

"Why is it I remember these moments so clearly? More than when he taught me to water ski, took me jet skiing. The street fairs where he bought me all sorts of candy. The first time he took me sailing. Not those times." My breath hitched and I averted my gaze out the window, to the palm trees whipping past us on the shore road.

Turo took my hand in his and kissed it. "Because the times he broke your heart cut deep." His voice low, husky, his touch tender. He knew what I was talking about, and I ached that Turo knew this sort of painful cut that wouldn't heal. I leaned my head on his shoulder.

"I get it, sweetheart." Turo's voice was low, soft. "I do."

I squeezed his hand and stroked his arm.

He kissed the top of my head. "You've got to accept them, those bad times, and just push them to the back of the memory line. Let the good ones move up front. Stop clinging to the crap. It won't change it, and you won't understand them any better."

"There's an idea." I'd never had this before, this genuine understanding and respect, and I wanted to offer him the same. Help him the same way he was helping me.

"Why did your mother decide on the adoption?" he asked.

I stroked the cuff of his jacket. "She had an undercover security guard following me that weekend I spent with my father. The next day she offered him money to get him to sign the papers for

Petros to adopt me. She didn't have to twist his arm. He signed and took the money."

"I like your mother more and more."

"She doesn't put up with bullshit, not like me."

"You want to see the good in people first. You search for it, cling to it. That's admirable, but it can get you into trouble."

"I used to think Mum was so cold when it came to my father, like she is with her business. Strategic, logical. But she was right. The constant giving in a little here and a little there only leads to a disaster. They lead you on, you lead them on. False expectations on all sides."

Turo's jaw stiffened and his gaze fell on our hands entwined. He kissed my hand once more as if he needed to in order to steady himself.

I needed him too.

I'd never shared any of this with anyone before. From a young age, my mother had ingrained in me the notion of never discussing "private issues," as she called them, with anyone outside the family; it was a dangerous thing when your family was in the public eye. Always the responsible one, I never had— until now. It felt good, it felt right to share it with Turo, and he understood without explanation, and I cherished that.

"Has Petros been a good dad?"

"Yes, he's a very good dad. Concern and generosity come naturally to him. It was easy to let him love me and to love him back. I never felt that he cared for me any less than my brother."

"You're lucky."

Turo's phone rang, and he took it out. "It's Alessio." He answered, putting his mobile on speaker. "Hey."

"I have news," Alessio said.

"Good," Turo said. "We're on our way." He shut off his phone and scowled at the traffic on the road.

"We need your driving skills, Lovely. This traffic is insane."

I laughed.

"What is it?"

"Remember when I told you that my father had taught me how to drive?"

"Yeah?"

"It was Petros, not Yianni."

"Petros is the former rally race car driver?"

"Yes. He was a good teacher, too. Very patient, very calm."

"There's a really good memory to bump up the list and push the shitty ones to the back of the line."

"Turo DeMarco, you are a very smart man."

40

TURO

ALESSIO'S WATERFRONT bungalow at the Grand Resort hotel in Lagonísi, its own peninsula on the other end of the Athenian Riviera, this one quiet, removed from the bustle of town, was pretty damned spectacular. Luca and four of his men were huddled at a table with Adri's two Greek bodyguards courtesy of Petros.

Alessio handed her a huge juice smoothie.

"Perfect, *grazie*." She sipped on it, curled up in a chair.

I crouched before her, a hand on her leg. My need to constantly touch her hadn't escaped me. Our touching was a balm for both of us. I could sense her energy charge and mellow under my touch, and I felt connected to her, to us, and I liked that. I fed off it.

Her eyes leveled with mine. So goddamn blue right now like the bungalow's infinity pool and the blue sea beyond.

"Are you okay?" I asked.

"Yes. I'm glad we're here," she said. "Seeing you and Alessio work together is a good thing."

"Oh, you like that, do you?"

She cupped my face. "I like seeing people I care about getting along and working together."

That wild heat she inspired in me kicked up in my blood. "All for you, baby."

Her cheeks reddened, her gaze falling to my mouth. That unassuming sincere appreciation of hers, that surprise and gratitude that people were doing things on her behalf set off sparks inside me. I wanted to show her my gratitude. That innocent grace of hers coupled with her wild, natural response to me in bed, her willingness to trust me to push her just a bit and then a bit more every time made me fucking wild. My guileless vixen.

Her thumb brushed over my lips, and I kissed it. A smile tugged on the corners of her mouth. "I'm going to check in with my banker and my mother."

No tears, no shuddering. No anxiety. The warrior goddess was here.

Alessio stood before us. "I have forty-thousand in the safe on the yacht, *Cara*. It's yours to use."

"Thank you, Alessio. I'll have it for you within days."

Alessio only lifted his chin at her. He trusted her completely. I liked him more and more, although his endearment for her in that growly sexual animal voice of his had me digging my heels into the floor, I'd get over it. He hadn't needed explanations about me and Adri. He saw us together, and he knew. Of course, Adri and I locking ourselves in a cabin on his yacht to fuck for the entire trip back to Athens had pushed the point home, as it were. Still, no drama from Alessio.

End of story.

"I'm going to confirm that with the bank now. For the fifth time," she said. "Greece isn't Switzerland."

I kissed her quickly and left her to it.

I crossed the room and sat with Luca. "What did you find on Fokas?"

"He's a former kickboxer hired by a crime boss years ago as

his muscle, collecting protection money from nightclubs, bars, restaurants. Eventually he formed his own gang involved in the same rackets and recruited young boxers and trained them as his soldiers. He expanded his activities to drugs, arms trafficking, and prostitution, bringing in women from the former Soviet bloc countries and Albania. Had his men hired as bouncers for the clubs that owed him protection. He even partnered up with a former bodyguard of the Minister of Public Order. Good one, eh? Big arms trafficker that one—explosives, weapons. This guy trained a group to rob banks, armored trucks, ATM machines with military precision."

"Is it the wild fucking west out here?"

A smirk edged over Luca's mouth.

"How do they launder their money?"

"It's a big market. Luxury cars, cruisers, yachts, jet skis."

"Yachts and jet skis," I murmured.

Alessio grabbed his brother's lighter on the table and lit a cigarette, a thick eyebrow arched high. "Sounds like someone we know?"

"Yianni must have been doing shit for them on his charter sailboat business as payback for that first loan," I said.

"Oh yeah," muttered Luca.

"I've seen it before," I said. "They get comfortable and think they're in, that getting more or getting special deals is easy. Makes sense he'd go to Fokas for the really big bucks."

"People don't trust banks here. They consider them a corrupt institution that steals from the people," said Luca.

I sucked on the last of my iced coffee. "Like the government, right?"

"*Si.*" A grin stole across Luca's face. "*Bravo, Americano.* This past year Fokas went big. His smuggling used to be only cigarettes through Cyprus. Now he's started bringing in cocaine from Latin America through Western Europe to Greece, hiding the drugs on fishing boats. He has a legitimate fishing business, rental boats. Not all the boats are used to hide the cocaine, but plenty are."

"Now the summer season is on and there's big demand for the drugs on the islands," said Alessio. "Mykonos was nuts."

Luca tilted his head. "Delivering and picking up in Greece is fun. All that coastline, all those islands, so many boats big and small, really fast, and not enough Coast Guard patrols to go around."

Alessio brought over three Pellegrinos and handed them to us.

"You said Fokas has been bringing in blow to Greece from Latin America via Western Europe?" I asked.

"*Si,*" said Luca.

"Where in Western Europe?"

He sucked on his Pellegrino, draining it, his eyes on me.

Ah, here it comes.

He set the bottle on the table. "Through my father in Napoli. You had asked me if I thought the shooting was meant for me."

"I did."

"I still think it might be."

"How?"

"My father beat out a rival to do business here. Ventura is their name. They were very pissed off. Also, one of their capo's girlfriends happens to love Alessio's jewelry." Luca laughed.

Alessio rolled his eyes. "She's a model. The week before we came here she did a naked modeling shoot in a magazine wearing only my necklaces and rings, and she sang my praises in an interview," said Alessio. "He got pissed, and had a couple of his goons trash my store window in Milano in broad daylight."

"I found him," Luca said, a hand down his chest. "He threatened me then. So yes, it passed my mind that they could be behind the shooting that night which is why I wanted to get on the boat right away."

"Does your father know?"

"*No.* I didn't want to bother him with this bullshit," said Luca leaning over, his arms planted on his legs.

"Maybe it's time you did," I said. "This isn't bullshit anymore."

"So now we wait for that fuck to call Yianni back?" Alessio asked.

"Yeah. We wait," I replied.

He cocked his head toward Adri who was still on her phone. "How is she really?" His voice was low. "First the shooting, now this."

"She's doing well, actually, all things considered," I said.

"If she's still with you, you're doing something right," he said.

"I do a lot of things right, Alessio. A fuck of a lot. Especially for Adri." That was the truth, and it settled in my chest, my gut.

"You be good to her. She deserves the best," he said.

"I know."

Alessio put out his cigarette. "You two stay here at the resort tonight so we're all together, eh? Get your own room though."

"I was planning on it." I turned to Luca. "I need a gun."

"Not a problem." He slanted his head toward his men. "Come." We went over, and one of them offered me my choice of weapons. I took the Luger and headed back to Adri who watched me and clicked off her phone.

"We need to stay here tonight," I said, crouching in front of her again, a hand on her knee.

"Yes, we should."

"I want to get out of here. I need a shower, a bed with you in it naked, your mouth on me—" She blinked, and I leaned into her, brushing her ear with my lips. "—all over me. And the only sounds I want to hear are the waves crashing on the beach and you moaning non-stop."

Adri stroked the side of my stubbly jaw, and I let out a breath, my eyes closing for just a moment, that moment under her spell.

"My indecent gentleman," she whispered, planting a kiss on my cheek.

I took her mouth, the taste of that sweet tropical juice on her tongue giving me a rush.

"Right. I'll arrange for our own bungalow." She put her empty juice glass on the table with a definitive *clack*. "My mother's company developed this property, and I was her intern that summer, and I've never spent much time here. They'll love that I'm actually staying here for once. All you need to do is enjoy. Massages, room service—"

I let out a laugh. "You arranging everything is turning me on like crazy, Lovely. Careful."

"No, no, no. I don't want to be careful, Turo. Not with you."

Absolutely fucking right. I grabbed her arm and her head snapped back at me, lips parted.

I said, "I don't want to be careful either."

41

TURO

She liked taking control.

And I let her. And for the first time in my life, I got off on a woman making decisions for *us*. This woman. Mine.

My dick hardened as she chatted up the reception desk agent in the main building. To say the staff "hopped to it" would be a poor description. We were ensconced in our own waterfront bungalow shortly thereafter. She ordered food and made it clear it was to arrive after the hour mark. The bell hop thanked me for the tip and left.

"Why so specific about the time, Lovely?" My hands went to my hips as I took in the heart-stopping blue, blue vista.

She whispered in my ear, "We need to fuck first."

I didn't think she used the word "fuck" as a verb very often, and her smirky grin told me so. She was pleased with herself.

"And then we eat and drink," she said, dipping a foot in the pool. "We'll be very hungry after." She brushed a hand down my back and my pulse wound up tight.

"Very hungry," I replied.

Adri took my hand and led me inside. With the drapes wide open, the azure sea and infinite sky filled the suite. She tugged my zipper slowly and got down on her knees between my legs, taking me in hand, exploring me with her mouth.

Cupping her chin, I raised her head, her eyes finding mine, her tongue still flicking over the head of my cock. "I want you naked for this," I breathed, my balls tightening. "I want us both naked."

A swirl of pink rose over her skin as she ripped off her jeans and blouse, got my clothes off me, then got back on her knees and took my cock fully in her mouth in the middle of the living room. I held her hair in my fist as she worked me, her fingers digging into my hips. So diligent. So committed to my pleasure.

To our pleasure.

"Dedicated aren't you?"

"Hmm." Her eyes lit up, her mouth moved quicker.

My orgasm built quickly, sharply. Pressing my thumb onto the side of her face, I slid out of her mouth which she held open for my cum. *No, baby.* I grabbed her up in my arms and with her legs cinched around my waist, I thrust my wet shaft deep inside her. My forehead slid against hers on our deep gasps.

That first moment of entry.

I'd never paid much attention to it before; it had always simply been the pass-through-and-go that signaled the beginning of the best ride. My ride. But with Adri, now, it was sheer ecstasy, pure, real excitement. Her taking me in, her unusual little moans, our flesh pressed together, our bodies seeking from each other's, all set off a euphoria in my blood that I'd never known before. Giving and receiving.

Her fingernails dug into my shoulders, and I buried my face in her throat. She murmured Greek words I didn't understand, yet we spoke the same language. We were one creature of need and lust and desire. And trust. So much trust.

I didn't know what tonight or tomorrow would bring. I didn't know if I'd ever see her again, if I should. After this daddy fuckup was over, and after I got what I needed, I'd be leaving, and we'd be done.

But now she was mine.

I brought us against the wall and pumped inside her fiercely. Her head arched back and she let out a long, savage cry. I loved her there, completely open to me and choosing to be so, relishing it.

A river of Greek.

A damp hand wrapped around my neck, holding on for dear life. Fierce blue eyes melding with mine. Each of us daring the other to go higher, harder, faster. My legs shuddered as I held her wrapped around me, our bodies sweaty, our skin hot.

After, we showered in the huge mosaic-tiled shower with a waterfall of water pouring over us. I washed her body, her hair, and brought her to lay back on the marble bench in the stall, and with the hair conditioner as my ambassador, nudged my finger past her tight hole as I ate her pussy. She moaned loudly, clutching at her breasts, her gorgeous wet body splayed out for me. My private feast. A storm in our steam-filled tiled jungle.

We dried each other off, donned the thick hotel robes, and the bell rang. I checked the peep hole at the door, gun in hand. The food had arrived. Adri directed the waiter to bring the cart onto the terrace. I tipped him and he left us to it.

We were starving, and thoroughly enjoyed the roast chicken and a steak along with grilled vegetables, a green salad and a selection of cheeses and breads. My phone beeped. A text from Alessio letting us know that Adri's cash had arrived and he had it with him in his heavily guarded bungalow. Adri called Yianni once again, but there was no answer. There was nothing left to do but wait.

The sun sank in a burning sky. Before us the sea transformed into a mellow blue and orange pink liquid cocktail. My hand slid under her robe and wrapped around her bare thigh. She covered my hand with hers, a low giggle escaping her lips. I stroked her warm, smooth skin and jerked open her bathrobe and kissed a breast, the other. I wanted to see her in the sunset, ravaged and satisfied, and mine. She stretched out, her flesh alive in the last glow of the afternoon light.

"The masseurs should be here in ten minutes." Her hand teased my hardening shaft. "Do you need anything until then, Turo?"

A hush had settled over the world, over me. I rubbed her thigh. "I've got it all, baby."

And that was the fucking truth.

It didn't take long to blow that satisfaction to hell.

42

TURO

A BEEPING SOUNDED. A phone. I shot up in the bed.

Adri reached out and grabbed her cell, answering in the dark, the light glowing in the bedroom. *"Parakaló?"* her voice unusually clipped.

"Marko? Élla, agóri mou—"

Her little brother.

Her breath cut off sharply, her body stiffened next to mine. She swiped the hair from her face and sat up on her haunches. A rush of Greek. *"Óxi! Óxi!"* she yelled.

She clutched at her phone and spit out another round of bitter, pointed Greek. Her eyes shut and she spoke, her tone lower. Was she agreeing to something? She cursed, throwing her phone on the bed like it was on fire.

"What happened?" I asked the question. But I knew the answer.

"They took Marko. They took my brother. Oh my God, Marko."

I gripped her arms. "Adri. Take a breath. Look at me."

Her wild eyes met mine.

"Tell me everything he said to you right now."

"They..." She gulped in air, swallowing hard. "They want to make sure I come with all the money. Real money, not counterfeit. No police, no detectives, no security. They want ten million euros for Marko. Ten million. Ten million..."

"Fuck. Yianni's been dicking them around long enough. They know you're in the game, they went for it."

"Now an innocent boy is going to pay for this bloody mess my father created?"

"Sweetheart, look at me."

She raised her tear-streaked face.

"When do they want the money?"

"In two days." She laughed. "Two days. Ten million in two days."

She touched my arm, her fingers running over the evil eye bracelet she'd given me. "All the charms in the world won't keep evil at bay. Nothing will. Nothing."

"Baby—"

She pulled out of my embrace. "I have to call my parents." She plucked at her phone, bringing it to her forehead.

"Hey." I lifted her face to mine. "This is not your fault."

"Isn't it? An innocent boy is in danger for his life. My brother is trapped in my—"

"In your what? Your father's bullshit? It's not your fault. He's the one who—"

"Yes, yes—he, him. My father, my blood, not Marko's. Mine. Maybe if I'd never given him money over the years, making him think that he could use me whenever he needed me, maybe this wouldn't have happened. A part of me always wanted to believe that we had a real relationship. If only I'd accepted the ugly truth that he can never see beyond his own needs and wants, then all this wouldn't have touched Marko. I brought this on our house, and my mother and Petros don't deserve it. They don't deserve it!"

"Neither do you. All you've done is try to be supportive of the man who spawned you. Yeah, you could've turned your back on him from the very beginning, but you didn't because you have a heart and a conscience. Because he's your father and you love him, baby. And that's a good thing. What could be more natural than a child wanting a parent's love? Wanting to preserve that? Wanting more of it?"

Her glimmering eyes filled with more water, and my chest constricted. I saw myself in those eyes. I'd heard my own voice, my words.

What could be more natural?

I had lived the same yearning all my life, hadn't I? The same striving, reaching, and the same goddamn disappointment. My strangling all that wretched want. Me striving to prove myself "worthy" of a relationship with Mauro, the Boss God. Adri hanging onto a relationship of threads at all costs. Both of us. At all costs.

So much cost. Always a ransom to pay.

"None of this is natural," her voice rasped. "There is nothing natural about any of it."

———

ADRI CALLED her mother and she held it together the whole time. Marko had been on an overnight field trip with his school in the countryside and gotten nabbed at a restaurant. I got on the phone with Petros and explained further about Yianni's gigantic cluster-fuck. I assured him Luca with his contacts and I were on it. That they should contact the police but keep them on hold. He agreed.

I put a whisky in Adri's hand and called Luca.

Bitter silence was his reply to my news about Marko having been kidnapped. "Fuckers took their opportunity," he finally said.

"I want Yianni to cough up some information about his Fokas buddy. We need to have our own chat with him. Specifically, you'll be doing the talking, Luca. You're going to make threats that your daddy would be proud of. Show him what the Alibertis are made of. We want the ransom lowered, and the kid released without a scratch on him, and no pieces missing. You be ready in the morning by eight."

Shutting off my phone, I finished Adri's untouched whisky. Her gaze met mine from where she was curled up on the sofa. "Can I get you something else?" I asked her.

"Hold me." Her voice was small but sure. I set the glass down and took her in my lap, in my arms, and my insides melted. I held her tighter, breathing in the warm scent of her skin, the fragrance of the shampoo we'd both used.

She rubbed her hands up the sides of my face, kissing me, wanting from me.

"Adri—" I grabbed her hands and held them fast.

"Make love to me, Turo. Part of me is spinning, part of me is numb. Make it stop."

I lifted her in my arms and brought her to the bed. She clung to me, aroused, ready. I kissed her, I entered her slowly, holding her gaze in the diffused light of the small lamp we'd left on in the living room. We breathed in the same breaths, we moved inside each other, building it together. One begging, the other giving. One demanding, the other devoting. Desperate. Untamed. Beautiful.

Shattering.

Afterward, I lay there spent on the bed, Adri's still, damp body pressed against mine, my fingers in her hair. A heavy, orange sun rose in the yellow sky over the pale blue water, and my heart, that once brittle organ that I'd fortified with fences and gates and checkpoints and clauses beat wildly in my chest.

And then it occurred to me.

Until now, I'd never realized that my heart could, all at once, feel both battered and full. Until now, I'd never realized that I had a heart that could burst.

I took in a deep breath.

A heart that could break.

43

TURO

FIRST THING IN THE MORNING, I sent Adri home to her mother and Petros at their fortified fortress of a villa—round the clock security, trained guard dogs, an electric generator in case the power got cut off, new security cameras, and outdoor lighting. Petros and Liana didn't fuck around.

Luca, Alessio, and I headed to Yianni's apartment.

Ciro, an unsmiling six foot five don't-even-think-about-fucking-with-me-Italian-muscle of a right-hand man with a shaved head pounded on Yianni's door. Muttering and loud voices rose on the other side.

The door swung open, and Yanni, his full head of thick hair standing on end, a platinum blonde young woman at his back.

"What do you want? It is so early! What the hell do you think you are doing?"

Ciro grabbed him by the neck and shoved him deep into his apartment. The girlfriend screeched, her tiny black nightie fluttering over her thonged ass as she scrambled down the hallway.

"Hey! Hey!" said Yanni. "Does my daughter know you are here?" His heavily accented English was not the crisp Queen's English of Adri, Liana, and Petros.

"*Sta'zitto!*" Luca shut him up as Ciro pushed him into a chair.

I planted my feet on the floor in front of Yianni. "Yes, shut up. You've been spewing more than enough bullshit for days now. Weeks. Years."

Yianni slanted his head at me and Luca and Alessio. "Which one of you is fucking my daughter, eh? All of you?"

Crack. I backhanded him. "Shut the fuck up."

Yianni's head hung, his chest heaving for air.

"Listen to me," I said, my voice firm. "Adri got a phone call from your friend Mr. Fokas."

"That's good, isn't it? He told her where to drop off the money? I asked them, but they never returned my call."

"Oh, did you hear that, Luca?" I said. "Yianni's been waiting, and Fokas never returned his call."

"*Ke katz.*" Luca yanked on Yianni's hair, pulling his head back.

"They have Marko now, Adri's brother," I told him.

Yianni stilled, his face set in stone.

"They figured they had Adri, thanks to you," I said. "Why not squeeze her for more? Play another hand for higher stakes."

"How much do they want for the boy?" Yianni asked. He didn't seem too upset by this new information. He was all business.

"Do you even know how old he is?" Alessio asked him.

"How much do they want?" Yianni only repeated.

"He's fifteen years old," I said. "About to be a man, still a child. Honor student, athlete. Polite, just like his father. Now he'll be marked forever because of you, a shitbag he doesn't even know."

Luca studied the water polo trophies lining a shelf. "They want ten million euros."

Yianni's face fell, his jaw hanging like a gate blown wide open by a sudden gust of hard wind.

"We need to talk to Mr. Fokas," I said. "And you're going to tell us where to find him."

"You can't just go talk to him," Yianni said on a sneer.

"You're such good friends, you said, Yianni. For years, from the very beginning," I said. "He wants this money, he'll see us."

Luca rammed a gun under Yianni's chin. "Start talking. And don't make up any little fairy tales. I've heard them all."

———

BLACK SKY GLITTERING, road lights flooding the long, winding seaside boulevard, palm trees stretched out like great big fans. It was just before midnight, and Luca and I were on the nightclub strip of Poseidónos Boulevard in Glyfada, a trendy seaside southern suburb of Athens, moving through the traffic. Nightclub after nightclub. Greeks loved a night out. They lived for live music, dancing, and every popular singer obliged. Billboard after billboard beckoned with huge, dramatically lit posters of male and female singers appearing at venue after venue.

Ciro directed the driver to pull into "The Lyra" which loomed ahead on our right, the parking lot jammed. "You stay in the car," Luca said to Alessio. "I don't want you seen or involved directly."

Alessio nodded and sank back in the leather seat.

Ciro, Luca, and I strode into the nightclub. Four bouncers blocked us at the brightly lit lobby, but Luca, in his Italian accented English, informed them of our need to see the *"affentikó."* The boss, in Greek.

Cell phones came out, murmuring, cutting glares. Pounding music, thick smoke. Greeks smoked a hell of a lot too. Everywhere you went. Thank fuck I didn't have asthma.

"Affentikó he cannot see you now," came the reply.

I got into the bouncer's sweaty face. "Tell your boss that we have the special delivery he requested, and if he wants it on time, he will see us right the fuck now."

The bouncer only blinked, made a face. This shit was complicated for him. His horrible, shiny, polyester-y, purple shirt was too tight at the neck, cutting off his goddamn circulation and any brain function.

Luca grabbed the phone from the bouncer's hand and shook it in his face. "Tell him one name. Tell him Aliberti is here." Luca smashed the phone in the guy's chest.

The guy peeled his phone back and made the call. He gestured down a dim hallway. "This way."

He led us to a far corner, up a narrow stairwell to a large door. He patted us down and took my and Luca's guns, unlocked the combination keypad, and we entered.

A thick cloud of smoke and the din of cards shuffling and snapping on tables, men speaking in low tones, the constant *clack* of high heels on tiled floor. Women in stripper clothes and heels served drinks. A mini casino.

"Here," said the bouncer, and we followed him to another stairwell that opened to an office. He closed the door behind us.

A large man with graying black hair and a gruff scowl sat behind a desk, a lit cigarette in his hand. His shirt collar open, a thick gold chain with a cross visible on his chest. Aside from a paunch in his waist, the former kickboxer had aged well.

"You don't stand up when you greet your guests, Mr. Fokas?" Luca asked.

"Why do you use the name Aliberti with me?"

"I am Tiberio Aliberti's son Luca. His representative here in Greece."

Fokas pressed his lips together, his glare scouring Luca. "How do I know you are who you say you are?"

"They took my gun at the door, this will have to do." Luca took out his European Union driver's license and held it up.

Fokas flicked his gaze over the card and Luca put it away. He leaned forward on his desk taking another hit of his smoke. "Please, sit. What is this about?"

"I was having a fantastic holiday here in your country, but then I got interrupted. You interrupted me."

"I interrupted you?" He let out a sharp laugh. "How did I interrupt you?"

"You took the boy. You shouldn't have taken the boy."

Fokas's dark eyes narrowed for a moment. "Why do you care about the boy?"

"His sister is my brother's woman."

I smoothed a hand slowly down my throat. Even though I knew it was all a scene we were playing, hearing those words out of Luca's mouth pissed me off, jerked and jangled my every fucking chain. Loudly.

"I had a point to make," Fokas said.

"*Si*. A point. Don't you think you made it when you shot at the girl?"

"I'm an impatient man, and I don't like being ignored."

"The money owed to you is ready. I have it," Luca said. His fingers flicked out at me, and I raised the briefcase in my grip.

"Hmm." Fokas smashed his cigarette in a full ashtray at his side and leaned back in his chair once more. "The ten million plus the hundred fifty-thousand?"

"Ah, I think you are being greedy," said Luca. "This, what you are doing now, will only bring terrible attention to your organization, and my father will not be pleased. It will ruin your agreement with him. All imports will have to stop. Do you understand?"

"No, I don't." His jaw stiffened.

"*Kírie* Fokas. I oversee the work in Greece for *Signor* Aliberti. I say who, when, where, and how to fuck yourself. There are hundreds of men like you looking to do business with my father. In fact, I met someone in Mykonos this past week who made me a very tasty offer for working that particular island. The best island, eh? But I'm a man of principle. You and I are already doing business, and I would like to be loyal to our agreement. You know, in the Ionian Sea I have new Albanian friends who service those islands with their power boats. Those boats could easily cross to the Aegean." Luca casually stroked his jaw.

Fokas's upper lip stiffened, he remained silent.

"You took the boy. Congratulations, you'll get money. Why shouldn't you for such an impressive act? But not ten million. His sister is my family. Be sensible. Take this—" Luca gestured at me, and I took the briefcase with the hundred and fifty and put it on the desk. I opened it, and Fokas's eyes darted to the cash and lingered there. "—it's what's owed you from that sailor friend of yours, yes? Lower the ransom for the boy to one million and you'll get it."

Luca and Fokas had a stare down, seconds ticking into minutes.

"These people have the money," Fokas said.

"You know," said Luca, his voice casual. "I hear the marijuana from the island of Crete is amazing. Maybe you could help me with that? I always need a fresh supplier."

More business opportunities. More bargaining. Fokas slanted his head in that particular Greek way.

Luca raised his chin at me. "Make the call." He turned back to Fokas.

I phoned Petros. "Hold please," I said, and then handed the phone to Luca.

Luca took my phone. "One million by tonight." He closed the phone and handed it back to me.

"The girl, Adriana, delivers the money to the drop off point." Fokas licked his full lower lip.

The fuck had tossed his match and the gasoline blazed in my veins. My muscles tightened, keeping the roar of my rage in check. It was Luca's place to respond. I had to remain unmoved.

"Absolutely not," Luca said through gritted teeth.

"She comes with the money or I keep the boy. Very simple."

"Why?"

"She may be between your brother's legs, but for me she is a star. And I want to see this star fall from the sky and come down to earth for a change. I want her and her fancy family to get their hands dirty for once, not to send their slaves to do their work for them. If she does not come, the price goes back to very, very high. You understand?"

———

"MOTHERFUCKER!" I spat out, climbing into the back seat of the car next to Alessio.

Luca slid into the front, Ciro slamming the doors after us.

"What happened? Did you see him? What did he say?" Alessio asked.

I filled him in as the driver swung the car out of the nightclub and back into traffic on Poseidónos Boulevard. Alessio's eyes blazed and he exploded in acidic Italian at his brother, hands waving in the air, punching at the seat in front of him.

Luca remained unmoved, his lips pressing into a firm line. "We'll be there with her, Alessio. He just wants a show. He wants to leave his mark like a fucking dog peeing on a tree."

"He's not going to leave his mark on her!" Alessio's voice boomed.

I scrubbed a hand down my face. "She can do it," I said. "She's more than capable."

"You are so certain?" said Alessio, his tone ironic.

"The Adri you know and the Adri I know are very different," I said through gritted teeth. "She can do this. She'll want to do it."

"If you say so," muttered Alessio.

"He wants to see her cry, be desperate, weak," I shot back. "She's not going to give that to him. No fucking way."

One by one, our fangs retreated and we slunk back into our corners, our black thoughts simmering in our heads, like boiling potions in a cauldron.

415

"You were very convincing, Luca," I said, breaking the silence.

"I've been doing this shit for my father since I was a teenager. Convincing people with my words, my gun, a knife." Luca let out a rough breath and trained his eyes out his window.

Violence, threats, murder, and shakedown made up family memories of growing up for Luca Aliberti. He didn't seem impressed with himself. It's just the way it was.

"He's always been good at this," said Alessio. "Some of us are made for it. Some of us aren't."

"How does your father feel about that?" I asked.

"He thinks I am playing at some sort of hobby. It doesn't matter so much to him that I got featured in Italian *Vogue* or an English rock star wears my jewelry on his concert tour."

"He is very proud of you, Alessio. Don't ever doubt that," said Luca. "He does not show it easily. He's difficult, it is his way. You know this."

"Hmm. I am lucky I have Luca and our brothers Emilio and Vittorio who are committed to the success of the dynasty, so my lack of direct participation is not so much of a sore point." He twisted his lips.

"Not so much," murmured Luca, that grin of his breaking his handsome face into something sly and self-satisfied.

"I suppose this is what drives me to succeed," continued Luca. "To prove to my father that I can do something of my very own and be a success and on my terms. My uncle Gennaro in America, he did this too with his hotels. He has built his own empire. I admire him very much."

His own empire. Alessio driven to succeed on his own terms and making it happen. At the end of the day, he had a father and brothers who had his back. I couldn't say the same for me.

"And you?" Alessio's voice filled the car.

"Me? What?" I took in a breath.

"What you have now with Guardino, is that good for you?" Alessio asked. Luca's eyes slid to me. "You like it?"

"Why do you care?" I said.

"Curious," said Alessio. "You've come all this way to clean up a mess of his son's. He must trust you. That's good, yes?"

"Yeah." I pressed a thumb down the cuff of my shirt sleeve. "He trusts that I'll get the job done."

"My uncle did not agree when you spoke, did he?" Alessio asked.

"It was our first conversation, but I think now he'll be more open to it." I met Luca's gaze.

"Once all this is done for Adri and her brother, I will help you with him so you can go back to Chicago with good news for your boss," said Alessio.

"I appreciate it," I murmured, a chill razoring through me. *Back to Chicago.*

A little over a week ago I would have been pleased as fuck to hear those words. Now they filled me with a cold heaviness in the pit of my stomach, like a hefty piece of Greek marble had settled in my gut. Because back to Chicago meant the weight of that same fight, that same unresolved tension between me and my father.

Because back to Chicago meant no more Adri.

An ache sprinted over my skull, and I ran a hand over my scalp to chase it off. "Is that where you'd prefer me to be, Alessio? Back in Chicago?"

He made a face. "I'm impressed you put yourself out there for Adri. Helping her, supporting her. You two have grown close, *no?*"

"That's fucked with your plans, has it?" I bit out.

Luca's heavy gaze slid to his brother.

"Relax, Turo," said Alessio. "I don't have plans for her. I only want her to be happy. To feel safe. She hasn't been either of those since I met her, and she deserves to be."

I shifted my shoulders in my jacket. "Yes, she does."

"I'm glad we're getting her out of this shit, eh?" Alessio said.

"Yeah," I replied.

Luca studied me, the beginnings of a smirk skating across his lips. He folded his arms and leaned his head back against the headrest and shut his eyes. Luca, Luca, Luca. Something gnawed at me about him.

My instincts were never wrong.

44

TURO

I HAD Ciro take us to an empty lot back behind some half built houses down the road from the resort. As Adri and I got out of the car, stray dogs stopped in their tracks and watched us warily. We didn't have any food on us, though.

Only guns.

"Have you ever held a gun before?" I asked her.

"Yes, I have. A few months ago my mother's security guard showed us both a few basics."

"Good." That was a relief. Something was better than nothing at all.

"I know you don't 'pull the trigger' but press it, squeeze it with control," she said.

"Very good. Let's review, shall we?"

"Turo—"

"I need to do this with you, baby. Please."

"Okay."

I propped up planks of wood that were littered in the abandoned yard. She took the gun in her hands and I showed her how to release the safety, had her do it once, twice, three times. I placed her fingers properly around the weapon.

"Gripping the gun high on the back of the grip will give you more leverage against the weapon which will help you control recoil when you fire."

"Right."

"Stand with your feet shoulder width apart and bend your knees slightly which will give you greater stability and mobility when you fire—good."

I stood to her side, just behind her. "Use your dominant eye to aim, and make sure you're only applying pressure to the front of the trigger and not the sides."

She aimed, fired, missed. Again. Again. Hit, hit, miss. Hit, hit.

"Good."

Her eyebrows quirked. "You're relieved I'm not half bad, aren't you?"

"Yes, yes, I am." I grinned.

She got more and more comfortable with the concept, with the weight of the gun in her hand, her positioning, the movement, got over the first shock of the sound and the heaviness. She paid attention, she didn't complain.

"How are you feeling?"

"Stressed but good, lots of adrenaline. I'm glad we did this."

I slid the gun in the back of my jeans and grabbed her, twisting her arm behind her, hooking an arm around her neck.

"Turo!"

"Now what do you do?" I said in her ear.

She twisted in my hold, she pushed.

"Before your attacker gains full control of you, you need to do everything you can to inflict as much injury as you can to get away. You hurt or be hurt. Get loud, push. Aim for the parts of the body where you can do the most damage easily—eyes, nose, ears, neck, groin, knee, legs. And conserve your energy while you're doing it. Your attacker's position and how close he is will determine what part of your body you'll use."

I showed her how to use her hands, fingers, her knees,

elbows, her head. How to leverage her weight strategically, get out of common holds and attacks.

Gesturing at Ciro with a lift of my chin, I released her. "Are we taking a break?" she asked, eyes wide, face flushed.

"Nope."

Ciro grabbed her from behind, and she twisted, her arm shooting out, the heel of her palm striking up under his nose.

"Go, baby," I murmured.

An hour and a half later we were floating side by side at our bungalow's swimming pool.

"Can we practice some more tonight?" she asked.

"Can you get the hotel to bring us gym mats for the floor?"

"After, can you show me maneuvers with your velvet tongue on the mats on the floor?"

Laughing, I gripped her ass under the water and pulled her body flush to mine. "Deal."

———

WE STACKED the money into a black duffel bag at Petros's villa.

They'd called with the location for the drop off, a rural area sixty miles north of Athens. After they picked up the money and the cash checked out, they'd call Adriana and tell her where her brother had been released.

Adri's hair was pulled back in a high, tight ponytail, the strain in her stiff shoulders evident. Her oversized black sunglasses masked her eyes, most of her face, leaving only the sharpness of her jaw, her pale lips. Lips I'd kissed just an hour ago in the privacy of our room, our bed, the car ride over.

Adri and I stared at one another across the courtyard through the group of private security agents, Alessio, Luca and his men. The servants of the house. Her mother hugged her, Petros. They'd been outraged at the demand that Adri delivery the money. But Adri had insisted she go. That she could handle it. She wanted to do this for her brother. For the sins of her father.

In the car over she'd confessed, "If something happens to Marko today, I'll never forgive myself. My parents cannot lose another child. I can't lose him."

I squeezed her hand. "We're getting him back, Adri. Believe that. There's no other option."

Now, across the courtyard littered with people and vehicles, she turned and caught my hard gaze. I raised my chin at her.

With her car keys in hand she strode over to me. My Aphrodite had transformed into the militant, determined Athena. "I need more from you."

"Anything, baby."

She wrapped her arms around my middle and kissed me, fingertips digging into my back. I fisted my hands in her hair, not giving a shit about what everyone thought. Nobody else mattered. "Never forget," I said against her lips, "you are Stefanos's great-great granddaughter. You can do this."

"I can do this," she replied.

"You call me after it's done, the second you get back in your car."

"I will."

"You will." Fuck, this was hard, fucking crazy. Harder than I expected. Hardest thing I've ever had to do.

My stomach squeezed together and twisted into knots over and over again. I should be doing this for her. Stepping into fire and smoke where she had no place. Letting her go was wrong, all wrong. My lungs squeezed together. But I knew she needed to do it and she knew it too—to face that devil, the devil that had killed her lover, the devil that had stolen the best part of her, the devil that now had her brother prisoner. She wanted to do this to prove things to herself, to redeem herself.

With a final look, she released me and strode over to her white BMW coupe, the car she hadn't driven in two years. She got in, fastened her seat belt, hands flexing over the wheel. She put the vehicle into gear and sped off, and a piece of me took off with her leaving me rooted to the spot. The churning burn in my gut told me what I already knew. I couldn't package these sensations and file them away. There were no files, no labels, no system where Adri was concerned. The BMW veered out of sight, and I took in a tight breath.

I had no control in keeping Adri safe, protecting her. It had all been ripped from me.

45

ADRIANA

I'D DROPPED off the cash in the bin with the pink graffiti on it and now I was supposed to wait for their call. My pounding heartbeat my only company, adrenaline my fuel. I parked in front of an abandoned kiosk, and I waited, pen and paper ready to take directions when the call came. After they counted the bloody money.

An hour went by.

Another forty-three minutes.

Another thirty-five.

My phone beeped. An unknown number. My mouth dried and I cleared my throat. *"Oríste?"*

"Asprópyrgos," said a husky voice. He gave me specific instructions to an abandoned warehouse parking lot, and I scribbled madly. Relief poured through me, beating down the anxiety. One step closer to Marko.

Click.

Asprópyrgos was an industrial area west of the city, and I knew the area. I'd been there once before, with Grigori for a rave party he had deejayed. A party that had turned into a riot after a fight broke out with a group of those right-wing anarchists who had shown up.

I called Turo and he put me on speaker so Luca, who was driving their car, could hear the directions as well.

"Are you okay?" Turo asked, his voice tight.

"Yes."

"You're sure?" he said.

"Yes. You go. Call me the minute—"

"I will. I will."

Turo clicked off the call, and I dropped my phone in the passenger seat next to me, letting out a heavy breath, but it did no good. My fingers curled tightly over the steering wheel as my brain replayed that hard, husky voice of the kidnapper that had drilled through me.

It drilled through me again. And again.

How had they been treating Marko? Had they beaten him up? Hurt him? Taunted him, been cruel? Was he hungry, in pain, in shock? All those questions that had tortured my mother and Petros. Those impossible questions with no answers had filled their eyes with thick, dark, heavy emotion.

My brother was a quiet, gentle boy. Life had been good to him. There were no creases, no jagged or crooked lines in his life up until now. Now, it would be a screaming wretched hell because of my father. Because I'd allowed my father in.

I'd done that.

Marko didn't deserve this. No one did, but especially not my little brother.

And especially not my mother and Petros who had already suffered the loss of an innocent child.

No more tragedy. Not again.

And not because of me.

My gaze went to the paper with the directions.

Not this time.

46

TURO

In a compact Toyota, Luca and I headed west for Asprópyrgo.

We got off the Elefsina highway and cruised through this neighborhood west of Athens. More like a postindustrial wasteland. Warehouses in ruins. Abandoned factories. Crumbling houses of another age alongside eroded and worn apartment buildings. Squatters, dark-skinned Romany children wandering the streets, their faces not soft in blissful childish unawareness, but focused, hard.

The roads were busy with delivery trucks, garbage trucks. Ratty pickup trucks collecting all sorts of rusty junk, old appliances, fencing, furniture, pipes. Sewage removal trucks battled with fuel trucks at an intersection.

Luca parked the car up a steep hill where we had a full view of the abandoned lot, more like a rocky field. The crooked, twisted street sign with the red and blue X on the left edge of the field was the designated marker.

"Now we wait," I muttered.

I leaned my head back against the headrest. The sun hit my face, its warmth heating my skin. Heat that poked at memories of light-drenched hours spent on beaches with Adri, not giving a single fuck except for grilled seafood and sun-washed wine, and where were my sunglasses, and holding her hand, and sucking down creamy iced frappés in the heat, and tasting her suntan lotion and the sweat on her skin. And kissing her, kissing her on the harsh rocks of those castle ruins, kissing her in that beach cave, our skin salty, our lips wet. And being inside her.

My fingers went to the inner pocket of my jacket and found the stone there, the smooth white stone she'd found in the beach cave at Vitáli. An ordinary thing, but so pure in its simplicity, like that moment had been, so many moments.

"Here's something."

Luca's grim monotone snapped me back into the present, my gaze following his.

A small, dingy-white Fiat van plowed into the rocky field where the rusty, no through street sign stood tilted. The Fiat jerked to a halt, a thin man dressed in a black hoodie and dark jeans, a black ski mask covering his head, opened the back doors and pulled out a teenage boy. Marko. The kid stumbled, a black scarf covered his eyes, his body hanging.

Had they drugged him?

The kidnapper dropped him at the base of the sign, squatting down and adjusting the scarf over Marko's eyes and mouth. He pushed the kid face down on the ground, and Marko's legs flailed in the air. He darted back into the van, where the driver waited for him, and the vehicle kicked into reverse, turned, and swerved off in a cloud of dust.

"Come on, come on..." I muttered under my breath, my eyes trained on the van slowly climbing up the opposite hill, waiting for them to be out of sight before I moved. "Make the call, Luca."

Luca didn't reply. The van finally vanished, and I lunged out the door, peeling off down the hill to where Marko lay motionless. A shot rang out and Marko rolled into a ball.

I blinked, my breath hitched painfully. A biting flame lit into my side. Stinging, searing. My stomach tightened. Pain scorched through me.

I'd been shot.

Clutching at my side, I stumbled on the dirt road, turning to see who the fuck—

Luca stood in front of the car, a gun raised.

A gun aimed at me.

"You run too fast," he said.

Warm goo filled my hands. Blood, my blood. "You're a lousy shot," I said. A chill spread over my flesh like watercolor paint soaking paper. "What the fuck are you doing?" I yelled. "Why?" My hand flew behind my back for my own weapon, my heart lurching in my chest.

"Your boss asked me nicely as an offer of compensation to Gennaro, but my uncle doesn't do this sort of shit, so I'm taking care of it. The things we do for family."

My own father put a contract on my life?

I gulped in air, rage flushing through me filling my lungs instead. Did this really surprise me? Had I become so much of an irritant, an unreliable factor in Mauro's Outfit? He'd sent me here on a fool's errand to kill me out of the country. Any traces of depraved paternal blood guilt on his hands would be far, far away, not in his face, not in his town. No reminders, no traces.

Cold, strategic Mauro. Practical, covering his bases. That was business. Good business. Had I pushed him too far with that last standoff with Valerio? That stupid encounter with Francesca under his own roof? I'd always be a problem for him, no matter what.

All I'd wanted was what was due to me, my piece, the piece I'd worked so hard for. The piece I'd turned my back on my mother for. So many pieces. Something, anything. How fucking pathetic. I didn't want a seat at his family dinner table, but this —this—

Luca standing there facing me with his gun, the gun he'd just shot me with, my blood filling my hand, told me the undeniable truth. *"Actions speak louder than words,"* my grandfather's voice hounded me. My throat cramped, the taste of copper filled my mouth.

"Mr. Guardino told my uncle to expect you," Luca said. "And as an apology for his son's rudeness and as a bond for their future business together, he offered your life. Very old school of him, eh? I liked that." A sharp smirk curled his lips. "It's perfect timing." He raised the gun again. "I'll blame it on the kidnappers."

Dizziness whirled through my brain. I blinked and blinked, willing the world to stay focused. Willing Luca and his fucking gun to remain clear.

Thick wetness filled my hands, seeping through the fabric of my white linen shirt. Not pink this time, but scarlet red. Crimson. My favorite fucking shirt. My shirt...

"It's wrinkled now."

"This is Greece in the summer. No one cares."

No one cares.

No one cares.

"I hope you die alone, you bastard, because that's what you deserve," Ciara's voice taunted.

I gulped in air. "Don't do this, Luca—" My eyes strained to stay on Luca in the sun, my vision blurry in its glare.

"Tell me, *Arturo*. Why does Guardino want you dead? What the hell did you do? Not curtsy properly? Criticize his haircut? His wife? Fuck his daughter?"

"It's a long, long sordid story. I could tell you sometime over a glass of Anisette."

"I like sordid. I hate Anisette."

"I thought you liked old school?" I smacked back.

He came closer, jaw set. "Tell me now. Tell me everything. I want to know."

"Why?"

"Your reputation is spotless. You get the job done, no matter what it is. Your work is very clean. You are an asset. So I want to know why he would send you all the way here only to have you killed? Why not in his own backyard? What did you do?"

My throat prickled with dry dirt and dust. "I'm his bastard son."

I told him about me and my father.

Luca's face darkened, an eyebrow flared. "So you have a—how do you say—attitude?"

"Yes, I do." I shifted my weight, pain ripping through me like a shearing knife. "Getting your uncle to come back to their table was supposed to be my good deed in return for a favor."

"You worked hard for Guardino, but remained the peasant, the soldier," he said.

I blinked, sucked in air. The taste of blood seeped through my mouth. The flavor of my mortality. "Yes."

"Listen carefully." His tone was grim and steady. He had my attention. I raised my straining eyes to his.

"I shot you," Luca said. "I tried to kill you. I told you he wants you dead. Your life flashed before your eyes. All true?"

"All true," I gritted out.

"You can't go back to Chicago." He stalked toward me.

My lungs heaved, a wheezing sound erupting from my chest. "You own me now?"

Luca pressed the gun against my forehead. The cool hardness of the metal shimmered over my skin. "Yes."

"Why?" I snarled at him, snarled at destiny. I pressed my forehead against the gun, pushing against Luca. "Because I'm a useful tool?" Valerio's words bristled on my tongue, hung in the dusty hot air between us. "Why should I believe anything you say?"

Luca's eyes gleamed in the hard glare of the sun. "Because you know deep in that black heart of yours, a heart as black as mine, that I'm telling you the truth." He fisted my shirt with his free hand. "I made Alessio stay in Athens longer than he wanted so you could find us and I could be done with you and we could get on with our holiday. But then Adri got shot at and you saved her. You being hired as her security and coming to the island with us was good for me—I needed you for my meeting with Berezin."

"That was a win for you either way," I muttered. "If I won Berezin's games, you'd get what you wanted from him. And if I lost, you'd still come out a winner. You'd be alive and I'd be dead for Guardino without you getting your hands dirty."

"Yes," came the velvet reply.

Luca's focus suddenly shifted behind me. *"Merda!* What is she doing here?" His grip on me relaxed a few degrees, his hold on the gun slackening.

I twisted slightly in his hold, my eyes narrowing in the dusty heat. A figure was running toward Marko. A tall woman, young, with a ponytail.

Adri.

My heart plunged in my chest, squeezing there. I turned toward Adri, every instinct commanding me to get to her. I twisted in Luca's lax grip and shot my elbow in his face. He jerked back, and I turned and kicked at the gun hanging in his hand. The gun flew. I grabbed my gun that was at my back and aimed it at Luca.

Luca lunged at me, tackling me down to the ground, my gun pitching from my hand. Wrapping an arm around my neck, he bound me in a chokehold. I bit his flesh, digging my fingers in his arm to pry it off me. A fist landed on my wound, and the breath knocked out of me, pain radiating through my body. I crumpled in Luca's vicious hold.

He swiped at his gun on the ground and shoved it against my cheek, dragging me up with him, both of us breathing hard. Luca raised his gun, he aimed at Adri.

"No! No." My vision filled with red, watery red. "Are you fucking insane?"

He pulled me up harder against him, his thick muscles pressing into me like a living vise—the fucker worked out hard for a reason. On a grunt, he shuffled his hold, pinning me to his side, extending his arm, the gun aimed at Adriana.

I reached out for the weapon, straining, fingers flexing but he kept me tight at his side. "Luca!" I could taste the metal, feel the sleek hardness. Inches away. *Goddammit.*

In the distance Adri ripped the ski mask off of Marko, wiping his hair back from his face. Hugging him, kissing him. His hands behind his back, Marko wavered, and she fiddled with the hand-cuffs. She tried to get him to stand, but he couldn't. He was dazed. Luca clenched me harder, choking me.

My heart banged against my ribs; it wanted to escape the prison of my chest. A cold sweat prickled my skin. The possibility of her suffering, her being hurt, her dying, gone from this world, from me, because of me and my not being able to stop it—

Impossible.

A small blue pickup truck coasted down the low hill into the lot. A figure in black—dressed just like the men who'd dropped off Marko—darted toward Adri and the boy. The driver got out of the van, gun in his hand pointed at brother and sister. Adri froze.

"Che diavolo?" Luca bit out.

I twisted in Luca's hold, blinking past the sweat on my face. The driver grabbed Adri, but she turned and slapped him, kicking at his legs, aiming for his balls and missing.

Relax, baby, think. Think.

I planted my feet firmly in the dirt, steadying myself, and shoved against Luca. "Fokas's minions want Marko for them-selves—for the big bucks."

"Now they've got Adri too." Luca's mouth came to my ear. "You want to help her," his voice simmered.

"Yes."

"You want to go to her."

"Yes."

433

"You want to fight for her."

"Yes!"

"Your heart's not so black after all, is it?" He released me and tracked over to my gun, scooping it off the ground. He gave it to me. "Cover me," he said.

"Seriously, you fuck?"

"I'm not going to kill you, Turo. Not after you saved my brother and Adri from those bullets, and not after you came through for me on Berezin's boat. There are only a few people I give a true fuck about and Alessio is one of them. There are only a few people I can work with, and you've proven to be one of them."

"So why did you shoot me?"

"I have a reputation. I couldn't just let you go."

"And how do you know I won't shoot you in the back right now?"

"You're much smarter than that. That's one of the reasons why I like you." He turned and charged toward Adri, his gun tucked to his side.

I slid the safety and trained my weapon on the fucker holding Adri. She'd spotted Luca and stiffened. Her searching gaze found me with my gun aimed in her direction. She yelled out in Greek.

Good girl.

Startled, the guy struggling with Marko spotted Luca coming at him, and releasing Marko, stumbled forward, gun in hand.

"No!" Adri shouted, pulling and twisting in her distracted captor's hold. Pivoting, she punched his throat. He staggered back on a howl, releasing her. The man with the gun jerked, facing Adri, arm raised, gun shaking.

I aimed. *Crack.*

He dropped in a heap, and Marko yelped. My weakened side shuddered with the force of the recoil and a dizzying rush flooded my veins.

Adriana rushed to her brother as the other man recovered from her punch, jacking up and lunging at her. Luca swiftly brought him down with a shot to the leg, his body rocking in a heap on the ground.

"Adri!" Luca darted toward Adriana and her brother, and I followed, holding my side.

Adriana scooped up the gun her brother's kidnapper had dropped, and twisting around, aimed it at Luca. He jerked to a halt, raising his hands in the air. "Adri. It's okay. It's over."

Her eyes were wild, glittering, feet rooted in the ground. No trace of fear, no shock. Only this ferocity. I tracked movement at her side. The guy Luca had shot in the leg moved, raised up, a gun in his hand.

"Ad—"

She pivoted, a flash of movement, and let loose a shot. The fuck flew back onto the ground howling. Her chest heaved as she lowered the gun. I darted to her, she remained stiff, her eyes on the fucker bleeding on the ground. I peeled the gun from her hand and held it out and Luca grabbed it.

"Kataraméne!" her voice seethed. Ancient curses howled in that one word. Luca kicked at the man she'd shot, and he grunted loudly in the dust.

"Listen," I turned her around, cradling her face. "We don't have much time," I said, my voice firm. "Are you listening?"

"Yes," she practically hissed. Her eyes leveled with mine. "Yes."

"Luca—is the other one dead?" I said.

"Si," he let out a heavy breath. *"Lui è morto."*

"One dead kidnapper, and another one shot and bleeding," I said.

"You are bleeding too—" Adri breathed. "Turo—" Her fierce eyes darted at Luca. "What happened, what—"

"It's nothing, I'm fine." My teeth scraped my lip, steadying myself. "The police would love a small victory in their ongoing battle with the anarchist underworld, and we should give it to them."

"I'm sure they would be very grateful," said Adri. "And Fokas needs a bite in the arse."

"Yeah, he does," I said. "This one's alive, he can talk. I say we use him. We turn him in, blame him for shooting me, and the rest just as it happened."

"*Bene,*" Luca agreed, wiping at his brow with the side of his hand.

"Adri? Do you understand? You were busy with Marko, but you saw him shoot me." I pointed to the kidnapper who moaned on the ground, his leg bleeding, the other leg twisted.

"This is what you want?"

"Yes."

"Okay."

"Luca put your gun in his hand," I said. "Take his so we can set this up for the police."

He scowled at me. "I know what to do, Turo."

"Then fucking do it."

Luca shoved at the guy's body with a quick kick. "He's unconscious now. He won't remember much." He patted the kid down, torso, sides, back, around his legs. He switched the guns.

My tongue was a thick, dry pillow blocking my mouth. My skull pressed in on my wobbling brain, and my head swirled in the heat shimmying off the stones. Luca approached me, a smirk barely visible on the blur that was his face.

I held out a hand. "Stay the fuck back, Aliberti."

He snapped open his cell phone. "You're getting paler."

"Am I?"

"Maybe you're wondering if your health insurance will cover you here in Greece, is that it? You Americans. Don't worry, they have national health here so—"

"*Skáse moré!*" Adri's sharp tone lashed at him and he shut up, punching buttons on his cell phone.

"Mr. Lavrentiou?" Luca spoke to Petros on his phone. "We have Marko—Yes, yes, do not worry, Adriana is here with us—" He glanced up at her. "No, they are both safe."

Safe, yes. That's what counted. That's what mattered. Adriana and Marko were safe.

My eyelids were suddenly heavy, threatening to close. So heavy. I tilted my head but it didn't help. My chest squeezed, and I couldn't breathe through the dust. The rocky earth tilted underneath me. Long hair flying.

"Turo!"

That voice.

My pulse sprang and bounced in my neck like an errant rubber ball. My hand fell from my bleeding side, and I sucked in a tiny breath, that throbbing pain barreling through my body. She grabbed my red-stained hand.

"Turo," her voice floated.

The sky twisted over me.

"Luca, get my car. We have to get to a doctor now! We can't wait."

Blue gray eyes swallowed me whole and I let them. I let them. A pair of cruel dark brown eyes took their place and my breath shorted.

Mauro.

All these years I'd assumed that I'd claimed a unique particle of Mauro's being, just the one, and I'd liked that. No matter how tiny that one, dark particle was, I knew it existed and I was there. I'd counted on that—I had to be there, I was his son. I'd liked the secrecy between us. It was a special darkness where only he and I met.

What did my beautiful girl once tell me about Dionysus?

"*Benefactor and Destroyer. The ancient Greeks understood that duality very well. In all their gods.*"

Mauro had been my god for so long. Mythological power, authority, influence. The high lord of Chicago.

My father.

My would-be destroyer.

Fuck no.

47

TURO

LUCA LIFTED ME UP, and with Adri on the other side of me, they got me in a car. Adri's car. Marko was in the back seat next to me, head against the window, folded in on himself. She drove fast and hard on a highway, through the winding, twisting streets of Athens with Luca on his phone, speaking in spitfire Italian.

The private clinic they'd brought me and Marko to had all the little luxuries and a very attentive staff. The bullet had passed through my side, and I'd been patched up, given blood, vitals monitored through the night, and given beautiful meds which chased away the pain demons. I'd answered the police's questions, told my story, and under the sunny warmth of Petros' influence combined with the police's relief over the outcome and joy at having captured a terrorist crew member possibly connected with the recent assault on a journalist, we were done.

Alessio was in my room when I woke up the next morning. Those warm brown eyes of his staring at me, his legs stretched out before him. He'd been here a while.

"I know he shot you first."

"Good morning to you too," I replied.

"Turo—"

"Don't get involved, Alessio. It's all good between me and Luca."

"Are you sure?"

"Nothing's ever for sure. But for now, it's good enough."

He only scowled, his formidable brow creasing.

"Any sign of the doctor?" I asked. "I'm itching to get out of here already."

Get out and go where, do what, I wasn't sure. I just wanted out of here though, and I wanted to see Adri.

"No, I haven't seen him," replied Alessio.

My phone buzzed and I reached for it. Marissa Derringer, my mother's lawyer. My scalp prickled. My mother had many lawyers, but Marissa had been her most trusted councillor for almost two decades.

"Marissa?"

"Turo. How are you?" Her voice tight, terse.

"Okay. Out of the country at the moment."

"Are you? I've been trying to reach you for several hours now. Must be it." Her breath hitched. She was collecting herself. A sharp chill jagged up my spine.

"Marissa? What is it?"

"There was a fire," came the answer.

Fire.

Fire.

Fire.

"And?" My stomach hardened.

"It's your mother. She and James were in the new restaurant, there was an electrical fire in the bar area. James is dead and Erin —Erin is—"

I jacked up from the bed, a stinging ache blazing through my middle, a cold tidal wave sweeping through my veins. "Erin is *what?*"

"She's in a coma, she's hanging on, but I can't get any more details. I need you here at the hospital. You need to see her."

"Which hospital?"

"Rush."

I tugged a hand through my hair. Rush University Medical Center. Top of the line.

"How did it happen?" I asked, the obvious already doing its smug tap-dance around me.

"An arson investigation is being conducted. There's been trouble, shall we say, in the neighborhood for months now."

"Erin told me. I saw her about a week ago."

"You saw her?"

"She called me, asked me to come by the office. She told me about my father giving her trouble."

"Trouble is right."

My heart pounded against my ribs, sending my head into a dizzying tailspin. Why hadn't I considered he'd go the extra mile with my mother? Why hadn't I assumed the possibility? All my professional life I'd been thorough, covered all possible angles, no matter how ridiculous they may have seemed. But I'd been arrogant where he was concerned, hadn't I?

Benefactor. Destroyer.

The fucking son of a bitch had gone for it. He thought he'd taken care of me, and then my mother was next on his list. Both of us in one day. *Motherfuckingfucker*.

"Turo, your mother is unconscious and as such, you are her designated successor."

"Say again?"

"You are now acting CEO."

My hand throttled my cell phone. "Are you telling me she never changed her will after she fired me?"

"No, she didn't. She'd never wrote you off. She always believed that you'd be back. That you'd be a part of her life again and that you'd work together once more. She had faith in you. You're her son and she loves you."

"You're telling me the explanation for this is that she loves me?" My voice was raw.

"Yes."

A whirlpool of adrenaline and madness pissed through me. "Marissa, the last ten years she and I didn't have much of a relationship, if any. She was cold, I was mean, etcetera, etcetera. You know how it was, how it's been all these years." I lowered my voice. "You know who I am and what I do. Who I work for. Everything she despised. I disappointed her, betrayed her."

"Don't think I didn't try to dissuade her," Marissa said. "But there was a piece of her that never stopped believing in you. She felt awful about how things had degenerated between you, how she could have handled things differently. She really did. She felt powerless."

"Erin Cavanaugh Bradley felt powerless?"

"As your mother, yes. She always put on a brave face, but she didn't want you in between her and him, ever. His constant threats over the years—"

"What threats?"

"Lately it's been all business. But when you were younger, he continually threatened to take you away from her."

"I had no idea," I said. Is that why she tried keeping me behind closed doors, at a distance? "Why would he have taken me when he's been adamant to this day about keeping me a secret from everyone?"

"Well, if you don't know that, who does?"

That stung. She was right. I knew he loved using his power to get what he wanted, to have the last word. Letting go of me and Erin had been easy for him, but she and I had become problems and that was definitely not him having the last word, and that he couldn't let go of ever.

"Turo, Erin worked hard to keep you safe, to give you the best of everything, shielding you and making her business a success so that she wouldn't have to rely on anyone or need anyone, not even her own father. She felt a great sense of failure when she forced you out, but she still believed in you. Never stopped wanting the best for you. That's what a mother's love is—an always proposition. Unyielding. Defies logic, practicality, legal advice."

My skin heated, my head pounded.

Marissa cleared her throat. "As Erin is currently incapacitated, the power of attorney goes to me and you to make decisions for the company. We've worked together before, but that was then, and I for one, don't trust you much."

"Understood."

"How soon can you be here? She needs you."

She needs you. "I'm in Greece right now."

"Greece?"

"I'll be on the first plane home. Let me give you another cell phone number to contact me. I'm shutting this number down."

"Go ahead," she said, and I gave her my alternate cell number that only two other people had. Two special contacts who I'd need the second I landed in the USA.

Marissa and I said our goodbyes, and I ripped the battery from my phone.

"What's wrong?" Alessio asked. "You look like hell all over again."

My eyes shuffled around the room. Metal bed, shitty sheets. Hospital room. My mother was in a hospital room all alone, thousands of miles away from me. Husband dead and vulnerable. Vulnerable to *him*. Him. Him.

"Turo?" Alessio grabbed my arm.

I flinched. "My mother. She's been in an accident. I need to be there. I need—"

"Turo, you can't go back to Chicago," Alessio said.

I had to go back.

I had to see Erin for myself. I needed to let her know she wasn't alone, because now she was all alone. All alone. And vulnerable to another hit from that fucker. It was up to me to protect her, and I had to let her know that I was there for her. He would try again, wouldn't he? Of course he would. He didn't like failing, and now this would be fail number two this week. He wanted to erase us, his mistakes, the two thorns in his side. And Mauro Guardino liked being the victor in any game.

Not this time.

Alessio put a light hand on my chest. "Hey, take a breath, man, come on."

I gulped in air, focused on the feel of his hand on me, and the thick, dizzying red diffused from my vision. I pushed his hand away. "Get rid of this phone for me." I gave him the pieces.

"Sure." Alessio pocketed them. "You need another or—"

"I've got one." I swallowed, but my mouth was dry. "I need to talk to Luca."

"Are you sure about that?"

I shot him a hard look.

"*Bene.*" Alessio got on his phone, yapped in Italian and clicked off. "He's on his way from the hotel."

Adri stood in the doorway, and a strange sense of relief washed with excitement flooded through me. I hadn't seen her since yesterday, since she and Luca had gotten me and Marko in her car and taken us to the hospital.

Alessio lifted his chin. "I'll go wait for my brother outside." He clapped me on the shoulder and left the room, giving Adri's arm a squeeze as he passed through the door.

I held out my hand to her. My anchor. I needed to touch her, feel her. Suddenly, time was ticking away, clock tower bells tolling, and not in our favor.

"Turo," she murmured taking my hand, brushing my cold lips with her warm ones.

I wiped the hair back from her face. "Adri, I have to go back to Chicago right away. My mother's been in an accident. She's in a coma, and her husband's been killed."

"No. I'm so sorry." Her eyes narrowed, eyes that searched mine for details, details I wouldn't give. "Was it really an accident?"

"I need to go find out."

"You already know," she murmured holding my gaze. She knew too. She knew that to have someone close to you hurt on account of you was a punishment, the worst sort of torture, a failure.

A smile flickered over her lips.

"What is it?" I asked.

"Dionysus went down to the underworld and saved his mother. He defied death and brought her out of Hades to Olympus to live with the gods."

Chicago, Hades, sounded about right. I would deliver her out from under him if it was the last thing I did.

"I'll talk to my father about sending you home on the company plane," she said. "It shouldn't be a problem. I'll take care of it for you."

I cupped her face. "You're good at that, you know."

"I know," she said, her lips brushing my fingers. "I love it when you let me do things for you."

"*Let* you?"

"You're overly self sufficient, but sometimes, *sometimes*, you let go and enjoy what I give you."

I kissed her fingertips, squeezing her hand between mine, and her breath caught. "Lovely—Athens to Denver."

An eyebrow lifted. "Denver?"

"Yes." I released her hand. "I need to meet someone there first, then I'll get to Chicago another way. A quiet way."

"Okay." She straightened her shoulders and got on her phone.

My head fell back on the pillow as I watched her talk to her father. How the hell were we going to say goodbye? How? I couldn't imagine not being at her side throughout the day, her hand always within reach, her lips mine to claim, her body mine to lose myself in, to worship. Her laugh tickling my ear, tickling my soul, enticing it to play.

But I was off on a fucking crusade, and her safety was definitely something I couldn't guarantee in Chicago right now, let alone for myself. She belonged here, with her family. That was safe. That was the best for her.

She clicked off her phone, turning it over in her hands. "You're all set for tonight. Can I come with you? Let me help you, be there for you. I could—"

"No, no, baby, you can't."

"Turo—" Her gorgeous eyes pleaded with me.

Jesus, this was a no win. Right now I couldn't harbor hopes or tender thoughts. Everything in me had to be focused on one thing only.

"Forget me, Adri, " I breathed.

Her face paled, an eye ticked. She wasn't sure she'd heard me correctly. Neither was I.

"You should forget me," I said slowly, pushing the words out of my mouth, forcing them out.

Since I'd arrived in Greece I'd been a marked man. But now, the cards had been finally laid down on the Blackjack table, the dice had been rolled, the roulette wheel had at long last stopped spinning.

She fingered the eye bracelet on my wrist, her voice a raw whisper, "I will never forget you, and I don't mean because you've taken bullets for me, protected me, saved my brother, been a true friend, a lover. Our time together—here, on the island, all of it, all of it—is very special to me."

So fucking special. Significant.

Her eyes held mine and her truth twisted and screwed tight in my chest.

"Your family needs you now, Adri," I managed.

"Yes, they do, and I need them. But you need me too, I know you do. You don't have to push me away."

I clutched the long, gauzy scarf she wore around her neck and pulled her close. "I have to. Give this to me, Lovely. I need it. I need to know that you're safe."

"I need to know that you'll come back to me," she whispered.

Our lips were breaths apart, the magnetic pull between us unmistakeable, unbearable.

I let go of her scarf. "Don't. I can't guarantee that. I can't." *I can't guarantee shit.*

She sat up straight, her gaze averted for a second then came back to me—cool, even, in control. She'd changed gears. "We're taking my brother to London in a few days to see a therapist who was recommended. Marko is emotionally numb right now, and we're all waiting for the explosion any day. Or implosion. I'm not sure which would be worse, him finally letting it out or never doing so."

"London?"

"Yes." She pressed her lips together.

London meant responsibility, London meant her entrenched in the professional family structure. London was what she hadn't wanted.

"London's good," I said. "Conquer, Lovely. Conquer. And don't ever let Yianni—"

"I won't. I've finally realized that keeping him at a distance is not wrong."

You're a smarter person than I am.

"His debt has been paid and he's in the clear. Now it's up to him to stay clean or not." She pressed her lips together. "I could take you to the—"

"Alessio will get me to the airport."

A nurse entered the room and said something in Greek which made Adri stand up. "The doctor's coming to check on you. I need to leave." She chewed on the inside of her cheek, but it didn't stop her lips from trembling.

"Goodbye, Adri," I said, my voice hoarse. "Goodbye."

48

ADRIANA

I NEVER KNEW BREATHLESSNESS, a racing pulse, could be a constant state of being.

Since I'd left his room, I'd had a good cry in the ladies and managed to last through a discussion of Marko's list of prescription medication with my mother and the doctor.

I was heading home to bring my mother a change of clothes, caught in afternoon traffic. My hands flexed around my steering wheel, and I laughed. No, I wasn't having a nervous breakdown. I'd never felt more clearheaded in my life.

Yes, Turo had made me say goodbye, pushed me away for all the right reasons, and I respected that. Understood it, intellectually.

I was shaking with so much wild emotion for him, for us. I was feeling these emotions, my body was feeling them, and I wasn't breaking or shattering or melting into a sorrowful heap. Yes, I would miss him. Yes, I was afraid for him. Yes, it felt completely unnatural and wrong to be separated from him, a chasm of forbidding proportions. In the handful of days that we'd known each other, *we had lived*. We had lived well, brilliantly, hotly. Honestly.

And that was everything.

I had chosen to be alone for so long, to hide, keeping everything at a distance, sabotaging myself along the way, but Turo had changed all that. I no longer felt stuck in that fear, that confusion.

And even if I didn't see him again, if he died or lived a new life with another woman or women, for that matter, I wanted him to know that he had left his mark on me. Not a scar, but a living, burning pulse. And it felt good.

I needed to give him that. He needed it, just as much as I did. If I didn't go to him now and give him *this*, he would never know.

My parting gift. Not just goodbye, not just letting go. I wanted him to know, that in his coming battle, facing his demon, my heart would be beating with his. That he had made a difference. That what we'd experienced was real and true and meaningful and not just some crazy whirlwind of stolen moments.

But those moments were a whirlwind. They were all connected and blended into one thing. One truth.

I checked my rear view mirror, eyes darting to the side, and turned the wheel and slowly, carefully edged my car into the far left lane, cutting off three annoyed drivers, and finally made a sharp U turn.

Airport, here I come.

49

TURO

CIRO DROVE me and Alessio to the hangar at the Athens airport north of the city where the Lavrentios jet waited for me. My blood slugged through my veins as Ciro handed my suitcase over and I gave my passport to the attendant at the desk. She glanced up at me, and I slid my sunglasses back down over my aching eyes. I wasn't going to think of this as an ending, but a turning point, a new beginning.

"My hoodie looks good on you," said Alessio, a smirk on his face, his hand thumping my shoulder.

I cleared my dry throat, my insides churning with sick. "Watch out for Adri. Please. Don't let her—"

"I know. I will."

I held out my hand to Alessio, but he quickly pulled me in to his chest and kissed me on both cheeks, the Italian way, the Greek way. *"Mio amico.* Get it done."

"Ciao, Alessio." I thumped his back.

He brought a ringed hand to the side of my face. *"Ciao."*

"Turo."

Alessio and I separated, our heads jerking toward the voice, her voice, and my stomach dropped, clenching. There she stood, in cutoff jean shorts, high leather, brown boots with a peep toe and a deep cut, silk red T-shirt with long beaded necklaces, a small, chocolate brown Birkin bag clutched in her grip.

My goddess.

"*Ach,*" murmured Alessio, slapping me on the shoulder. He raised his chin at Ciro and they took off.

"Adri, what are you doing here?"

"I had to come. I had to see you one last time." She swallowed hard as she moved toward me. "Please don't be mad at me for coming. I know you have to go and do what you need to do, and I want that for you. That's who you are. I came because I need you to know that you touched my life. You've changed me."

"You did that, Adri. She was right there all the time. You just had to believe in her and let her loose."

"I love you," she said.

The world stopped moving. Only my heart thudded in my chest, its heavy beat resounding in my ears.

"I had to come and tell you, I had to—I don't expect anything in return, but I had to tell you, I—"

I kissed her.

Her beautiful, full, warm lips. Lips that I'd made my own. My hand dug in her beautiful hair and I pressed her into my chest. We were wound together, she and I, coiled around each other like wild vines, tangled like twisted silk ribbons pulled tight. Intricate. No beginning, no end. But it had to end, and I had to let go.

I released her. "You're in my blood, baby. But right now, I need to take care of business, and you need to be separated from all that. I need to know that it won't touch you, because I couldn't handle that. That would fucking kill me." My voice shook with the truth.

Yes, the fucking truth.

That truth quaked through my veins, had my heartbeat hurtling at a dizzying pace. A cold sweat prickled over my skin.

Her eyes widened. "I want you safe too. I want so much for you—"

My fingers touched her lips, stopping them from continuing, from articulating dreams and hopes and wishes that we both knew might never come true for us.

A cold, brutal, Aegean wind tore between us. Right there in the airport terminal we were on a cliff. Our Andros castle cliff. Her beautiful eyes that choppy, dark blue sea we swam in.

She entwined her fingers with mine and smiled. "We only had a week or so together, but I *feel*, and it's because of you."

I feel too, baby.

"And I'm not afraid of it anymore. I'm embracing it, the good, the bad—" She swallowed hard. "I love you."

Her words squeezed around my heart. She'd changed the water into wine. I tightened my grip on her hand and breathed fire, "I can't promise you anything right now, Adri. And fanciful promises should never be made to a woman like you with the sea in her eyes and the sun in her heart. You belong here, conquering. Stefanos had promised Natalia he'd be back, and it took him a lot of years to return and he lost her. I can't—" My throat closed. A low grunt escaped my lips. I was leaving, charging into a firestorm I might not survive.

I didn't want to lose her to another man or to death. *So fucking selfish.* "I can't hold you to a promise I can't fulfill," I continued, the words a jagged knife shearing through my gut. "No matter how much I want to make that promise to you right now."

"You're going to war, aren't you?"

"Yes."

She wiped the hair back from my face and kissed me, my mouth filling with her taste, our tongues tangling, devouring. My body would never be the same again, would never know this desire again. Adri resided inside me. Her passionate kisses, her touch, bold and sweet, trusting and daring, had awakened me to a new world.

The urge to grab onto her and pull her close, smell her hair, inhale the scent of her skin that had become my very own tore through me. Feel her arms around me, hear her throaty Greek whispers tease me, plead for my mercy, for my ruthlessness, for more.

Just once more.

I released her. "Go."

Adri's watery eyes glimmered at my sharp tone, her chin raised. She stood still, a thousand flaming words yet unspoken. But in our hearts they were there. I knew. She knew.

"I will never forget you. You gave me something beautiful that I will always treasure no matter what," she said slowly, carefully. "This I wanted you to know."

"Go," I begged, my voice raw.

Her shoulders eased. A hand on my chest and she leaned closer, whispered in my ear, *"Adío, agápi mou."*

I shut my eyes, and she let go. Like a boat setting off from a dock, heading out to sea, my beautiful, resilient girl took off. A harsh sting snaked through me, and I winced. She vanished in the glare of the sunlight filling the glass terminal.

Gone.

Gone in the blur of my unsteady vision.

My hands jammed in my pockets, and my fingers closed around the smooth stone I'd taken from her at the beach cave at Vitáli. I shut my aching eyes, and I saw us walking the cobble-stoned streets of Chóra hand in hand, the uninhibited grin on her face as she danced, her laughing at me when I was annoyed, hair flying as she put the jeep in gear and we climbed those twisting mountain roads that very first time, her body clinging to mine as we swam together in the aqua sea we'd had all to ourselves. I felt that gentle kiss in the ruins of a stone castle on a rock above the sea.

Adri. Adri. Adri the wind called to me.

"Goodbye, my love," I whispered on that wind, repeating her

words. Words that seared whatever was left of my soul, my heart. My hand went to my chest where hers had just been. I couldn't breathe through the smoke those burning words had left behind.

Adri had made me hers forever. Adri had bound me with moonlight and jasmine, sunrises and cold wine, the press of her hand in mine, the rapture of her sigh, the warmth of her skin. I had to leave her on the other side of the globe, and if I survived, I would lift the world on my shoulders and tilt its axis to bring her back to me.

"This way, sir," the stewardess said pointing to the door that led outside to the tarmac. I followed her to the plane that waited for me.

I was going to cross the sea again, return home. I'd risen from my battlefield, my own blood dripping from my side, and that cold elixir, truth, had finally seeped into my veins, my very bones.

Unlike Hamlet, I had no ghosts warning me, telling me what to do. No arras to hide behind. I didn't fucking need them—I knew what I must do, and I would face my quarry eye to eye.

The rest will not be silence, Hamlet, not for me. My purpose and ire are sharpened and heavy and ready for blood. Blood speaks louder than words, young prince. Blood. His, mine, hers.

I settled in my seat, fastened my belt, refused the offer of a drink. Door sealed, the pilot spoke, engines roared, and we taxied down the runway. The plane rose in the sky, curving, and we soared above mountains, shoreline, blue, blue sea.

My heart thudded in my chest, and I closed my eyes.

High on a cliff, Adri told me a myth born of blood and saltwater, written in the tears of a man and a woman, in a blue sea far away, far, far away. A sea of pirates and conquerors. A sea of ancient heroes.

I listened, and it told tales of boldness and daring.

Of swords and cannons.

Of smoke and fire.

Of deep love and savage longing.

Of a dagger.

I heard its wild song. Alluring, unforgiving.

For me there would be no rest, none of Hamlet's angels singing, only the flights of demons filling the night sky with their roar as I moved from under my shadows.

I am ready.

In my heart the rhythm of that song, in my blood the exultant wine.

In my hand, that dagger.

DENVER

50

TURO

I FROZE my ass off on the never-ending flight, no matter the blankets, the heat, the hot coffee. Without the distraction of other passengers, the small plane seemed like a narrow white cave where there was no escape. Excruciating.

I slept. I didn't sleep. Visions of my mother's bloodied and mangled body wrestled with my sanity. Clung to me like stinging jellyfish that wouldn't let go. Mauro's face, swollen, smug flashed through the circuits of my exhausted brain. Valerio jeering at me. An overly made up blonde ordering veal Marsala, the smell of that cloying sweet wine sauce. Ciara stomping out of my apartment, mirror smashing in her wake. The new prostitute assuming her submissive pose in my guest bedroom.

"What can I do for you, sir? How can I please you tonight?"

Evgeny's cruel, cold, expectant smile as he gripped Adri's arm.

The taut chords of violins, violins, violins in the darkness.

The clink of two icy, ouzo filled glasses in the sunlight.

I felt my nakedness to the elements, the heat, the cold, the wet, the burn. I was stripped bare.

"You have a choice to make, Turo."

459

My mother's ultimatum that had once sent me reeling now gave me a rush. *Yes, Mother, I've made my choice.*

The Rocky Mountains spread out before me, and the plane's engines groaned as we finally descended. I sat up straight in my seat and put the hood of the designer black sweatshirt hoodie jacket Alessio had given me over my head. What did Hamlet say on the boat back to Denmark from England after he'd narrowly missed assassination?

"From this time forth, my thoughts be bloody, or be nothing worth."

Fine words. But again, no action.

I'll show you bloody.

———

"LONG TIME NO SEE," his voice growled at me behind a cargo warehouse at the Denver airport.

A tall, bearded, tattooed biker with a scarred face and leather gloves hiding the fact that he was missing both middle fingers stood before me, hands on his hips. A President's patch was stitched on his worn leather jacket over his formidable body. The mere mention of his name in underground circles made people shudder. So many wild colorful rumors flew about his cruelty, his ruthlessness.

And they were all true.

Yes, when pushed, men like Finger pushed back. Hard, brutally hard.

We both had been pushed.

"Finger," I said, shaking his powerful hand. "Thank you for meeting me on such short notice. I appreciate it."

"Not a problem. Not far. Figured you flying out here, asking so fucking nice, it's big."

"It is."

"Hey," Mishap said, his chin lifting. He was a smaller version of Finger, fewer tattoos, no such obvious ugly scars on the outside, but his eerily calm demeanor and terminally haunted eyes hinted at deep, ugly scars on the inside. He was an old friend of Finger's, a former Special Forces assassin and now a special anonymous contractor for hire.

I nodded. "Mishap."

"What do you need?" Finger asked.

"An assassination," I replied.

Mishap's big eyes flicked up to mine. His specialty.

"It needs to look like the Tantuccis did it," I continued. "It has to have their signature. I have a former soldier of mine I want clipped, and I want you to use his dead body any way you see fit. There's a Tantucci snitch I worked over recently you could use as well."

"The target?" Finger asked.

"Mauro Guardino."

Mishap stilled, his body tightening, his focus.

Finger said on a low whistle, "Not a small request."

"I know."

"Gotta ask why? All these years you've risen in the Outfit."

My chest expanded. "Just a puppet with a short shelf life. He tried to have me killed, came after my family. I have to stop him before he does it again."

"Runs deep," Finger murmured. "Know that one. Know it real well." His dark, almost metallic eyes held mine. "By the way, I liked the way you sent Med to hell."

"My pleasure. Did it myself," I said, my voice low.

His eyes narrowed, his jaw tensing, the long lines of his facial scars deepening. Scars that Med had put there. He averted his gaze for a moment. He knew I'd done it for *her*. Had he found her? Were they finally together again? I hoped so, for both their sakes, but fuck it, it wasn't my business. I was here for one reason only.

Mishap took out a pack of Marlboros, the *click* of his lighter the only sound between us. Finger's dark gaze found mine again. "You gonna take over Chicago now? Be the fucking king?"

"King?" I let out a laugh. "I have something else in the works. And whoever survives is going to hate it."

Finger's lips tipped up at the edges. "You starting a war, DeMarco?"

"I'm ending the goddamn war."

CHICAGO

51

TURO

I MADE it back to Chicago with Mishap on his bike, and I'd had my suitcase FedEx'd to my mother's office. Being a former Special Forces soldier, Mishap knew how to tape me up properly for the trip, and I swallowed the last of my pain meds. Riding on the back of his bike from Colorado had certainly not been the most comfortable, but that was meaningless. I got to Chicago undetected, and that was key.

"I don't have no guest room. Couch okay for you?" Mishap bolted his door behind us, his heavy boots tracking through the stuffy basement room that was his apartment.

"That's fine," I said.

The acrid odor of pot and tobacco was thick in the airless room. We got on the phone with Finger for updates and further refining of our plan. After, I called Marissa and told her to meet me at Rush.

Mishap and I got on his bike again, helmets on, and he took me to the hospital in the heart of the city. He would shadow me, wait for me until I was done.

I pushed open the door to my mother's room. She was motionless. Face bruised. Lips pale pink. One arm had burns, a leg fractured. Lung punctured. Lots of blood lost. Lots of blood transfused. Tubes and cables connected to her, bleeping, monitoring.

"Mom." I slumped forward on the rails of her hospital bed, my head dropping, my shoulders giving way. "Dear God. Mom." A groan escaped my lips.

This wasn't my Erin Cavanaugh.

This pale, lifeless, helpless form was not my mother. My heart thudded loudly in my chest. She couldn't die. She couldn't. I still had to tell her that I regretted hurting her, that disappointing her had pained me. *I wanted—*

I took her cool hand in mine and stroked it. Leaning in close to her, I whispered, "Mom? Mom, it's Turo. I'm here."

An eyebrow jumped. Yes, she heard me. Recognized me. I knew she would. I knew.

My fingers ran through her hair. "You're being taken care of, and I'm right here. I've spoken with Marissa. We've got this. But we need you. You wake up. You've got to wake up though. Make that choice." And when she did wake up, she'd learn the horrible truth that she'd lost her husband.

I planted a kiss on the side of her face, and my vision blurred. I sucked in a breath. "I'll be right here with you."

"Turo?"

I jerked back, pivoting. Marissa. Short dark blonde hair, blue eyes gleaming, elegantly cut suit over a slim figure. We shook hands. "Marissa. Good to see you. Unfortunately."

She let go of my hand. "Yes, it's a huge shock." A heavy breath heaved from her, her glance averting to my mother. "Absolutely horrible," she whispered.

"Yes," was all I said as she moved to the table in the room and opened her briefcase. She opened a folder and slid it in front of me. "James is gone. You are the only beneficiary in the will other than a number of her favorite charities. You would get the personal and commercial real estate holdings in the city which include their apartment, the parking garages James owned, the house in Michigan, the condo in Aspen—"

"Marissa—"

Her gaze flicked up at me. "You need to be prepared if she does pass."

Acid seeped through my mouth. I only nodded.

"We've worked together before, Turo. You know what it takes to run Erin's corporation, and you know her style. You've been on the inside. Your instincts were always good, and I'm sure with your recent professional experience, they've only sharpened." She paused, the silence crackling, her eyes opaque, an eyebrow arched. "But, again, I don't trust you."

"I don't blame you. One step at a time," I replied. "Know that I'm committed to making this work for my mother."

"Good." She tucked the folder back in her briefcase and snapped it shut. "She was never afraid of him, you know. No matter what he said to her, or did. I'll bet it pissed him off, made him keep trying to hit her harder, in new ways. You need to know that she always fought for you."

"Now it's my turn to fight for her."

Marissa pushed back from the table. "I'll see you in the office tomorrow morning?"

"I have something to take care of first. No one can know I'm back in Chicago. Our meeting today is between you and me." I got up from the table. "I'm trusting you, Marissa."

"Nobody will know. I promise," she said.

"Our priority is that the new restaurant be cleaned up and fixed up, I don't care how much it costs. We're opening on schedule."

She shook my hand firmly. "I'll get right on it."

52

TURO

THE FADED JEANS bunched and wrinkled at my ankles. The waist gapped. I ripped off the black hoodie, the surfer boy sunglasses and threw them on Mishap's lumpy couch.

Mishap's clothes didn't fit me properly. He was much bulkier and taller than me, but I didn't give a shit. They were clean, and I was dressed appropriately for my day.

My one burner phone beeped with a text message. Marissa.

Got your suit & shoes—will have them at church

She'd bought me a black suit and shoes as per my specifications from Barneys. I'd change at the church. I couldn't go to James's funeral dressed in a hoodie and jeans.

I flicked a thread off the thick cotton black T-shirt. So many funerals in my future.

Mishap had been gone for the past two days, laying down the plan we'd come up with along with Finger while I stayed put at his place except for a quick errand just now. Marissa kept me informed of what was going on at the company, and we'd

469

arranged for James's funeral for today. Erin's vitals remained strong and steady. There was hope for her to wake up very soon.

Wake up, Mother. Please wake up.

My other burner phone beeped. Finger.

"Yeah?"

"Grandpa's all settled in at the nursing home," his distinctive, deep grumbly voice filled my ear.

Mishap is in place.

"Glad to hear it. I look forward to seeing him," I replied.

"I know you are. I got him the minestrone soup. My special recipe. I made plenty for everybody."

The Italian deli was a go ahead, and Finger had designed the explosives himself.

I was getting the Finger VIP treatment. I was going to owe him in a big way, and it would be worth every fucking cent and particle of sweat off my back.

"You think of everything," I said. "You're the best."

"Oh, hey—" he continued our code conversation. "Our baby cousin showed up just like you said. "

He got me Little Anthony.

"Great."

"A friend of mine from the old neighborhood is coming too."

He was taking the opportunity to involve a member of his enemy bike club, the Smoking Guns, Med's club, the Tantuccis' gopher boys. Fuck yes. Like me, Finger was an excellent multitasker.

"Glad to hear it. The more the merrier," I replied.

"So is your girlfriend coming?" he asked.

"She's picking out an outfit as we speak."

The prostitute from my stable who I'd hired for Med's last moments on Earth was on standby, well rehearsed and ready to do as I'd instructed.

"She bringing her special cupcakes, I hope?" Finger asked.

"You bet. Can't have a party without those cupcakes."

I'd gone to the bank earlier and accessed into my safety deposit box. I had saved DNA evidence from Med's corpse, his clothing, that motel room, all in professional police-grade packets. Saved it for a rainy day.

Forecast for today in Chicago: Clouds. Rain. Heavy thunderstorms.

————

THE DENSE MUSK of salami assaulted me the moment I stepped through the door of the shop. Such nostalgia. I'd always disliked it, that overabundance of cured meat, damp sawdust on the floor, the sour odor of pickled everything in this pre-war grocery, but I'd grinned and bore it. Only Sal's prosciutto had ever enticed me, the parmesan, of course, and his rosemary scented focaccia. Not today, though.

I felt his eyes on me the moment I stepped through the doorway.

"Hey kid, what can I get ya?" said Sal. His swollen face scrunched in a frown. "Turo, that you?"

A hush fell over everyone, the chewing even stopped.

Mauro sat at his usual table, his close compadres and capos Oscar, Tony, and Beni sitting with him, smoking and drinking coffee and beers. Mauro's eyes widened as I came to a stop in front of his table. His jowl got fuller, jaw tenser.

"Good morning, Mr. Guardino," I said.

He took in a deep breath, scanning me from head to toe. Toe to head. He'd expected never to see me again. He expected me to be dead and gone. "Turo," his voice was sharp, taut, and a shot of adrenaline went through my veins, spiking my pulse even higher. "You're back."

"Yes. I wanted to tell you the good news myself," I said.

"What's that?" he said.

"The doctors are very hopeful that my mother will be waking up from her coma."

Mauro tilted his head slowly, his eyes on me. "Terrible accident."

"This neighborhood, just isn't what it used to be," I said.

He sat up straighter, eyes narrowed. "How was your trip?"

"Eventful," I replied. "Full of surprises."

"Oh yeah?"

"It opened my eyes to a great many things." Planting my hands on the table, I leaned over. A hiss escaped Tony's mouth as he inhaled on his cigarette angling toward me. Mauro raised his palm, and Tony and the others stiffened.

I stood up, raised both my hands in the air, my unzipped hoodie opening to reveal only a stark black cotton T-shirt fitted to my torso. No gun, no weapon. Mauro flicked a finger, and my eyes held his hard gaze as Tony got up and searched me, his big hands patting down my chest, middle, sides, my back, my legs.

From the beginning, our dealings were always in private, shrouded, between us.

Not now. No more.

"He's clean." Tony remained standing.

I said, "I told you to leave my mother alone. I asked you to let it go, for me. But you couldn't do that, could you? For years now. You had other plans, bigger plans. For her, for me."

In the corner of my eye, I caught Tony's hand moving across his middle, slowly oh so slowly. Oscar's too.

"Your point?" my father said.

My pulse raced at a high pitch, an L train screaming down a black tunnel. I held his drilling gaze and gave him a grin. "You always taught me, like a good father should, that no enemy should ever go unpunished."

Pop.

One burning hole in the middle of Mauro's forehead. The

pinpoint accuracy of Mishap's aim from a distance was extraordinary.

Mauro's body shuddered perversely, dropped forward on the table over a plate of cheeses. His beer glass crashed onto his ashtray, liquor splattering. Yells ricocheting. Shouts, hollers.

I swiveled and Mishap, a steady rock in the center of the deli, threw me a gun.

"Mauro!" Sal yelled, a gun raised.

I shot Sal in the chest, and he crumpled to the tiled floor in a messy heap. Tony's eyes hardened, his gun raised, and I shot at his head. His neck jerked back and he fell over on the table, his head crashing on the tray of sweet rolls and ham slices, his gun going off. Rolls flew, the old Depression era lamp hanging from the ceiling shattered. A shower of splintered glass.

Chairs stumbled around me, Oscar lunged at me. My leg shot out, my foot slamming into his throat, knocking him back. He let out a howl, and I fired at his head. His body fell like a heavy stone over a chair, the chair collapsing under the shock of his weight.

Mishap charged over the bodies and debris toward the back door, and I followed, hurdling over the stacked three liter cans of olive oil in the narrow hallway, out the back door. We dove into the waiting car.

Bwoom. Boosh.

Our vehicle rocked and shook. An orange-black mushroom cloud of fire and smoke rose in the gray sky. The Dumpsters rattled out of their spots, bricks flying. Particles crashed and pelted the car windows as we took off around the corner, down another side street. Screams, alarms, sirens blaring.

Motherfuck.

Finger had told us we'd have a seven second window to get the hell out of there. His exactness shot my adrenaline level even higher.

I rubbed at the gun handle with my hoodie and handed the gun to Mishap. He tucked it in his boot and dismantled his weapon into small parts. I tore off the hoodie and Mishap grabbed it. My gaze flicked back for just a moment. That little deli, the original cornerstone of Mauro Guardino's empire, had been obliterated, and him and his right hands along with it.

It was done. He was done with. And I had done it.

Destroyer.

53

TURO

THE DRIVER DROPPED me off about two blocks away from the church. I'd made my way through the back entrance, and found Marissa in the special room reserved for brides and their bridesmaids before a wedding. I scrubbed my hands, my face clean, got dressed in the new suit and shoes she'd brought me, rolled up the clothes I'd been wearing into tight rolls and tucked them into a plastic bag and then into the oversized handbag Marissa had brought with her upon my request.

Marissa's phone rang and she answered it, her eyes popping wider. "I'll let him know, thank you." She grinned at me. "She's awake. She's awake. Thank God, she's awake."

I glanced back at my reflection in the mirror and took in a breath, my every muscle relaxing. My heart drummed in my chest, sending a new high seeping through every vein. I grinned back at Marissa as I buttoned my suit jacket.

So many friends and associates had showed up for James's funeral, all dressed to the nines, all saddened and shocked, and all surprised to see me. The social set, politicians and local government officials I knew from my days working with my mother, and those I'd gotten to know from working for Mauro.

All here under the glorious roof of this great cathedral. Incongruities gave me a thrill. The service concluded, the priest introduced me, and I stepped up to the lectern in front of the altar.

"James Bradley was a good man, a kind stepfather," I said to the crowd at Notre Dame de Chicago, my voice steady, firm. "James made my mother very happy," I continued. "And as her son, that has always been the most important thing to me no matter what. My mother's happiness. She can't be with us today, but I'm very pleased to announce that she is conscious, recovering, and getting stronger."

A jovial murmur moved through the crowd like a gentle wave.

"I know I make her proud by standing here, in her place, where she would have been, sharing with you how her husband will be deeply missed. He was a dependable, trusted partner, a cherished stepfather, and a beloved husband. His loss will be deeply felt and grieved by his wife and all of us who knew him."

The dour faces before me in the church nodded. My gaze landed on Marissa in the front row, her dark red lips curled in a discreet smile, an eyebrow raised. In the third row behind her was the police detective who was investigating the "accident" at my mother's new restaurant. He looked at his watch and lifted his chin at me.

At this very moment the police were searching Valerio's house. They would find the photograph of Med's dead body that he had showed me and Mauro, that he and Mauro had touched. They would find Med's DNA on a pair of his shoes, in a shirt crumpled at the back of his mudroom closet in his McMansion. At my former soldier Little Anthony's apartment, they would not only find his dead body and evidence incriminating Valerio in his death, but also more of Med's DNA in one of Little Anthony's gym bags.

I returned my attention to the paper before me on the podium and began to read the poem "Ithaca," from the Greek poet Cavafy, one of my mother's favorites. I recited the verses about not hurrying to arrive at the island, that the journey there needed to be full of adventure and knowledge. That one should enjoy the delights of summer mornings, enjoy the precious riches the voyage itself has to offer. To always keep this Ithaca fixed in your mind.

My breath burned in my lungs.

I hadn't expected my trip to Greece to offer me pleasures or riches.

But it had.

Oh, it had.

I recited, and with every verse, Adri's hand squeezed mine, the glittering Aegean before us. Her rich laugh over glasses of wine. Her hair draped on my breathless body, warm lips on my skin. Her trust. The gift of her love that she'd given me freely, asking nothing in return.

I agreed with the last verse of the poem that left my lips. I had gained a particle or two of wisdom from my voyage. I had crossed the sea. I had charged forward on a fool's crusade where there was no Holy Grail to be found. I had been betrayed in the cruelest way, yet had returned, alive.

I had killed for Mauro Guardino's greed.

For my greedy ambitions.

For Serena's justice.

For Evgeny's entertainment.

Now I had killed my father—who was no father—for my mother. For me.

"They tore Dionysus up and ate him, but his heart survived and he was resurrected."

Mauro had tried to oppress me and destroy me, but it was my heart that had remained, and my heart had made a choice.

Resurrected, yes. Liberated. Empowered.

Folding over the sheet of paper, I lifted my head, taking in the hundreds of faces, breathing in the bittersweet hush in the vast cathedral that waited on me. In the very back, against the wall, I spotted him. That know-it-all smirk of his saying, *Salut, fucker.* Luca Aliberti. Next to him a man who was a darker, meaner mix of Luca and Alessio. Their older brother, Emilio.

Luca would now sit at a Guardino business meeting instead of me, and he would take the heat, distract, and Emilio would conquer, destroy, usurp. I would be their silent partner.

Luca and Emilio left the church, and I tucked the poem in my inside jacket pocket.

Stin iyiá mas.

54

TURO

I WENT STRAIGHT to Erin's hospital room from the church once the service was done and the condolences had been dished out. She'd been conscious about four hours already, and I couldn't wait to see her myself. To talk to her.

I took her hands in mine and told her about James. She'd turned her face into the pillow and cried silent tears.

"I'm so sorry, Mom. So sorry. He didn't deserve that." I held on to her, her breathing choppy. I told her about the funeral, and she was distraught that it had happened without her.

"He did this, he did this..." she hiccuped.

"It's over, Mom."

"It won't ever be over, Turo. He'll never—"

"It's done."

She gripped my arms, her eyes searching mine. "What are you saying?" she breathed.

I leaned in closer to her. "He won't ever come after us again."

Her face paled, her lips opened as if she had something urgent to say.

I slanted my head, shaking it once, twice. "Don't."

She shut her eyes, wincing. Her head fell into my chest, and I held her, and we grieved for our transgressions and our might have beens. Together, we sank into some sort of gentle, hazy relief.

I handed her a bottle of her favorite water from the side table and she drank. "I didn't want you to have to do this. That's not what I wanted," she said.

"For you to have asked for my help in the first place, that meant things had gotten extreme."

"Yes but—"

"He'd been threatening you for years and you never told me."

"I had to protect you. But I failed because eventually he got to you."

I pressed my lips together. "He tried to have me killed the other day. The next day he hit you at the restaurant. So don't mourn the man you think your son should have been."

Her eyes blazed. "He tried to kill you?"

"Set me up. But things worked out quite differently."

She threw her arms around me. "I love you," she whispered into my neck.

"I love you too," I whispered back, my heartbeat steadying in my chest in a way that it hadn't in a long time.

———

"YOUR FIRST MEDITERRANEAN RESTAURANT? How did that happen?" I asked my mother, changing the subject, changing it forever.

She leaned back into her bank of pillows and wiped at her eyes. "The Mediterranean diet is huge now. Two islands in Greece, in particular, have attracted serious attention from scientists as well as tourists. Greek food is much, much more than *souvlaki* and *moussaka*. They have their own rich tradition of appetizers, like *tapas—mezé,* they call it. Their sense of simplicity with seafood, with grilling, the herbs they use, their olive oils.

They have an incredible variety of vegetarian dishes too. It's all about what's in—"

"In season."

"Yes. In season, exactly." She let out that knowing, rolling laugh of hers. It had been a long time since I'd heard it, felt those particular sparks go off in my gut. This was us in sync in the workplace, in sync as people. I never realized how much I valued that until right this moment.

I cleared my throat. "Actually, since we last saw each other, I've been to Greece, would you believe?" I said.

"Really? Lucky you."

"Yeah, very lucky," I murmured, my gaze going to the sea of tall, metal and glass buildings scraping dense, gray clouds out the window.

"How ironic, but very fortunate for the new restaurant," she said.

I met my mother's eyes once more. "Tell me everything about the new restaurant."

She told me, until the nurse kicked me out a few hours later.

———

I KEPT MYSELF BUSY, pouring over details of the restaurant, from replacing the destroyed fixtures, to overseeing the cleaning and restoration from the fire, smoke, and water damage. Staff training picked up again. We'd be ready to open. Maybe forty days after Erin's originally planned date, but we'd open.

Every morning at home, I amused myself with an espresso reading the newspaper reports about the investigation into the destruction of the Guardino crime family, the chaos, the disarray left behind. How the bomb used at Sal's *salumeria* had the signature of the Smoking Guns, an infamous motorcycle club associated with the Tantucci Outfit. Arrests had been made, and multiple investigations by local police and the FBI were under way.

Finger had killed his bird with our mutual stone.

I didn't hear from Luca again. I continued to be "distraught" over my boss's demise and kept very busy running my mother's company during her recovery and being with her at the hospital and then the rehab facility. From what I read in the paper, from what my former right-hand man, Paul, had told me, Emilio was cleaning house and holding the reins tightly in his fist. Paul also told me that the new boss was going to dissolve my operation.

"Really? I think I'll make him an offer," I'd told him.

Of course, that had already been agreed on between me and Luca, but we had to make it look good for everyone else. Luckily, I could afford to buy.

"So, you're out now?" Paul asked after the deal was done.

"Aliberti is consolidating and cutting the fat. I bought the gig for a hefty price, but it was worth it to me. I'll be paying him a protection fee, of course, but it's all mine. He's bringing in his own people, reorganizing. He's not going to trust me. Anyway, I'm very busy with my mother's company right now. The timing is right for me to move on. Believe me, I know I'm lucky to be able to move on."

"Yeah, sure." Paul shifted his weight.

"Thanks for everything you've done for me, Paul. I told Aliberti that you've been solid. That he can rely on you."

"'Preciate it, Turo." We hugged, slapping each other on the back.

Over lunch at my mother's steakhouse, I told Tricia that I'd bought the escort business outright and offered her a choice.

"You want to stick with me and this business or you want out?" I asked, cutting into my rare rib eye.

She put down her fork and oversized steak knife. "What kind of question is that? Of course I'm sticking with you. Fuck yes! Does this mean we can make those changes we've discussed?"

We'd wanted to go upscale for a long time. Less in and out whore for the ordinary john, more highly qualified escort experience for the client who could appreciate and could pay.

"All the changes."

Her face beamed, a beacon cutting through the fog. "Waiter!" She ordered a bottle of Bollinger.

———

TODAY I WAS FINALLY SITTING down with Dean, the chef of the new Greek restaurant, in his new kitchen.

Dean was a Greek American in his twenties who'd worked in New York and Athens for a summer and had returned to his Chicago roots. He was relieved that I was committed to opening. We reviewed his different menu plans for the coming months, discussed his culinary vision as he cooked for me in the kitchen.

"Erin has been amazing, really supportive," he said as he plated three large grilled shrimp on a long, bright blue dish and scattered oregano over them, then flakes of salt. "She has her opinions, I have mine. We don't always agree, but she's always willing to listen. It's obvious that she's dedicated to great food and great service, not just making a splash and a buck." He drizzled olive oil over the shrimp. "And that's been huge for me in this whole crazy process."

"This is your first restaurant, right?"

"Yeah." He let out a breath of air as he wiped the edges of the plate. "In here I know what I'm doing, what I need to do. Out there—" he slanted his head toward the dining room, "—not so sure. Not yet at least." He slid the plate before me.

"How'd you come up with the name 'Porto'?" I asked, peeling back the shell on the shrimp, my mouth watering at the sight of the perfectly cooked texture, the grilled aroma.

"Erin did. Although it's the Italian word for 'port' there are a lot of Greek beach towns named Porto this or that, so it implies seafood, which is a big focus of what we're doing here. Erin liked the idea of a harbor beckoning the weary traveler to enter, and when he does, he passes through this "portal" into a completely new and brilliant world of flavor and taste."

My mother the romantic poet, my mother the sharp, mature businesswoman supporting her artists in the right way. A flutter of emotion streaked through me at Dean's words, at the creamy tenderness of the shrimp filling my mouth, the perfect burst of sea fresh and sweetness. I swallowed down a crisp white wine from the island of Lemnos that Dean had poured for me earlier, and I savored the satisfying swirl of warmth it left behind.

I wiped my mouth with a napkin. "I like the name Porto. It's evocative multilingually. Smart."

"Right?" Dean planted his elbows on the counter. "And how do you like my shrimp?"

"Also very evocative. What kind of salt are you using?"

His eyebrows quirked up his forehead. "What kind?"

"Yes."

"It's top notch *fleur de sel.*"

"From France?"

"Uh, yeah. I've also got Peruvian pink on hand, have you tried it? It's just amazing, it's—"

"No."

"No?"

"I was on the island of Andros recently, and their natural sea salt is very special. You need to be using Greek sea salt. Find it, order what you need. You speak Greek?"

"I get by."

"Good." I wiped my fingers on the napkin. "I'm heading over to the hospital in half an hour to see my mother. Make her lunch and I'll bring it over. She must be suffering."

Dean let out a laugh, his eyes lighting up. "I'll bet she is."

Sure enough, once I got to the hospital, a nurse flagged me in the hallway. "She won't eat. She needs to eat."

"I'll take care of it."

I entered my mother's room. "I hope you haven't already eaten, because I brought lunch from your new chef." I placed the full shopping bag on her bed.

A smile of true pleasure lit her face as I handed her the boxes and she opened them. Grilled sea bass and garlicky stewed chickpeas. A salad of baby arugula and spinach topped with a grilled soft white cheese.

She bit into the cheese. "You see? There's more to Greek cheese than just feta."

I laughed. "I know." I unwrapped the silverware from the restaurant's cloth napkin and handed it to her. "You wouldn't believe the cheese I had over there."

"I think I would." She sliced into the roasted fish and ate. "So good. Have you tried? Dig in." She handed me the fork and I ate.

I handed the fork back to her. "That's good."

"You didn't happen to bring any wine, did you?"

"No wine, Erin. Not yet."

She made a face. We ate, and I cleared the mess. I adjusted her pillows for her and she leaned back. "Tell me more about Greece. Did you see the Parthenon? Did you have a chance to go to an island?"

I told her about all the touristy things I'd managed to do.

Her eyes narrowed at me. "Did you meet someone?"

"Why?"

"There's this wistful quality to the way you told me about the island. And you're not the wistful type."

"Wistful?"

"Hmm. Then there's Marissa telling me how invested you are in every detail of the restaurant from the font we chose for the menu to the light bulbs, to the food, especially the food. Every damned detail."

"Did you think I'd become some raging bureaucrat only interested in the bottom line?"

She touched my arm. "No. Your attention to detail always pleased me."

I put my hand over hers. "The entire team is committed to the opening. That's my only focus. You need to focus on getting stronger so they'll let you out of here sooner rather than later."

"Okay," she whispered, and my heart squeezed in my chest. This was vulnerable Erin, grateful Erin. An Erin I hadn't experienced in I don't know how long.

"Okay."

"So, is she Greek?"

I grit my teeth. "Erin."

Saying her name would conjure Adri before my eyes, here in this hospital room. Something I hadn't allowed myself. With everything going on, I'd pushed her into a vault and locked her up tight, so I could concentrate on the tasks at hand. But she was real. And I fucking missed her.

"Her name is Adriana."

"What a beautiful name."

"She is very beautiful."

I told my mother about Adri, about meeting her, the yacht, Mykonos, the getaway to Andros, all the damned food, all the wine.

None of the blood.

"Andros sounds extraordinary," she said. "I'm glad you had that. And to have experienced it with someone you care about."

I opened my mouth to say something, to refute as would have been my usual response. But there was nothing to refute. Only that my feelings for Adri went beyond mere caring, didn't they? An ache that had begun to hurt as the days wore on had rooted itself deep in my chest and would not be plucked like some weed. Unyielding and strong.

"Turo, you can't hide it. You can't. Oh, look at that—" Her voice softened considerably and she touched my chin, and her hand slid down my arm and squeezed.

"Mother, stop."

"No, honey. You and I, we're done with stopping and not discussing the important things. We have a lot of catching up to do, and we're going to do it."

———

MARISSA and I met at seven in the morning three times a week organizing ourselves and maintaining the company's flow. The first weeks of my full-time management, I'd met with each department director, toured each restaurant at lunch, cocktail hour, dinner time and during the day, spoke with the chefs, the managers, the bartenders. I wanted them to see the face, feel my handshake, hear my voice. Be assured that Erin's ship was under firm command.

Most evenings I spent at the different restaurants, having meals, checking on quality, watching the staff in action with either Marissa or Tricia or many times on my own. On one of those evenings, Charlotte, the attractive blonde sommelier at the steakhouse, propositioned me.

She stood close to me at the bar where I was nursing a Cabernet. I could smell her sweet perfume, noticed the tip of her tongue skirting her matte red lips. I knew it was coming, and yet, I had no reaction—no swell of heat, no tick of the pulse or shift of the cock, no smug satisfaction at the thick, expectant attention from such an attractive woman.

Charlotte slid her empty wine glass to the side. "I get off work in an hour. I'd love to show you this terrific wine bar in River North. They have an incredible new selection of reds from Latin America I think you'd really like."

"No, thank you. I have an early day tomorrow."

"Oh, okay." Her lips pursed and she stood up straight. "Well, have a good night, then."

"You too, Charlotte."

She wasn't the only woman who tried. There was a restaurant hostess, a special events planner, a bartender, a lawyer from the Mayor's office. But all their pheromones were an unscented mist. Their flirting, teasing, grins—no power, nothing.

No, not nothing. Their attempts didn't entertain me, nor did they please me, they only set off an ache, a literal pain in the center of my body that radiated through me. It was acute, this pain. It hurt.

I walked home, alone on the streets in the hustle of a Chicago Saturday night and stopped at a bookstore to get a copy of *The New York Times*. Foreign magazines lined two shelves by the cashier. British gossip magazines with royals and soccer studs and models on the cover. *"What are the young, beautiful, and rich shopping for this summer?"* trumpeted one magazine cover. A photo of a young English royal holding a bright pink leather designer bag and another of a singer's embroidered denim jacket. Her face jumped off the glossy periodical at me. Blood rushed to my head, my mouth dried.

A photo of Adri in a long, dark linen coat, flat sandals, her hair loose, lips painted burgundy, black sunglasses, her arm through Marko's who was holding several Burberry shopping bags, his hair much longer than the last time I'd seen him. I grabbed the magazine.

Rifling through it, I finally found the inane article, but there was only one other photo of Adri and Marko—the two of them getting into a chauffeured car outside a restaurant with a mention of how she was keeping a quiet profile since her and Marko's return to London. I flipped back to the cover photo again. I'd bet she knew she was being photographed; her stride was confident, head tilted toward her brother, mid conversation, a slight smile on both their faces. She was not giving a fuck, she was living, doing her thing.

The way it should be.

I tucked the magazine back on the shelf, tucking that sudden wave of emotion back inside. My hands settled in the pockets of my jacket, my fingers finding that talisman that I took with me everywhere.

Outside, the buildings and damp streets flared with light from the huge store windows, blinking traffic lights, the flow of cars. I looked up at the sky. No crown of stars visible. No stars at all. Rubbing a hand around the back of my neck, I headed home.

Nothing was the same anymore.

Not my Chicago, not the crowds on the streets, the familiar blare of traffic, not the refuge of my apartment, a good meal, a glass of fine red wine.

No, I was no longer the same.

55

TURO

MY MOTHER'S LATEST CREATION, Porto had finally opened.

The business had turned into a media favorite since the attack, with my mother's survival and James's death, my crime lord mystique. From a marketing standpoint it was sheer gold. Me as the new face of the Cavanaugh Group added all sorts of dark, intriguing luster.

Mauro was dead, three of his capos, five soldiers. Valerio was under arrest and under investigation for the murder of Little Anthony, and a meth-making biker associate of the rival Tantucci Outfit. The Tantuccis landed immediately under the telescope for their role in the mass killings of the Guardino chiefs. The two men who had survived the deli bombing hadn't seen anyone suspicious. At the time of the shooting, these two illegal immigrants had been in the basement stocking jars of pickles and bricks of heroin. And I'd been at a funeral across town in a well-fitted black suit and new shoes, eulogizing my stepfather.

Porto's menu was spectacular, the food beautifully presented, the staff poised. Fresh seafood flown in from Greece was the highlight, non-GMO locally grown organic produce. Authentic

Greek products from beans to lentils to nuts, artisanal breads. And a Greek only wine list.

I made sure my mother's friends and associates on the Mayor's task force for neighborhood renewal had known that I fully supported their work by attending a meeting in Erin's stead, assuring them the restaurant would open. Confidence and relief flared in the stodgy air in that boardroom like a whiff of fresh perfume making everyone blink and sigh.

Half the mayor's office wanted to suck my cock, the other half had their fingers poised to dial 911 at the sight of me. I'd made many political contacts while working with Mauro. I'd also known many while working with my mother. Then there was the one committee chairman who was a steady client of one of my ladies of the night.

The neighborhood renewal project was full steam ahead. Other business owners had put their projects on hold at the first sign of trouble; on hold no more.

Emilio had chopped up the Guardino octopus. Threw a few chewy tentacles of the syndicate to the fire, others he kept for himself, marinating them carefully with his own special vinaigrette. Emilio was the new guy in town. New guard from the old country wiping slates clean, doing things his way. The brutal way.

Show them how it's done, Aliberti. *Andiamo.*

———

"*Amico?*"

My insides tightened at the sound of that melodic accent, and I swiveled to my right and grinned. Alessio was a sight to behold here in Porto's bar. Heads turned, admiring glances tossed his way by both men and women.

"Alessio." I clapped him on the back, shaking his hand.

He lifted his chin at me. "*Eh, compagno. Come va?*"

"I'm good. I'm good," I replied. "This is unexpected. What are you doing here?"

"A last minute trip. I've been in Miami for a photo shoot."

"Photo shoot?"

"A shop there is going to be selling some of my jewelry. It was an opportunity to go and meet them personally, have fun in South Beach with my uncle, and do the advertising campaign. Of course, I couldn't leave America without coming here to see Emilio. And you. It's been over two months since you left Athens."

"Sit with me." I gestured at the empty chair next to mine.

He sat, stretching out his legs. "This restaurant business is for real, eh?"

"Would I lie to you?"

His chest shook with laughter.

Alessio took out a pack of cigarettes from his jacket pocket. "Can I smoke in here? I can't keep track of the rules anymore—Italy, Greece, here, fuck."

"No, you can't. Drink this." I handed him a frothy lemony ouzo cocktail from the bartender. I drank from mine.

"Hmm." His tongue rubbed over his front teeth. "That's... different." He put the drink down and scanned the bar lounge where we sat. "This place is crowded."

"We got solid reviews from all the right critics opening week. This *meze* bar lounge is proving to be a real hotspot for the young professionals after work. The tasting menu in the dining room is attracting a diverse clientele as well. Let me get you something to try."

"No, no. I'm good." He waved a hand at me. "I just had dinner with Emilio."

"How's he doing?"

His fingers rubbed the pack of cigarettes. "He misses home, but he loves it here. Likes being his own boss. And our father is thrilled at how everything worked out, of course."

"Of course."

"He's so proud. You'd think Emilio got into Harvard and graduated in one year." We laughed. He wiped a hand through his hair. "It rains too much here. I've been here three days, and rain, rain, every day rain."

"Yeah, I know," I said. "Luca's back in Naples?"

"*Si.* He might meet me in Mykonos the first week of September."

"Business good there since the big party?"

"Yes. The store on the island is doing good. Very good. And you? You are the restaurant king of Chicago now?" A wide grin broke his handsome features. Facetious prick.

I leaned back in my chair. "No, I wouldn't say that."

"They obviously like what you're selling. Greek food, eh?" He let out a laugh.

"Ironic, I know."

"You put on a very nice show for them. This is a wonderful theatre that vanishes once the customer's meal is over and they leave, isn't it? You offer carefully orchestrated flavors and an environment to evoke certain feelings, right?"

"Yes, that's right."

"But we know better." He picked up his glass, swirled the cocktail around, sniffing at it, and swiftly plonked it down on the table again. "When you've had the real thing, all this is only imitation, eh?"

Yes, I'd had the real thing. The pure thing.

I licked my lips and the ouzo flared on my tongue once more, diffused between sugar, lemon, and rum. Something pinched and twisted in my chest at the memory of me and Adri, that first lunch in Andros, celebrating our escape, our self imposed exile with *meze* and ouzo on the rocks with a dash of water on the sea, sun pouring over our skin.

"*This is how it should be enjoyed. You should keep all this in your* heart right this very second so that every time you take a sip of ouzo wherever else you may be, you will enjoy it the right way."

Sliding the ouzo cocktail away, Alessio caught the bartender's attention and ordered a whisky,

I took in a tight breath and raised my glass. *"Yiá mas,* Lovely," I murmured to myself and drained what was left of the suddenly absurd drink, my eyes closed.

"Keep all this in your heart," she whispered.

She was in my heart. She was. And this tarted up ouzo was bullshit compared to crisp, bright, pure ouzo with Adri on those beaches, on that island, our hands touching, our lips. Souls.

I texted her.

I'm drinking ouzo & it's crap without you

We texted once in a while. It was immediate gratification, light check-ins, masking yearning, need. I was here, she was way the fuck over there. And that sucked, in plain English.

I checked my watch. It was four in the morning in London, so, no, she wouldn't see my message and text me back right now. Unless she was out clubbing with friends. On a date with a man. Fucking somebody. My fingers tightened around my glass, knuckles whitening.

Alessio's whisky arrived and he quickly took a swallow. *"Grazie Dio."* He wiped at the edge of his mouth. "Don't you miss it, Turo?"

"What's that?"

"What you tasted in Greece."

My eyes shot to his. A slight grin curved his lips. "Tell me you didn't fall in love."

I rubbed my cool, slick glass, my teeth scraping my lip. Yes, I fell in love. With Greece. With her.

Yes, yes, yes.

I cleared my throat. "She's in London, getting her brother settled at school, working at her father's office."

"I know," Alessio said, his mouth twisting. "She's determined to start over, if you call that starting over. She said it was time to be sensible."

"Sensible?"

He let out a dry laugh and swallowed more liquor.

Adri was trying to buckle down. For the family business. For her brother. I could imagine her buttoned up in a suit, those long legs in sleek boots or tights with heels underneath a desk. Hurrying through London's damp streets in the coming fall. Bundling up against the chilly air, thick scarf around that glorious neck.

Fuck no.

Adri's coppery brightness belonged in the sun, that broad smile brightening her face, warming me.

Me.

She was my sun.

My mouth dried. "Alessio, is she with someone? Is she—"

"*No.*" His face grew serious as if it were an impossibility beyond reason. He put down his glass, shaking his head. "When I first met Adri, she was a—how do you say—*un fantasma.*"

"A ghost?"

"*Si*, a beautiful ghost. Nothing touched her. She would not let it. Wasn't eating very much. I tried to make her laugh, and I did, but it only worked so far. She wanted me to cocoon her, I did."

"Shut the fuck up now."

"Listen to me, Turo—" his tone was sharp, firm. "She was doing okay for a while, floating. But that shooting in Athens— enter Turo DeMarco and everything changed. With you she began to live again. To feel things. She stood up for herself, finally faced that father of hers. I have seen *una trasformazione.*"

Transformation.

"Come back to Europe, my friend," said Alessio.

"And do what? Be her bodyguard?"

"Ah." His head spun back, and he sent a stream of Italian curses flying to the ceiling.

"What now?"

"Her money is a problem for you, eh?" he asked. "It is for most men."

"No, her money doesn't bother me. I grew up with plenty, and I'm very familiar with the lifestyle. Not on her level, of course, but I have my own trust fund, and I'm very, very comfortable."

"Then what are you doing here? Go, be with her. Fuck like bunnies, be happy."

"A part of me feels it's better to let her go. It would be easier now that we're apart, so far away. She's young. She has so many choices she could make, and I don't want to hold her back or limit that."

"You think too much. She's like that too. You've got a new future now, asshole. Make it with her. She's yours, isn't she?"

"Yes, but—"

"But what?"

"Does she still want me? Could it even work?"

Alessio studied me, waving his glass in my direction. "You are afraid."

"Not afraid. Apprehensive." I swallowed cold water to drown the dregs of that cocktail from my mouth.

"Why? You go there, grab her, and you—"

"I don't want to fuck it up," I gritted out. "It was damn perfect, but it was this dream-like sliver we had cut out of time together. Maybe it was just a Greek island vacation high and the drama of running off on our own."

"Maybe, maybe, maybe." Alessio waved his fingers in a mocking flick.

"Fuck you."

"Don't throw away the chance to find out, Turo. Don't. It is easier for you to risk your life over and over for assholes, than it is to be with the girl of your dreams? Adriana is not a dream. And your time together was not a dream. All of it—real."

I eyed him, crunching the ice from my empty water glass.

"Hmm." He slanted his head. "You see, I am glad I came. You need me."

"I need you?"

"Oh yes." His eyes narrowed at me. "Are you running anything for my brother or are you out?" he asked.

"I don't run anything for anybody else anymore. That's over. Never again."

"Glad to hear it."

"I'm Emilio's silent consultant with local issues, the characters involved. He sold me my business, I get his protection, and I'm going to expand once I'm not working at my mother's company full-time anymore."

"When will that be?"

"Another month, probably. She's doing very well, in fact."

"Good. This other business of yours is successful?"

"Very. For years now. It's a well-lubed machine, but I want to take it to another level."

"You like it?"

"I do. I turned it into something much, much better than it was originally. And I want to see it grow in a new way."

"You know, I worked for my father for a few years. Gambling, garbage, drug dealing—" Alessio drained his whisky, a slight wince lining his features. "—Not my thing. The world of pleasure and beauty, *that* is my thing. And I believe you have a very fine appreciation for it as well."

"I do."

His voice lowered. "I've been living in my father and brothers' shadows all my life. I love them and they love me. We are family and that never changes, but I'm not interested in what they do. Stepping away was not easy. It was unusual, awkward, insulting to them. I've had to prove myself to them with my success." He shrugged. "Mostly, I think my father was worried I was gay."

"You're definitely not gay."

Rich laughter erupted from him, and I grinned at the sound.

"Ah, Turo. I want more. More of my own creations. It makes me happy that my work gives others so much pleasure, and I like making my own money. Why not continue to create more and different things? Mykonos was fantastic for me. Now this Miami thing may turn into something. I want to do more of this."

Alessio's family seemed to be tight, supportive, and I was glad for him. But both he and I had a need to step out of the shadows into our own sun.

"I know how you feel, Alessio," I said.

"I can sense this in you. I know these things," he said. "You must come back to Europe." He slammed a hand on the bar. "I'm going to be in Greece in August. Come with me. Remember the Greek singer Elektra from my party?"

"Sure."

"She will be singing at the same club. An end of summer party, and Adri insists I go."

"Good for the brand."

"Yes. Close out the season on Mykonos with a bang, get some press. Adri had me design a special necklace for Elektra for the concert."

"Nice. Adri is going too?" I asked.

"She'll be there." He held my gaze. "She and Marko are meeting their parents at their house on Mykonos for a quick holiday before Marko starts school in London. It will be her birthday then too."

"Her birthday?"

"Hmm. I invited her to this private island thing, but she wasn't interested. Just wants to be with her family."

"What private island thing?"

"Ah—this new friend of mine who I met in Mykonos at my party in May, his family owns their own private island in Greece."

"Really?"

"Yes." His eyes lit up. "He is the son of a Sheik from the Gulf who bought himself a small Greek island, more like a big rock, a few years ago. They've built a house there, only accessible by boat of course. He's having a small party there and then we'll all go to Mykonos together on his daddy's yacht."

"You know the right people, Alessio."

"I do." He grinned. The cat had nabbed the mouse and mightily enjoyed the tasty treat. "Get us another drink. Your bartenders are way too busy. This drink was shit and you know it," he said to me, gesturing at our ouzo cocktails.

With an unhappy look on my face, I signaled a waitress and she immediately charged over. Alessio ordered two single malt whiskies, and she took away our glasses. Our drinks arrived and he raised his glass.

"Are we drinking to anything in particular?" I asked him, holding up my whisky.

He clinked my glass with his. *"La trasformazione."*

56

TURO

"This feels good, and I'm not ashamed to say it." My mother spread her hands out over her desk and heaved a sigh. Satisfaction, exuberance. The Queen was back on her throne.

"No shame for workaholics like us," I said.

Six weeks had gone by since Porto had opened. My mother was finally allowed to come back to work, for a few hours a day for the time being. Her face beamed at me, rivaling the beauty of the flower arrangement on her desk next to her. I crossed my arms at my chest and admired her, enjoying her pleasure.

"I have something for you," she said, laying a thick envelope on the desk.

"What's this?" I picked it up. Travel agency. I pulled out the papers. An itinerary for a one way first class flight to Athens.

"Erin?"

"I know I haven't been a good role model to you in the relationship department." She came around her desk and stood before me. "I could have been fairer about your father to you, instead of spouting my form of vitriol at every opportunity, instead of pushing me away."

"You did that to keep me safe."

"You were just a boy. A boy without a daddy and not much of a mommy." She smoothed a piece of my hair at the side of my face. "I should have bit my tongue more often."

"Don't apologize for him."

"I'm apologizing for me. It's very late, I realize. You're a grown man now."

"Mom?"

"You're passionate about your work, just like me. And that's a good thing. But you can't mistake that passion for love in your life. A good love. It's not the same. By that I mean a true one, one that pulls all your loose pieces together and makes them fit. One that's a beacon for you, physically and emotionally." Her hands rested on my shoulders. "I want that for you. You deserve to experience it and to hold on to it. If Adri could be the one, you need to be together."

"Jesus, Mom. You make it sound so easy."

"It definitely isn't easy, but you have to try. You must. Otherwise what's the point of fighting to stay alive?" Her voice pleaded with me, her eyes searching mine. She was right; My mother was a fighter. So was I.

She let out a breath. "Have you ever been in love, Turo? Really in love?"

I shook my head. "Once I thought so, but this, this was so different. So much more."

"Have you told her how you feel?"

"No. We both realized it was something—something that really mattered—but circumstances, reality got in the way and then I had to leave. She has a lot of family responsibilities and she's stepping up—"

"Just like you've been doing."

"I suppose. I didn't want to interfere with her—"

"No."

"No?"

"There'll always be interference of some kind, but that's

where you shine. Fighting through it, clearing the deck. I had no illusions about James. He wasn't a fighter. I did the fighting there for both of us. Never a good thing." Her gaze drifted to the window. "It wasn't an ideal relationship, but it worked in many ways."

"I know," I said tersely.

She pressed her lips together. "I don't want that for you. I don't want you to ever settle because you've been hurt, or it seems like the practical thing to do. Real love only blooms if you risk, if you take a leap of faith. Love soars in that leap. It's in that soaring that you savor its unique flavor and texture, the one only the two of you share.

"I need you and that's a good feeling," she said. "It tortured me these past ten years, but I deserved it."

"Don't—"

"It's true. But now that's over, and I'm letting myself actually enjoy needing you for a change and it's sweet, not bitter." She cleared her throat. "But now is your time to soar. Take a moment and give whatever it is you feel for Adri a chance to grow. That wistfulness I noticed when you first told me about her has turned into a workaholic denial. I know that shit all too well, and I'm telling you, don't allow it to happen."

"Is this a mother power play here?"

She squeezed my arm and held my gaze. "Take it as my simply pointing out an alternative direction to you."

"And make a choice?"

Her face fell. "Turo—"

"It's true. I need to make a choice. My choice."

"Yes, yours. We both know there's no time to waste in this life. This is new to you, and it may feel awkward and uncomfortable, but you need to try."

That voice beckoned me, *"Get uncomfortable with me."*

My mother leaned in closer. "I do need you, Turo, but I love you more." A kiss on my cheek.

"I love you too," I breathed.

She released me. "As current CEO, I'm officially transferring your title to "consultant." Go to Greece and explore some new ingredients Chef Dean could use at Porto or old traditions he could put his spin on. Maybe a winery that hasn't exported yet. Take your time."

"Actually, I do have a new business idea I'd like to research in Europe."

"Do you? Fantastic. Go."

"Mom."

She held my gaze. "You need to go, Turo."

I rubbed my hand across my jaw. "She's in London right now. Not Athens."

"Marjorie can have the ticket changed."

"Mom—"

"I'm fine. Go."

I scanned the itinerary. "Jesus, the flight is tomorrow?"

"Yes, tomorrow."

"Such a tenacious bitch."

"You and me both."

LONDON

57

ADRIANA

"DAVID, I need to have that quarterly report on Khalid Enterprises before four today. Mr. Khalid just informed me that he's flying in from Doha tomorrow afternoon instead of next week, and I have to be able to give him the specs he wants to see."

"Oh, damn. I'll start on it now."

"Thank you."

My assistant David was an efficient sort. My office was run efficiently. I was an efficient component of Lavrentios Shipping, Ltd., London headquarters. *Efficient.*

I let out a heavy breath as I hunted for the right file on my computer. The only thing that wasn't "efficient" was my constant daydreaming, an electric flutter of memories that frequently interrupted my train of thought, derailing me over and over again. Turo's brittle but hearty laugh, the brush of his lips on my skin. Waking up in the morning with him wrapped around me. That yearning for him that now twisted and pulled at my insides, the intense feelings he evoked in my body, in my soul.

Working here filled me with pride, and I heard that pride in Petros's voice every time we spoke. In my mother's voice. In the way my uncle, Petros's older brother who headed the offices here, had discussed in great detail a new investment with me earlier this week. And it made me feel good that I gave them that.

I glanced at the framed photo on my desk of me and Marko on the London Eye just last week. His smile was huge. A rare smile after everything he'd been through. He'd started to tell me details of his capture, and I'd ground my jaw together at the new shudder in his voice, sentences that would often drift, his far off looks that were too frequent for my liking.

We lived together at the family flat in Mayfair. We did things together. Either cooking at home or takeaways from his favorite restaurants and snuggling on the couch in front of the telly, or going to movies, museum exhibits first thing in the morning, a classical music concert once, but the crowd and noise had proven to be too much for him.

He was quiet most of the time, and yet once our parents flew back to Athens weeks ago, he had become a bit more talkative and relaxed, mostly because their constant state of concern had seeped into the atmosphere no matter the smiles on their faces. Thankfully, he was enjoying summer school and would be entering a private school north of London in the Fall.

Our mother had wanted to stay with us, but I'd convinced her otherwise. "Please, go home, *Mamá*. We'll be fine."

"Are you telling me my own son and daughter don't need me?" she said, her fatigued eyes tightening, lips pursing.

"No, God no. I'm telling you your son and daughter need each other now and please give us this time."

She fell on me, hugged me, and for the first time in what seemed like a long time, neither of us cried. Just held on tightly.

Today the sky outside my bank of windows at the office was streaked with puffy gray clouds. Raindrops still streamed down the glass from a quick shower earlier today. Bloody hell, it was the height of summer and it was cloudy here with a chance of rain this afternoon. I stretched out my neck and lower back and went back to preparing for my meeting with Mr. Khalid.

"Miss Lavrentiou?" the receptionist's voice rose from the intercom on my phone.

"Yes, Claire?"

"A man is here to see you. He doesn't have an appointment, but he's quite insistent."

I groaned inside. Greek reporters still tried to talk to me at the office, but I didn't go anywhere without my security team. To gain access to me at the office, you had to go through a two stage check and pat down.

"His name?"

"Marino Dandolo."

My heart stopped then banged in my chest. My fingers tightened around the pen in my hands, and I let out a laugh. *That perfect sense of humour of his.* The Venetian lord of Andros had arrived. My conqueror, my crusader was at the castle gates.

"He says you know each other," Claire said. "And that he's just flown in from Chicago to see you."

I tossed the pen on my desk. My insides ached, knotted. My mouth dried, my fingers suddenly cold as they pressed down on the intercom button. "Yes, Claire. I know Mr. Dandolo. Please send him through."

I ran a hand through my hair. Checked myself in the tiny mirror in my top drawer and dabbed on a swipe of my favorite plum gloss. My once long hair was now a little shorter and still stick straight after my morning blow out. His beach naiad was gone.

I swept the folders, newspapers, pens, my cell phone into neat piles and stood up, my legs shaky in my heels. I smoothed a hand down my snug charcoal gray pencil skirt, across the chest of my silk, sleeveless, beige blouse.

I waited. My lungs burned. I burned.

The door opened.

Those sharp eyes of his held mine, taking me in. I could feel the swell and pull of them, and I took in a breath. That crooked smile broke over his lips and my pulse leapt. A dark suit. Crisp pale yellow shirt. Spotless leather shoes. And that fantastic scruff on his angular face.

That heat reverberated between us, created a buzzing thing that had a life all its own, sending groans, touches, kisses of another lifetime now dancing in my chest, trying to break free.

"*Signor Dandolo,*" I said, and my blood stirred to life at that dark look that passed over his features at the sound of my Italian. "Are you here to seize and conquer?"

He stood there, still, as if he were overwhelmed by the sight of me. "Have you missed me?" he asked.

Cheeky sod.

My fingers grabbed the edge of my desk. "I miss you all the time," I replied.

His smile transformed into something wicked that filled the room, wrenched at my insides, swelled in my soul. "I miss you all the time too," he said, his voice low. He smoothed a hand down his lapel. "Thorough security check."

"Oh I do hope they didn't muss you up too badly."

"I'll live." His smile got huge, brilliant once more and my breath short-circuited. I couldn't move.

"Your mother is well?" I managed.

"She's very well and back at work." His gaze returned to me, his eyes blazing with a dash of his signature wickedness. "She kicked me out, in fact."

"What? Why?"

"It's time for me to pursue my true passion."

"Ah, and so you came to London?"

His gaze went to the model reproduction of the company's first mega tanker encased in plexiglass. "Yes," he said, his attention settling on me.

The silence between us crackled as we both drank each other in. Brisker, headier than any champagne.

My heart banged in my chest. "A haberdashery business? I know someone on Savile Row I could introduce you to—"

"No." He stalked toward me.

He got closer. That cologne of his wafted over me and my knees quivered, my insides tightened.

"Ah, you're opening a pub or a teahouse in Chicago and need to research the real thing?"

He shook his head, his eyes narrowing. "No." He stood before me, so close I could sense his body heat.

"Fish and chips?" I breathed.

He scented me, carefully, with his whole being. An animal taking in his mate. "You. You, Adri."

My lips parted, no words came out.

"You came to the airport in Athens and told me you loved me," Turo said. "You gave me that gift freely, not asking for anything in return, knowing you might never see me again. Your gift kept me warm and sane and inspired in that darkness."

I reached out and cupped the side of his face. "I'm glad," I whispered, my heart thundering in my chest.

He brushed my hand with his lips. "Now the time for battle and grieving is done," he breathed. "You told me in that castle in Andros that you've always believed in love. I believe now, too. You made me believe. I love you, Adriana Lavrentiou."

My breath shorted, my hand slid down to his chest to steady myself, to touch him. He covered it with his own, connecting us, and his warmth bolted through me.

"We shouldn't be separated by continents, an ocean, a sea. We should be traveling them together," he said.

His words rushed and swirled like a living, breathing thing between us. Expectation, anticipation, possibility.

My throat burned.

He tilted his head at my non-reply. "Maybe your parents already have a royal prince lined up for you?"

"That was the year before last," I stuttered.

"Ah. Maybe now you're dating an age appropriate Greek shipping heir?"

"No, no. Been there, done that, as you Americans say." I touched the seam of his lapel. "There's no one else. How could there be?"

The edges of his lips tipped up but the grin quickly faded into something almost delicate and shattering. He took my hand in his and placed a small, leather, purple box in my palm. "A gift for my lady." A box embossed with Alessio's medieval double "A" logo in gold on the top.

My heart knotted in my chest. "What's this? The conqueror's bargain?"

"A declaration. Especially designed for you."

I snapped open the box, and my eyes flared at the spectacle in my hands. A ring. A ring unlike any other. A raw aquamarine stone, and wrapped around it as the band and setting was a gold dagger.

"Turo..."

"You told me that your great-grandfather threw his lover's precious dagger in the sea because he had to let go and move on."

"Yes."

"Because the battles he'd fought and won with that dagger were finally over. But unlike Stefanos and Natalia, we aren't lost to each other," he said.

I nodded.

"You and me," he said, his words a rush of liquid fire. "We've let go of the past, but we can keep our dagger, lovely. This is *our* declaration of love. This is our gift to each other, and it should shine like the brightest star."

"I love it. I love the ring."

"I figured you had plenty of diamonds."

"Too many," I said, my voice shaking.

"This is a jewel for my beach goddess. You need a piece of the sea and the sun on you all the time. Our piece."

"Put it on my finger," my voice shook, my hand shook. He slid the sea jewel on my ring finger and I stared at it, my heart pounding.

"Baby, do I need to fuck a response out of you?" he asked.

"I love you," I said, my vision blurry. "I love you. I love you."

"Adri, will you—"

"Yes!"

He got down on his knees, his hands skimming up my stockinged legs, inside my skirt.

"W-what are you doing?"

He shoved the material up my hips and found the soft bare skin of my upper thighs. "I want to seal this moment with a kiss." His eyes darkened.

A cry escaped my lips, and I trembled, my pulse pounding at the feel of his heat over my suddenly very sensitive flesh.

"Ah, fuck," he rasped, fingering the garters that held my stockings, the sliver of my rosy pink knickers covering me. "Here's my Lovely—delicate and decadent pink hidden under all that crisp gray."

Goosebumps rose on my skin under his careful caresses, the warmth of his breath on my sensitive flesh.

"Your skin is much too pale, baby." His lips brushed a thigh and I quivered. "This northern climate is no good for you."

My head fell back and I laughed.

His thumb breached the silk fabric of my knickers, finding my wet flesh. "Fuck, I missed you," he breathed.

My hips twisted in his hold. "I missed you too. So much." His thumb swirled gently. "Turo—"

"We belong together. Dwell with me in my underworld, Persephone."

My core hummed with sensation, my every nerve ending on

fire. "Will you be good to me all those months in your darkness, my Lord?"

"I will, baby. Always." With his eyes holding mine, he yanked the damp fabric aside and his tongue lashed over me, a swipe of velvet, and my hips tilted to meet his mouth. I wanted him, ached for him. All of him. How long had it been? For-bloody-ever.

"Oh...Turo...Turo..."

His lips, his tongue turned hard, savage, a whirlpool of sensation throbbing inside me. His mouth let go of me and he rose, lifting me onto my desk.

"*Stásou*—wait!" I blinked, pushing at his chest. "The door's not locked."

He unzipped his trousers, his hard length bounding free of his boxer briefs. "Then you'll have to be quiet this time, Lovely. Do you think you can do that?" He pressed against me, his wet tip teasing my entrance.

I whimpered. "I don't want to be."

"Try, just this once. I'm too fucking impatient." He thrust into me ruthlessly, and the two of us gasped.

Pure ecstasy.

His forehead slid against mine, and my insides shuddered. The world made sense again. Something shifted in my chest, tightening, erupting. Everything had led me here, everything; the bad, the screwed up, the frustrations, the tears, the fuckups. Turo was perfect. Perfect. My insides hugged his gorgeous, powerful cock as he moved inside me, groaning.

His thickness filled me, and he moved more urgently, cutting off my breath. "Yes, yes—"

"You were meant for me, Adri. Only me. All for me."

My heart beat faster at his words, his possession. "All for you." I kissed him, his taste lighting me on fire and soothing me all at once.

Turo's fingers dug into my hair, pulling tight as he ground into me, filling me. My legs hooked around his waist, keeping him close. My fingers clawed at his taut arms, and he encouraged every scratch, hushed cry, and moan he elicited from me on his every harsh thrust.

The two of us, together. Inside each other. Claiming a new life, new dreams.

Against the hot, damp skin of my throat, he growled, "All for me."

58

TURO

THE HOUSES OF PARLIAMENT towered regally across the Thames, the sun's afternoon glow washing the old stone in dark brassy gold. The sun was setting upon London. People had gotten out of work and were swarming the roads, the bridges. It was Friday, there was excitement in their rush of activity. Off to shops, bars, restaurants, the theater.

But Adri and I weren't in any rush. We enjoyed an aimless stroll, her arm through mine, as we ambled down the South Bank of London, the ornate lampposts dotting the tree-lined riverside walkway our companions.

"You've been to London before?" she asked.

"Twice before. On family vacation, and another time when I was in college. I liked it very much. Beautiful city."

"It is. A great combination of the very modern and the very historical. I like the energy here, it's unique. I've never been to Chicago."

"I look forward to showing it to you."

"Me too." She reached up and kissed my lips.

I held her chin. "It doesn't matter where we are as long as we're together. I want to give you the world, Adriana."

She squeezed my arm and pressed in closer to me.

"What would you like to do tonight? Where should we eat?" I asked her.

"Actually, I don't want to share you. I think I'd like to cook dinner at home tonight. Is that terribly boring of me?"

"Sounds perfect."

We got into a black cab which took us to her tony Mayfair neighborhood. All the townhouses looked alike along with rows of similar luxury SUVs parked up and down the streets. We went to a fancy butcher boutique and she chose beef filets.

"We need to make mashed potatoes with that," I said. "The real thing, not from a box."

"The horror," she said on a dramatic shudder as I held the shop door open for her and she passed through.

Back at her incredible apartment that was filled with bold contemporary art and delicate antique furniture, colorful rugs, and heavy damask curtains, we set up shop in the magnificent black and white kitchen. She marinated the thick slices of organic Black Angus beef in crushed peppercorns, olive oil and wine, while I peeled the potatoes, cut them up and added them to a pot of salted boiling water along with a couple of garlic cloves. She'd lined up Irish butter, Jersey cream, and English mustard for me on the marble counter which stood waiting for my mash mastery. She created a salad out of mixed greens and thin slices of parmesan.

"Having dinner parties is a way of life here in London," she said as she set down plates on the enormous marble island in the center of the kitchen. "It's become theatre, rather competitive theatre at that. Everyone gets caught up in outdoing each other, making the biggest splash. They get obsessive about the prestige and the glamour of it. I went to a dinner once where the entire meal was made from truffles."

"The entire meal?"

"Yes. The starters, the salads, the main course. The dessert.

All of it. The novelty wore off quickly for me, and I couldn't eat after the second course. "

I made a face. "Jesus, that must have cost a fortune."

"It was crazy. In fact, she'd hired a truffle agent—"

"A truffle *agent?*"

"There is such a thing for London's elite—an agent for every delight you can possibly think of. This one's quite famous, all word of mouth. She buys the truffles directly from sources in Italy and brings them here to sell herself."

"She does well, this agent?"

"Extremely well. With private clients only, mind you, not restaurants. There are agents for smoked hams and sausages, different cheeses. Oh—then there was one who sells trout and salmon that's smoked while the smoker—who is also a jazz pianist—plays. He claims the music affects the tenderness and the flavor of the fish."

We both burst out into laughter.

"It's true, I tell you!" she said. "I've eaten it myself."

"And how was it?"

"It sang in my mouth, darling."

I kissed her, nipping at her lips. "My mouth is going to make you sing tonight, Lovely." She kissed me. "The obsessive pursuit of the finest pleasures," I murmured.

"Hmm."

I made the mashed potatoes, she plated the beef. I poured the wine, we ate.

We got the plates into the dishwasher, the cutlery. I said, "There's something I need to tell you about my work, how things have changed for me."

She wiped her hands on a towel. "All right."

I lifted her up onto the kitchen counter and stood between her legs, my hands on her thighs. "I'm out of the business in Chicago. Luca and Alessio's brother, Emilio is running it now."

"Emilio? Really?"

"Really. Luca and Emilio made the transition of power...definitive."

"I'm sure they did."

"It was a good deal for me and very good for them, this foothold in America. And I like having the Alibertis on my side."

"And your boss, your father?"

"No more," I said evenly.

She held my gaze, steely. Understanding. Accepting. "I see."

"If Luca or Emilio need my opinion on anything, my insights into the local players, they ask me, I answer," I said. "But that's as far as that goes. Luca sold me the business that I always ran for Guardino and it's all mine now. An escort service."

"Oh." Her eyes widened and settled into a knowing smirk. "You must like this business if you've bought it for yourself?"

"I've made a good living off the obsessive pursuit of illicit pleasure. I have a friend from business school who I run it with, and for years we've wanted to expand, upgrade, take it to another level, but we were unable to. Now that it's mine, I plan on doing that. Like this truffle agent."

"How do you mean?"

"There's a whole secret underworld out there of desires desperate to be fulfilled."

"From wild mushrooms to sex, it would seem."

"And more. I want to offer something unique that I know people want, people who can afford to indulge, but aren't sure how to get it or how to get enough of it."

"People who are more than willing to pay for this unique. And you would be the agent?"

"Yes. Consensual sexual entertainment in a private, exclusive setting."

"Like what we saw on Evgeny Berezin's boat?"

"No. That was a gaudy circus. I'm interested in creating an experience."

"An experience," she murmured. "Which includes a high-class escort service?"

"That would be one part of it, yes. Women and men who are not only attractive but well-dressed, educated, can hold a conversation and listen—to accompany a client on a vacation, a business trip, any kind of social event. A companion tailored to your tastes and interests."

"Not just a fuck," she said.

"That's right. Everybody's busy multitasking now, mobile phones are everywhere, gaming, online gambling, porn. People are forgetting how to touch, how to feel, connect."

"But their bodies haven't. Their bodies crave," she said, her cheeks reddening.

I brushed my thumb along her lip. My baby had hungered and craved and didn't know how to reconnect until me. My inner caveman roared.

"The spirit craves too," she said.

"It does." I kissed the side of her face.

"And what's the other part?"

"A private club, but not at one location. Members from all over the world, small numbers, keeping it exclusive, a surprise even. We have special parties on private properties, leased yachts all over the Mediterranean. Luxury all the way. Alessio told me about this new friend of his whose family owns their own island. That got me thinking, and it pulled together all these ideas I've been having for a while now."

"That island this Sheik owns is in the Ionian Sea, part of a chain of a few tiny islets. It's quite impressive what he's created. The original owners had been trying to sell it for years, the taxes —" she made a face "—you can imagine. He built this incredible mansion there. It's well guarded, supremely private. Naturally, you can only get there by boat. He arrives with his yacht, it makes the national news."

"To rent a place like that for a week, ten days..." I said.

"Maybe Alessio could talk to him about renting or even sponsoring an event. The Sheik has two wives, but he has four sons and two bachelor brothers who are all notorious players. They and their circle might very well be interested in such a club."

"Let's get Alessio in on this."

"That would be smart. He lives that lifestyle of riding the taboo, and he's able to combine this underground aesthetic with luxury cachet."

"You played a huge role in creating that."

"I did." She smiled. "And it's what you need. What happens at this club over the weeklong stay?"

"Organized activities either with the escorts or members' own partners to experiment with, reconnect, to swing. We provide something for every taste and desire: straight, gay, menage, orgy, bondage, whatever the hell it is, it's on the menu."

"Maybe a different menu or theme for every occasion," she said. "Really special, very extravagant. A compelling experience. And how often? Two sessions a year? And at extremely different locations. Create that buzz and they will feel they must be a part of it."

My insides tightened like a drum. "You like this?"

"You said, 'We' and I like that."

I cupped her chin. "You like the illicit too, baby."

"I like it with you." Her tongue flared across her lip and my breath snagged in my throat. "Your excitement is infectious. Now, would you only want experienced people as members or novices as well? A mix?"

"A mix. You'd want to make this good for first timers. That's key. They may react anxiously. They'll need time to warm up to the reality, and then they'll get into it. I've seen it in Chicago, especially with the celebrities or politicians. Once they feel comfortable that their privacy is ensured and they have one good experience, they take off. They keep coming back, they spend, they get comfortable, they stretch their wings. Knowing they can afford this sort of thing is a high for them."

"The unique factor of the setting will make them feel they *need* more, that there's always another level for them to experience, something other."

I grinned. "Exactly."

"I say a big initiation fee plus a yearly membership fee. Every member signs a contract ensuring privacy, making them feel safe to express themselves freely and to enjoy without fear of exposure. They'll play by the rules as there would be too much for them to lose personally and professionally. A bond of secrecy wrapped up in privilege." She picked up her wine glass and polished off the last of it. "Rather delicious."

"I see this as a medium not only for entertainment, but exploration, learning, discovery. We could have a tantric sex guru come and show couples the light. Sexual massage."

"Shibari." She cocked an eyebrow, hooking her feet around my legs, pulling me closer.

"Shibari, huh?"

"I found it on the internet."

"You'd want to keep it small, a tight group in the beginning," she continued. "Members could nominate other potential members, but they'd have to pass our approval. You could even do some sort of initiation, a purely hedonistic little ritual to seal the pact." Her eyes literally sparkled.

"Which would go to emphasize that this is a shared, special experience for the very few."

"Ooh, we should have Alessio design some sort of charm or necklace as a sign of membership for the ritual."

"Great idea. A tactile logo."

"Would you need to hire just the right women and men to play the roles, satisfy certain interests?"

"That's where Tricia will come in."

"Tricia?"

"My madame in Chicago. She keeps track of sexual trends and shifts in fads and fetishes."

"Now there's a job." She nodded. "Then there's branding, pricing, scheduling, coordinating, communications..."

A rush tipped my system. "Work with me."

"I'm already your sex slave," popped out of her mouth.

"And I'm yours," I breathed, standing perfectly still.

A flash of hunger, dark desire crossed her features. My skin heated as my body remembered her initial tentativeness, her embracing my rough, her willingness to go farther every time, to submit, to take control. That hunger inside me that yearned for Adri flared painfully.

She wrapped her arms around my neck, pressing her body into mine. "So you're saying I should leave my job here for this sinful, indecent adventure?" A smile dawned on her lips.

"You wanted to break out, didn't you? You've worked in shipping, in oil, real estate, fundraisers. You're multilingual, you're an amazing special events planner, your instincts for publicity and PR are spot on. You're able to juggle a thousand details all at once, and all the right details, and make snap decisions in a crisis. There's a huge market to be tapped, and you know the players we'd like to target, you're a part of their world. More than that, you would be amazing at this, you would shine."

She let out a small laugh. "Shine?"

"Oh, so fucking bright."

"Your belief in me has always meant a lot, Turo, from the very beginning. It helped me see things differently, see myself differently. You never coddled me or let me hide. You dared me, teased me. Thank you."

"I've always believed in you, Adri." I brushed my lips with hers, a hand around her pulsing throat. "We should talk to Alessio about this tomorrow."

"He gives good face and attitude." She let out a laugh. "Always an asset. I think he'll really like this idea."

"It's the next level," I said. "I have plenty of clients in America who'd be interested in an experience like this. An alternate vacation from their hectic schedules. An adventure."

"Our adventure." She caressed the side of my face and a low moan escaped my throat. "So you wouldn't mind living like a gypsy in the Mediterranean for half the year, maybe more?"

"If it's with you, nowhere else I'd rather be."

She kissed me.

I nipped her bottom lip. "I like brainstorming with you."

"We came up with so many good ideas," she said. "We should write them down so we can review them tomorrow. See if they hold up in the light of day—"

"No writing—fucking." I brushed the side of her neck with my lips. "Let's fuck on it tonight, see how we feel in the morning."

She laughed as I scooped her up off the counter and brought her into the living room and down to the floor. I wanted her naked, on my cock, and covered in my cum on that antique silk Persian rug.

———

I PUT the suede pouch in her hands.

"What's this?" Adri sat up from the floor.

"Early birthday present. I can't wait. I want you to have it now."

"Turo," she murmured, grinning as she opened the small pouch. Turning it over, the necklace fell into her open palm. She studied the midnight blue cord entwined with another of slate blue. Little brass cubes and balls, crystal beads along with tassels and charms—stars, starfish, an abstract sun, a *máti* evil eye charm trimmed in gold.

Our beach. Our sky. Our Andros.

"I'd gotten it for you in Andros, that last morning. But in the rush of everything going on, I didn't have a chance to give it to you. Then I felt the moment for it had passed, that it was better not to give it to you. I found it in my suitcase once things calmed down in Chicago and I've kept it in my pocket ever since. Everywhere I go."

"Everywhere?"

"Everywhere. Along with the stone from Vitáli." I took the necklace from her and put it over her head, smoothed it over the tops of her breasts and kissed it, kissed her warm skin. "This is where it belongs."

"It's beautiful," she breathed. "Perfect."

"You're perf—"

She kissed me, a slow kiss, gentle, and led me to her room where she threw back the covers and pulled me into her bed. Moonlight gleamed through the open shutters, casting a silvery sheen on her body. I traced a delicate circle over her skin, down her middle. Her scar was no longer a distraught wound that she cut at as her pent up emotions dictated. She'd finally let it heal. I kissed the whitened scar and she let out a sigh. The mad Bacchanal had finished, the frenzy was over, yet I remained possessed and mesmerized by my lovely girl, my Adriana, and I knew I always would be.

She held me, and I laid my head down on her chest, a hand cupping a breast, her heart beating with mine. This was accomplishment, this was real ecstasy, deep joy. Peace. This was where I belonged.

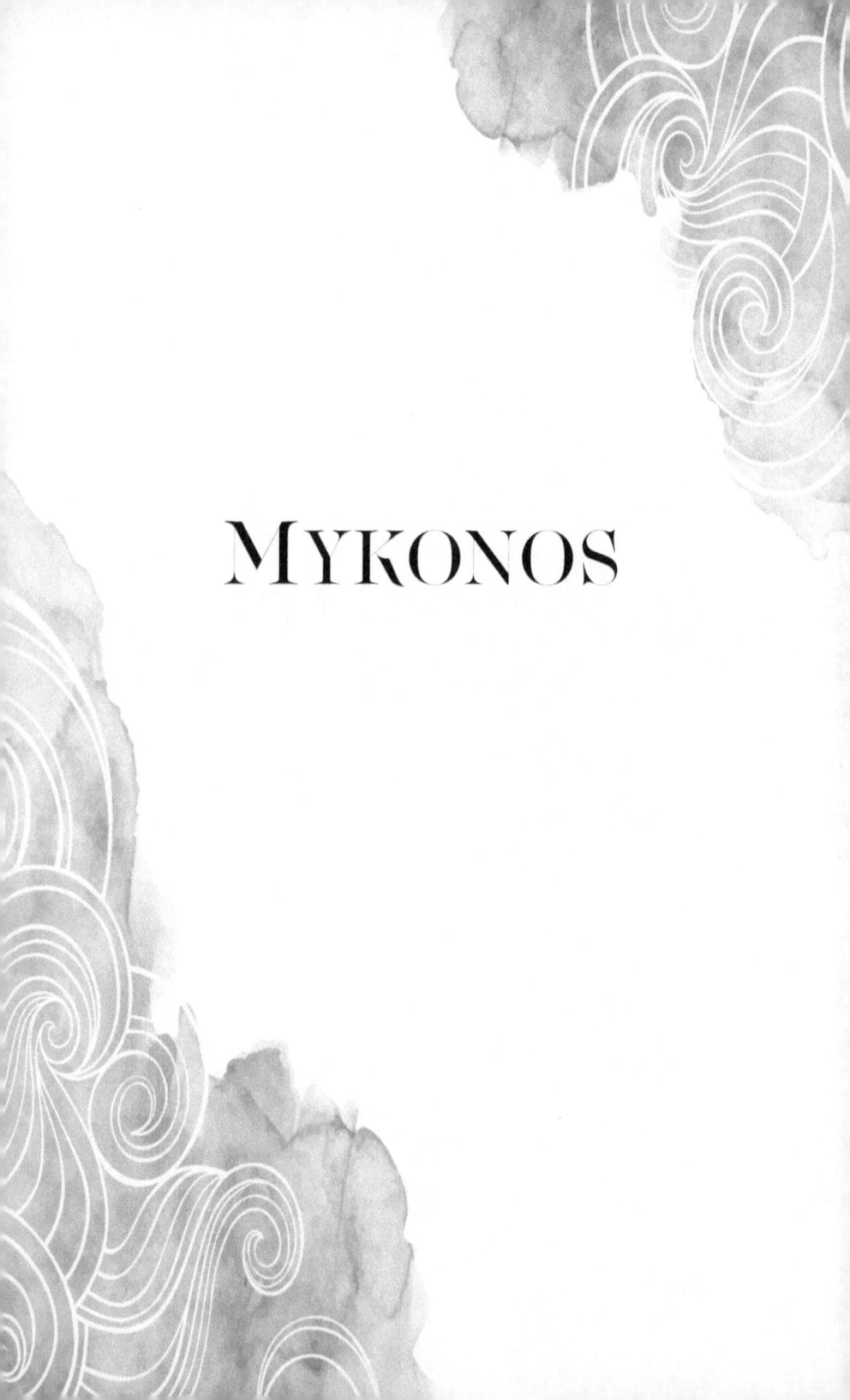

MYKONOS

59

TURO

WE CALLED Alessio and told him about our private club idea and he loved it. So much so, that he wanted to be a full partner.

"Count me in," he said, the excitement obvious in his voice. Adri had him on speakerphone.

"Wonderful. We'll see you in Mykonos in three weeks for Elektra's concert and that's where we'll start to suss out potential members. That whole weekend on the island will be ideal for that. We'll see who might be interested, how they respond, and we'll be able to put together our first list of desirable members and work from there," said Adri.

"When are you going to Rashid's island?" I asked him.

"A week or so before the concert."

"Perfect," said Adri. "We need that island for the first club event, Alessio. Talk to Rashid and set up a meeting. Turo and I will stop there on our way to Mykonos."

"*Si, Si, contessa.* You be ready to dazzle."

"I will."

"I'll call you. *Ciao,*" said Alessio. Adri shut down her phone.

I contacted Tricia and told her the club idea.

"I want you to be my full partner in the Chicago operation," I said. "The upgrade you've implemented is working out beautifully and I want it to continue. Hire more support staff because I need you as manager of operations on this club. Come to Mykonos for this concert party, meet Adri and Alessio, and we can all discuss concepts, details, test theories, and you can get the lay of the land and get some sun."

No response.

"Tricia? Are you there?"

"Just...speechless. Give me a sec."

"Get over it, and get on it."

She laughed.

———

RASHID WAS interested and wanted to talk.

After three weeks together in London, Adri, Marko, and I jetted directly to the Ionian island of Zakynthos where Alessio met us with a motorboat to take us to Rashid's private island retreat.

We met Rashid who gave us the complete tour. Alessio and Marko wandered on the property while Adri and I discussed details with Rashid. Afterwards, he left us on the sandy shore to discuss on our own. Alessio and Marko found us on the sweeping stone terrace which led out to the beach.

"This place is insane!" said Marko, dragging a hand through his long hair.

Alessio rested an arm on Marko's shoulder. "And what do you two think?" he asked.

What did we think?

Complete privacy and an extensive monitored alarm system to rival any other on a small uninhabited island. Twenty bedrooms and almost every detail plated in gold. A huge formal dining room, a grand staircase, commercial kitchen. Marble everywhere. Pristine beaches, natural coves, ancient olive orchards, a citrus grove, landscaped garden with pine trees, towering cypress trees, idyllic palm trees—the urge to fuck my woman in every location had me licking at my bottom lip, cock twitching.

Alessio interrupted my reverie. "Will it do for the club?"

Adri's eyes danced and she let out a warm laugh as she squeezed my hand.

I said, "It's perfect."

———

AFTER SPEAKING MORE with Rashid and Alessio, Adri, Marko, and I headed back to Zakynthos where we boarded the family plane for Mykonos. We'd have a few days to ourselves before Elektra's concert. Then Adri's parents would be arriving the following week for a short vacation before Marko had to return to London to start school.

We arrived on the "Island of the Winds" and a waiting taxi brought us to the house. The moment I stepped inside the roomy, airy structure, I was rendered speechless. It wasn't just the incredible view of that infinite Aegean blue from the open portico which wrapped around the house. It was...everything.

The polar opposite of the historical aristocratic house in Andros, this house was a sprawling flat roofed and whitewashed set of stone cubes—a contemporary castle of stark white walls and earthy accents of raw stone and wood. All simple austerity and organic, sleek forms etched into an arid bluff overlooking the Aegean. The sharp, pure white color of this and all the buildings on Mykonos deflected the scorching rays of the intense sun but was also an arresting contrast to the rich blue of the sea. Stimulating, relaxing all at once.

It may have been simpler and much less varnished in style than Petros and Liana's lavish, elegant house in Athens, but there was nothing plain or unsophisticated about this house. Furniture made of textured, organic materials, the hushed blue and gray color tones of the walls and accessories, the long, diaphanous white curtains swelling in the breeze, the pale polished marble floors, and the few pieces of art, the infinity pool stretching out over the bluff and taking me with it—all of it seamlessly created a soothing, tranquil aesthetic.

But it all came down to that sea, always that sea. It hovered, embraced. The sea was the guest, the star, the soundtrack. The sea was the soul of this house. I stood rooted to the spot in the center of the great room, my entire body breathing in the Aegean, the air, the light.

"What do you think?" Adri came up behind me, her arms wrapping around my waist.

I only leaned back into her, taking in a deep breath, my hand clasping her arm which tightened around me.

Marko promptly put on his bathing suit and parked himself in one of the many pale wood sun loungers around the pool out back in the outdoor living area overlooking the sea. He stacked three paperbacks on the low table at his side and plugged himself into his iPod.

"Marko's got the right idea," I said.

The three of us spent the entire afternoon swimming and pool lounging. When the heat got too much, we retreated to the shade of the wooden canopy where we flopped on oversized rattan sofas gloriously padded with huge white pillows. Siesta time.

That night, after a dinner of grilled fish, hand cut potatoes fried in olive oil, and a tomato and onion salad all prepared in the outdoor kitchen by the chef and Magda, the housekeeper, an exhausted Marko tracked off to bed early. Adri led me to a lounger by the now lit pool where we finished a bottle of fantastic white wine from Santorini. We stargazed and kissed and felt each other up like teenagers.

Adri turned her head toward the house. "We're finally alone."

"Are we?" My eyes closed and I let loose a long sigh.

"The lights inside the house are off. Magda's gone home."

"Hmm."

A hand squeezed my stiff cock that had already tented my shorts, and I chuckled, my eyes popping open.

Adri straddled me. "Marko's bedroom is on the opposite end of the house from here." She undid the button on my shorts, my zipper. A warm eager hand slid under my boxer briefs and found a very grateful cock. "Oh yes," she murmured, her lips brushing mine. "I feel like it's been forever since we—"

"I fucked you this morning, didn't I?" My tongue lashed at her lips and she let out a soft hiss. "Woke you up bright and early with this tongue between your legs and then—"

"Yes, yes." An evil grin blazed over her lips as she cupped my balls.

"Shit." My muscles clenched.

"But that was over fourteen hours ago, my love. Take off your shirt."

I complied, tossing my Polo shirt to the ground. "Shameless girl. It must be the sun here, the fresh air, the wine."

"Must be." Her face slanted over mine and she took my mouth, devouring me. She ripped off her blouse, chucked her bra, stood up and shimmied out of her cut off jeans which revealed a panty that was nothing more than a web of dainty, silk, pink straps stretched over her pussy, slung low on her hips.

"Whatever you do, do not take off that fucking thong," my voice growled.

"Do you like it? I bought it and others especially for this trip. For you."

The feral urge to bury my face between her legs overwhelmed me, and I grabbed at her hips.

"*Óxi, óxi.*"

She pushed me back on the lounger and tugged on my shorts and, helping her, we got them off me. She sat back, her fingernails tracing lines on my legs, her nipples delectable pebbles I needed in my mouth.

"That's better. Now show me how much you like my knickers, Turo."

My flesh heated under her hungry, expectant gaze, and I took hold of my cock and stroked, my eyes holding her gleaming ones. My strokes grew rougher, quicker, my tip engorged, wet. Her teeth scraped over her bottom lip as her hand kneaded a breast. *Fuck, fuck, fuck.*

She wanted to kill me tonight.

And I would let her.

On a grunt she pushed my hand away and took my cock in her mouth. "Damn, baby..."

She sucked me long and slow, faster, harder. I dug my fingers in her beautiful hair, my head reeling back against the lounger. Her mouth released me with a sucking *pop*, and my lungs crushed together as she climbed on top of me. I yanked the damp panty to the side and she tucked my cock inside her, filling herself with me in one rocking move.

Majestic.

"Ah fuck..."

Adri rode me, rode me, and I worshipped her there under the stars. The incremental strokes of my cock, my fingers, my filthy words lifted her, fed her, met her every demand. My goddess claimed what she wanted, bestowing on me the gift of her radiance, her rapture, *her*. I drowned in her, I breathed her in. We soared.

Wrapped in each other's arms, skin to skin, our rough breaths finally slowed down. *Fuck yeah* had just met tranquility.

"I love you, Adri."

"I love you," she said quietly, her voice raw, and her murmured Greek words that followed caressed my skin.

We dozed off and were awakened by the Cycladic wind whipping at our damp bodies. We stretched out and dove into the swimming pool.

"Ah, that feels so good." I kissed her as we paddled in the water.

"I need ice cream," she said. "Don't you need ice cream?"

I let out a laugh. "Yeah, I do actually."

We got out of the pool and dried ourselves with towels and headed to the outdoor kitchen naked. She opened the fridge and grabbed a small carton from the freezer and opened it.

Her eyes lit up. "Parfait. My favorite."

"Parfait?"

"Ice cream, but richer, thicker." She grabbed a spoon. "*Élla,* try." Adri scooped up a spoonful of the vanilla dotted with nuts and brought it toward my mouth. The ice cream slid off the spoon and landed on her tit, a splatter on her thigh.

"Oh, baby, that's too bad." I chuckled and sucked it off her breast, pinching the underside, my lips taking in her hardened nipple and she cried out. "That. Is. Extraordinary. Parfait," I said, my tongue grazing her nipple over and over.

"And that is an extraordinary tongue," her voice was breathless. "More?"

"Yes, please." I lifted her up on the marble kitchen island, held her leg open, and lifting my gaze to her blazing one, lapped at the ice-cream on her thigh.

She leaned back and shook the spoon over her tummy. Drips of creamy white pooled on flesh. "Oops."

I grabbed the small carton of parfait from her and put it on the counter. "Lay back."

Her eyes flashed and she immediately laid down. Taking a long, thin kitchen towel from the counter, I twisted it around her wrists, bringing her fingers to the faucet behind her on the small sink. "Hold onto the faucet and don't let go."

She licked her lips as her fingers wrapped around the faucet, her luscious tits at attention. I put another towel over her eyes, tucking it under her head, and she let out a low moan. The light illuminating the swimming pool created a luminous glow over her flesh. My chest heated as I admired my nymph splayed out for me on her island altar.

"Turo?" she breathed, her back arching.

"Shh." I dipped the spoon into the icy cold dessert and brought the back of the spoon, coated in ice cream, over her swollen clit, applying pressure, rubbing her. She cried out at the cold shock, the unlikely friction, her pelvis rocking, and I nipped at her wet pussy lips, lapped at the ice cream dripping between her legs. I scooped more parfait into the spoon and ate.

"So good." She moaned as I scooped up more and brought it to her mouth.

"Lick."

She did, ravenously. I kissed her, licking the ice cream from her lips, her tongue searching for mine.

I dipped the spoon in the parfait again and repeated the stroking around her nipples. My licking and sucking.

Her body shuddered, she panted, "Oh, Turo, oh, Turo..."

"Do not let go of that faucet, Lovely."

I offered the spoon, touching it to her lips but pulled it back from her mouth. Her tongue fluttered to reach it, her back arching off the marble. A rush of heat engulfed me. *Desperate for me. Begging for me.*

Dribbling the last of the parfait over her writhing body, I licked, suckled, nipped, and finger fucked her until she came. I brought my ice cream and Adri-covered fingers to her lips.

"Suck on me."

She sucked hard, and my balls tightened painfully as her teeth grazed my fingers, the wet, tense suction of her mouth unbearable. Positioning myself between her legs, my hands gripping her thighs, I nudged my tip at her entrance, sliding my shaft up and down her wet.

"You want ice cream, baby or you want cock?"

"Give me that—"

I thrust deep, and jagged gasps ripped from us both. Pinning her legs up high, I pumped into her wildly until we both came.

"You've exhausted me, woman."

"I can't move," she whispered, her head rolling to the side, the towel falling from her face. "I can't."

"You have to, sweetheart." I chuckled, biting the inside of her knee. "Get us to your bedroom."

She laughed.

The next morning I detected the maid stifling a smirk with a huge grin as she served us our iced *freddos* on the patio. It all came back to me. Adri and I had neglected to clean up the outdoor kitchen island after our parfait fest, and we'd left our clothes and towels strewn on the ground by the pool.

Oh well.

60

TURO

ALESSIO ARRIVED in Mykonos as did Tricia, the two of them staying at a resort nearby. Marko had a couple of good friends over to swim in the pool and have lunch, while Adri and I, Alessio, and Tricia discussed business in the small dining room inside the house. Rashid's island paradise was a go ahead, and we were planning on all the details of our premiere event set for next May.

Tricia was all set to cast the right escorts for the club and would communicate with contacts in New York and Paris to find the right men and women along with two she had in mind from our Chicago stable.

"I really like the name," said Tricia, shutting down her laptop.

"Me too," said Alessio.

"Good. Club Dionysus, it is," I said.

"I'll do a few sketches of a Greek "D" for the logo and the necklace, and I'll email you," said Alessio.

"Don't forget," said Adriana, "one as a sign of their member-ship and their pledge of privacy, the other on a very long, strong chain for activities."

"I won't forget, Adri. Trust me," said Alessio with a wink,

pushing his chair back from the table. "Tricia and I are going back to the hotel to get ready for the concert. We'll see you there."

"Yes, we'll see you there," said Adri.

We showered and changed, and Marko was at the front door waiting for us. Dressed in black jeans and high tops, a black graphic tee, his long hair in his face. "I changed my mind. I want to go to the concert with you."

"Really?"

He hadn't wanted to do much since we'd arrived but stay home. He hadn't come with us for lunch in town or to a beach club yesterday or the day before.

He shrugged in that Greek way that said, *isn't it obvious?* "It's Elektra. You don't miss a live of Elektra's."

"That's right, you don't." Adri smiled huge. "Let's go then."

We made it to the Delfini Beach Club which was crawling with people and loud as fuck. We found Tricia, Alessio, and Rashid and his friends at a table. Many people came over to Adri and took pictures with her. Adri introduced me and Tricia to most of them, Tricia making notes in her Blackberry and conferring with Adri. Marko and I sat together and sipped on sodas. He seemed uneasy at first in the crowd, but then he settled, especially when a friend of his came over and sat with us.

Thunderous applause and cheering roared through the club as Elektra took the stage. Electric guitars and synths exploded and her strong voice filled the air. Her energy was off the charts. She was a remarkable, athletic performer, prancing on the stage, her incredible voice piercing our hearts. Her joy in reaching out to her fans was palpable. She gave her audience everything, singing a mix of her own original rock ballads and pop hits, and many Greek classics, from what Marko told me, for over two hours to a thrilled, throbbing crowd, all of them on their feet, swaying, dancing and singing along. Arm in arm, Adri and Marko sang together.

"She is hot as fuck!" Alessio whooped and applauded.

After her final set, Elektra found us, and the photographers in her wake swarmed her and Adri and Alessio, the three of them showing off their new Alessio jewelry. Alessio kept his arm tightly wrapped around Elektra holding her close as the lights flashed over them, talking in her ear as she laughed. After, I asked Adri if Elektra was still seeing that young actor.

"No, that's over. I think Alessio may be in for a good time tonight."

"Here's hoping," I quipped.

Fireworks went off over the shore, behind the stage, cracking and popping their fiery colors in the sky over us, their reflection in the sea electric. My arm slid around Adri pulling her close. The last time we were here, things had been so different, what we'd believed about each other, about ourselves.

Adri turned her face up at me, the flashes of light washing over her beautiful, relaxed smile, gleaming in her eyes. Color and brilliance. *My lovely, lovely girl.*

She kissed me, her lips whispering against mine, "Take me home."

———

THE NEXT DAY Adri's parents arrived in Mykonos to celebrate her birthday.

"You're positive you don't want to go out for dinner, darling?" Liana asked, settling into one of the easy chairs in the shaded outdoor living area, her gaze darting to the outdoor kitchen where Chef Pavlo and Magda were busy grilling and arranging dishes.

"I'm positive," Adri replied, handing her mother an iced tea. "I chose the menu with Chef Pavlo and we're all set. I'd much rather we stay here and enjoy ourselves. I want you all to myself."

"Sounds perfect to me," said Petros sipping his glass of beer, his eyes on Marko who was swimming laps in the pool. "How's Marko been doing?"

"Very good," said Adri. "He's been staying here mostly, reading, swimming, listening to his music. He and Turo play that Playstation all the time. A few of his friends have been over, and he came with us to Elektra's concert last night."

"Did he?" Liana said, eyes widening. "Did he enjoy himself or—"

"He had fun, he really did," I said.

"Thank God," she let out a breath.

I caught Adri's gaze and, clearing my throat, I stood. "Adriana and I have news to share with you." Adri came over to me, a hand sliding around my bicep.

"News?" Petros said, removing his sunglasses. Liana slanted her head at us.

"I've asked Adri to marry me—"

"And I said yes," Adri said.

"That's wonderful!" Petros stood and Adri hugged him. He extended a hand to me and we shook.

"This is sudden," said Liana.

"When you know, my love, you know, isn't that right? That's how it was with us. And I've never seen our daughter happier, more confident and relaxed. Have you?" He kissed Adri on the cheek.

"I am happy, *Babá*. Very happy."

Liana released a breath and a smile curved her lips.

"Look, *Mamá*—" Adri extended her hand to Liana, showing her the ring. "Isn't it fantastic? It's for *Papoú's* dagger. Turo designed it, had it made just for me."

"It's quite beautiful," said Liana.

Petros took Adri's hand in his and studied the ring. "How remarkable. Well done." He raised his chin at me.

"A remarkable ring for a remarkable woman," I said.

Petros clapped a hand on my shoulder. "Congratulations to the both of you."

Liana kissed her daughter and came over to me and kissed me on both cheeks. "Do you have a date in mind?"

"No, we haven't really decided on that yet, but we will. We have some new business plans too, but we can discuss that later," Adri said.

Yes, later. We would tell them about our special events company providing exclusive entertainment in the Mediterranean, but not share the sex club aspect.

Marko got out of the pool and we all sat down at the dining table which was beautifully decorated with small vases of white flowers and laden with amazing dishes. Garlicky eggplant carpaccio, muscles in a white wine broth with plenty of parsley, zucchini flowers stuffed with minted rice and pine nuts, succulent large shrimp, langoustines, octopus tentacles, and calamari all charred on the grill and doused in lemon and olive oil. Salads of every color along with a selection of cheeses in boldly colored plates. Chunks of freshly baked crusty bread. Then there was the tiramisu birthday cake specially made by Adri's favorite local pastry shop.

Petros brought over a bottle of Veuve Clicquot from the wine refrigerator and opened it. Magda scurried to the table with a tray of champagne flutes, and he filled them. We raised our glasses.

"To our Adriana. Happy birthday my darling. *Xrónia sou pollá.* And congratulations on your new life together."

We drank.

Petros insisted on buying us a house in Athens as a gift. "You don't have to to do that," murmured Adriana.

"What? *Have* to? I want to," Petros said. "As the father of the bride, I can give whatever gift I like!"

"*Babá!*" Adri laughed, sliding an arm around Petros's shoulder, burying her face in his shoulder. "There is one thing I want. One perfect thing."

"What is it, Adri?" asked Liana.

"The house in Andros," she replied.

I held my lover's beautiful eyes and my heart swelled in my chest with her beaming smile.

Adri said, "That's what I'd like. The house in Andros."

ANDROS

61

TURO

Three Months Later

I DIDN'T UNDERSTAND what the priest was saying, what the Byzantine hymns he chanted meant, but it didn't matter really. I could feel their ancient power thrumming in my chest as Adri and I listened, standing together, hand in hand, the incense floating around us, filling the church with its smoky sweetness. Our wedding was in full gear at the tiny church in Chóra down the stone path from our house in Andros.

The club's first event was in six months, and we were determined to get married before then. Adri insisted she didn't want a huge planned out extravaganza. Liana wasn't thrilled but she gave in. Liana was all for Mykonos, but Adri was adamant on Andros.

A few days before my mother had flown in to Athens. She met Adri and the family and we showed her the town. Then we all came to Andros together.

Now the priest blessed a small silver cup and held it up to me. I drank. Sweet wine. He gave it to Adri and she drank and smiled at me, squeezing my hand. We shared the wine like we would share our joys and sorrows, our successes and failures, hopes and fears in our new life together.

Marko, our best man, stood behind us holding the two gold wreaths of bay leaves entwined with small pearls attached together with a thick satin ribbon. On the priest's nod he placed them on our heads, crowning us. Adri and I were the King and Queen of our new household, of our own family, and three times the priest repeated his chanted prayer, three times Marko switched the crowns on our heads. We held hands, locked gazes. Adri and I were joined, united, connected.

With the Gospel book in one hand, the priest grabbed my and Adri's clasped hands and led us in a procession around a small table set with candles before the altar, two little cousins of Adriana and Marko's in puffy white dresses held lit candles leading the way. This was the "Dance of Isaiah" Adri had told me about. Our literal first steps together as husband and wife. I gave in to the urge and my gaze went down to our feet. My polished black shoes, Adri's delicate white heels peeking from the hem of her flowing white gown. Together, stepping together, moving forward.

Rice and flowers flew through the air, raining over us, our guests hurling handfuls from the little satin pouches the tiny bridesmaids had passed out when they'd entered the church. I knew this moment was different, this climax of the service, this ritual within the ritual, because when he led us forward, the priest's voice rang out louder than before in a powerful and upbeat tone and everyone's voices joined his in singing the Byzantine hymn. Three times we circled the table together. A celebration.

My mother's face flashed by me, her eyes wet, her smile wide. She stood with Liana and Petros, all of them throwing rice and flowers at us. Alessio next to them. Adri's cousin Silia who'd designed her beautiful wedding dress with her husband and a handful of other relatives.

As we danced this ancient dance, I held on tight to my wife's hand and she to mine, our simple gold bands shining in the candlelight. We were now one. Forever one.

———

AFTER THE WEDDING CEREMONY, we'd had an amazing evening of endless food, drink, dance, and *bouzouki* music in town. Our parents spent the night at a beautiful hotel in Chóra while we spent our first night as husband and wife in our house.

The moment Adri had told her parents she'd wanted the house in Andros, her mother made calls and set the wheels of renovation in motion. Over the course of three months, new furniture, repaired roof, upgraded kitchen and bathrooms, painted inside and out, new appliances. Even the small jacuzzi in the garden was in the throes of getting itself a long lap pool to keep it company. Our island home was our private paradise.

It was almost six in the morning by the time we got home from the wedding party. "Let's go up to the castle," she said. "I want us to see this sunrise together."

I could tell it was more than simply watching a sunrise by the set of her jaw, the press of her lips together. "Okay, sure. Let's do it." We changed into shorts, T-shirts, and sneakers. Adri grabbed a straw tote bag and we were off.

Pink washed over the slate blue sea, filling the sky with gentle light. The precious hush over the town made every brush of our feet over the rock loud to our ears. As we climbed, slowly, slowly. Almost imperceptibly, that light changed color as the pink orange ball of the sun emerged, rising to prominence in the sky. We finally got to our spot by the hole in the stone wall overlooking the sea.

My eyes caught a haze of movement on the edge of the rocks, the very edge, where no sane person would stand, only a very brave one. A chill crept over my flesh and I blinked. He was there.

It was him. I recognized Stefanos from that portrait in the living room. The legend, the hero, the rebel stood at the edge of the cliff facing the sea that hundreds of years ago had claimed him body and soul. The sea upon which he had built an empire.

The rebel hero turned, large blue gray eyes meeting mine. My breath crushed in my lungs, a burning fullness surged inside me, and I knew.

I *knew*.

After the cannons fired, after the smoke cleared, love is what we had left, love remained; love was the great inheritance. To choose to fight for that love was the good fight; to choose to nurture that love so it takes root and thrives in this stone-littered earth the greatest victory.

Tears and regrets and vendettas had been tossed from this cliff—Stefanos's, ours—and buried forever in these waters. Stefanos had triumphed in so many battles, but he had lost his true love.

But I got my woman.

And his great-great granddaughter got her man.

Adri took out her wedding bouquet from the straw tote bag. A thick cluster of luscious, pale pink peonies wrapped in a wide satin ribbon at the stems.

"Baby, what are you doing?" I said.

She smiled. "When a ship sinks and souls are lost, sailors toss wreaths of flowers into the sea at the spot. I want to do that now to honor Stefanos and Natalia. To honor their dagger. To relieve them, give their souls the peace they so deserve. To appease the bloody fates because only we can. Our blessing is theirs too."

"Do it."

Taking in a breath, she turned and threw her beautiful flowers, and they soared, a riot of pink against the pale sky, down to the sea below. Turning to me, she held out her hand, her aqua ring and wedding band gleaming in the day's first light, and I took her hand.

We held each other on that cliff in that castle as the sun grew stronger and bolder reaching its full height in the sky. Gold fire blazed over the infinite swathe of sea. The water transformed before us. Luminous mauves and lilacs and cobalts swelled and churned into one blue. Vivid. Redefined.

We kissed.

The blue-eyed specter turned toward his Aegean once more. He fragmented in the sunlight, vanishing from sight.

The
End

BOOKS BY CAT PORTER

- LOCK & KEY SERIES -

LOCK & KEY

RANDOM & RARE

IRON & BONE

BLOOD & RUST

LOCK & KEY CHRISTMAS

LOCK & KEY - THE COMPLETE SERIES BOXED SET

FURY

MC Romance Standalone Spinoff

- LEGENDS OF MEAGER SERIES -

THE DUST AND THE ROAR

THE FIRE AND THE ROAR

THE YEAR OF EVERYTHING

DAGGER IN THE SEA

Mediterranean Romantic Suspense Adventure

WOLFSGATE

Historical Romance

ACKNOWLEDGMENTS

This book would not have been possible without these special people in my life. My deepest thanks and gratitude for your precious time, energy, and support. I love and cherish each of you.

Tina, working with you on this was, as ever, sublime. This one was hard. So hard. You pushed me off the right cliffs. Your instincts, your passion, your articulate precision were my beacon in the storm.

Jenn, thank you for your clarity and pure instincts, my dearest friend. You at my side and in my words means the world to me.

Lori, Lori, Lori for your design magic, for getting me from the get go, for all the laughs, for startling me with every piece of art you came up with after each of our brainstorming sessions. This was truly a collaboration, and a satisfying one, and I loved every minute of it.

Rachel, Alison, Needa, Jan, Lena for beta reading and giving me your time, precious insights, and the best pm's and emails ever!

Penny for your vigilant proofreading and going over the

action scenes with me step by step. Could not have done it without you.

Jan Hoodlum for giving me Turo's Chicago and to Mindy Milner-Downey for your firearm insights. Thank you for these precious details, my loves!

Alison for your support, enthusiasm, and efforts on my behalf halfway across the world. Love you, girlfriend!

Linda R. Russell and everyone at Foreword PR for having my back. One day, a real Starbucks together.

Bloggers who make the book world go around—we writers could not do this without you. In particular, iScream Books, The Book Bellas, Book Babes Unite, Dirty Book Girls, Totally Booked, Triple B, EDGy Reviews, LABB, Perusing Princesses, Schmexy Book Girls, That Transylvanian Chick Book Blog, Kinky Girls Book Obsessions, and so many more. And to the bookstagrammers on Instagram who create such beautiful images and share their book love. My deepest thanks for the astounding work you do.

My Cat Callers who cheer me on and kept the adrenaline flowing as I worked. I loved sharing Turo with you every step of the way— #TakeMeTuro ! Ellen, Kimber, Kandace, Korrie, MJ, Soulla, Cindy, Sammy, JoJill—your enthusiasm and hearts are so bright, and I thank you for all the shout outs and for your friendship, most of all.

To all the wonderful fans, bloggers, and authors I met at RARE Berlin and London, and you, dear Amy Jennings! And to my fellow authors who inspire, support, answer my questions, and share, share, share, I thank you from my very full heart.

Special thanks to authors Willow Aster, Leylah Attar, Carian Cole, Autumn Jones Lake, Victoria Paige. To Katie Larsen for that sprint (my first!) that got my head and my revision straight, and to Karina Halle for our romantic suspense discussion in Seattle.

To actor Bill Kwikowski who blew my mind in his acting class when he declared he hated Shakespeare's Hamlet. I've never forgotten it, nor the lessons I learned in his class which have informed my writing craft ever since. (I'm sorry that play-wrighting class I took didn't work out. I wasn't ready back then!)

To all my readers for sharing the book love, your personal notes, taking the time to leave reviews. Your enthusiasm and reader satisfaction mean everything to me. Thank you for loving my bruised characters and their difficult stories.

To my three children for believing in me. To my husband for insisting on Andros last August.

To my father who lit my heart on fire from an early age by sharing with me his love of travel and discovery, history, mythol-ogy, and suspenseful tales. You would've loved this one, Dad. This is the one you were waiting for.

And to Andros. Oh, how you bewitched me.

ABOUT THE AUTHOR

CAT PORTER was born and raised in New York City, but also spent a few years in Texas and Europe along the way, which made her as wanderlusty as her parents. As an introverted, only child, she had very big, but very secret dreams for herself. She graduated from Vassar College, was a struggling actress, an art gallery girl, special events planner, freelance writer, restaurant hostess, and had all sorts of other crazy jobs all hours of the day and night to help make those dreams come true. She has two children's books traditionally published under her maiden name.

She now lives on a beach outside of Athens, Greece with her husband, three children, and three huge Cane Corsos, freaks out regularly, still daydreams way too much, and now truly doesn't give AF. She is addicted to reading, classic films, cafe bars on the beach, the Greek islands, Instagram, Pearl Jam and U2, bourbon she brought home from Nashville and whiskey she brought home from Ireland, and realllllllly good coffee. Writing has always kept her somewhat sane, extremely happy, and a productive member of society.

for more more more
www.catporter.eu

Join my CatList
for exclusive content, book news, sales,
special giveaways and offers

Visit the "Dagger in the Sea" inspiration board on Pinterest

Follow me on BookBub & Amazon

Join Cat's Facebook groups:

Cat Porter's Cat Callers

Dagger in the Sea Beach Bar

Email me at catporter103@gmail.com

facebook.com/catporterauthor
twitter.com/catporter103
instagram.com/catporter.writer
amazon.com/author/catporter
bookbub.com/authors/cat-porter
pinterest.com/catporter103

www.ingramcontent.com/pod-product-compliance
Lightning Source LLC
Chambersburg PA
CBHW051202120726
47905CB00004B/957